REVEILLE

Harry Borg, every nerve on fire, every muscle convulsed into full readiness, stood in the center of the room. He had never been more terrified. To awaken suddenly to a piercing scream, to find the hideous mouthparts, the great fangs of an enormous spider looming just above his face was the stuff of a nightmare beyond imagining.

He watched the spider crouch to spring. The fangs came up like lance points, aimed at Harry! The spider leaped—

God! How quick the thing could move!

a novel by
Ward Hawkins
RED FLAME BURNING

A Del Rey Book

BALLANTINE BOOKS • NEW YORK

A Del Rey Book
Published by Ballantine Books

Copyright © 1985 by Ward Hawkins

All rights reserved under International and Pan-American Copyright Conventions. Published in the United States by Ballantine Books, a division of Random House, Inc., New York, and simultaneously in Canada by Random House of Canada Limited, Toronto.

Library of Congress Catalog Card Number: 85-90712

ISBN 0-345-32121-9

Manufactured in the United States of America

First Edition: August 1985

Cover art by Ralph McQuarrie

CHAPTER 1

But the last Jassan—

"Damn it to hell!" Harry Borg had time to whisper.

And that was all the time he had. For the last Jassan, the one Lori had clubbed, had remained upright and had brought his sidearm to bear on Harry. Harry saw it coming and knew it would get to him before he could bring his own piece around. He felt the explosion erupt enormously at his left leg, then another explosion at his right arm—those fine, powerful, beautifully muscled limbs that had been his for such a short time were torn off and blown away—and he was driven to the floor, not yet suffering pain, only enormous shock.

"Oh, God! Harry!" Lori screamed as she saw him fall. "Don't—don't!" Her fear was total, but she ran to him and threw herself onto him as if she might be able to hold him there.

Harry could see the Jassan who had fired the shots that had destroyed him standing motionless, yellow, vertically slitted eyes wild, long tongue flailing—but immobile, as if in great shock of his own. "You won, you bastard..." Harry whispered. And then he found Lori's grief-distorted face close above him.

"Some kind of a hero—I turned out to be..."

"You tried, Harry. Oh, God in heaven, you tried!"

"I blew it..."

And that was the end of it for Harry Borg.

1

Lori's face, and all else, simply went away.
As if forever ...

Harry Borg was sitting in a darkened room, quietly rocking.
There was enough light leaking in around the drawn venetian
blinds—it was still only a little past four o'clock in the afternoon—to show the hard-scrubbed, austere, almost cell-like quality of the apartment Harry now called his home.

A bookcase used most of one wall, and there in perfect align-
ment were reference volumes dealing with a variety of scientific
and engineering disciplines. A drafting table served as a desk,
as well as a place to design, a tall stool as a place to sit. Immediately before Harry, against the wall, was a large television set,
but it was dark now, silent.

Just through a doorway to his left was a bedroom. A single
bed made up to drumlike, GI tautness, a footlocker at the foot
of the bed, and two pairs of shoes, hard-polished and carefully
aligned, gave the place a barracks look. A bathroom opened off
the bedroom, and there towels hung squarely on rods, and the
bathmat was folded carefully over the rim of the tub. Tub, com-
mode, and washbasin all gleamed with a cleanliness that again
spoke of service training.

Through the door to Harry's right, a portion of a small kitchenette could be seen—cupboards, counters, sink, refrigerator,
stove—and all that, too, was excessively neat. Except for the
half-full quart bottle of vodka and the shot glass, which, though
clean and carefully squared to the doorway, were certainly not
GI.

Harry Borg had spent three years in the Air Force a long time
ago—World War II, a fighter pilot, in fact; almost forty years
ago, now, wasn't it?—and in some ways he had reverted back
to those days. He had liked the orderliness, the feeling of security
he had known then, and now, in the face of all else that had
gone wrong, he could laugh at himself: "At least, I'm a *clean*
old man."

And he was as neat about his person as he was about the
place in which he lived. A tall, spare man, almost sixty-five, he
had dark blue eyes, quiet and gentle, behind round spectacles,
and thinning, brown hair that had receded well back on a wide

and prominent forehead. He favored suntans, now that he no longer had to wear business suits, white shirts, and ties; because suntans laundered well, and when one does one's own laundry, that matters a lot.

A beep on his digital wristwatch told him it was time again.

He got out of the rocking chair with a practiced movement that caught the chair at the peak of the forward thrust, enabling him to take a steadying hold on the frame of the door to the kitchenette in one stride without risking a fall. Then another stride took him to the counter where the vodka bottle came easily to his right hand and the edge of the counter to his left. He held the counter for a moment, drew a deep, ritualistic breath and let it out slowly. Then, satisfied that he was capable of the task at hand, he poured a careful two ounces of vodka into the shot glass, capped the bottle, and set it down so carefully there was hardly a clink when the bottle touched the tile. Lifting the shot glass smoothly, he quickly swallowed the vodka, then waited, quite still, until he felt the bloom of heat begin to glow in his stomach.

"All right!" he said.

Retracing his steps, he settled into the rocking chair in the shadowed, middle-class apartment, in an old but respectable building on a quiet, tree-lined street, before the dark television set, and again resumed his slow, metronome-like rocking.

Harry Borg, thirty-two years a design engineer for Lockheed, after his war service, and one of the good ones. Harry Borg, husband to a wife who had divorced him and cleaned him out within six months of the day Lockheed had fired him. Harry Borg, father of two grown sons who hadn't come near him since the divorce. Harry Borg, grandfather to the child whose framed picture stood on his bedside table. Harry Borg, a helpless, hopeless alcoholic.

Rocking in a darkened room.

Alone.

Well, not quite alone...

One thing about the booze, Harry had found, one of the good things in spite of all the tales of sweat and terror he had heard, were the DTs. The delirium tremens. The hallucinations.

He had thought they were going to scare the living hell out of him when they finally came, as he had known they must sooner or later, since he hadn't spent a day entirely sober in the past thirty years. But the DTs hadn't scared him at all.

When had they finally arrived? About a month after Ruth had turned him out and he had settled here. Six months ago, wasn't it? Eight months ago? No matter. But it had seemed to him that when the DTs had finally come, they had come to entertain him as much as anything else.

They had appeared the first time, there in his room, as little cowled, monklike creatures that marched across the top of the kitchen doorframe from right to left out to the center of the doorway, where they dropped off, becoming as they fell large, black spiders, spinning a single strand to slow their fall. At a point about halfway to the floor, the spiders exploded, *poof!*, like soap bubbles, disappearing, to march again across the top of the door, quiet, orderly, friendly. They were company for him, if nothing else. Watching them gave him something to do. And they were far better to watch than anything he was able to find on television.

Harry had watched them for hours on end. Muddle-headed, of course. Sometimes he was only a little muddle-headed, sometimes he was very muddle-headed. With his steady intake of vodka, what else? But they always gave him enjoyment. It had gotten so he was able to call them up almost anytime he felt the need for company. But for the past few days he hadn't wanted or needed them, because for the past two days he had had something else to entertain him.

Something far better.

What he had now was the last half of a metal screw suspended in midair, just to the left of the television set. Now *that* was something else!

That was something a man could spend a lot of time with, wondering, trying to figure, guessing...

What could it be? *How* could it be?

Suspended in the air at least two feet from the wall or any surface of any kind—come *on*! Even a hallucination had to make some kind of sense!

But that screw did not.

That screw he could touch!

That screw he could scratch a finger on!

How about *that*?

The way it had started, he'd been sitting in his rocking chair, rocking and drinking—his usual, everyday drill—when a pounding on a wall had begun, a pounding as if the guy next door was putting up a picture, or a shelf.

Harry Borg smiled at that memory. "All right," he'd called out. "Y'don't need to beat a hole in the wall!" But the pounding had gone on, and Harry had gotten up to discover the pounding was going on in the air. *In the air!* Three feet inside the wall! Inside the room! He could even walk behind the source of the pounding. He could stand behind it, so that he was between the pounding and the nearest wall, the wall behind him!

Un-flippin'-believable!

He'd laughed out loud. What were they putting in the vodka these days? Some kind of happy dust or something? No. He knew better than that. Scotty, the guy who owned the liquor store and delivered his booze by the case, was a friend of his. The booze was all right. You could depend on Scotty. The vodka was poison, of course, like all vodka, but it had to be pure poison, or Scotty wouldn't sell it.

What then?

"Beats the hell outa me," he'd said solemnly, and had teetered a careful way into the kitchen to brace himself with a short one.

Being an engineer, he had found he could spend hours trying to figure out the pounding on a wall that wasn't there. Then, before he'd gotten tired of it, the screw had appeared.

First, there had been a light tapping. Then he'd heard the familiar grating sound a screw makes when it's biting into wood or plaster. And then the point of the screw had appeared, coming into view out of nowhere, turning a half twist at a time, pausing as it would while a screwdriver was being reset, until, finally, there it was, coming through at an angle, the bungled work of a lousy mechanic, but snug enough for all of that. A half an inch of an inch-and-a-half metal screw.

In midair!

And you could scratch your finger on it!

Goddamn interesting, is what it was.

For anybody.

For an engineer, it was fantastic. What he had there was a mechanical impossibility, and how often did a man get a chance to study and ponder a mechanical impossibility?

One you could scratch a finger on?

His wristwatch beeped—it was time again.

He gauged the motion of the rocking chair again, timed it nicely, and propelled himself to the doorframe and into the kitchen. "Good show!" he complimented himself, pleased he was so capable, even when drunk as a goat. He very carefully poured another two-ounce shot of vodka and very carefully knocked it back.

And so the rest of the afternoon passed for Harry Borg— rocking, studying the screw through the drifting, shimmering, alcohol-induced haze, and having another. He never seemed to get more than two-thirds totally drunk, and certainly never two-thirds totally sober. When the light had gone from the venetian blind, Harry got out of the rocking chair long enough to prepare and eat a small dinner of precooked frozen food thawed in a microwave. Feeding himself, like keeping his quarters clean, was a ritual Harry rigidly observed. He knew it was necessary if he was to stay alive.

If staying alive was important.

And just now, for the first time, it was.

"Got to stay alive," he said, solemnly, viewing another shot glass full of vodka, "until I figure out about this goddamn screw."

The food also prolonged his ability to continue the drinking. He became more and more muddle-headed, of course, as the drinking went on, and the shimmering haze through which he saw the world became an oily blue and more shimmery. But he would go on enjoying himself, all by himself, until his lights went out, which on most evenings was around nine-thirty or ten.

About nine o'clock on this particular evening, the pounding began again, somebody hammering on the wall again, the wall the screw was fixed into, the wall Harry Borg couldn't see, the wall that wasn't there.

Harry was delighted.

The screw *had* become a little boring.

It didn't *do* anything.

But pounding, now . . .

Pounding was different, Harry thought. Pounding brought you a whole new element entirely. Somebody or some*thing* had to be *doing* the pounding—right?

"Godfrey mighty!" he said, as the pounding got louder. He

could talk pretty well, even smashed. "The guy's going to bust a hole there, sure as I'm a foot tall!"

And he was right.

A few more pounds and a hole *did* appear.

In the wall that wasn't there.

A large hole, jagged, perhaps two feet in diameter, as if a section of a thin and fragile wall had suddenly given way under the heavy pounding of a hammer in the hands of a very inept mechanic.

But it wasn't a hammer. Harry could see it wasn't a hammer, now that there was a hole to look through. It was an angled piece of metal, entirely unsuitable for use as a hammer. And it was not being held by what could be called a hand. At least, not a human hand.

"Great balls of fire!" Harry exclaimed. "Well, shoot!"

The hand had a whole bunch of fingers. Eight, or so.

"Goddamn!" Harry said. "Would you look at that?"

Then the head and shoulders of the owner of the hand with all the fingers appeared framed by the hole.

"Suffering sassafras!" Harry whispered, awed.

The owner of the many-fingered hand was like nothing Harry had ever seen before. It was a *lizard*—kind of. A man-size lizard. A man-size *lizard*?

"What the hell's goin' on here?"

After a moment, Harry began to believe that his lizard-man was manlike in more ways than one. He was willing to swear the lizard-man was surprised at the way he'd knocked the hole in the wall, and, what was more, that he was embarrassed at having done it. Embarrassed! The lizard-man was, it seemed to Harry now, a typical, klutzy, do-it-yourself home mechanic, who had knocked a hole in a wall while trying to nail up a shelf with a piece of angle-iron he'd picked up to use as a hammer—

A lizard-man. *Really?*

How about a man in a lizard suit? Like Godzilla, only not giant size. No, Harry decided, not a man in a lizard suit. You could always tell one of those. Faky, you know? This had to be for real.

A man-size lizard-man.

Okay?

Scaly-looking skin; yellow eyes, slitted up and down; forked tongue. Dig that tongue! Might be as long as a foot, split-ended, whipping in and out. But he was not ugly. He was not what you would call repulsive. At least Harry didn't think so, though, granted, Harry was in a very mellow condition. The lizard-man's skin, for instance, though scaly, looked polished up, smooth and warm. And it seemed to Harry that the lizard-man might even have some kind of man-type sense.

It figured, didn't it?

A man-type lizard *would* have man-type sense. Of course it figured. Stood to reason. Nobody could argue a thing like that.

Harry, feeling quite confident now, spoke to the lizard-man, trying to sound serious.

"I was afraid you were gonna break that wall, the way you were banging on it," he said. "The wall sounded flimsy to me right from the start."

No answer.

"Couldn't you tell it was a flimsy wall when you put the screw in there?"

No answer.

"It was you put the screw in there, wasn't it?"

Then he got what might have been an answer. The lizard-man ran his forked tongue out straight *at* Harry and sucked it back. He did that a couple of times while looking straight at Harry with those yellow, glowing eyes with the up-and-down slits, slits like the slits in a cat's eyes.

"I'll buy it," Harry said.

The lizard-man was staring steadily at Harry like he couldn't believe what he was seeing. He turned his head, looking back into the room on his side of the wall with the hole in it, as if to make sure his side was there, safe and secure, then he looked back at Harry's side again, and at Harry. Then he touched around the edges of the hole, as if to make sure it was what it seemed to be. When he was satisfied that it was a hole, he put his head through it, into Harry's room, to peer at everything he could see. The way he did it, as curious, as puzzled as any human would be, he was as near human as anything Harry could imagine.

"I'll be dad-bobbed!" Harry said, delighted, slurring hardly at all. "Son of a gun!"

The lizard-man went on looking around, stretching his neck

to put his head through the hole as far as he could, checking out Harry's quarters—living room, kitchen, bedroom—peering this way and that to see all he could. Then he put his entire arm and shoulder through the hole and patted around, as if he was trying to figure out the makeup of what was from Harry's side an invisible wall with a large hole in it.

"All right, already!" Harry said, settling back. "Now I'll believe anything!"

The lizard-man backed into his room a slight distance away from the hole, as if to give himself a better view of it. Then he shook his head in a gesture that said clearly he was having as much trouble as Harry believing what he was seeing.

"Believe it," Harry said smugly. "I'm seein' it too!"

Returning to the hole, the lizard-man gave Harry his full attention, flicking out his forked tongue again and again, his head tipped. Questioning?

Had to be, Harry was sure.

"Name's Harry Borg," Harry said.

No response.

"What's yours?" Harry asked.

He hadn't really expected an answer. But the forked tongue kept flicking out and back.

"Well, okay," Harry said agreeably.

And in all truth he had never felt more agreeable. He was one of those agreeable drunks, as a matter of fact. The drunker he got, the more agreeable he got. And he was very agreeable right now. The blue shimmery haze, the feeling of warmth, the pleasant buzz—fine as silk.

As friendly as could be, he said, "Come on in and let's get better acquainted."

No answer.

That was okay.

"Come on," he said, gently, coaxing. "Give 'er a try. Nothin' here to hurt you. Nobody's gonna come botherin'. Ain't been a soul come 'round here in I can't remember when—"

And then, as if he had understood everything Harry had said, the creature broke away more of the flimsy wall, enough to give him a hole he could climb through.

And damned if he didn't do 'er!

He climbed through!

He came right on through that hole in the invisible wall and stood erect right there, in Harry's living room. Stood right there! Right where Harry could see him fine. And he looked real enough to touch.

"Ain't *that* a pistol?" Harry said.

When Harry got the lizard-man back in focus, he saw that he looked to be about as tall as himself. Maybe not quite. But he was built about the same. Head, shoulders, arms, trunk, legs—all about GI. A good build, you would say, whiplike, on the slender side. And no tail! Harry took that as a good sign. The lizard-man's rump looked like anybody else's.

Say! Harry wondered suddenly. *Male or female?*

No way to tell with what he could see. Because the thing was wearing clothes. He had on a silk shirt and some sort of a vest, short pants and soft boots . . . *Pants?* Harry's muddled mind did a double take.

Pants on a *lizard*?

A lizard, even a lizard-man, wearing pants! Great day in the morning! What was coming next?

"Don't know if I can stand it," Harry said.

He decided the lizard-man had to be male. He sat quietly now, twisting his head to follow as the lizard-man began to explore the apartment. The lizard-man moved carefully, but he didn't seem afraid. He checked everything—walls, furniture, doorways, floors, pictures, books.

The window held him for several long moments when he had finally figured out you could open a slot between the slats and look through. What he saw held him sharply interested. And he could see a lot of things—the tree-lined street, the other apartment buildings, the parked cars, the occasional passing car. Harry couldn't tell what the lizard-man thought of what he saw, because all he did was flick his split tongue in and out.

The kitchen was next.

The sink, the water that ran at the turn of the tap, the stove, the refrigerator—they all got the lizard-man's attention. And then the vodka bottle came to his hand. He unscrewed the cap, flicked his tongue down into the bottle, tested the contents, and reacted with some surprise. He looked at Harry. Was it questioningly?

Harry thought so.

"That's booze," Harry said. "That's my downfall. Have one if you want, but I would advise against it. Once you get started on that stuff, you can't quit. Ask me, I know. I'm your A-number-one, copper-plated, dyed-in-the-wool, hopeless alcoholic. Got me maybe another month to live, then I'm gone and soon forgotten."

No response.

So what did you expect, Harry? Tears?

The lizard-man didn't seem to care a hoot. He capped the bottle and came into the living room where the TV set caught his eye. He looked it over, felt it, looked at Harry.

"That's a boob-tube," Harry said. "The sober man's booze. Turns your head to scrambled eggs. Here, I'll turn it on for you."

He managed—but not with the first try, or the second—to get out of the chair, to find the right button, and to turn the set on. The sound came on immediately; the picture followed. The lizard-man was startled, and, more than that, Harry was sure he was impressed. He looked at Harry, back at the set, then back at Harry again as if to say, "Well, aren't you the smart one!"

Archly modest, Harry said, "Nothing, really. Just a bunch of wires and a tube—"

His watch beeped—it was time again.

Harry rocked himself out of the rocking chair, to the kitchen, to the vodka bottle, and had himself a substantial belt. He offered his visitor a drink, but on getting no reaction he decided that, to keep things on a roll, he ought to have another one. And that was one too many.

He rocked back on his heels, then rocked forward, making a slow run for the bedroom door. Halfway there, the floor tipped up, slowing him to a stop—but then it tipped down again, allowing him to sail right on through the bedroom door and to fall across the bed.

"Ah, yes . . ." he sighed.

It was time for bed. And it felt good, so good. He got under the covers, closed his eyes blissfully. Then he opened his eyes a little to see the lizard-man through the deepening blue shimmer, a distant blur now, bending over him, looking down, flicking his long tongue.

"So . . . sorry," Harry mumbled. "End of the day . . . Back

tomorrow . . . same time . . . same station . . ." And then another thought wandered through his fading consciousness, and he whispered, "Y'all come back, now . . . hear?"

And then his lights went out.

CHAPTER 2

When he awakened, there was daylight in the room—a great, blinding lot of it. "Oh, my god," he whimpered through head-splitting pain. Open blinds! Who the hell would do a thing like that? Could easy kill a man in a weakened condition.

"S'criminal, 's what it is."

In the morning, Harry Borg was always in a weakened condition. Maybe not as weakened as he was this morning. God-almighty, he had a head this morning! He felt his head and found a very sore spot on the back of it. A spot scraped clean of hair! Took a fall, is what he must have done. Hit his head on the corner of something. That, and the kind of vodka they sold nowadays, had gotten him a head that really boomed. And that was not all by a long shot. His insides were shaking like a short-haired dog in a blizzard; his mouth felt like chickens had been dusting in it. Mercy! Harry tried to sit up, couldn't make it, and fell back.

It's finally here, he thought. *My last day on earth!*

"Good morning, Harry," a quiet voice said.

Harry almost jumped out of his skin.

Who the hell was that?

Coming around in the morning? In his apartment? Nobody he knew came around. Not in weeks. Maybe months. Panic began to shake Harry's already shaken mind. It could be an

13

enemy. It *had* to be an enemy! Who else would open blinds and
let all that daylight in on a dying man? He wasn't going to open
his eyes and get the hell scared out of him—no way! What he
needed was a bracer. First.

"Stand aside," he groaned.

Then he lurched up, eyes still clamped tight shut, ran a track
he knew blindfolded to the kitchen, to the vodka bottle. Never
mind the shot glass, there wasn't time. He tipped the bottle
straight to his lips, took a couple of long swallows, then a couple
more. Eyes still shut, he followed the track back to the bed and
collapsed there, breathing heavily, to wait for the booze to knit
up his raveled sleeves.

Then, voice hoarse, eyes still closed, he asked, "Who're you?
Anybody I know?"

"I was here before," a voice said.

A voice?

What voice?

Harry's fuddled, stricken, pain-filled mind struggled, fighting
panic again. He kept his eyes squeezed tight shut. "Say something more—anything."

"Don't be frightened," he heard after a moment.

Ah-ha! It wasn't a voice. It was like *thinking* in his head.
The two large belts of vodka had worked into his bloodstream
and were bringing swirls of pain-killing balm to his brain, soothing, relaxing. He lay quietly as the pain receded.

I know who it is, he thought behind closed eyes. *Sure—who
else?* Reassured by his realization, he began to chuckle quietly.
*Yeah! It's my old buddy the lizard-man back again! How about
that?*

He opened one eye carefully.

"There you go!" he said aloud, very pleased. Because, bending over him, tongue flicking out now and then, was the lizard-
man, sure enough.

"Glad you're back."

"Couldn't stay away."

Harry closed the eye he'd opened. He was right. It wasn't a
voice. It wasn't sound. It was in his head. Like thoughts. Like
he was talking to himself in his head.

How could that be? he asked himself.

Feeling better, he opened both eyes.

And there the lizard-man was, still looking down at him, and Harry was willing to swear the glowing, yellow, vertically slitted eyes were friendly, even concerned. He might have been smiling, though it was hard to tell, because his face was, generally speaking, pretty much the face of a lizard. Kind of a long muzzle, no nostrils. But there was a forehead. Yes, definitely there was a forehead. No hair, though. Scales. Soft, smooth scales with a little blush of pink behind them. A warm-blooded reptile, for chrissake? Yes, apparently. The DTs came in all shapes, colors, and sizes—ask anybody.

"You got a name?"

"Yes, of course. My name is Guss Rassan. You could call me Mr. Rassan. Or Rassan. I'd like it if you'd call me Guss."

"Guss it is," Harry said. "I'm Harry Borg."

"I know."

"Well, say—" Harry sat up in bed. "How did you—" He grabbed his head just before it fell off. After holding his head tenderly, he trusted himself to shake it carefully. "We're talking—and I'm the only one making any noise! It can't be!"

"It is."

"Aw, come on! No way!"

"Harry! I'm telling you! It is!"

"How could it be?"

"Because I can't, as you would say, talk out loud. We use telepathy."

"We? Who's we?"

"We are essans. I am an essan just as you are a human."

"You look kind of like what we would call a lizard."

"So I understand," Guss said, then went on with his quiet explanation. "My country is called Jassa. I'm a citizen of Jassa, a Jassan, if you will. A sissal-player by profession. I come from around Larissa—that's on the west coast of Jassa—" He broke off, waving his many-fingered hands. "Let's just say I'm a visitor for now, and let it go at that until you feel better."

"Yeah." Harry closed his eyes. "Yeah, till I feel better . . ."

He was needing again.

"If you'll excuse me," he said with an apologetic half smile, "I've got to have me a couple of blasts." He got up and stood, wavering. "I'm a little loose and rickety in the mornings sometimes. But I'll be all right when I get myself nailed back together."

He indicated the kitchen.

"Sure, Harry," Guss said, and stood out of the way.

Harry tipped back, then lurched forward and shambled quickly into the kitchen. There he had a long drink straight out of the bottle, and stood motionless while the booze worked its way down. Then he glanced at Guss, who was standing in the doorway, watching with interest.

"Gimme a half hour, will you?" Harry said. "Fix myself something to eat, get a bath, shave, clean clothes, y'know? I'll be like a new man."

He had another belt. Ummmm, better! He could feel the shakes slowing down, the pain going away. And then he remembered his manners. "You want something to eat? Eggs? Bacon?"

"No," Guss said. "Not my kind of food, thanks."

"Figures," Harry said. He rubbed stiff, shaking fingers into his forehead. Lizards ate bugs, didn't they? Or mice? Something like that.

"I'll watch your television, if you don't mind."

"Be my guest," Harry said.

When Guss went to turn on the TV and settle himself in the rocker, Harry stood at the counter, keeping a firm grip on the vodka bottle. He had a nip. Then he stood staring at the cupboard door a foot in front of his face.

Easy does it, he told himself.

"Way to go!" he said aloud.

"What was that?" Guss asked.

"Nothing," Harry answered. "A figure of speech."

He drained the vodka bottle, got rid of the empty, and broke the seal on a fresh quart. Short or long, this was going to be a day full of surprises.

"Gonna need plenty of juice."

"Juice?" Guss asked from the other room.

"Juice of the grape," Harry said. "Booze."

Steadied up, nailed back together by the vodka, Harry went past Guss, who was comfortably rocking, watching a Woody Woodpecker cartoon. He went into the bathroom, showered and shaved—he wondered only vaguely why his beard was like three days' growth instead of one—and put on clean clothes. He felt better then. Almost good. He found his glasses, polished them, set them on his nose. He made his bed—drum tight, of course—

wiped his shoes with a shine rag. Dusted. And that brought him to the bedside table and the framed picture of his grandchild, a girl, four years old, blue eyes, golden hair.

So sweet. So fair.

"I'm sorry," he whispered, as he did each morning.

Guss was still in the rocking chair, watching TV, when Harry went back to the kitchen. Coffee, toast, a couple of scrambled eggs, and he felt as near normal as he'd ever felt in the last thirty years. He could think straight, he was sure, talk straight, and he could even drive a car, if he had to. He was wrong on all counts, of course; but, like all drunks, he was blissfully unaware of the fact. He laced a cup of coffee with a liberal dash of vodka and carried it into the living room. Guss turned off the TV.

"Go ahead, watch it," Harry said. "Y'can get a game show pretty quick—that'll show you we're a race of babbling idiots."

"I've seen enough for now," Guss said.

"Know what you mean," Harry said. "Coffee?"

"No, thanks."

Remembering, then, Harry looked. The hole Guss had come through was gone. "Now, look there," he said, with excessive good humor, a man going along with a joke. "You got no way to get back!"

"It's been repaired," Guss said. "It's a door now."

"Repaired," Harry said carefully. "A door now."

"I didn't think you'd like a hole there."

"Why, no! Of course not!" Harry had a quick sip of the vodka-laced coffee. "Who'd want a hole in his wall—even if his wall wasn't there." He blinked several times. "All right," he said. "I appreciate that, I surely do. A nice door I can't see in a wall that isn't there. You shouldn't have gone to all that trouble."

Guss tipped his head back and opened his mouth in what could have been a smile. At least Harry got the feeling Guss was amused.

"You don't believe I'm real," Guss said.

Harry thought a moment.

"Well, let's put it this way," he said finally. "I've been drinkin' pretty hard. And I've been havin' hallucinations—the delirium tremens, y'know? And it's got so I really can't tell real from phony." He picked up his cup and gestured with it. "Holes in walls that aren't there, lizard-men that talk to me with telepathy—my friend, the whole routine is pretty goddamn farfetched to be real. Odds are like maybe ten-to-one the whole sketch is a hallucination. I've gone bonkers, I guess. Not that it matters."

He had a sip of his laced coffee.

"Why do you do it?"

"Do what?"

"Drink that booze?"

"Why not?"

"It affects your mind. And it's going to kill you, if you keep on."

"You're right. Might even kill me today."

"Then why?"

"I can't quit! That's why!" Harry was a little angry at being asked such a stupid question. "I'm hooked! For the past thirty years I've been hooked! Hooked and can't get loose! That answer your question?"

"I don't know what 'hooked' means."

"It means when I try to quit, I hurt. I hurt so bad I like to go out of my cotton-pickin' mind. It's like I'm being tortured to death! It's the pits!"

Guss said nothing, waiting.

Harry had another sip.

"A few times I did," he said, gazing at nothing, remembering. "Quit, I mean. I'd be dry for a couple of months, maybe more. Everybody thought, 'Hey, look at Harry. He's a new man!' Sure. Bright-eyed, rosy-cheeked, bushy-tailed, sharp as a razor—that was me. What they didn't know was that every damned minute of every damned day I was thinkin', 'Let's have a drink, Harry. Maybe a short one. Who's gonna know? Get a short pint, slip it in your desk drawer. Some breath mints . . .'" Harry shook his head resignedly. "It was no damn use. Sooner or later I'd have me a quickie, y'know? To test myself. And that would be all she wrote."

"All she wrote?"

"The end of fighting the booze."

"It's going to kill you soon."

"I know it, I know it!" Harry looked at Guss, then away. "With you showing up—no offense, of course—but with a DT as bad as you, a man can't have much track left."

Guss, with what might well have been sudden exasperation,

got up to pace the room. Harry moved quickly to get his place in the rocking chair before Guss got back to it. His rocking chair was *his* place. He felt at home there, secure. He could rock and sip. But he didn't want to be rude about it. He tried to pretend it didn't matter one way or the other.

"You were saying?"

Guss looked around the apartment, then made a gesture that included all of it as he sat down on the sofa. "Where is this place?" he asked.

"This apartment?"

"Everything. This—what I can see out the window."

"Oh," Harry said, understanding. "Like you were from another world, right?"

"Right."

"Gotcha," Harry said.

He was into the swing of it now, enjoying, ready to play the game to the hilt. He finished his spiked coffee, put the cup down, and lurched out of his rocking chair. At a closet, he rummaged for a moment, then returned with an inexpensive world globe.

"Here's your planet Earth," he said.

Guss's reaction was one of immediate and intense interest. He almost snatched the globe from Harry's hands. He took it with him, to sit on the sofa again, to study the globe minutely, his yellow, slitted eyes sharply intent, fingers tracing continents, oceans.

"The planet Earth is one of eight planets," Harry said. "Or is it nine? I forget. Anyway, they all orbit the Sun." He was talking like a slightly inebriated sixth-grade schoolteacher, but he wasn't aware of it. "The Sun is one of billions in the galaxy called Milky Way, and the Milky Way galaxy is one of billions in the universe."

Guss went on studying the globe. "Where on this Earth are we?"

Harry reached out to spin the globe. He planted a finger dramatically. "North America," he said. "The United States, the state of California, the city of Los Angeles, the suburb of Canoga Park. Seventy-eight forty-three Charleston Street—there!"

Guss spun the globe, looking further. "How big is the Earth?"

Harry held his hands up, a foot apart. "That's a foot," he said. "Five thousand two hundred and eighty of those makes a mile. And the Earth's about twenty-five thousand miles around the middle there. You follow that? I mean, miles?"

"How many of you live on it?" Guss asked.

"Four billion, give or take a few."

"And other—what? Creatures?"

"We've got all kinds. Insects, birds, fish, mammals. And reptiles, like you—only, well, different—the crawly kind." He hoped he hadn't offended, and apparently he had not. "You try to count all the kinds we've got, and you'd end up with zeroes clear off the page."

Guss seemed to be only half interested in what Harry had been saying, lost in discoveries and speculations of his own. He finally put his thoughts into words.

"It's practically the same!" he said, shaking his head in wonderment and disbelief.

"What is?"

"Your planet, Earth. It's the same as our planet, Essa, as near as I can tell from this globe."

"What're you saying?"

"I'm saying it's the same."

"You got a world like ours?" Harry's voice had gone a little shrill. "You're putting me on!"

"Land, oceans—" Guss indicated the globe. "Not enough difference to matter."

"It can't be!"

"It is, though."

Harry stood back on his heels, waiting for Guss to relent, to tell him it was all a joke, a put-on. But Guss didn't. Instead, he seemed to be as amazed as Harry was.

"All right," Harry said, turning belligerent. "If it's the same as our world, where the hell is it?"

Guss looked around the apartment, searching. Searching for an answer, for understanding. And he found neither. At last, reluctantly, he said, "It's here."

"Come on!" Harry scoffed. "*We're* here!"

"And so are we."

"I'm an engineer," Harry said warningly.

"What's that supposed to mean?"

"It means you can't con me!" Harry drew himself up with a

great show of righteous dignity. "Two objects cannot occupy the same space at the same time—that's the law!"

"Law? What law?"

"The law of phys—physics!" That's a hard word to say when smashed, but Harry got it said and with some authority. "Any kid knows that."

"And I know that."

"So don't try to con me."

"You're getting drunk," Guss said.

"I'm always drunk!" Harry said indignantly. "'S a way of life around here. But that don't mean— Oh, wait a minute! You—you're—"

"That's right," Guss said. "You saw me come through the hole from my place, remember? Right over there. Didn't you? The screw? The pounding?"

"Yeah! Yeah! Yeah!"

Godfrey! Harry said to himself.

"Hold your fire," he said to Guss.

He did a right-face, took aim on the kitchen, straightened his spare, suntan-clad body, set his glasses squarely on his nose, squared his shoulders into a military brace, and barged into the kitchen. It was time, clearly, for direct action. He poured a belt of vodka into the shot glass, knocked it back, and poured another.

"One more," he said.

And he knocked it back. Then he turned around.

"I'm still here," Guss said.

Defeated, Harry made his way back to the rocking chair, sat down carefully, and began rocking slowly. He ignored Guss, and as he rocked, he worked at getting himself and his mind straightened out. It took a few moments, but presently he was sure he was as sensible as anybody.

"All right," he said. "So you've got a world that's just like this. Okay. So what about inhabitants?"

"Two billion like myself," Guss said. "No more, no less."

"Exactly?" Harry asked, disbelieving.

"We've got a very strict population control."

"Y'must have, if you can stick to two billion. Don't get me wrong. If you've got it, and stick to it, it's a good thing. The best. Look at us. We go on multiplying, which is the root of

most of our troubles. The fight for food and space, y'know?"
Then, to be agreeable, he said, "What about animals? I mean,
beside yourselves."

"Of course," Guss said. "All kinds. And a great many like
you. We call your kind bassoes. We use you for—" He decided
not to go on in that direction. "Never mind. We've got insects.
Some very big ones we've domesticated, some small, marine
life—all that."

Harry put a finger beside his nose. "And all this clutter is
living in the same space we are. Only we don't know it. Can't
see 'em. Can't feel 'em. Is that about right?"

"Looks that way."

"It's impossible, you know."

"I know," Guss said. "And I know Klasson is right over there,
using the same space your kitchen is using—or a lot of the same
space."

Even muddle-headed, Harry had heard something he could
pick up on. "What's a Klasson?"

"An—an—" Guss seemed to be searching for a word
in Harry's language. "An estate, that's it." Now he seemed a
bit reluctant. "My family's for centuries. The government took
it—" Again he was searching. "—Back taxes? Yes. I have just
redeemed it, and I've been—working on it." He gave up. "It's
a place like this."

"And you're a klutz, right?"

"Klutz?"

"With tools. You try to set a screw, you get it in crooked.
You try to put up a shelf, you knock a hole in the wall."

"That's right," Guss admitted. "I never was any good with
tools. Not my line of work."

"You got a line of work?"

"Of course!" Indignantly.

"Like what?"

"I play the sissal."

Harry laughed. "What the hell's a sissal?"

Guss was offended. "I'm an entertainer," he said. "And not
what you would call small-time, either."

"I still don't know what a sissal is."

"It's something I play." Then he threw up his hands. "You
haven't got words for it, so how can I tell you?"

"Does it make music?"

"That's close." Guss apparently saw he was not going to get out of this without some kind of an explanation, so he made an effort: "The instrument doesn't make what you call sounds—it's more like odors."

"Stinks?" Harry tried to keep his face straight. "No, it wouldn't stink. Makes nice smells, right?"

Controlling his obvious exasperation, Guss replied as patiently as he could. "To us, very beautiful odors that we take in through our tongues." He extended his long, forked tongue for Harry to see, and it was rather nice, the way he could flex it about and then withdraw it. "And I entertain thousands."

"I'll be trampled to death by a duck!"

"What does that mean?"

"It means I'm baffled," Harry said. "But I ain't gonna fight it. If you say that's the way it is, that's the way it's gonna be with me."

Guss seemed to brighten. "You don't have any idea the excitement me busting that hole"—he nodded toward where the door would have been, if it had been visible—"caused on my side."

"I'll bet! Everybody's goin' bananas, right?"

"Not everybody!" Guss said hurriedly. "Just a *few* know about it! A few big, biggies. A couple of scientists. And they're keeping it very hush-hush. And I don't think they *really* believe it yet. Well, think what it would mean, Harry—another world like ours, billions of your kind, right next door, so to speak. It's *big*, Harry!"

"Sure would be," Harry said, unimpressed.

"What d'you mean?"

"If it were true."

"It *is* true!"

"Yeah, yeah," Harry said, soothingly.

He looked at Guss and saw that the lizard-man wanted very badly to be believed. Some kind of a DT, that was for sure. But what the hell? Why not? "It's a wonder *they* believed you at all," he said with a straight face. "It's a pretty wild story, you know."

"They didn't believe me at all, at first," Guss said. "But they let me talk to a doctor friend of mine—thought I was nuts, y'know—and I convinced him to take a look."

"When was this?"

"When you were asleep—passed out, I guess you call it."

"I was asleep," Harry said with some dignity.

"Whatever," Guss said.

"And this doctor believed you?"

"I brought him in here. And, well, there you were! There all this was!" Guss waved his multifingered hands in exasperation. "How the hell could he *not* believe it?"

"So?"

"So he's got clout enough that he could get the big, biggies—high government officials, y'know—to look. A group came over and looked around for themselves. They took you over to our side and gave you a physical you wouldn't believe, Harry. And they gave your TV a workout. There were two or three of them watching your TV all the time you were gone."

"Gone? *I* was gone?"

"Only two days, Harry," Guss said apologetically.

"Two days!" Harry said. "You got a nerve!"

"You weren't harmed, for Chrissake! And they wanted the time to watch your TV, to learn as much as they could."

"You learned about us from TV? From *Diff'rent Strokes*? From *Happy Days*? From *Laverne and Shirley*? You got to think we're a nation of mutton-heads!"

"What's a mutton-head?"

"Never mind," Harry said. "While I was gone—that was when you learned to talk inside my head?"

"It's a little device," Guss said, again apologetically. "A kind of what you call a radio receiver. Sassan—he's my doctor friend, a very famous surgeon—he put it there. Gave you a little head-ache's all. At first. It won't bother you again."

"Imagine that!" Harry said, more pleased than not. "Now I can talk to lizards!" Then, after a moment's thought, he said, "You don't talk very good English, y'know. Too much slang."

"It's the way you talk."

"No way! I'm an educated man—" He stopped, mildly cha-grined. "Y'got a point. It's the TV," he explained. "You watch enough of it, you begin to talk like Fonzi, y'know?"

"You talk different, I'll talk different."

"Okay! Okay!" Then, as a realization grew, Harry said, "If

all this two-worlds business is so big, big, big, why isn't all hell goin' on *right here, right now*? Why all the hush-hush?"

Guss became very uncomfortable. "Harry, I don't know how to tell you this, but your world's in one helluva mess."

"Everybody knows that!"

"It's maybe worse than everybody knows," Guss said, almost apologetically. "When our scientists found out how bad it was—and they've got ways—it scared hell out of them. They don't want what's going to happen to you to happen to us "

"So what's going to happen to us?"

"You're going to blow yourselves out of existence. With those nuclear bombs, y'know. Maybe this year. Maybe next. Within ten years, for sure."

"Funny, that's what I've been saying."

His watch beeped—it was time for another.

He rocked out of his chair again, made it to the kitchen counter and to the vodka bottle without a stumble. Two ounces of vodka knocked back and he was on a glide again, those lovely fumes swirling through his brain.

"So *I* don't have to worry," he said over his shoulder.

"Why's that?" Guss asked.

"I'll be long gone," Harry answered, almost with satisfaction, as he poured another one. "Booze is gonna do 'er first."

"That's up to you."

Harry agreed. "And it ain't a bad way to go. If you got a choice, I mean. Booze or bomb, I'll take booze anytime."

He had the other one and made his way with increasing unsteadiness back to his rocking chair. "How do you folks explain it?" he asked once settled, making pleasant conversation. "This business of two worlds being in the same place at the same time?"

"We can't explain it," Guss said. "The best guess is that the catastrophic event that wiped out our kind, what you call 'reptiles' on your world—" He paused and looked at Harry sharply. "They were the dominant species on your world, you know."

"I knew, but I didn't know you did."

"Anyway, that catastrophic event—whatever it was, probably a collision with a meteor the size of a small planet—caused it. How? I don't know. Nobody knows. There are a lot *more* things that we *don't* know than we *do* know."

"That's the wisest statement I've heard yet."

"And I know less than most. I'm a sissal-player, not a scientist. I believe in accepting things the way they are without a lot of questions and arguments."

"I'll drink to that—next time I'm up."

"In our world we're still the dominant kind," Guss said with a pride that verged on smugness.

"You're dominant over people?" Harry's eyes became round behind his glasses, even owlish, though not sharply focused because of the booze. "I don't believe that."

"It's true."

"How could that be?"

"Your kind—the bassoes—they're not intelligent. They're like, well, your cattle and sheep."

"Is that a fact!" It was an exclamation, not a question. "What do they look like?"

"About like yourself; almost identical."

Harry was amazed. "And they're dumb?"

"Yes."

"How could that be?"

"I don't know!" Guss was obviously distressed. He got up to pace to the window, to pretend to look out. "Evolution! Why didn't your cattle become intelligent?"

"Beats me," Harry said.

He rocked for a moment, pondering the vagaries of the evolutionary process in a muddled, booze-fogged way. Who could say why one species developed in one way and another species in another? Luck of the draw?

"What do these dumb people do?" he asked. "If they're as dumb as cows and sheep, what good are they?"

"Harry, I—" Guss began.

And the doorbell chimed.

Surprised, Harry said, "Whaddayuh know?"

"What is it?"

"Somebody at the door. A visitor? I haven't had one in weeks! A salesman, prob'ly. He'll go away."

The doorbell chimed again.

Harry went on rocking.

Then a hard rap was followed by a pleasant but firm voice. "Police officer. Official business. May I speak to you, please?"

"It's the fuzz!" Harry said. "How about that!"

Harry rocked himself out of the chair. "Stick around," he said to Guss. "Only be a minute."

Harry made his way down a short hall, staying in the center of it by touching walls a time or two. He lifted the chain and opened the door. A large young man in uniform was standing there, blue-jawed, with friendly dark eyes and a pleasant, though concerned, smile.

"Sorry to bother you, sir."

"S'all right."

"We're canvassing the neighborhood," the officer said. "A young lady and her child are missing from the next building. A Mrs. Lori Calder and her daughter, Tippi. The daughter is thirteen years old. You know them, by any chance?"

"No, I don't."

"Here's a picture."

He showed Harry an eight-by-ten portrait of a very pretty young woman of about thirty and a daughter about eleven or twelve. "It's an old picture," the officer said.

Harry blinked at the photograph.

"You haven't seen them? Or know anything about them?"

Harry was holding on to the door with one hand, steadying himself, looking at the picture, moving his head back and forth a little to keep it in focus.

"Sorry. Missing, you say?"

"Since yesterday. No reason, no trace."

"Looks kind of like my granddaughter," Harry said. "The daughter. Older, of course. Same hair, though. Pretty."

The officer was looking closely at Harry, still in a friendly way but missing nothing. And there was a lot not to miss. Harry was smashed, obviously, and the officer knew from the manager that Harry was a reclusive drunk, a ding-a-ling, some would say.

"Sir," the officer said, kindly, "d'you mind if I come in and look around?"

"No, no, not at all," Harry said. "I was going to ask you if you'd like a cuppa coffee, maybe a drink."

"No, nothing to drink, thanks," the officer said as Harry stood aside for him. "I'll only take a minute. Just a formality. I promise I won't be a bother."

"You see a fella in there looks kind of like a lizard, he's a friend of mine. Name's Guss." After a moment's thought, he shook his head. "Can't swear he's real, though. Could be a DT. You know, a hallucination?"

"You getting hallucinations?"

"Yeah. Weeks now. This one's outa sight, though."

He followed the officer, half expecting to find Guss waiting. But the lizard-man was nowhere in sight. Neither was the wall that wasn't there, the opening, or any trace. So Guss had been a DT, after all. Harry was not surprised, and only mildly disappointed.

"I know about the DTs," the officer said. He was going through the kitchen cabinets, the refrigerator, the broom closet. "Seen a few people havin' them. They're no joke."

"I liked this one!" Harry said, half serious. "I could talk to him and he talked back. Told me all about where he came from— ah, but you wouldn't believe it. You'd have to be drunked-up pretty good to even start believing it." He was standing beside the rocking chair, holding on to the back of it to steady himself.

The young officer checked the bedroom, the closets, the bathroom. He was impressed by the GI cleanliness of the place, and concerned about Harry's condition.

"Thanks for your cooperation," he said, pausing on his way out.

"Anytime!" Harry said grandly.

The officer stayed on, searching Harry's face, smelling the vodka. "You know I could call an ambulance and get you to a hospital. You're in pretty bad shape."

"Naw, I'm okay. A little drunk's all."

"You ever try a Care Unit? The AAs?"

"Nothin' works, friend."

"Sorry."

"'S all right," Harry said.

After another long, doubting pause: "Promise me something?"

"Sure. Anything."

"Stay home," the officer said. "Don't go out? Don't drive? All right?"

"Y'got it!"

"And if you hear anything about the lady and her daughter, give us a call. We'd appreciate it."

"Promise."

Harry locked and chained the door after the officer had gone. He went back through the living room to the kitchen, to the vodka bottle, and had a tot.

"To the cops..." he toasted quietly.

He'd just talked to one of the good ones, he knew. They were all good—some better, though. And that young fella had been one of the better ones. He cared! You could tell looking at him. He cared who Harry Borg was, and how Harry Borg was making it. You could count on the fingers of one hand who cared about Harry Borg.

"To Harry Borg..."

Funny thing, though. They all thought that when he was smashed he couldn't think straight. And that was where they were wrong! Falling-down drunk, he could think as straight as anybody. Maybe he couldn't walk straight, or see very well, but sometimes he could think even better after a drink or two. Lockheed couldn't understand that. They'd fired him. And they'd fired a damned good man.

"To Lockheed, a fine airplane company..."

He drank to that, shuddering only slightly, then poured himself another. He lifted that glass and offered another toast.

"To Guss," he said solemnly. "As fine a DT as any drunk ever had!"

He barely got that one down. But it stayed, after he'd swallowed a time or two to keep it there, and after the glow hit him he knew the lights were about to go out again. He turned, tipped back on his heels, then tipped forward and trotted straight through the living room and into the bedroom, where he flopped onto the bed.

His eyes closed.

He began to snore.

CHAPTER 3

Harry Borg's sleep was dreamless, and he had no idea how long it lasted. When he awakened in early evening darkness, he awakened slowly. It was a pleasant awakening, different from any he had known since he had been very young. His mental awareness was fresh and clear. And, of course, the first thing his mind became aware of was that his head didn't ache and his mouth felt clean.

"What's goin' on?" he asked aloud.

There was no reply. Neither was there an explanation of why he didn't have his usual ball-breaking hangover. He hadn't been sober in thirty years. And yesterday, as he remembered it vaguely, he hadn't made it clear through the day. He remembered getting smashed out of his skull before noon, and managing to crash-land on his bed.

Yet here he was—no hangover! Feeling like a kid again! He took a deep breath. His lungs filled up wonderfully. His body felt bigger. He ran his hands over his chest, shoulders, and arms—and what he discovered scared the hell out of him. He reared up, eyes flying open. My God! He was different all over! He had muscles on top of muscles. He leaped out of bed— *leaped*? He hadn't leaped out of anything since he'd been sixteen! He groped for a light and turned it on. He lunged for a mirror and saw the answer.

30

He had changed!

He was wearing a short, neatly trimmed beard. He had a tanned, healthy-looking face. He had clear, sharp eyes of a darker, more intense blue than he'd ever had. He had a thick column of a neck; broad, powerful-looking shoulders; strong, heavily muscled arms. And when he checked his waist, he found it lean and hard, and he found his legs were powerful, easily flexed, and full of life. He had been like this once before in his life, and that had been during his third year at U.S.C., when he'd been a weight-lifting, powerhouse fullback, an All-American— but that had been so long ago. This was now! The person he was now couldn't be Harry Borg, the sixty-five-year-old alcoholic. Couldn't possibly be him! Then who the hell was he?

"Can't be me!" he said in an awed, disbelieving whisper. "It can't be! But it is."

He turned away from the mirror. He found fresh suntans, fresh underwear, sox, shoes; and, dressing hurriedly, he found to his amazement that they all fit, though they were not—to his even further amazement—of quite the same material as the clothes he'd been wearing.

Moving quickly, then, he went into the bathroom, then into the living room. Everything was the same—but, no, it was not the same. There was a thin layer of dust on every flat surface. And, looking down the short hall to the door of his apartment, he saw his mail piled neatly on a hall table. All the letters were bills, he found, and three were bills from the same company bearing postmarks dated for succeeding months—the last on the first of September.

September!

"What about July and August?" he asked. "What happened to them?"

He went into the kitchen. A bottle of vodka and a shot glass were sitting on the tile counter where they belonged, thank God! He grabbed the bottle, twisted the cap, and began to pour—and stopped.

"What the hell?"

He didn't want a drink.

He stood a long moment, staring at the bottle in his hand, unbelieving. He didn't want a drink! Never before in his adult life had there been a time when he didn't want a drink, or, at least, hadn't been perfectly willing to have one. And here, now, didn't *want* one. More than that, he was *unwilling* to have one. And even more than that, he would *resist* taking one!

The full realization of what it all meant was several long moments sinking in. And when it finally did, he was filled with a joy so intense he wanted to shout out loud.

"Jumping Jehosophat!" he exclaimed. "I'm *free!*"

He was loose from the juice!

After thirty torturous years chained to a bottle, he was free! He could turn to the sink with that bottle, still two-thirds full—and he did just that. He could tip the bottle and watch the vodka gurgle down the drain—not with an agonizing despair at losing it, but with a beautiful, uncaring glee, knowing he could watch all the booze in the world go down a drain in the same way without even a shadow of regret.

"Un-goddamn-believable!" he whispered.

Then the doorbell rang.

It was followed by a knocking, tentative at first, then demanding. Harry fought to control himself. He finally managed a serious, controlled mien and went to open the door. The landlord of the building, Joe Lansky, was standing there. A short, rotund, balding man with round, rather bulging eyes, Lansky fell back a step at the sight of Harry.

"You—you ain't Harry—Harry Borg."

"So?"

Lansky didn't know whether to be apologetic, angry, or afraid at finding this young, athletic, even powerful-looking, man, instead of the elderly, totteringly alcoholic he had expected. There was a faint resemblance to Harry Borg, he saw now. But—

"I heard the toilet flush," he said, "and I thought it was Harry come back, and—" He broke off, staring hard at Harry. "You kind of look like Harry. You his brother, or something?"

"Brother," Harry said, glad he had been handed an explanation for his changed appearance.

"So where's Harry?" Lansky asked. "He die?"

"No, he didn't die."

"Glad to hear that!" Then the landlord realized he hadn't introduced himself. He did that, then said, "I've been worried as hell about Harry. He just took off about three months ago without tellin' anybody."

"Is it the rent?"

"No! No, not that," the landlord said hurriedly. "He was paid up for the rest of the year. It's just I *liked* Harry. Sure, he was a helluva lush! But he never bothered anybody. He was clean. A good tenant. What he did to himself was his business, I always said."

"I felt the same way."

"He go into de-tox?"

"Uh, yes!" Harry was again glad for the help. "He finally decided to take a cure. Takes a while, you know. Bad as Harry was, it'll probably take a long time." He looked back into the apartment. "I came back to check up—to see if his place was all right, that nobody had broken in."

"I've been looking after it," Lansky said. "After about a week, I got the cops and we came in—to see, you know. All those disappearances we had about the time Harry left, it was cause to worry."

"Disappearances?"

"First we had Mrs. Calder and her little girl—they lived in the next building. Then right after that five young men—football players, gettin' ready to go to college—they disappeared. All in a bunch. Found their car in the alley back of this building. Then, when Harry took off, we thought he was probably another. But we found his suitcase, clothes, and shaving gear were gone, so . . ."

"Yeah," Harry said. "Well, thanks for your concern. I'll tell Harry. He'll be touched."

"Fine. Anything I can do—Mr. Borg?"

"Yeah—Jerry Borg."

"Just give me a ring, Jerry."

"Thanks. I'll do that."

After the landlord had gone away Harry closed the door, hooked the chain, and moved slowly back into the apartment. He turned off the lights, went to his drafting table and stool, and sat in a room lighted only by the small glow of the street-lights.

"Three months," he said.

He had been gone that long?

Gone where?

His mind was lucid, clear, completely serious, deeply concerned. He was not quite afraid, but almost. He could not remember anything of the past three months—the three months in which he had, by some miracle, been cured of acute alcoholism. In which he had, by another, even greater miracle, been physically rehabilitated. More than rehabilitated—*rejuvenated*! He had been given the same body he had had as a college athlete!

In the name of God, what had happened?

Had he collapsed, finally, and been taken to a detoxification center? And had he then, afterward, physically reconditioned himself? And had his brain, horribly damaged by alcohol, lost all memory of those months, dropping them neatly out of his mind by some strange quirk, only to regain awareness here and now?

No, of course not!

Utterly impossible—all of it!

What then?

He could remember with perfect and total recall the time *before* his mind had stopped.

He could remember Harry Borg, the hopeless alcoholic. Harry Borg, rocking in that chair, day after day, bottle after bottle, killing time, killing himself with booze. He could remember enjoying the delirium tremens while he waited.

The little monk-spiders? The ones that had walked across the top of the kitchen door? Yes, he remembered those. And the screw that had come through in thin air? He remembered that, too. The hole in the wall that wasn't there, the lizard-man that had appeared—Guss? He remembered Guss very well.

"The DTs," he said aloud. "What the hell else?"

With a clear mind now, looking back, he knew Guss and Jassa and all that had to be the hallucinations of a deeply disturbed mind, a mind brought almost to the verge of total destruction by alcohol, totally unable to sort fact from fantasy. Had to be! Because, if it were not—

Good God!

The alternative was so enormous, so incredibly beyond any acceptable reality, that Harry could not even begin to consider it.

"It can't be—it can't be—"

And yet it had seemed so real.

That other world. Two worlds existing in the same space, but not in the same dimension—there could not possibly be such a place!

Could there?

A world on which reptiles had evolved into the dominant race? A world with a corner that had somehow, by some incredible chance, intruded into his apartment? A world from which a lizard-man who had called himself a Jassan had come? A Jassan who called himself Guss?

No, of course not!

"Never, never, never," he whispered.

And yet now, cold sober, it still seemed real.

Harry Borg got off his stool and went to stand before the area where the lizard-man named Guss had broken a hole in a wall that wasn't there. He stood on braced legs, his hands balled into fists, angry, yet feeling like a fool.

Right or wrong, real or fantasy—he had to know!

"Guss!" he called out harshly. "If you're there, come back. Now!"

Nothing happened.

Then he remembered about the telepathy. Guss had said that the Jassans communicated with telepathy. They had put a receiver in his head. He felt and found the faintest trace of a scar under the hair at the back of his scalp.

He put all the strength of his mind into a thought command.

"Guss! Come back! Now!"

Still nothing happened.

And then, in the wall that wasn't there, Harry saw a crack of light appear. The crack became a band of light, widening, until it had grown to a block of light the size of a rather wide door. Harry waited, braced, half in anger and half in fear.

Long moments passed.

"Guss," Harry finally managed in a strain-clogged voice. "Are you in there?"

There was another long moment of silence. Absolute silence. No sound of any kind. Not a thump, a bump, or even a scraping. Silence. Complete. Empty. And then, with perfect, in-the-same-room clarity, but tentative, even reluctant, an answer came.

"Yes. I'm here."

That familiar voice echoing in his mind worked like strong medicine on Harry's near-panic to bring the fear down to a level he could control, changing his anger to something more akin to exasperation than fury.

"Guss, you—" He drew a ragged breath and let it go slowly, heavily. "Why the hell don't you show yourself? You've scared the living daylights out of me!"

"*I'm* scared, that's why."

"What've you got to be scared about?"

"*You!* You're *angry!*"

"You better damn well believe I'm angry!" Harry said. "I got a right to be!"

Guss had to be just inside the doorway, obviously, standing with his back against the wall, out of the path of anything shot or thrown through the open door.

"So, maybe you have." Guss's tone was conciliatory.

"So come in here!"

"Oh, no! Not till you control yourself."

"You think I'm going to hurt you?"

"You could. You're bigger than I am, stronger. Or haven't you noticed?"

"I noticed!"

"Look again. Please!"

Harry looked down at himself again—and became less angry. Six-foot-two, weighing about one-ninety, flat-bellied, trim, hard— keerist! A round mirror in the living room gave him back the face of a young man. Hard, square jaw, covered by a neat, curly brown beard. Eyes a clear, dark blue.

"So?" Guss asked, after a moment.

"So what?"

"You'd rather be the way you *were*?"

And Harry had a flash memory of that. Harry Borg, the aging drunk, no more than a case of vodka from the grave.

"Good God, no!"

"So what are you angry about?"

After a moment, Harry capitulated. "I'm not angry. Not now, anyway. I was, but I'm not now. Come on in. I won't lay a hand on you. That's a promise."

"Back up a little. Give me room."

Harry backed up a few steps.

A yellow, vertically slitted eye peered around the frame of the lighted doorway. "Back up to the sofa and sit down," Guss said. "Keep your hands where I can see them. Then I'll come in."

"All right, damn you!"

Harry turned, angry again, strode to the sofa, and sat down hard, back against the back of the sofa, his hands open and firmly clasping his knees.

"Come on, now!"

"You've got a shock coming, Harry." Guss was still only an eye, peering. "You know that, don't you?"

"What kind of a shock?"

"The way I look," Guss said. "I don't think you believed I was what I am, when we talked in your apartment the last time." He paused briefly. "Did you?"

"You're some kind of a lizard, right?"

Guss's voice became mildly offended. "You say that like I'm some kind of—well, what d'you call it? Crud?"

"I didn't mean to offend you," Harry said with exasperation. "I'm no bigot. So you're not like us, so what the hell? Come on, show yourself!"

And with that, Guss stepped into the lighted doorway, into the room. He stopped, turned so Harry could see him plainly in the light that spilled in through the doorway. He seemed embarrassed, self-conscious, like someone posing who was not accustomed to posing, stiff and a little awkward.

Harry stared at him in awe. "I'll be go to hell," he whispered.

"What's that supposed to mean?" Guss asked, still mildly offended but becoming irritated.

"It means I can't hardly believe you."

And he couldn't. There, before him, standing about five-ten, was a lizard. A reptile of some kind, at any rate. A manlike lizard. Head, torso, arms, legs—all distributed in a way almost identical to humans.

The eyes were most compelling. They were quite large, yellow, the pupils vertical slits, like the eyes of a cat. Just now they seemed to be wary, as they looked at Harry, wondering, doubtful, almost fearful. Was Harry going to like him? Was he going to run, screaming? Was he going to attack?

"Relax," Harry said. "I'm just shook, is all."

Guss relaxed and let Harry continue to look.

And Harry thought that Guss's face, considered as a whole,

was not really frightening. It was reptilian but refined. The skin was smooth, only faintly scaled, a dark gray color, faintly pink. A warm-blooded reptile? The structure of the face was a very acceptable muzzlelike configuration extending forward from a forehead—yes, there was very definitely a forehead—from eyes widely spaced to a slightly upturned nose-tip with small nostrils. The mouth was generous, with nicely formed lips and white teeth: it was a mouth capable of expression. And there was a tongue. Good Lord! Was there ever a tongue!

The tongue was forked, to be sure. There was, as nearly as Harry could tell, about a foot of it, moistly gleaming, red in color, the outer four inches of it split into two independently sensitive tendrils. Guss used it constantly, particularly when agitated, as he obviously was now, flicking it out toward Harry, drawing it back, with graceful curls and twists—testing odors, Harry supposed, because he understood reptiles used their tongues for that purpose—in a way that was not unattractive at all.

"Well, for godsake!" Guss protested. "Are you going to sit and stare at me for the rest of the night?"

"Sorry!" Harry apologized without losing any of his exasperation. "You are different, you know!"

His attention had gone to Guss's clothing. Made of silk and fine leather, dark brown in color, the garments were simple but attractive—a shirtlike covering, open at the throat; what might be called a vest; short-legged trousers, well tailored to fit slim hips and lean, muscular legs; and moccasinlike boots.

"You've got eight fingers on each hand," Harry said. "I remember that now."

"Sure, sure," Guss said impatiently.

"And opposable thumbs."

Guss waited a moment, then spoke with exasperation of his own. "Can we sit down and talk now? Like a couple of rational beings?"

"Be my guest," Harry said.

Guss took the rocking chair with obvious relief that the worst moments had passed. "We do have a lot to talk about," he said.

And what had to be a smile lighted his yellow eyes, moved his lips. It was an attractive smile; it held friendship and warmth.

"Do you believe I'm real? That I exist?" he asked.

"Yeah, I do. There you sit!"

"Now tell me how you like yourself. Your *new* self."

Harry looked down at himself, felt his jaw. "No booze," he said. "Younger by thirty years. What's not to like?"

"You *do* like?"

"Hell, yes!" Harry leaned toward Guss. "You figure out a way to put what you did to me in a bottle and give it a nice label, and I can make you rich beyond your wildest dreams!"

Guss laughed. Harry knew that was what he had to be doing, because he tipped his head back, opened his mouth to show a pink interior—he had to be warm-blooded—a lot of white, very capable teeth, and a waving forked tongue, even though there was no sound. No sound at all. But there was laughter, a kind of a high, girlish giggle, inside Harry's head, telepathic, the way Guss's words were telepathic.

"You couldn't get Sassan in a bottle," Guss said finally. "He wouldn't stand for it."

"Sassan?" Harry asked.

"He's a surgeon. Does organ transplants." Guss's tone became apologetic. "You were in pretty bad shape, Harry. All that booze all those years. Your insides were about shot. Once Sassan started replacing organs and glands, he couldn't quit. You're like new, he tells me. Inside and out."

"And I feel like it," Harry said.

"Glad to hear it."

"How did I get this way? In this kind of physical shape? It would take me months of pumping iron, even years, to get like this." He frowned with a sudden realization. "I don't remember anything like that. I don't remember a damn thing about your world!"

"Your memory was blanked, Harry."

A new thought leaped into Harry's mind, pushing aside the first. "Where'd he get the new organs?" Harry asked. He was suddenly very serious. "Your kind are all like you, aren't they? Reptilian, right?"

"Naturally."

"And I'm a mammal." Harry looked steadily at Guss, who was becoming uncomfortable now. "You can't put reptilian parts into a mammal, now, can you, Guss?"

"Harry, I'm not a surgeon—"

"Guss!"

Guss looked at Harry a long moment, flicking out his long, forked tongue, wiping the air with it. "I suppose not," he said weakly.

"Where'd he get the parts, Guss?"

Very uncomfortable now, Guss squirmed in the rocking chair. Then he got up suddenly and went to the window, where he parted the slats and peered out, obviously trying to find something else to talk about, something to distract Harry.

"Harry, what I'd—"

"Guss!" Harry's tone was ominous. "You're going to tell me, or I'm going to unscrew your head. Where did this surgeon get the mammal parts?"

Guss turned from the window, very distressed, almost pleading. "Harry, we're getting into something I didn't want to talk about just yet. There's so much that's different ahead of you I— uh, well—I'd like to take it one step at a time."

Harry's dark blue eyes had become cold. "I'll jump a couple of steps for you Guss. So listen up." When he was sure he had Guss's undivided attention, he said, "We're missing some mammals around here. They disappeared just after you showed up. A young woman and her child. And five young men. Do you know anything about them?"

Guss's tongue flickered with great agitation.

"Harry, if you think your parts came from them, you're wrong! I can prove it—I *will* prove it!"

"But you *did* take those people?"

"Not me, Harry!"

"But your kind did!" It was a direct challenge.

"Harry, you've got to believe me! I didn't have anything to do with it! I wouldn't be allowed. And, anyway, I wouldn't do a thing like that! We're friends!"

"Stop ducking," Harry said. "Some of your kind took our people. Right?"

"Yeah," Guss admitted finally. "They did."

"And cut them up for parts."

"No! No! No!" Guss couldn't have been more vehement. "Your people are all right! They're even better than all right,

Harry. They're like museum pieces." Guss waved his eight-fingered hands. "Think about it a minute. Wouldn't they be? *Intelligent* mammals. Would we cut up something as unique as that?"

Guss was pacing back and forth now, and if it were possible for reptiles to sweat, he was sweating. Harry's grim, cold stare was unrelenting. Then, suddenly, Guss came to sit beside Harry on the sofa and make what had to be a salesman's last desperate pitch.

"You've got no idea what I've been through these past three months to keep you alive. To get you repaired. To keep that door open between our worlds."

"So tell me about it."

"I had to talk my way past I don't know how many stupid minds. Hundreds, Harry. Maybe thousands."

"Why was that?"

"When they found out what's ahead for your world, your kind, it scared the living hell out of my—what you call government. They're scared silly that when you blow up, we'll blow up. They wanted to seal that door shut. Tight! Forever! And if it hadn't been for me, they would have done it!"

"What are you, a world of craven cowards?" Harry asked.

"Cowards is a little strong," Guss said. "Wary is better. Yeah, very, very wary. If it hadn't been for me, they would have locked that door shut—forever."

"Is that a fact!"

"True, I swear it."

"Who're you that you could do something like that? Talk your government into big decisions? You're a sissal-player, or something, aren't you? An entertainer?"

Guss looked sharply into Harry's eyes. "Think of an entertainer, big, with a young audience, very popular in the last twenty years. All right, I read Elvis Presley." He sat back. "Among my kind, I rate like Elvis Presley did with your people. I'm somebody. Okay?"

"If you rate like Elvis, you're somebody."

"And I do. I am. I got the attention of important Jassans, and *they* influenced the government. Or most of them. Been a fight all the way, believe me. Two days ago I had to rush you back here, just to keep you alive." Then, hastily he said, "But it's all right now. Sassan—that's the surgeon who rebuilt you—he got his crowd together and they went to the very top. And now they want you to come back."

"Why?"

"To, uh—" Guss became very agitated again. He got up and went to the window. "Harry—I—I can't tell you. It's—well, it's still in the planning stage. There was to be a period of— what would you say? Observation. That's it!"

"I'm a freak, right?"

"In my world, yes. What am I in your world?"

"Y'got a point there."

"Will you come with me?"

Harry was silent a moment. "On one condition," he said finally.

Gus was suddenly nervous. "And that is?"

"You take me straight to see that Mrs. Calder and her child. And then those five young men."

"Why, Harry? Listen—"

"I'm going to bring them back, Guss," Harry said. "If they're still alive, I'm going to bring them back. And if they're not alive, I'm going to take you apart piece by very small piece, if it's the last thing I do."

"Harry . . ."

Guss tipped his head up. His long, forked tongue flailed upward in an excess of emotion. He seemed to sweat, or at least to be in a sweat of considerable proportions. He waved his multifingered hands; he shook his head.

"The humans have not been harmed, I promise you."

"But there's something else?"

"It's a whole different world, Harry."

"So?"

"If you—what d'you call it? Blow your top?—you'll get us both killed. I mean that. I promised I could—could control you. If it turns out I can't—" He made a sharp, cutting gesture.

Harry got to his feet. "Let's go!"

"Have I got your promise?"

"Nobody *controls* me."

"I didn't mean it that way. I meant—"

"I know what you meant, Guss. Let's put it this way: I'll do my best to keep us both alive. All right?"

Guss lifted and dropped his arms in a gesture of worried resignation. "If that's the best I can do . . ."

They moved toward the lighted door.

CHAPTER 4

There was a *snap* as Harry Borg, following Guss, crossed from one world into the other. It was as if the division between the worlds was a membrane without elasticity, so thin it was without dimension, a one-plane singularity that could not exist except in a theoretical sense.

He felt it, though. He did indeed.

And then they were crossing through what seemed to be a bedroom in what had once been a fine home, worn now after years of usage, needing repairs and replacements. But it was clean, Harry noted. Even broken things were polished.

Guss followed Harry's gaze, reacting, it seemed to Harry as they moved on to larger rooms, like a nervous housewife whose home was being inspected.

"You say this is your place? A family estate?"

"The government's for the past twenty years—they'd taken it for back taxes, and they let it run down, like everything else that belongs to the government. Since I, uh, became . . . well off, I decided to get it back. I was thinking I'd use it for a . . . hideaway."

"So you could be alone?"

"Being a celebrity sometimes—well, you know."

"I don't know, but I can guess."

The walls were blue, softened with age. The windows, floor

to ceiling, dark now, were sparkling clean. Recliners of various sorts were scattered about and looked comfortable, though in need of new upholstery. The floor covering, once rich carpeting, was showing worn pathways.

"Looks comfortable," Harry said.

A door opened as they approached it, and they moved out onto a terrace and into a warm night softly lit by a near-full moon. A moon, Harry was pleased to discover, no different from the one he'd always known.

"We put some men up there," he said, indicating the moon, and unable to resist being smug about it.

"Did you now?" Guss's tone held disbelief.

"Want to hear about it?" It was a challenge.

"Maybe later," Guss said after a quick glance at Harry, and several testing tongue flicks.

He began to move away, but Harry caught his arm.

"Hold it just a sec."

"What now?"

"I want to look." He was looking upward. "There you go!"

"What?"

"The Big Dipper. Polaris. We're in the Northern Hemisphere, below the forty-fifth meridian."

"What's that mean?"

"It means I know where I am—if your world's identical to ours, and I think it is. At least, the night sky's the same." He noted the temperature. Mid-fifties, Fahrenheit. He looked at the land. Gentle hills, dotted with oak, shrouded in what he felt sure was coastal fog, rolled away into the darkness. "I'd guess we're near the central coast of what we call California, not far from the bay."

"Pretty smart," Guss conceded grudgingly. "Larrissa's off that way a couple of hundred of your miles. A big city on the coast— a big harbor."

Harry grinned again. "San Francisco Bay, sure as you're born!"

"Whatever," Guss said. "Let's go."

Guss's sharp response caused Harry to reorder his priorities. The way back had to be number one. He *was* going to come back, of that he was sure. Possibly at night. Possibly at a dead run ahead of God only knew what kind of a pack. And he wanted the pathway to this place charted in his mind with utmost clarity.

"So much to see, to learn," he said, chidingly. "Guss, old buddy, don't hurry me. I've got a thick head—it takes time."

"Stubborn, yes," Guss said, about half surly. "Thick you are not. I'm beginning to see that now."

"Three minutes," Harry coaxed.

He looked back at the building they had just left. It had the look of a country home that someone with a pocket full of money and a Disneyland taste in architecture might have built—a long time ago. The airy grace of the building was blurred, colors faded, archways sagged, roofplates were missing. And the grounds had gone to weeds and tall grass and overgrown ornamental shrubs.

"Sure run-down."

"I had hoped to change that." Guss's thoughts saddened. "But now with this gateway to your world and all—well, the government has taken it back again. Lost to me for good now, I guess." He tugged at Harry's arm with sudden urgency.

"Come on!" he said.

Guss led him to a small paved area where a two-seater vehicle was parked. The pavement was cracked, and weeds grew from the cracks, and since there were no roads or paths leading to it, Harry had to assume the vehicle was an aircraft of some sort. Short, stubby wings did seem to bear out that assumption, but it sure as hell didn't look like it would fly. There was no rotor. On closer examination, he found there was a jet exhaust beneath the craft, and other exhausts pointing forward and rearward. While all the surfaces of the craft showed the dents and scrapes of age and hard usage, it still managed to look serviceable.

"Is this thing going to fly?" Harry asked.

"Fly?" Guss was still in a hurry, still impatient. "Of course it's going to fly! It damn well better!" He indicated a door on Harry's side. "Get in."

Harry got in and found himself in a worn though reasonably comfortable seat. Before him was a strange-looking instrument panel. A duplicate set of controls extended from beneath the panel, convenient to hand. Harry stared at the dials on the instrument panel a long moment before discovering they were the usual—artificial horizon, bank-and-turn, compass, air speed and altitude, among others—but with lettering in a strange language.

"I just realized you reptiles have a written language," he said, amused at his own tardiness.

"We can count, too," Guss said sarcastically.

His attention was on getting the craft started. And it proved not an easy task. He flicked a large OFF-ON switch, then waited expectantly. Nothing happened. He flicked the switch off, then on again. Still nothing. He hit the panel in front of him hard with the heel of his eight-fingered hand, and Harry heard what had to be Jassan profanity explode in his head. A third, even harder, hit did produce results. A low hum began, and with it came a steady vibration. Harry saw Guss relax, still angry but relieved.

"That's it?" Harry asked. "It's running?"

"It's running," Guss said disgustedly. "My craft's being serviced, and this is a loaner. I told them about that switch, and they said they'd fixed it." He flicked another switch that turned on the lights. "You think *I'm* a klutz. Wait'll you try to get something fixed in Jassa. In less than a week, and right the first time."

Harry laughed. "Sounds like I never left home." But he was still impressed. "Even if this rig works only half the time, it's hard to believe you could build it."

"Why's that?"

"You're reptiles, y'know. In our world—"

"In your world," Guss cut in, with very marked exasperation, "we're creepy-crawlies. I know. I read you loud and clear."

"Guss, I didn't—"

"Hang on!"

Harry tensed, expecting something dramatic. But there was only a slight increase in the humming and vibration as Guss drew back on the controls and the craft lifted straight up from the pad, smoothly, with no apparent effort, and kept rising to an elevation of about a thousand feet. There, Guss moved the controls forward, turned them, and the craft spun about until the compass showed a bearing, Harry noted, of 310 degrees. A slight movement of Guss's finger and the craft headed out, reaching a speed of a hundred knots in a few moments' time, still without apparent effort, still with just quiet humming and vibration. Harry was more than impressed.

"I'll be go to hell!" he said.

"Now what?"

"This—this aircraft! It's something else!"

His admiration was wholehearted and undisguised, and after all of Harry's negative reactions that had gone before, Guss was more than pleased. He was still giving most of his attention to the dials, as if not quite certain all was as it should be, or that it would continue to be as it was for any length of time, but in a few more moments he was able to relax and enjoy.

"Just a little something we reptiles whipped up on a lazy summer afternoon."

"I'll bet," Harry said. "No matter how long it took, it's a great little machine. We don't have anything even close."

Then Guss sobered. "We've got a problem."

"Yeah? Tell me."

"In your world, we reptiles are creepy-crawlies, something you'd step on and wipe your shoes after. Okay?"

"Not that bad!" Harry said.

"Almost," Guss said. "What I'm trying to get you braced for is this: Your kind rates about the same in our world as my kind rates in yours."

"Y'mean that?"

"You're chopped liver, Harry. Zilch!"

"Chopped liver! Zilch!" Harry protested. "Where you getting all that slang? I don't talk like that. I'm an educated man."

Guss gave the protest some thought. "It must be the television," he said finally.

"Television?"

"The hookup in your head translates what I think into *your* speech patterns," Guss said. "And your speech center is imprinted with a mishmash of rubbish you've gotten from watching too much television. I can't help what comes out. If 'worthless' translates into 'chopped liver,' that's your fault, not mine."

"You got a point," Harry conceded. "Give us another twenty years of the boob-tube and we'll be a race of idiots." Then, after a moment: "That gadget in my head only works on speech? You can't read my mind?"

"No way can we read minds," Guss said. "It's been against

the law ever since anybody can remember. Think about it. Wouldn't it be a crock if everybody knew what everybody else was thinking?"

"We'd all be in jail."

"So your thoughts are private, believe me."

"Glad to hear that."

Harry was relieved. He was very much relieved, because just now he wanted to know something, and he didn't want Guss to know why he wanted to know it. He forced a tone that was no more than friendly interest.

"I had a commercial pilot's license before I bombed out on the booze," he said. "You think a man with that kind of experience could learn to fly one of these rigs?"

"If you can fly a rocking chair," Guss said, "you can fly a Cassal. Those controls in front of you are the same as these in front of me. Take hold of them."

Harry grasped them gingerly. He found the controls were warm to the touch, almost alive. Two triggerlike buttons fell easily under his forefingers.

"Gently now," Guss said. "Pull toward you for up, push away for down, turn for left and right. Right trigger is go, left trigger is stop."

"And that's it?"

"That's it."

"Jet-powered," Harry said, marveling. "But not by air—and not by gas."

"Some kind of energy," Guss said. "Don't ask me what kind—or any of that."

"I know. You're a sissal-player, not a mechanic."

"You got it."

Harry manipulated the controls gently and smiled at the smooth, sure way the craft responded. "If I go hands off or the engine quits, what happens?"

"Nothing much," Guss said. "Like this."

He took control, lifted his hands. The craft lost speed, smoothly, braking, stopped, and remained motionless without loss of elevation.

"Sonofagun!" Harry said, amazed.

"Just a little something—" Guss began.

"I know. On a lazy summer afternoon."

"About two hundred years ago."

"Two hundred! Good lord! We were still looking at the tails of horses from the front seats of wagons!" He shook his head, marveling. "I got to hand it to you."

Guss got them under way again.

"What about fuel?" Harry asked. "And mileage?"

"A charge's good for about a thousand..."

Guss's voice had trailed off, his attention going to one of the dials on the instrument panel, a movement Harry found easy to recognize because it had to be the same in whatever civilization.

"You're about out, right?" he said.

Guss gave him an embarrassed glance. "I should have a half charge, anyway. Haven't gone anywhere to speak of." He rapped the dial with a long finger, his tongue beginning to flick with agitation.

"When the gauge says OUT, you're out," Harry chided, with ill-concealed amusement.

"Could be stuck."

He rapped the gauge hard.

"Don't fight it, my klutzy friend," Harry said. "You're about out of gas. Pull into the nearest pump."

"You know what time it is?" Guss asked angrily. "An hour before daylight. There's nothing open." He rapped at the gauge again. "We're still running, aren't we?"

"But not for long," Harry said.

And he was right.

In just a few more minutes the vibration faltered, then stopped. The craft came to a halt smoothly to hover, humming quietly, at an elevation of about twelve hundred feet. Guss seemed unconcerned about the height above the ground. But it made Harry nervous.

"Well?" he asked.

"Well what?"

"You going to set us down?"

"Why should I?" Guss asked.

"Because we're out of gas," Harry said angrily. "I don't know about you, but when I hit the ground from this high up, I splash."

"We won't fall!"

"We got a skyhook or something?"

"We've got a safety feature," Guss said, trying to be patient.

"You can't run into a mountain with a Cassal. Or a building. You can't fall out of the sky."

"And that safety feature?" Harry asked. "It works *all* the time? Like the switch, maybe?"

"The switch—"

Guss, reminded, began to look out the window at the moonlit landscape below. "If you're going to be nervous, I guess I could put down on that hill over there."

"If we're *both* going to be nervous," Harry said.

Guss didn't argue. He put the craft into a long glide that brought them to a gentle landing on the crest of a hill that overlooked what seemed to be cultivated farm area. And he did it with a sigh of relief. He saw that Harry had noticed the sigh.

"All right," he said defensively. "With the kind of mechanics we get nowadays, it doesn't hurt to be careful."

"I'll buy that."

He watched Guss lift a microphone very like the ones used in small planes on Earth and heard him ask for help. He got a response that promised help would be along shortly. Putting the mike back on the hook, he settled back in his seat.

"Be an hour before he shows," he said with some disgust. "You'll see."

"What time've you got now?"

Guss checked a timepiece on his wrist. "Four thirty-five, the way you figure it," he said after a moment's calculation. "The sun'll be up in less than an hour."

Harry set his watch.

There was already light in the east, and as it spread rapidly, Harry began to make out the details of the valley below the hill. He found a switch that lowered the window on his side, to let in the fresh, morning air and allow a clearer view. The land he could see below seemed rich and fertile, most of it under cultivation. Crops were planted in easily irrigated rows running north and south in areas as large as fifty acres, and now Harry could discern a large irrigation ditch in the near foreground. In the valley, there were trees planted as windbreaks, dividing the planted areas, and more trees, mostly oak, grew randomly in the hills.

There were habitations and what had to be farm buildings on the slopes immediately below and perhaps a quarter of a mile from the hill where Guss and Harry were waiting. A roadway emerged from the trees a hundred yards below, crossed, and disappeared into more trees. Harry sat listening to the sounds of awakening birds, saw a few of them flying from tree to tree—jays, he thought, or blackbirds—and thought it wouldn't take much imagining to believe he was sitting on a hill that overlooked the San Joaquin Valley in central California.

And then he heard the sound of voices.

It was a kind of chattering and chirping that was certainly human, and he became alert, searching for the source. Guss became nervous, then agitated. Harry heard him curse quietly, saw him hit the control with his hand. His tongue was flicking in that rapid way that spelled serious agitation.

"Harry," he said. "You've got to take it easy."

"What's the problem?"

"I said you were in for some shocks, but I didn't want you to get hit with this one so soon."

"What're you talking about?" Harry asked, his eyes searching for the source of the voices. "Who's out there? Sounds human."

"It is human, Harry."

"What the hell? I mean, how could there be—"

He looked at Guss and found Guss looking at him, his yellow eyes full of active worry. His long tongue was flicking very rapidly, almost a blur.

"You've got to brace yourself, Harry."

"For what?" Harry's eyes went back to searching the slope below.

Guss turned his eyes heavenward. "Everything happens to me!" he complained.

"Like what, for instance?"

"I've got to set us down here! Of all places!"

"So what's wrong with here?"

"It's farm country, Harry." Guss was trying to reason now. "What would you expect in farm country? Food products, right? Vegetables. Meat."

Harry's jaws grew tight. "Yeah . . ."

"That's what they raise here. Listen, Harry. Your kind have been raising meat animals since time began—cattle, hogs, sheep—like that."

The sounds of the human voices were coming closer, though

still a hundred yards away. They were very clear, almost like the trilling of birds in the stillness of the quiet morning.

Guss was watching Harry anxiously.

"Harry, you're getting upset."

"Damn right I'm getting upset!"

As the voice sounds grew more audible, Harry realized that they had no particular words, no meaning. The hair on the back of his neck began to crawl. The sounds were like the *baa*ing of sheep, the lowing of cattle. They were not the voices of *communicating* humans. They were mindless! The makers of the sounds were on that portion of the road that was still concealed by the overhanging branches of the trees, but they were approaching the clear area and would emerge onto the open road in a few more moments.

"Harry, you promised you'd control yourself."

"And I will! So tell me what's down there."

"Bassoes," Guss said. "What I did was, I set this damn Cassal down on a farm where they raise bassoes. For, uh, market. My rotten luck every time." He began to talk fast, because the sounds were moving closer. "I wanted to break it slow. Harry, listen! I was trying to say, you raise cattle for food. Have since the beginning of time. And we've raised bassoes—"

"People!" Harry said, tightly. "Not bassoes!"

For the herd—it had to be called a herd—of people, not bassoes, had straggled into view, moving out from beneath the trees along the road. They would cross fifty yards of open road before disappearing into trees again.

"Holy Christ!" Harry whispered, shocked.

CHAPTER 5

Harry Borg was more than shocked.

What he began to feel now was horror. Chilling, mind-numbing, sickening horror. But he couldn't turn his eyes away. Those creatures down there were humans. People! They were naked, of course, male and female about evenly divided. They looked frail in stature and build, like slowly developing sixteen-year-olds. And they were not unattractive. Their features, as well as Harry could tell at this distance, were very like the humans on Earth—though, especially in the older males, verging toward the coarseness of the Neanderthal. And their bodies were covered with soft gray fur.

"I can't believe it," he whispered.

Most of the creatures in the herd were young, though Harry could tell the older ones—large genitals on the males; well-developed, even sagging, breasts on the females—and all were completely docile. They moved along as a band of sheep might move.

"My God!" Harry exclaimed suddenly.

For he had just discovered that the humanlike creatures were being herded by a pair of—*beetles*! The beetles were the size of sheepdogs, and they were ranging on either side of the herd as sheepdogs would, nudging the stragglers, as they wandered off the road, back into the herd.

Then the shepherd came into view. The shepherd was an old Jassan, judging from the bent way he moved and from the way he leaned upon a staff as he plodded along in the rear.

"Insects?" Harry whispered incredulously. "To herd them?"

"Harry, I tried to warn you," Guss said.

"But *insects* to herd *humans*!"

"They're, uh, very smart insects, Harry."

"Good Godalmighty." Harry was at a loss for words.

He watched the herd as it moved along the road until it had passed out of sight in the trees again. Their vocalizing, as meaningless as the *baa*ing of sheep, faded gradually from hearing. And still Harry sat, stiff, tense, unbelieving.

"Come on, Harry," Guss said, almost pleading.

Harry drew a deep, ragged breath, wiped his face with a hard palm, and looked out over the valley, avoiding Guss's gaze. "Y'mean to tell me there's nothing in their heads, Guss? Nothing at all?"

"Like your cows," Guss said. "Like your sheep."

"What'd you *do* to them?"

"*Do* to them? Harry, they've been that way since time began. We didn't *do* anything to them. It's the way they are! The way they've always been!"

"I can't believe it."

"All right," Guss said. "Let me ask you this: Why are the reptiles on your world like the bassoes are on our world? Was it the luck of the draw? Roll of the dice? You tell me."

Harry scrubbed his face again.

"Godalmighty, I don't know!"

"D'you hear me groaning because we're crud in your world?"

"No."

"There y'are! It's something you've got to take in stride, get used to—whatever you call it. And there's something else. We're trying to *help* the bassoes. We really are! They were dyin' out, gettin' littler. And they don't multiply like they used to. That's why we took those five males. To improve—"

Harry turned on Guss, suddenly furious.

"Harry!" Guss said quickly, alarmed. "*I* didn't do it."

"But you reptiles did." Harry was snarling. "You took those five high-school kids, young men, for *herd bulls*!"

"The gene pool needed help," Guss pleaded, struggling. "That's what they told me. That's all I know. You could see the bassoes didn't look healthy, like you humans—" He broke off, waving his hands. "How do I get out of *this*?"

"You don't!"

"Quit blaming *me*," Guss said, his voice almost a shout inside of Harry's head. "*I* didn't have anything to do with taking those males. I'm a sissal-player, remember? And all the ones in charge are trying to do is save the bassoes from becoming extinct!"

Harry, face as grim as death, was staring out over the valley again, shaking his head slowly, as if fighting an inner battle he was by no means winning.

"Sonofabitch," he kept muttering. "Sonofa-flippin'-bitch! I can't believe it!"

"Geez!" Guss said, helplessly.

Guss's yellow eyes were glowing, the vertical slits wide in what must have been total frustration. He began talking, putting words in Harry's head, but in a way that indicated he was only bitching out loud.

"I don't know how the hell anybody can blame us for doing something we've been doing since time began. Especially when it's not a damned bit different from what the humans have been doing since time began. They eat cattle; we, occasionally, eat bassoes."

Harry's shoulders slumped in a kind of surrender. "All right. Maybe I shouldn't blame you. But it takes a helluva lot of getting used to."

"Fair's fair, right?"

"Right," Harry agreed reluctantly. "But I'll tell you something—the humans in our world don't eat reptiles." Then, being an honest man, he had to qualify that statement. "Except your rare ding-a-ling human. Your regular human wouldn't think of it."

"Why not?"

"What d'you mean, why not?"

"Just what I said. Why *don't* you eat reptiles?"

"They're nasty, that's why," Harry said, cornered.

"Nasty?" It was Guss's turn to become furious. "What's nasty about us?"

"You're snakes!"

They were facing each other now in the narrow confines of the aircraft. Harry's dark blue eyes were hot; Guss's yellow eyes were blazing, his long tongue a blur. Harry was yelling, and Guss's voice in Harry's head was just as loud. They were almost at the point of blows.

"What's wrong with snakes?" Guss demanded. "We're just as good as humans. Better! You make my ass tired, with your high and mighty—"

"*I* make *your* ass tired!" Harry yelled. "Listen, my scaly, forked-tongue friend—"

There was a rap on the window on Guss's side.

Outside, peering in, was a Jassan. He was a greasy-looking Jassan, clad in greasy-looking coveralls. He was motioning to Guss to lower his window, while staring at Harry and flicking his tongue.

Harry looked through the back window. He saw that another aircraft had landed behind them. It was obviously a tow-truck kind of an aircraft—battered, oil-spattered, with crane, hooks, and cables. When Guss had lowered the window, the mechanic forgot Harry and spoke to Guss with a sudden excited recognition.

"Say! Ain't you Guss? Guss Rassan, the sissal-player?"

"I'm Guss Rassan," Guss answered with a smug glance at Harry. "And I'm out of ergan. Fill it up for me, please."

"Yeah, you bet!"

But the mechanic was too overcome with the fact that Guss, the celebrity, was in fact sitting right in front of him to do anything about the empty tank at the moment.

"You know, I never miss one of your shows if there's any way I can get to it. Sometimes I travel a couple of hundred miles just to get to one of your shows."

Guss looked at Harry. "See what I mean?"

Of more interest to Harry at the moment—of startling impact, really—was the fact that not only could he hear conversation between two Jassans perfectly, but that it was coming through in his own vernacular, complete with the television-type slang and bad grammar.

"What's he going to do?" Harry asked. "Kiss your hand?"

"*He's talking!*" the mechanic yelled.

The mechanic's discovery pushed all else from his mind; he fell back another step. He stared at Harry, his yellow, slitted eyes about to fall out of his head, his tongue whipping in and out of his mouth in a blur.

"That bassoe *talked*!"

He continued to stare at Harry a moment longer. Then he sidled closer to the window on Guss's side.

"You got a talkin' bassoe, Mr. Rassan!"

"I know it."

"Wherever in the hell," the mechanic wanted to know, "did you find a thing like that?"

"None of your damned business," Guss told him.

The sharpness in Guss's voice escaped the mechanic entirely. His shock now turned to eagerness. "You gonna take him on the road with you, Mr. Rassan? What an act! You and a talkin' bassoe!"

"Fill the goddamn tank!" Guss yelled at him.

And that sobered the mechanic. "Sure, sure!" He stumbled hurriedly away. A connection was made. And a few minutes later they were under way again.

And Guss had control of his temper again.

"Sorry about that."

"About what?"

"The mechanic—acting like you were a freak."

"I don't know," Harry said, pretending to be serious. "That greaseball might have something. Think about it. 'The Guss and Harry Show' in bright lights. No. 'The Harry and Guss Show' in bright lights. We'd be a smash, Guss. Big time!"

"Cut it out," Guss said.

"You don't think it's funny?"

"Not for one damned minute!"

"How do you like that?" Harry asked nobody in particular. "I've got a stiff on my hands!"

Then he became serious.

"Back to business," he said. "We're not mad anymore?"

"I'm not, anyway."

"Neither am I," Harry said. "We can leave it this way: You reptiles have got a nasty practice eating humans, and we humans have got a nasty practice thinking you reptiles are something to step on. But, basically, deep down, we're both nice. Okay?"

"Harry, for chrissake—"

"And we've got a helluva lot of work to do," Harry pressed on, "starting right now. So tell me. Where are we going now?"

"I told you."

"Tell me again."

"To see that female and her child—to prove to you they have not been harmed."

"Good! Good! So where are they?"

"In Larissa. The big city by the bay."

"Great!" Harry said, filled with a kind of cold eagerness. "A Jassan San Francisco—this I've got to see."

They entered the area high, at an altitude of about five thousand feet, from the south and east, and Harry had the weird feeling that it wasn't that much different from any morning flight of PSA or United, L.A. to San Francisco. The landscape below seemed identical. There was the Golden Gate, the Bay, the Sacramento River, the Oakland area. But the city was not San Francisco.

It was Larissa.

And Larissa was so very much different.

Even from this altitude, Harry could see the fairylike architecture of the building that held the door to his world repeated in the buildings of the city, though on a massive scale. The tallest of the buildings were as tall as any New York City or Chicago had to offer, and spired on top of that. They were many-windowed, the early morning sunlight glinting off what had to be glass, and separated by what had to be a grid of streets where traffic moved. Walkways, some supported by suspension cables, connected many of the buildings at various heights, a kind of webbing that, again, suggested a fairyland that a Disney artist might have imagined.

There were water-craft visible on the surface of the bay, some quite large and slow and others quite fast, to judge by the character of the wakes they left scarring the surface. As Guss brought the craft down in a sweeping turn, Harry could not resist a needle.

"We've got a bridge," he said, "right across there. We call it the Golden Gate Bridge. And we've got another across there, the Bay Bridge. And a vehicular tunnel from there to there."

"Good for you," Guss said, unimpressed.

"How come you don't have 'em?" Harry asked, hoping Guss would reply that they didn't have the mechanical knowledge and ability to build them.

"They rusted out and fell down like, oh, three or four hundred years ago," Guss said. "We never bothered to replace them. Pneumatic tunnels work better, faster."

Harry looked at Guss a long moment.

"Smart-ass," he said flatly.

"You asked me," Guss said innocently.

"It's the smug tone that bugs me."

Guss mimicked: "'We've put men on the moon.' How about that?"

Harry grinned. "We're a pair of smart-asses, right?"

"Right."

Guss had found a landing site atop a building in what, in Harry's world, would have been called Nob Hill, and he was hovering above it now, clearly concerned. Looking down, Harry could see a number of Jassans moving about. A group of a half dozen emerged from a penthouse sort of building above the main building to wait near a painted landing spot—a reception committee, apparently. They appeared to be friendly, though some, because of identical apparel and sidearms, had to be police.

"We gonna be under arrest?" Harry asked.

"Not exactly," Guss said. "The police are for your protection as much as anything. A visitor from another world, you know? Like from outer space. Only a few are supposed to know about you, but word leaks out."

"Sounds familiar."

Harry felt a tightening of muscles and nerves—he was alone, *alone*, in a strange world, among the strangest kind of inhabitants.

Keerist! he said to himself. *Me! In the Land of Lizards! And I haven't even got a buggy whip to defend myself!*

Guss was making a deliberately slow business of landing the craft. While they were still a hundred feet up, he disclosed his reason. And it was not that he was concerned about his fellow lizard-men.

"You're going to follow my lead?" he asked Harry.

"I'll follow." Harry's voice was tight.

"They're going to be *very* curious about you, Harry. You were here before. All these ussles—you'd say people—know you from back then. What they don't know is what a bassoe with smarts is going to be like when he walks around with his smarts working. So take it easy, okay?"

"They going to think I'm something to eat?"

"Geez!" Guss said. "Well, all right, the thought might occur to some of them. But for most of them you'll be only a talking bassoe."

"A talking cow?"

"Something like that," Guss admitted feebly.

Harry was tautly furious. "And to me they'll just be a bunch of talking lizards."

"Damn!" Guss hit the controls with an exasperated hand. "What a stubborn jackass!"

"What d'you expect? Them calling me—"

"Harry!"

Seeing that Guss was genuinely upset, Harry managed to get control of himself. He clamped his jaws together. Guss checked him a moment.

"You cool?" he asked warily.

"I'm cool," Harry said. "Take us in."

They landed.

Six of the larger, uniformed Jassans moved up at once to form a protective shield between the craft and the civilians. They showed no fear of Harry, only the same caution they might show toward a potentially dangerous animal—a bear, perhaps, or a prize bull. One of them opened the door on Harry's side of the craft while the others waited, alert, eight-fingered hands unobtrusively near sidearms, tongues flicking.

Harry got out of the craft and stood erect, shoulders in a military brace, every trace of fear perfectly concealed. He was a fine example of the human race—tall, lean, and powerful. His closely trimmed beard gave added maturity and strength to a face that really had no need of it. Dark blue eyes under straight brows met the vertically slitted yellow eyes of the Jassans with a direct, not quite challenging, stare.

He watched the forked tongues flicking toward him, testing, and felt the presence of many minds waiting for the first words he might speak. He let them wait for several long moments.

"I mean you no harm," he said then, portentously, in spite of himself: "I come in peace."

He heard a heavy sigh of relief from Guss, who had hurried around the craft to stand beside him while he faced the Jassans for the first time on their ground as an equal. The uniformed Jassans moved smoothly aside as the civilians, reassured, moved forward. One of them, the highest in authority obviously, and an older, heavy Jassan, took an additional step forward and spoke with equal portentousness:

"We welcome you, Earthman."

I'll be goddamned! Harry thought.

CHAPTER 6

There was going to be trouble, Harry realized, in ever telling one Jassan from another. Like Orientals to the unaccustomed Western eye, they all looked very much the same. The Jassan who had come forward and spoken to him did seem to be older, and did have the look of authority about him—was it the very noticeable corpulence and the age, instead?—but his features were not *that* much different from any of the others: yellow eyes, possibly a little bulging and bloodshot, a muzzle darkened with age, wattles that went with the good life and advancing years. His garments seemed a finer quality, and he wore a badge of some sort on his left breast. To signify high office? Most probably.

His voice, as it materialized in Harry's head, might have been the voice of a politician on Earth, one of importance, possibly a mayor, even a congressman, and it came through in the expected vernacular.

"My name is Kass," he said, "and I am privileged to welcome you to our world as a guest." His long, forked tongue seemed to be missing nothing as it scanned Harry. "If you will come with me, I'll show you to your quarters."

"My friend goes with me," Harry said.

"Rassan?" Kass asked. "Of course, if you wish."

"Mr. Guss Rassan," Harry said. "And I wish."

Kass lifted a finger in Guss's direction. "Come."

Guss moved in close behind Harry, and Harry felt a slight goose and heard a murmured, "Thanks, pal," as they were led into the building, Kass leading the way and the armed guards forming a protective pouch behind and around them. The first area was no more than a hall that led past a bank of open doors to an elevator, the door of which stood open and waiting; but there were a dozen or more Jassans in different kinds of dress—some, because of softness of appearance, obviously female—pressing in the doorways to stare at Harry with intense interest.

But it was not until they were inside the elevator and the door was closed that Harry felt the full impact of where he was and how alone he was. Four of the armed Jassans had entered the elevator with Kass, Guss, and Harry, and they were crowded in the small space. The body odor of the Jassans was different from that of *Homo sapiens*, Harry discovered—rather like the smell of the long dried earth of a root cellar or a cave floor. *They don't sweat*, he told himself, and when he noticed that their long tongues were almost licking him, he added, *but they seem to like those who do*.

A pneumatic sigh closed the door; another caused a sudden loss of weight as they plummeted downward.

The yellow, vertically slitted eyes of the Jassans averted when Harry looked at them, or took concealment behind the gray veil they could move across the eyeball at will. Standing with them so closely pressed about him, Harry became aware of facial differences that would enable him to recognize individuals. Guss had features more refined than any of the armed guards: He was, Harry had just discovered, a damned good-looking Jassan—a Tom Selleck of his kind—while Kass definitely showed the mottled brown, the sagging flesh, the corpulence of advancing years.

And then a truly hair-raising realization came to him. The uniformed guard closest to him, the one who tried the hardest not to look at him, and who failed most obviously in the trying, was salivating! He wanted to sink his teeth in Harry's neck so bad he could hardly stand it. He wanted to drink Harry's blood, to eat his flesh. And they were all like that, all fighting to control themselves. To them all, Harry understood now with perfect clarity, he was, first of all, a choice morsel of food: He was candy, a top-sirloin steak, a walking, talking shish-kabob.

Damn! he thought. *All I need's an apple in my mouth!*

The elevator stopped; the door opened. They moved out in the same formation across what Harry discovered was a subway platform. There were many Jassans here, and when they saw Harry, they began a rush forward—driven by curiosity or hunger, Harry was not sure which—and were held back at what seemed the last moment by drawn weapons in the hands of the guards and a crackle of orders that almost burned out the sensor in Harry's mind. Sweat was beginning to glisten on Harry's face and neck by the time they reached a waiting tubular vehicle, and once inside with the doors closed, Harry could take some comfort in the fact that here there were only half a dozen who would like to eat him.

Again, Harry's engineering mind took refuge in observing and recording. A pneumatic underground, Guss had said, and this was obviously a car designed to fit exactly in a tube and to be pushed, or sucked, by a column of air. The car seated them all comfortably, with room for perhaps a dozen more. They moved slowly into darkness. The lights in the car came on as a sudden, smooth, and powerful acceleration pressed hard against their backs.

Guss spoke to Kass with a tone that did not lack in respect yet held a certain authority: "We were to be taken directly to the Earth female—that is the contract signed by the Issles, Mr. Kass."

"That's where we're going," Kass answered, untroubled, soothing. "Sos Vissir has taken her to his summer residence." He looked at Harry. "You will find her in perfect *health*."

He said it in a way that suggested there might be an area in which she was not perfect. Harry picked up on it at once, and so, for that matter, did Guss.

"But there *is* something wrong?"

As Kass looked at Harry, the gray membrane crossed his eyes, giving him a bland expression. "Her intellect seems to be fading—which, I suppose, is to be expected. A bassoe with an intellect at all is remarkable enough."

Guss, troubled, leaned in front of Harry. "Being alone among us, she's just upset. Once she sees you, she'll be all right."

"How about the child?" Harry asked, voice tight.

"Perfect health," Kass said.

Guss's eyes were on Harry's taut face. "We'll be there in about five minutes, Harry. Just take it easy."

"Yeah, sure. Sure." Harry's voice was thick.

He used the remaining moments to gather further data: Clean but very old, needing repair and replacement—and that, he realized again, described almost everything he had seen thus far. The aircraft, the buildings, the elevators, the subway platforms, the tube car they were riding in—all needed replacing, fixing, painting, repairing.

"You got a run-down country, Guss. You know that?"

"I know that."

"How come?"

"Bad management," Guss said. There was a grim sort of delight in his voice. "You think *I'm* a klutz? I'm a whiz kid compared to our leaders. A few centuries ago they decided they could spend their way to prosperity, and it didn't work out." His tone became needling. "Isn't that right, Mr. Kass?"

Kass looked uncomfortable. "I don't care to discuss our problems—particularly not in the presence of an alien."

"He's sensitive," Guss said. "I don't blame him. He's got plenty to be sensitive about. About a hundred years ago, the ruling class—and Mr. Kass here's one of the ruling class—decided the easy way out was to have a war. You know, a small one. To make jobs, keep the population down, give the poor something to think about besides their empty stomachs."

"Didn't work?"

"You can see for yourself."

"What went wrong? A nice little war always works in our world, as long as you keep it little. Matter of fact, if we had a sudden attack of peace, every economy on Earth would collapse."

"But you've got to win, right?"

"If you start fighting," Harry agreed. "But just the threat of a war is the best way to go. Keep it a threat, an active threat, and you've got a real economic stimulator."

The tube car broke into light, slowed, and stopped, much to Guss's relief. He had, Harry knew, been keeping him diverted and out of trouble with the talk about economics; and while it had been helpful with Harry, easing him through some difficult moments, it had gone badly with Kass. As they waited for the door to open, Kass fixed Guss with a hard stare.

"If you value your freedom, Mr. Rassan, I'd suggest you show a little more respect for your country and your leaders."

Guss was not intimidated. "You'll make a report, and I'll hear all about it," he said.

"Yes, you will."

They got out of the car, formed up again with Kass leading the way and the armed guards enclosing the rear, and moved through the small room, through an exit, to a waiting ground vehicle. This one was very similar to a sight-seeing bus, and it took them a mile or so along a drive to a castlelike building, complete with spires and high windowless walls, lacking only a moat.

"Some kind of a summer residence!" Harry said. "What's his main residence look like?"

"Bigger," Guss said. "More expensive."

There was sarcasm in the exchange that did not escape Kass. "Sos Vissir is a very important and very respected member of our community."

"Owns about half of it," Guss added.

"I know the type," Harry said. "We've got a few."

They went through a large gate, into a paved courtyard, and stopped before an entrance where several unarmed, uniformed Jassans, whom Harry assumed to be servants, were waiting. The servants escorted the entire party into a vaulted entryway, up a long, curving flight of stairs, and into what looked to Harry like a throne room. A raised dais occupied the far end of the room, a long walk away. They went to stand before it, to wait silently, and then, after what to Harry was an almost comical dramatic effect had been achieved, Sos Vissir appeared.

I'll be go to hell, Harry thought. *The Grand Vizier, the Wizard of Oz, the Great Poobah himself!*

"Watch it," Guss whispered. "He can have us both for dinner."

Sos Vissir wore a caftanlike garment, shimmering gold, trimmed in crimson, that reached the floor. A plumed turban rode on his head, and his fingers wore rings that flashed with what had to be diamonds. He came down the two steps from the dais with what was obviously intended to be a regal manner. Harry read it as something else.

He's a fruit, Harry thought. *Got to be*.

But he stood quietly as Sos Vissir walked around him, inspecting him with a kind of curious disdain, tongue flicking steadily.

"So this is the male," he said to Kass, who waited, obsequious, anxious. "Good specimen, I suppose. Big. Strong. A good breeder, d'you think?"

"I'm sure of it!" Kass said.

"And intelligent?" Sos Vissir asked, unbelieving.

"Speak to him, sir," Kass replied, almost coaxing. "You'll be surprised."

Sos Vissir stood in front of Harry with the amused, doubting attitude of a man about to start up a machine he is more than half sure won't work.

"Say your name," Sos Vissir said, testing.

"My name is Harry Borg," Harry said. "I've got all the intelligence you've got, and probably a good bit more." Sos Vissir backed up a step, startled. "I didn't come here to perform for your amusement," Harry went on. "I came here to see the human female and her child. And I want to see them now."

The flat, biting tone alone was enough to frighten Sos Vissir, who clearly was not the bravest of Jassans. He moved several steps back; his servants moved quickly forward. Kass looked angrily at Harry and apologetically at Sos Vissir.

"He's not dangerous, sir."

"I should hope not!" Sos Vissir said, recovering. He continued with a feigned amusement. "I wasn't alarmed, only startled. One doesn't expect a voice from a bassoe! A thinking mind!" He looked at Harry a moment longer from a safe distance, then waved his hand doubtfully. "But can he be trusted with the female? I mean, do we dare put him with her without a testing period."

"He won't harm her," Guss said.

But Sos Vissir was still doubtful. "The female is extremely valuable. If this male should get out of control and cause any injury to her—"

"It won't happen, sir," Guss said.

Sos Vissir stared at Harry, his tongue, as well as his eyes, measuring every aspect of Harry, his height, the width of his shoulders, the strength of his arms, and, most particularly, his genital area.

"When aroused," Sos Vissir murmured speculatively, "he must be formidable." He thought about that some more, then put aside the thought, almost reluctantly. He finally waved his hand in dismissal. "Put him with the female, then."

The servants moved forward to take Harry's arms; Harry shook them off easily. "You don't lead me," he said sharply to Sos Vissir. "I walk. And where I go, Mr. Rassan goes."

Sos Vissir looked questioningly at Kass.

"He has permission from the Issles, sir."

"Orders from the Issles," Guss amended.

Sos Vissir was doubtful. "But—will they breed with one of us present? Some of our bassoes are—"

"What the hell is he talking about?" Harry asked Guss. "Does he mean what I think he does?"

"Cool it, Harry," Guss said anxiously. "The humans have different customs," he told Sos Vissir. "They are more like ourselves than bassoes. They're sensitive about mating; certain rites must be gone through."

"Well, whatever," Sos Vissir said. "Get on with it."

He motioned with an impatient hand, the servants indicated a direction, and Harry followed them with Guss at his side. Harry was seething, furious.

"We've got a problem, Guss."

"I can see that, Harry," Guss said, even more anxious now. "Your temper, that's the first problem."

"If they keep treating me like a prize bull at the county fair, somebody's going to get his face broke."

"Harry, give them time. They've got to learn you're an equal. And they will! The same way I did."

"They damn well better—and soon!"

Another corridor had led them to a closed door, where two servant types waited, obviously guards. Before their guides could open the door, Harry said, "I want all of you to stay out here. I'll go in by myself."

The servants looked at Guss.

"You heard him," Guss said. "Open the door."

The door was opened, and Harry walked into the place where the human female was being held. A place of comfort, first of all, then of beauty. The floor covering was soft underfoot, silken draperies covered the walls, tall, glistening windows admitted

light. Azure blue and pale green were the primary colors, taste-
fully blended in varying shades of intensities. Deeply, softly
upholstered furniture offered almost sensuous comfort at every
hand. There was nothing worn here, nothing old, nothing in need
of repair. A luxurious prison. An expensive and beautiful cage,
newly built to contain a captive creature of great value.

Harry advanced to the center of it ᴛᴏ stand quietly. He heard
nothing, saw no one.

"Mrs. Calder," he said, quietly. "Are you here?"

There was no response for a long moment. Then he saw her
through an archway, rising from a large bed—a young woman
in her early thirties. Beside her was a girl child of about thirteen
years. What impressed him first were the eyes, two pairs, at
once frightened and unbelieving, staring at him. The woman got
up slowly, moving toward the archway, the child following.

"I'm real, a human being," Harry said quietly, trying to reas-
sure them. "Don't be afraid of me. I'm here to get you out of
this."

"My God—my God—" the woman whispered, a shaking
hand moving to her face, the shaking fingertips at her quivering
mouth. "Really? Really—for sure?"

"For sure," Harry said.

He could see hysteria in the woman's eyes, a near insanity,
and he knew he had to establish somehow the reality of himself,
a human, a man, in this world of lizards. And fleetingly he
thought the fact she had *not* gone totally insane was testimony
to her mental strength. He held his arms out to her, hands open,
and moved toward her, his voice gentle.

"Come here, touch me—see for yourself."

She came finally, the child close behind her, to touch his
hands, her eyes wide, afraid to believe.

"Really?" she whispered. "Honest Injun?"

"My name is Harry Borg," he said. "I lived at the Armstead
Apartments, not far from where you lived. And I'm real, honest
Injun."

A deep, shuddering groan escaped her, and she suddenly
threw herself at him, threw her arms around his body and clung
to him in a fierce hug—a desperate victim clutching a tree to
save herself in a flood—and he held her against him, feeling
her shake. Her child, eyes huge and round, came in to stand

close to her mother. Harry included her in the warmth of his arms.

"It's going to be all right," he told her.

After a moment the woman's shaking began to lessen, and Harry loosened her grip and held her away a little to look at her tear-streaked face. It was a strong face, really, making the emotional wreckage even more tragic—good bones; wide, long-lashed gray eyes; a generous mouth; a straight nose. And the shoulders under his hands were firm and spoke of an active, even athletic life, a woman of substance, of strength and beauty and grace. She was looking at him almost hungrily.

"You *are* real," she said. "I had given up."

"I can believe it."

"I woke up and I was in a world of monsters. How did I—did we—Tippi and I—how did we get here?"

"You were kidnapped—drugged, I suppose."

"But—but why?"

"I'm going to tell you."

"And how did *you* get here? Are you one of them? You're *not*, you *can't* be!"

"No, I'm not one of them." Harry led her gently toward a divan and persuaded her to sit down, the child, Tippi, on the far side of her. He still held the mother's hands. "One of them brought me here to see you. His name is Rassan—Guss Rassan. He's outside. I want you to believe me when I say he's a friend, your friend and my friend, the only one we have."

"One of *them*?" she asked. "A *friend*?"

"I'll explain it all," Harry said. "He's in some danger for befriending us, and I'd like to bring him in now. Don't be upset."

"You—*talk* to them?"

Her eyes were growing wide again, with suspicion, with returning fear. Harry knew then that he had to take the time now to tell her much of what had happened. He took both her hands in his and held them while he explained how he too had been kidnapped, how he had been physically rehabilitated, and how the speech sensor had been implanted. A good part of it, of course, had to be left for a later telling, but he managed to calm her again, to win her trust.

"Just a moment," he said.

He went to the door and opened it to find Guss lounging there with the two suspicious guards. He brought Guss inside and closed the door. Then, as they stood in the entryway, Guss whispered with concern, "She's the first human female for me, y'know. You've got to tell me what to do."

"Be your own sweet self," Harry said, with just a little sarcasm. "I've told her you're the only friend we've got in your world—all you've got to do is act like it."

"You know I can't talk to her."

"I know." Then Harry had another thought and laid a restraining hand on Guss's arm. "I don't know if she knows your kind eat our kind. Try not to give her any reason to think so—I mean, don't salivate, okay?"

"C'mon, Harry! Give me a little credit!"

"Sorry."

They went into the large and luxurious room where Mrs. Calder and Tippi were waiting with obvious apprehension.

"This is Guss," Harry said gently, drawing Guss up beside him. "I promise you he's on our side—and I've known him long enough to know there's a kind and gentle personality behind that formidable face."

Mrs. Calder was silent, wide-eyed, wary. Tippi, though still huddled behind her mother's protective arm, was more curious than frightened. Perhaps she'd grown used to seeing Jassans. And Guss, Harry was pleased and amused to see, made a genuine effort. He bowed at the waist, covered his eyes with the gray film, and flicked his long, forked tongue with polite deference.

"I'm pleased to meet you," he said.

Only Harry heard him, of course. "He says he is very pleased to meet you," Harry told the woman and child.

Mrs. Calder looked bewildered, frightened.

"I didn't hear anything."

"He thought it," Harry said. "In our language. That thing in my head—remember?"

"Oh. Yes."

Then, hesitantly, Mrs. Calder spoke to Guss. "Tell him that I am glad to meet him, too. That I'm glad to find a friend among—them."

"Jassans," Harry said. "The country is Jassa, these—people—are Jassans."

"People?"

"Whatever," Harry said. "Just think of them as Jassans."

He let the tension relax for a few moments while they all became accustomed to each other. Then he turned to Guss. "Can you get us something—some food, soft drinks, so we can sit down together?"

"Coming right up," Guss said, and turned away.

"I don't know your first name," Harry said to Mrs. Calder.

"Lori," she said. "Lori Calder. Single."

"And this is?"

"Tippi. She's twelve years old."

"Going on thirteen," Tippi said.

The child was coming out of the fear she had picked up from her mother rather faster than her mother was recovering from her own. A large-eyed, small edition of her mother, she was not shy.

"I hate it here," she said. "I want to go home."

"I'll take you home," Harry said. "That's a promise."

"How are you going to do that?" Lori Calder asked. "Are you going to pay a ransom? Or what?"

"Well—" Harry looked and found Guss returning. "We'll talk about it later," he said quickly, softly. "Just now, let's keep it secret." He looked at Tippi. "Okay?"

"I won't tell," the child said.

"Good girl!"

The next hour was one of nerve-twanging tension for each one of the four who sat on comfortable cushions around a low table that very quickly became laden with food and drink brought by the servant-type Jassans. The food was fruit—recognizable peaches, plums, grapes—pastries made of grain-flour and fruit, and a variety of cheeses. There was no meat at all. The drink was winelike—totally lacking in alcohol, Guss hastily assured Harry, but containing, Guss admitted, a substance that would induce a mild euphoria.

"The female is scared to death," Guss told Harry. "I had to do something."

"Just so it's mild," Harry said. "We call it a tranquilizer."

"Tranquilizer," Guss said. "Yeah. That's what it is."

Harry had stopped speaking aloud to Guss, or to any of the

Jassans, for that matter. It wasn't necessary, once he'd acquired the skill of putting his end of the conversations into thoughts alone. But Lori found the long pauses, the moments of silence in which Guss and Harry might, or might not, look at each other during the exchanges, nerve-wracking in the extreme.

"For God's sake!" she said. "I don't know if you're talking about me or not. So cut it out already! At least *you* can speak out, can't you?"

"I'm sorry."

And Harry did make an effort to remember to voice his end of the conversation, and to translate Guss's thoughts into words that Lori and Tippi could understand. But it was rough going no matter how it was done.

Lori Calder could not bring herself to fully trust the man who called himself Harry Borg, and the Jassan—her name for them was *lizard-men*—she trusted not at all. And with cause.

"I went to bed," she said in response to Harry's questions, "in my apartment on a night just like any other night, with Tippi asleep in her bedroom—and I woke up in the middle of the most godawful nightmare I've ever had, and I've had some beauts! Tippi and I are alone in a world where everybody has all of a sudden turned into lizards! Can you imagine anything as horrible as that?"

"No, I can't," Harry said. And then, for Guss, "He agrees it must have been impossibly cruel."

Lori couldn't believe that one. "Lizards know what cruelty is? Come off it! I never knew a snake or a lizard or a reptile of any kind had any feelings."

"Guss does," Harry said. "At least, I think he does. Well, he says he has feelings."

"And I do, damn it!" Guss said impatiently.

"He says he does," Harry told Lori.

"*You* can talk to them," Lori said. "Tippi and I *can't*, and that makes a difference. Believe me! You look at those yellow, up-and-down slitted eyes, and see that long tongue zipping out at you, and you *know* all they're thinking about is what you're going to taste like."

"There you go," Harry said silently to Guss. "We call it women's intuition." Aloud, he said, "I can believe you. It must have been terrifying."

"It still is," Lori said.

"I'm not scared anymore," Tippi said. "All I want to do is go home. They shouldn't keep us here."

"Not without your permission," Harry said. And to Guss, silently: "We call it kidnapping in our world. In some cases it's punishable by death."

"Sorry about that," Guss said. "If I had my way, I'd send her back."

"Why not get your way?"

"Sos Vissir outweighs me. Like a hundred times. To him, this lady and her child are prize possessions. Like—" He groped around in Harry's head for a comparative value. "Like the Mona Lisa. No, like a female giant panda and her cub. You know what I mean?"

"You're talking about me!" Lori said angrily.

"Yeah, we are," Harry admitted. "I was looking for a way to get you and Tippi out of here—and back home."

"Well?" she demanded.

"I'm workin' on it."

Harry was as uncomfortable as a man could be. There was so much he didn't want to tell her, so much he didn't want her to know, so much that would scare the living hell out of her.

"Y'see, the Jassan who owns—I mean, who has possession of you two," he stumbled on, "it's like he's got the Mona Lisa all to himself, to show off to his rich friends, to flaunt at them—whatever—and it's not going to be so easy to talk him out of you, if you know what I mean."

As Harry stumbled along, mixing half-truths with pure fiction, Lori Calder knew, she found herself measuring the man in some detail. And what she found was to her liking.

Look out, she told herself. *After what you've been through, you'd kiss the hell out of the Hunchback of Notre Dame!*

But this Harry Borg was more than just a human being. *And keep your fingers crossed on that one; he might be a lizard dirty trick,* she told herself.

He looked like a comic-strip hero: handsome as hell, built like Arnold Schwarzenegger. Those dark blue eyes could turn a gal's backbone to spaghetti if she let them look at her too long, and he was looking at her now. And right there she decided he was human for sure. Because he was trying so hard, fumbling around with what he had to say like a high-school kid on his first date.

No, this one was for real.

"Tippi," she said to her daughter. "I'm beginning to like Mr. Harry Borg."

"I'm glad," Tippi said. "I like him too."

"I heard that," Harry said. And then, in confusion, "I'm sorry. Talking silent to Guss, hearing him when he doesn't say anything, hearing you when you do—well, anyway, I'm glad you said that. Because the feeling is mutual." He covered Tippi's hand as it lay on the table with one of his, and Lori's hand with the other. "I want you to trust me, most of all."

"Have we got a choice?" Lori asked, smiling.

"Nope," Harry agreed. "I'm the only one around."

But there was warmth in the exchange, warmth Guss did not fail to notice. He pushed to his feet, nodding his head toward Lori and Tippi, flicking a polite tongue at each of them.

"Time I got out of here," he said to Harry. "I don't know much about you humans, but this looks like you're about to get something going."

"He says he has an appointment," Harry translated for Lori Calder. "He's enjoyed meeting you and Tippi, and hopes to see you again real soon."

"Do come back," Lori said to Guss, trying not to sound sarcastic.

Harry took Guss's arm and steered him toward the door. On the way, he put his thoughts into words only Guss could hear: "What the hell do you mean, 'About to get something going'?"

"Come off it, Harry!" Guss said.

"Spell it out."

"You're goin' to mate with her, right?" Guss asked, almost plaintively, perhaps pleadingly. "That's how come you're here. I sold Sos Vissir on the idea that if he'd let you see her, you'd mate, and he'd have a whole litter of intelligent bassoes to show off before he knew it."

"Damn you, Guss! Damn you all!"

"Harry! You wouldn't be here if I hadn't done it." It was Guss's turn to be angry. "I don't know how you do things in your world," he almost snarled, "but in ours we go one step at a time. Anyway, I do! Now, if you want to go back to your world and leave her here, I can maybe fix you up. I don't guarantee it, but I'll give it a shot."

"All right, all right!" Harry said.

They stood there glaring at each other, dark blue furious eyes and yellow, slitted eyes locked. Harry knew Guss had done the only possible thing, but he did not yet have enough control of himself to admit it. Guss was in no mood to give him any relief.

"Well?" he demanded. "Are you going to?"

"To what?"

"Mate with her, you dummy!"

"Guss, so help me——"

"You'd better," Guss said. "Or, *you*, anyway, could end up on somebody's breakfast table."

Harry stared at Guss a moment longer. "And that's got to be the best argument for fooling around I've heard yet." He gave Guss a shove toward the door that was at least half friendly.

"Whatever it takes," Guss said.

"One thing," Harry said at the door. "Human females are very flighty. Any little thing turns them off, y'know."

"No, I didn't know."

Conspiratorially, now, Harry said, "Well, it does. So if Sos Vissir wants action, he's got to see that we get privacy. I mean, *total*."

"I'll tell 'im."

"That means at least two, maybe three days. Nobody comes near. For any reason. Y'got that?"

Guss shook his head, more in wonderment than in dissent. "When we get a little time, you've got to tell me how you humans do it," he said. "Three days!" He shook his head again. "With us, ten minutes is plenty."

"Get outa here!" Harry said.

CHAPTER 7

Harry closed the door and went back to Lori Calder and her child. She was looking at him, worry—not fear or distrust—in her wide gray eyes.

"What was that all about?" she asked.

"What do you mean?"

That Harry Borg was embarrassed about something was obvious enough that even Tippi could see it. Lori was determined to find out what it was.

"If you want us to trust you," she said, "you can't have secret discussions about us with the lizards. So what did you and Guss decide was in store for Tippi and me? Come on now."

"Whoo, boy!" Harry said.

Lori became more determined. "Mr. Borg."

Harry still ducked.

"Harry," Lori said warningly.

He was acting like the school kid again. Men could be such clumsy clods, especially when—then a light began to dawn. She looked at him with new interest.

"Oh," she said. "Now I get it."

Harry suddenly needed a drink of the mildly tranquilizing winelike potion that was still on the table. A long drink. And then another.

Tippi was looking from one adult to the other, her eyes wide, and then, when Harry put off the necessity of a response with another long drink of wine, she grinned with delighted amusement.

"I know," she said. "They want you and Mom to make a baby! Don't they, Mr. Borg?"

Harry looked at Tippi, shocked, then at Lori with amazement. Lori returned his look with a shrug of wry, mildly embarrassed amusement.

"They grow up quite young," she said.

"She's only—" Harry said.

"Twelve, going on thirteen," Lori agreed. "But she's right, isn't she? About what they want?"

"Well, that was what—what they hoped."

"And you told them?"

"Just so I could get them to leave us alone," Harry said anxiously. "I told them I—we—needed a couple of days, at least. You know, so I'd have time to figure a way out of here. That doesn't mean I committed you to anything. Believe me!"

"I should hope not."

Tippi was disappointed. "But Mom! I think—"

"Hush," Lori said.

Tippi recognized a final word from her mother when she heard one, and she subsided, lower lip out, to watch the grown-ups and to listen. Her mother was looking at Mr. Borg as if he had done something very bad. And Mr. Borg was getting desperate or something.

"All we've got to do is make them think—you know, that we— Well, that we—" Harry gave up. "I need a little time, that's all."

And then Lori smiled. "Harry, it's not all that serious! It really isn't. There's no need to act like a schoolboy."

Relieved, Harry grinned shamefacedly. "I guess I'm old-fashioned," he said. "I used to be, not long ago, a man in his late sixties. And in my day..." He didn't finish, because he didn't know where to go with it.

Lori was amused, her gray eyes knowing. "Late sixties," she murmured without belief. "I must say you are the best-preserved late sixty I've ever seen. Come. Sit down. Tell me about it."

"I think I kind of knew you back home," Tippi said when they were seated.

"You did?" They both looked at her.

"Armstead Apartments, that's where you lived, right?"

"Apartment three-ten," Harry said.

"You know Sandra Higby," Tippi said to her mother. "And Mrs. Higby? The big fat lady, her mother?"

"Of course."

"I know Mrs. Higby," Harry said. "First floor in the back. Not very tall. Had a weight problem, though. Quite heavy. Right?"

"We talked about you sometimes," Tippi said with an una-bashed grin. "If you're the same Mr. Borg. You hardly ever came out, because you were drunk all the time." And then doubt clouded her eyes. "You were old, though."

"I was old," Harry said. "And I was a drunk."

"I can't believe it," Lori Calder said. "Just a few months ago, and now look at you! They—these lizards—did that for you? You've got to be putting us on!"

"Nope. It's the truth."

"But how? How could they?"

"Trans—" Harry began, and then, realizing where that would lead, he changed the subject. "All that we'll save for later. What's important now is we were neighbors back home, and that's better than complete strangers, isn't it?"

"Proves you're not a lizard dirty trick," Lori agreed.

"So tell me about yourselves," Harry said. "How you got here, what you've seen and heard."

There was much to tell, and through the rest of that morning, and through the afternoon and evening, Harry Borg and Lori Calder told each other about themselves in considerable detail. While Lori was able to believe only a part of what Harry had to tell her, she didn't ridicule him for the part she didn't believe.

"Sixty!" she kept saying, and with increasing interest. "You can't be a day over thirty, and for a physique like yours." She looked him up and down. "Jack Youngblood, eat your heart out."

"You mean that Ram football player?" Harry asked, pleased.

"He's the one," Lori said. "One of the biggest, one of the toughest, one of the best. If not *the* best."

Harry couldn't help it, he went completely aw-shucks! After

what he had been, to have a pretty lady tell him he was a regular Jack Youngblood was almost too much. He tried to return the favor.

"You're not exactly chopped liver, you know."

"Gee, thanks," she said, amused.

"What about me?" Tippi said. "Don't I get some of this gooey guck?"

Lori and Harry both laughed, and Harry roughed Tippi's hair with a big and gentle hand. "A button should be half so cute," he told her.

With that—and was there not perhaps something aphrodisiacal in the winelike drink when taken in sufficient quantity?— Harry Borg and Lori Calder found, after Tippi had gone to bed, that living up to the Jassan's expectations was not at all difficult.

"Would you believe I'm in love?" Harry asked afterward.

"I believe," Lori said. "If you're not, please go on faking it the rest of our lives."

Perhaps an hour later, with moonlight streaming in from a balcony window, with a cool breeze blowing softly across their naked bodies, the phrase "the rest of our lives" sounding steadily in his mind brought Harry Borg back to the reality of their predicament. "I'll get you out of this," he had promised Lori Calder and Tippi, and that was still to be done.

Lori was sleeping now, probably for the first time in a long time, sedated by the winelike drink and the lovemaking, but most of all because she had found reassurance in him. Her confidence in him—or perhaps more precisely in the superman's body he was using—had placed a burden of responsibility on him he couldn't escape. Nor did he want to, he found: He wanted to test his new strengths, to use his potential. And what greater test could there be than to get the three of them safely home?

Gonna take some doing, he told himself.

And he recognized that as the understatement of all time. They were high in the castlelike building. There were uncounted Jassans, many armed with weapons of an unknown kind, between this apartment and the entrance of the building. They were two hundred miles, at least, from the building that held the only gateway between the land of the Jassans and the land of the Americans.

A lot of doing, he corrected himself grimly.

He got out of bed quietly, slipped into his clothes, and moved silently across the soft carpet to the window that was admitting the moonlight and breeze. The window was actually a glasslike paneled door that opened onto a wide balcony, which overlooked a sleeping countryside. In the distance he could see the glow of city lights reflecting on clouds, and thought that was probably the bay area. As he watched, he saw the moving lights of aircraft going to and leaving the bay area; commercial aircraft, he was sure, busy with the same kind of commerce that occupied aircraft in his own world.

He turned his attention to his own position. The balcony was thirty feet below the top of the building and easily a hundred feet above the ground. As a young man, Harry had done considerable rock climbing, and with that practiced eye he scanned the wall below.

Possible, he thought. *Barely.*

The wall was rock and mortar, well laid but suffering from the same erosion of weather and time and lack of repair evident throughout Jassa. And there were embellishments and decorative effects to offer grips and purchases for a man with enough strength in fingertips and toes to manage a descent. How much was enough? Harry made claws of his fingers and tried them on the edge of the balustrade, trying to lift his weight and support himself on his fingertips alone, and found he had strength he'd never had before. But enough for an hour's descent? Or even longer?

Only one way to find out, he told himself.

He felt a grim, cold eagerness to accept the challenge, but a sober thought held him back. If he were able to make the descent, what would he have accomplished?

"Zilch," he whispered. "Zero."

One man, alone, on the ground, somewhere north of what in his world was the San Francisco Bay, in a world of civilized and intelligent reptiles, who considered the likes of him as nothing so much as an entree of a banquet—that man would last about as long as ice cream at a picnic.

And Lori and Tippi would be left alone.

"No way," he said. "No damned way!"

He was turning away with the thought that there had to be a way out from the inside when he saw the lights of an aircraft approaching. The craft was low, barely skimming the treetops when it caught his eye, a small craft much like the one Guss had used to bring him into the city; as Harry watched, it slowed, then dropped behind trees at a distance of about three hundred yards. Other lights appeared then at ground level. And in a matter of fifteen minutes all the lights went out, leaving only darkness and silence.

"Well, now," Harry whispered, suddenly, fiercely eager. "A whole new ball game!"

He went back inside the room where Lori Calder lay, still sleeping. He touched her shoulder, awakening her gently. She was blurry for a few moments; then, when she saw that he was dressed, she became sharp and concerned.

"What's going on?"

"Quiet, now," Harry cautioned. He sat on the edge of the bed and took hold of her shoulders. "I've found a way to get us out of here—I think."

"How in the world—"

"You and Tippi get dressed," he said. "Wait for me. It'll take maybe an hour, maybe less. But I'll be back with one of their aircraft and either land on or hover near the balcony outside to take you aboard. And I know the way out of this world—the way I came in."

"You're out of your mind, Harry," she said. "We're halfway to the sky!"

"I can climb down that wall."

"Oh, my lord! You'll kill yourself!"

"Not with any luck at all."

"You'll kill yourself and leave Tippi and me alone!"

"No I won't."

"I couldn't stand it, Harry! I'd go insane—stark, raving mad—if you didn't come back. I know I would!"

"I'm coming back," Harry said fiercely. "Now show me you've got some guts. Do what I tell you."

He turned away, but she clung to him, making him drag her out of the bed. Angrily, then, he stood her on her feet and shook her hard.

"Stop the damned nonsense!" he said.

"I—I—"

She faltered, caught by the blaze in his dark blue eyes, the whiplike crack of his voice. Then she forced control upon herself with a deep and shuddering breath. Fully awake finally, and in possession of all her wits and courage, she returned his stare. He saw strength come into her eyes, a coldness that turned the wide gray eyes into the hardness of slate.

"Now," he said. "Now you've got it."

"You're really going to try to climb down."

"I am."

"All right, idiot," she said. "I won't even watch."

"Better not."

"And if you don't make it—been nice knowing you."

"And if I do, you'd better be ready to go."

He turned away from her and strode out to the balcony. She watched him go to the balustrade, slip out of his shoes, knot the laces, and hang his shoes around his neck. Without even a glance in her direction, he swung a long leg over the balustrade, paused a moment, a dark shadow etched against the distant city lights, then dropped smoothly and silently from her sight.

She closed her eyes and saw him in her mind's eye, a small figure clinging to the stones of the almost sheer face, a hundred feet above the ground, in darkness. "Oh, my God," she whispered, as chills of fear shook her body and nausea welled up in her throat. She uttered a low cry, turned, and ran to the bathing chamber, where she was desperately sick for long, gagging moments.

Thirty feet below the balcony, Harry Borg began to know the same kind of fear. The first thirty feet had been the distance he had been able to scan from the balcony in the darkness and had found possible of descent—barely. And he had gone down it with relative ease, reveling in his new strength, holding his weight with ease on little more than the tips of fingers and toes. A genius, that surgeon, Sassan. A damned genius!

Until he found himself in that most dreaded predicament of climbing: no next move. The way back was closed to him; it permitted descent only. And he could not at this moment see a purchase point that would permit even a fingertip's grip that would support his weight enough to allow his toes to seek purchase further down. So he clung there, pinned to the sheer face by his own lack of ability, or lack of will, or lack of courage, as a white panic—was it a remnant of the old, decrepit, hopeless alcoholic Harry Borg, overlooked by the surgeon Sassan, still lingering inside him?—a white panic that welled up inside, choking him, bursting in a sudden, slick film of cold sweat that bathed his skin.

He looked down between his legs and saw only darkness. He felt the cool draft of air that rose out of that darkness, filled with the scent of earth and shrubbery, as it flowed up past him, telling him the ground was a long, long way below, waiting to accept his plummeting body when his strength finally failed, as he knew it must inevitably if he continued on here much longer, unmoving. He felt a trembling begin in the calves of his legs, a trembling that came of holding this one precarious position too long without movement, a trembling that would grow, he knew full well, to a shaking that would dislodge him and send him down, unless— unless—

You bastard! he whispered savagely. *You worthless bastard! Do something! Anything! Even if it's wrong!*

And then, gripping with the fingers of both hands and the toes of one foot, he extended his left leg down, searching for a crevice, a toehold, and at full length he found none. That was it. He was not able now to retrieve the leg. Defeat? Final defeat? He suffered that for several moments—a lifetime, it seemed to him—before he went further, to that fractional point that lies beyond what is possible, that can be reached by those with the courage to reach for the impossible. He stretched his leg beyond full length and his toes found a crack where mortar had decayed and washed away, leaving room for strong toes to slip in far enough to support weight.

Sonofagun! he breathed silently.

He held his weight on those five toes, dropped his hands smoothly and carefully down to new and lower grip points, then lowered the other leg to thrust toes into the same crevice that provided a safe hold for the first. Then his eyes saw a route that with two more moves would take him to a cornice above a lower balcony. Beyond that, he could not see, but he knew there couldn't be anything more difficult than what he had just been through. For hadn't he just faced the impossible and survived?

Like the man said, he told himself, *"the possible we do right now. The impossible just takes longer."*

But it seemed that beyond each insurmountable difficulty lay another, and by the time he finally reached the ground, at least an hour after he had begun the descent—Arnold Schwarzenegger or not; a Jack Youngblood or not; or even a Superman or not—he was a sweating, trembling wreck of a man who had to sit on the ground, back against the wall, shaking, panting for twenty minutes, before he was sure he had enough strength to cope with whatever lay ahead.

It was two forty-five by the luminous dial of his wristwatch, and there were still a couple of hours before daylight would begin to eat away the darkness in the east. He pushed to his feet, shook the tremors from his legs, and began the approach to the airport. His eyes, well adjusted by this time to darkness, took him easily through what once had been ornamental shrubbery and was now wild growth, thinned by centuries of its own needs, by animal trails and ancient, weed-grown walkways. In ten minutes he found himself coming up on a low building—a hangar, he soon discovered. Following the wall on silent feet, he reached a paved landing area, an open doorway. There was light above a workbench against a far wall, and in the cone of light, working at an engine part, was a Jassan in greasy overalls. And, parked between Harry and the mechanic, facing outward with an engine covering raised, was an aircraft that was almost identical to the one Guss had flown away from the gateway building.

Damn, Harry whispered.

Even if he were able to overpower the mechanic without raising an alarm, there would still be the problem of the engine part, broken, malfunctioning, whatever. Harry could only wait, sweating, counting minutes. Would the mechanic make an all-night job of the task? Would he fool around, like Earth mechanics, kill time? Would he—

Ahhh, Harry breathed.

The mechanic had turned with the part. The upper portion of him went out of sight beneath the raised engine covering. Two minutes passed. The mechanic went back to the bench for a tool, then returned. Another three minutes. And then the mechanic straightened to wipe his hands on a cloth from a hip pocket, an unmistakable indication of a task completed. He closed the engine covering, tossed tools on the bench, then got in the aircraft. Harry heard the humming sound he recognized as that of an activated engine, heard it run for a few moments, then stop. The mechanic got out, turned off the light, left the hangar, and disappeared into the night.

Harry moved quickly across the hangar entrance and turned into the area beside the aircraft. He was looking for the handle to the craft door when he heard the footsteps of the mechanic returning and froze against the craft, breath held. The mechanic went straight to the workbench, flicked on the light, found a small metal box he'd apparently forgotten, and turned to find himself face to face with Harry Borg.

"The bassoe! He's loose!"

Harry heard the words, almost a yelling, in the voice receptor planted in his brain. And he knew sudden fear and panic when he heard it. He knew the mechanic was terrified, knew he would yell for help with his next thought, so he lunged at the mechanic, an offensive tackle on a hard drive.

The mechanic twisted, hissing a loud, rasping hiss through widely gaping mouth, forked tongue flailing, just as Harry's hands caught at his throat. The mechanic managed to break partially away; his eight-fingered right hand caught up a heavy wrench and lifted it, clublike. Harry's left hand caught that upraised wrist, his right hand gripped the mechanic's throat, and they fought for leverage, chest to chest. The Jassan's yellow, vertically slitted eyes were fierce with pain and fear and anger, his mouth gaping open, tongue lashing, fanged teeth slashing the air, trying to find flesh. Harry applied strength to the hand gripping the Jassan throat, all the strength he had, driving the Jassan's back against the workbench, bending it, bending it more, and still more—until there was a sudden sound like a stick breaking and the Jassan went limp, the gray veil drawing across his yellow eyes.

Back's broken, Harry whispered. *Killed 'im.*

He laid the mechanic on the floor gently and waited until he was sure the creature was dead. The film remained across the slitted eyes; the long forked tongue was limp and motionless.

And now the stuff will really hit the fan.

Now it was going to be a life-or-death fight to stay alive, he knew, not just a question of capture and return. And he had no weapon. He hefted one of the wrenches—no good. Looking desperately, he saw a row of lockers beyond the bench. They opened easily. *Bingo!* A holstered side arm lay on a shelf, belt and all, and when he pulled it out to buckle it around his hips, he found there was a short sword in a scabbard on the opposite hip. *Damm me! The sword that built the Roman Empire, as I live and breathe!* How the Jassans had found their way to the short sword in their evolutionary process he didn't know or care. It was a winner—that he knew.

He examined the sidearm. Like an automatic pistol, it had a long barrel, a chamber, sights, a trigger, a safety. He tried pointing and aiming it, but he didn't move the safety and didn't fire. The piece might be silent or it might make a hell of a bang—he had no way of knowing. He holstered the weapon, glad for the comfort of having a weapon on his hip, usable or not.

Moving quickly, he dragged the Jassan's body to the locker, stowed it carefully out of sight, and closed the door, latching it securely. Then he doused the light and got into the aircraft. It was a duplicate of the one he and Guss had flown, he found, and gave a heavy sigh of relief. He pushed the OFF-ON switch to ON and the gentle vibration began. A slight draw on the controls and the craft lifted effortlessly; a slight grip on the right trigger and the craft took him out of the hangar; and then, flying almost as silently as an owl, he took the craft away from the hangar and up toward the balcony.

He was delighted, in a fiercely excited way, in the way the craft flew. "Those suckers can build a plane!" he said. "Look at this little mother go! So quiet! So easy! And they had this a hundred years ago, maybe more. While we were still looking at the rear ends of horses, they were riding the skies!"

He was at the level of the balcony where Lori and Tippi were waiting. He could see them, darkly outlined against the dim light, heads and shoulders above the balustrade.

"And what else do they know?" he asked aloud, the engineer in him irrepressibly awakened again, stimulated perhaps by these moments of success. "Harry, lad, you've got to come back! There's more gold here than ever there was in the Yukon. Surgical rejuvenation, alone—*think of it*! Instant wealth beyond your wildest dreams!"

He brought the aircraft in, easily and silently, to land on the balcony, and reached across to open the door. Both Lori and Tippi were wide-eyed, scared as hell, and jubilant with excitement.

"My God, Harry, you *are* a man of miracles!"

"C'mon, c'mon! We're a long way from home."

With them crowded into the small plane, a plane intended for only two passengers, there remained one question: Could the power source, whatever the hell it was, lift them and fly them?

"Let's go, baby," he whispered.

The craft moved sluggishly, but it did rise, and once airborne and moving, it seemed perfectly capable under the added load. Harry dropped it down as close to the ground as he dared fly with lights out, heading southeast over the darkly shadowed, open countryside.

"We're a little north and east of what in our world is the Bay Area," he said. "Those lights over there would be San Francisco and Oakland."

"I don't believe this," Lori Calder said flatly. "I don't believe even one single minute of it. I'm going to wake up pretty soon; you'll see."

"How about you, Tippi?" Harry asked. "You having a nightmare too?"

"Some nightmare!" the young girl said. She was stiff with fright, afraid to look either left or right, and especially not down. "What keeps us *up*?" Her voice was drawn thin with hysteria.

"Easy does it," Harry soothed. "An energy force field of some kind."

"Magic, Tippi," her mother said. "Magic, like flying-carpets magic, like Disney flying-Volkswagens magic." She held Tippi tightly to her. "We can believe in that, can't we? We always did, remember?"

"I *never* did."

"Aw, c'mon! You cheated!"

"Well, I'm not a dummy. You can't tell me things can fly without wings—or propellers—or jet engines."

"This one does," Harry said.

Whether she believed it or not, the talk brought some relief from the almost overpowering fear, and the girl began to relax, to look around, to watch as hills approached them—hills studded with the black shadows of scattered oak trees, hills that were higher than they were, making it seem certain a life-taking crash was only a breath away, before the slight movement of Harry's hands drove their bottoms into their seats, and their stomachs, too, as they swooped upward effortlessly, to reverse the process as they crested the hill, dropping again, to lift them out of their seats and push their stomachs into their throats.

"If I live through this," Lori gasped, "nothing can kill me."

"Come off it," Harry chided, lying cheerfully. "You're sitting in God's pocket!"

"That, I'd like to believe!"

"You sure you know the way home?" Tippi asked.

"Absolutely," Harry said. "We may have to grope a little, but we'll get there."

On the way in with Guss he had memorized course and distance, and by circling widely around the bay area, he was able to cross the path they had used going in. Turning there to 130 degrees, he was on a reverse course that was at least parallel to the one Guss had taken, maybe to the left of it, maybe to the right.

And that, he told himself mentally, *cuts 'er down to just a couple of haystacks hiding the needle.*

He saw lights on other craft going toward or moving away from the Bay Area, and none seemed to show the slightest interest in them. Most probably they hadn't seen them running dark against the ground. And how long before someone went looking for the Jassan mechanic? How long before they found him dead and sounded the alarm?

Any damned time!

And he said that silently, not wanting Lori and Tippi to know that falling out of the sky or running into a hill was the least of their dangers. If they couldn't find the building on the lake and get through the door before the Jassans discovered the body, or discovered they were gone, their chances of escape dwindled almost at once to two: slim and none.

Because where the hell else could they go, except to the only doorway that opened into their world? Set down and hide in the bushes? No way! Once the doorway was guarded against them, they were dead turkeys.

This certain knowledge, as the minutes crawled away, set a drip of cold sweat running down Harry Borg's spine, though he kept a light, running, pilot-to-passenger talk going: "And on our left, if you will turn your attention in that direction, you will see the lights of what would be Stockton in our world."

"Keep jiving," Lori said. "We're needing that."

She was tense in the seat beside him, and he knew her good gray eyes were searching, as his were, for the lights of approaching or searching aircraft. He felt her hand creep onto his thigh, grip and discover the tense muscles there; felt a reassuring, hang-in-there kind of thump of a clenched fist. She didn't know about the dead mechanic, but she knew that when their absence was discovered the Jassans would move immediately to head them off at the pass. With radio communications, with a sure knowledge of where the pass—the escape door—was, they would have no difficulty in cutting them off.

Light was beginning to outline the hills ahead of them. Full daylight was no more than an hour away. *Come on, baby,* Harry whispered to himself. *Give me a reference point—any kind of a damned marker.* And not three minutes later, in the growing light, he saw the hill where he and Guss had landed after running out of fuel, saw the bassoe ranch.

"Hot damn!" he said to Lori. "We're right on course, believe *that* or not."

"I believe it! I believe it!"

She was so emphatic, Tippi looked at her. "You don't sound like you believe it," the youngster said worriedly.

"If you say something hard enough, you can make it true—didn't you know that, sweetie-pie?"

"Nope. I sure didn't."

"This time it worked," Harry said. "There'll be a house on a lake in a parklike setting in just a few more minutes, coming in right under our bow. Watch for it!"

"I'm watching! I'm watching!" Lori said.

The house on the lake appeared so suddenly, Harry almost overran it. He went off the throttle and braked. "There's the needle," he said. "Sticking right out of the haystack."

"Needles!" Lori said. "Haystacks! What a liar you are! What a faker!"

"A lucky, lying faker," Harry said grimly. "So far." He brought the aircraft around in a low, sweeping search. "You see anything on the ground—plane, car, pickup truck—sound off."

She scanned the ground. "Looks clear."

"Going in," Harry said.

"Still okay." Lori was jerking her head this way and that, poking her eyes into every place that might conceal a Jassan. She saw nothing. And yet . . .

A moment before they touched down as near the entrance of the building as Harry could bring the craft, he said, "Remember, now. Straight through to the doorway. The lock's on the left, the handle's in the center of the door."

"I remember, I remember," Lori said, about ready to jump out of her skin with tension.

"I'll be right behind you," Harry said. "Don't stop for anything, okay?"

"Gotcha, for goshsakes!"

The aircraft bumped down. Harry cut the switch; the doors popped open.

"Go!" Harry said.

Lori and Tippi hit the ground, stumbling, then recovered their balance and ran for the door. Harry paused the briefest of moments to check the sky and the surrounding shrubbery for some sign of Jassans. Lori and Tippi had reached the front entrance. Lori jerked open the front entrance—and found herself face to face with a grinning, uniformed Jassan.

"Harry!"

Her cry was a squawk of fear and anguish and dismay—after all they'd dared, after all their fear and striving, that grin said they had had no chance at all from the very beginning. *The very beginning.*

Turning at her cry, Harry Borg drew his sidearm. Lori fell on Tippi, driving her down to the paving stones to one side, leaving Harry a clear field of fire. He leveled the piece, aimed as the Jassan began to draw his own sidearm, and fired. Damn! there was no muzzle blast, no recoil—but a section of the door above the Jassan's head exploded.

"A helluva piece," Harry thought wildly.

"Bassoe's armed!" a Jassan voice screeched in Harry's head. "He's shooting!"

A Jassan head appeared at the door's edge, ducked back. Harry placed another shot through the door, heard it strike explosively on a back wall. Lori and Tippi were scrambling on all fours out of the way. And Harry heard an exchange of Jassan voices from within the building. He counted three. There was no time for schemes. They would summon help, if they hadn't already. They could go out the back and come at him from the sides. The only way to go was straight ahead.

"Coming at yuh!" he yelled.

The short sword in one hand, the sidearm in the other, he charged straight through the doorway. "Harry! For Christ's sake!" he heard Lori scream at him. Inside, he hit the floor, rolling hard. A shot blasted through a wall after passing over him. He straightened to find a Jassan had leaped and was diving onto him, and he had time only for a thrust with the short sword—and that was enough. The sword went in smoothly, cleanly, and the Jassan died on it, but the weight of the Jassan bore him down in a tangle.

He fought clear, only to be struck a crashing blow with some object, possibly a chair, that disintegrated after striking him on the head and shoulders, knocking him almost unconscious.

"Grab him!" a Jassan screeched.

"Get his arms." Another Jassan.

"Kill him! Kill him!" yelled the first.

"Harry!" The voice was Lori's.

And as his vision cleared, Harry saw that Lori had come in, had caught up a part of whatever had broken on his head, and had clubbed one of the two remaining Jassans. The other had drawn a sidearm and was leveling it at Lori—and Harry blew a hole through the chest of that one with his own gun.

But the last Jassan—

"Damn it to hell!" Harry had time to growl.

And that was all the time he had. For the last Jassan, the one Lori had clubbed, had remained upright and had brought his sidearm to bear on Harry. Harry saw it coming and knew it would get to him before he could bring his own piece around. He felt an explosion erupt enormously on his left leg, knew that leg had been blown away. Then another explosion took off his right arm. He was driven to the floor, not yet suffering pain, only enormous shock.

"Oh, God! Harry!" Lori screamed as she saw him fall, bleeding. "Don't—don't die!" Her agony was total, but she ran to him and threw herself onto him as if to defend him against more wounds.

Harry could see the Jassan who had fired the shots that had destroyed him standing motionless, yellow eyes wild, tongue flailing, but immobile, as if in great shock of his own. "You won, you bastard . . ." Harry whispered. And then he found Lori's grief-distorted face close above his own.

"What a lousy hero I turned out to be."

"You tried, Harry. Oh, God in heaven, you tried!"

"And blew it . . ."

That was the end of it for Harry Borg.

Lori's face, and all else, simply went away.

CHAPTER 8

A fantasy world, Chad Harrison decided.

That was the only description that fit. Fairyland would be another, except that here all the inhabitants were monsters. What else could you call the lizzies? They acted like humans. They treated you as civilized humans would, civilized humans who had to keep you imprisoned for your own protection, who provided you with every comfort imaginable, but who were, beyond any doubt, lizards masquerading as humans.

He was lying on a recliner in the early morning sun, stark naked, adding more tan to the substantial tan he already had. Stark naked, because what was there to be modest about in a land where the only other humanlike creatures, the fuzzies, wore fur and went naked too? The lizzies showed some interest in his genitals, but it was, he suspected, a scientific curiosity rather than any sexual interest.

Chad Harrison was nineteen years old. He was a lean six-one when standing, a young man with the sun-bleached blond hair of a surfer, with gray-blue eyes under unexpectedly dark brown eyebrows, a cleft chin, and, when he chose to use it, an absolutely charming smile. While he had done more than a little surfing, the thick column of his neck said that his real interest was football. His size—and, of course, he was still growing—his very

95

high IQ, and his near perfect physical coordination had qualified him for scholarships to almost every major college in the country.

But all that had been back on the planet Earth, he mused now, with only an amused sort of bitterness, if there was any bitterness at all. Before the UFOs. Damn! How many recruiters from how many colleges had he had sitting in cars out in front of his house, waiting for him to get home each day? That new, yellow Ford Mustang convertible? Sucker bait, right? His if he signed, and the Big Ten could worry about the violations of recruiting rules tomorrow.

All shot, now. Gone.

But—what the hell?

The sun was getting hot.

He was going to have to move pretty soon. But not yet. He had to know for sure what the lizzies were building out there. Oh, he knew, but he wanted the final proof. They'd been working on it for a month now, grading, sodding, enclosing it in more electric fence. Since they couldn't talk—they only flopped those long, forked tongues at him—there was no point in asking. But the shape of it was unmistakable, and when he had realized what they were up to, he'd been absolutely flabbergasted. Apart from taking them back home, there didn't seem to be anything the lizzies wouldn't do to keep them happy.

To begin with, lizzie-land wasn't all that different from planet Earth. Where he was lying right now felt like August in California. It even *looked* like California. Somewhere out in Ventura County, he would say: the same sun-browned hills, the same scattering of oak, and, in the steeper hills, the same chaparral. The buildings across the way could be a university. And the housing for them here was tops: Each had his own room, good beds, comfortable chairs; a rec room with games; a dining room with fine chow. And clean! Spotless didn't even begin to tell about it. The crew of lizzies—in white smocks and gauze masks, of course—kept it absolutely CP.

It makes you wonder, now, doesn't it, Chad, baby? he said to himself. And he answered, *It do, it do!*

But—what the hell?

Behind him he could hear three of the others arguing in the rec room, Arnie insisting he was right about the rules of the lizzie game they were playing. Arnie had never been in doubt about anything in his entire life, Chad knew. Even when he was wrong, Arnie knew he was right, and he was wrong about half the time. Homer liked to put him on, good-humoredly, of course. And Eddie had to defend Arnie. That loud belch that came from the third window down was Barney—Samuel Barnstable. A big, good-natured bull of a man, Barney, and one hell of an offensive tackle. But he did have that streak of cheerful vulgarity. Liked to shock people.

"Hey, Chad! Where are yuh, Chad?"

It was Arnie Garrett, still heated with the argument Homer had laid on him, looking for an arbitrator. He came out of the rec room and onto the terrace where Chad was lying, watching the lizzie construction below. Eddie Cole was right behind Arnie.

Homer, who had had no real interest in the disagreement from the beginning, and had even less now, came to push Chad over for sitting room, to look down at the lizzie construction. "Well, lookie here, now," he said to Chad with surprised amusement.

Arnie, because it was a matter of principle, persisted. "Homer says you can hit a black ball with a red ball, if the white balls are gone, and I say he's full of bull. Am I right or not?"

Chad peered at Homer lazily from under the brim of his pulled-down baseball cap. "You full of bull, Homer?"

"Yup," Homer said, unperturbed. "Up to here."

Arnie, realizing the big, soft-talking farm hand had been putting him on again, leaped on Homer and clamped a headlock on him with pretended fierceness. "Unscrew your goddamn head!" he yelled. "Jerked me for your last time!"

Homer let him try all he wanted, a large dog patiently suffering a wooling by a smaller one. Arnie was five-ten, one-eighty, and very strong when he wanted to be—a very good running back; Homer was six-two, two-ten, with shoulders as wide as a farmyard gate and hands as big as shovels—a superlative center.

Chad grinned at Eddie. "Gonna help Arnie?"

"Naw," Eddie said. He was black, a very handsome, lean greyhound of a black with large, black-almond eyes, a graceful mover, a leaper of amazing ability and therefore a wide receiver who could make a hero out of any quarterback. His real interest was radio; he'd grown up in a mom and pop electronics store.

"Scufflin' ain't cool, man." He only talked jive to amuse the others.

"Right on!" Chad agreed. Then he indicated the lizzie construction project. "How about that?"

Eddie looked. His eyes widened with delight. "All right!"

And there was enough delight in Eddie's voice to cause Arnie to quit twisting on Homer's unresisting head, to look, and to instantly forget his pretense at anger.

"Goddamn, a football field!"

"As you live and breathe," Chad agreed.

"Those lizzies're something else!"

The Jassan construction crew was now erecting the pipe framework they'd put together at one end of the field. Goalposts! What else? And the markings another crew was laying down were boundaries and yard markers.

"They've got it right, too," Eddie said. "Or very close. Hundred yards between goals, sure as can be."

"Where'd they get the dimensions?" Homer said to Chad. "They didn't have it when we got here."

"They went back!" Arnie said, surprised, incredulous.

"I think so," Chad said. "And that gives us a line on how long it takes for them to go from this planet to our planet. A month, would you say?"

"Impossible," Eddie said. "They'd have to exceed the speed of light a dozen times to get between any two solar systems in a month."

"Correct," Chad said. "Makes you think, eh?"

"How about Mars?" Arnie asked. "Those eggheads might be wrong about Mars . . ." His voice died out as he saw the negation in the faces of the others. "Guess not."

"No way," Homer said.

"Been sitting here the last half hour, trying to guess where we are that they could get to Earth and back in that short a time. I never see anything that suggests they have space travel, or any of that Star Wars crap."

"Their fly-buggies are slick," Homer said. "When they ain't broke down. Maybe a big one?"

"I'll go with Einstein," Chad said. "Nothing faster than the speed of light."

"Me, too," Eddie agreed.

"So—what the hell?" Chad said, which was his way of accepting a situation beyond remedy, or a question beyond answering. Which was not to say he had given up. It just meant he had put the matter aside until new data came to hand.

"But they went and brought back a football field, of all things," Homer said.

"That's for sure!" Arnie said less thoughtfully.

"And for our pleasure," Eddie said.

"For our exercise," Chad said. "For our good health." His gray-blue eyes, like Homer's brown ones, were very thoughtful. "I don't know if you gents noticed it or not, but a month ago, as a group, we were doing very poorly. Scared, at first. Lying around a lot. Listless. Not eating. Losing weight."

"Took a while to get used to being here," Arnie said, defensively. "Christ! Wouldn't anybody go off his feed? Not so bad, now we got kind of used to it. Got things to do. Ridin' them birds is a gas—that's what saved me! It's one way I can beat the ass offa Eddie."

"You can like hell!" Eddie came back immediately.

"Take you on right now!" Arnie challenged.

"Deal!" Eddie said. "But first I got to hear what's buggin' our quarterback."

"Jiggin' again," Arnie said. "You're yellow!"

"Yeah," Eddie agreed. "Goes purty with black."

"Listen up," Chad said. "This is important. Any of you ever ask yourself why the lizzies treat us so good?"

"Sure," Arnie said. "We're like in a zoo. Even a lizzie'd take good care of animals in a zoo."

"You buy that, Homer?" Chad asked.

"Sure," Homer said.

"And what else, Homer?" Chad insisted.

Homer gave Chad a slow grin. "Keep askin', you're gonna get an answer."

"That's what I want."

"In front of the children?"

Arnie was immediately belligerent. "Hey, listen, wise-ass! Who're you puttin' down?" He made another lunge at Homer.

"Cool it, Arnie," Chad said.

Homer was holding Arnie at arm's length, and he smiled at the young, tough face of the smaller youth. "Back home on the ranch," he said, "the only critter that gets the kind of treatment we're getting here is Jeffrey. That's Lord Jefferson of Wyandotte, the Third. He cost the old man eighteen thousand dollars, and he's a registered Hereford." And he looked at Chad. "That answer your question?"

"Yeah, it does."

"When did you figure it out?" Homer asked.

"The second physical," he said. "Before it, I had a hell of an urge for sex; after it, none—for three days. Felt laid back, lazy."

"What're you guys sayin'?" Arnie demanded with a growing understanding, a growing horror.

Eddie had understood. His black, almond-shaped eyes were fixed on Chad. "They're telling us we're seed bulls, old buddy, that's what they're saying."

"Seed bulls!" Arnie was outraged. "Does that mean what I think it does?"

"Yeah, it does," Homer said quietly.

Arnie and Eddie continued to stare hard at Chad. "When we're taken for a physical," Chad said, "they blank us out and strip us of seed, just like we were seed bulls."

"Jesus Christ Almighty!" Arnie said. "They can't do a thing like that! Not to me, they can't!"

"Seems like they've been doing it," Eddie said.

"Well, they ain't gonna do it again!"

"You goin' to fight 'em, hothead?" Homer asked.

"Betcha goddamn life I am!" Arnie yelled. "Nobody does that to me without I say so!"

"They'll do it without your say-so," Chad told him. "Or you better hope they do. Because if they can't get semen from you, you're no damn good to them anymore. And if you're no damned good, why would they keep you around?"

"Holy smoke!" Arnie said, as that truth sank in.

"Where does the seed go, O wise man from the city?" Homer asked Chad with a good-humored, mocking tone that was old between them.

"You seen anything besides the fuzzies it would work on?" Chad asked. "If it works on them, that's supposing."

"Nothing," Homer said.

"They're trying to improve the breed," Eddie said. He was

giving very serious thought to the idea that semen taken from them was being used to fertilize the fuzzies. "That's why they've been running a half a dozen in here each night—they want us to screw 'em."

"Right on," Chad said.

They had all wondered about the nightly admission of well-scrubbed fuzzie females into their compound—a different group almost every night—and after the initial shock, which had been, in fact, quite staggering, they had come to think of the creatures as entertaining pets. About the size of smallish sixteen-year-old children, they were well, if immaturely, formed—cute, pert breasts, swelling hips, rounded bellies, inviting pubic area. Their faces, though covered with soft fur, had the regular features of human female children: straight nose, normal lips, straight, white teeth. The eyes were where the difference was most obvious. Their eyes were wide, clear, uniformly brown—and quite without expression.

"The lights are on," Arnie had said, talking about those eyes and feeling a great pity, "but there's nobody home!"

And the aimless *baa*ing, soft and untroubled, that was the limit of their vocal ability seemed to bear him out. Of one thing, however, there could be no doubt: They were sexually active and sexually receptive to a very marked degree. Since the fuzzies were "animals" to the young men in the sense that sheep were "animals," they had all, except Barney, said they would not copulate with them. Barney had said, "Hell, yes, I'm liable to service one of them little critters—if I get lonesome enough." But then Barney was always joshing.

What the others did in the darkness of night, in the privacy of their own rooms, was, again by mutual consent, not a topic of conversation.

"These nightly visits by the fuzzies could serve two purposes, to their way of thinking," Chad said. "One, we could impregnate a few in our spare time. And, two, it would keep us from getting antsy from lack of female companionship."

"Why are fuzzies important to them?" Homer asked rhetorically, as if expecting no reply.

Chad pointedly made none.

"Pets?" Arnie asked tentatively.

Chad and Homer exchanged sober glances. Then Chad pushed

up. "Lemme get some pants on, and I'll see which one of you gladiators can ride a bird best."

"Yeah!" Eddie said immediately. He gave Arnie a hard thump on the side of the head. "C'mon, short stuff! Get your ass in the saddle."

The lizzies had provided the five young men from Earth with a stable of the riding animals the young men called "birdies," but which were actually reptiles that had apparently become stranded in the evolutionary process at a point halfway toward becoming birds. They were the size of camels—but with eager, ready-to-please dispositions—and were built like flightless birds with two very powerful hind legs and only rudimentary fore-limbs, which, with better luck, might have developed into wings.

Being vegetarian, the birdies were essentially harmless—though, as Arnie had discovered, they could kick hard enough to lift a man over a high fence. They had tall, scrawny necks, snakelike heads, and, unexpectedly, because of their otherwise reptilian character, large, movable ears and excellent hearing, proving once again that the vagaries of evolution were beyond comprehension. The birdies could run a steady thirty miles an hour for several hours. When exhausted, they died in full stride, at top speed, crashing to the ground, causing the rider great inconvenience, if not fatal injury.

The birdies served the Jassans as horses serve humans, for both utilitarian and recreational purposes. They were ridden for fun, they were raced, and they were harnessed to carts, wagons, and buggies. A stable and a circular track of about a half mile had been a part of the property the Jassans had converted into a compound for the Earthlings, and both stable and track had been retained for Earthling use.

Three Jassans, obviously professionals in the raising and train-ing of the birdies, had spent three days with patient sign language teaching the young men how to go about using the creatures. One had to strike the birdie a light blow while jerking on a halter rope, for example, to get them to squat for bridling and saddling and mounting. Once aboard, the rider found he was mounted on a wind splitter. The birdies loved to run, loved to compete against each other, loved to win, and for these qualities they had gained the unqualified affection of the young men from Earth. "They talk my language," was the way Arnie put it. "Hard triers, every one of 'em."

When the birdies saw the young men approaching the stable, they began to kick the walls in eagerness, thumping hard, then turning to poke their ugly heads out over the doors to their stalls. The Jassan trainer who had remained on as a permanent caretaker came out of his quarters at one end of the building, followed by his "bug," as the young men called the giant beetles the Jassans used as watchdogs and shepherds.

Chad, Homer, and Barney took seats on the top rail of a fence, leaving the racing to Arnie and Eddie, who had a thing going between them. After races that must have numbered in the hundreds, Arnie claimed an eleven-race margin of victory, which may or may not have been true. The competition was what really mattered, because if they kept it heated, it occupied their minds fully, leaving little room for thoughts of loneliness, or realizations that could spout geysers of sheer terror within them in the dark hours of the night. And they kept it heated white-hot, arguing, fighting furiously for any small advantage, cheating outrageously, loving every minute of it.

Arnie and Eddie went to the stable-keeper. "Hey, pal," Arnie said. "Today we want two birdies. You savvy 'two'? Carter for him, Reagan for me. Okay? Chop, chop! Saddle quick!"

It didn't matter, really, what he said. The Jassan knew what they were there for and turned to bring out the birdies.

That Barney yelled, "Your mother eats her own eggs!" at the Jassan didn't matter either. The Jassan couldn't hear voices. And even if he had been able to, it still would not have mattered, because if any harm came to the humans through any action or inaction of his, it was very likely his own life would be taken a few moments later.

Chad, Homer, and Barney, sitting on the fence, watched as the birdies were brought out, the tall, leathery animals frisky at the end of their halter ropes like colts. But they were tractable, even eager, squatting without being asked, getting up, squatting again. Even though Arnie was five-ten, the top of his head came only to the underbelly of the birdie he was to ride; mounted, legs securely pinned behind the rudimentary forelimbs, he looked dwarflike.

"Hah-*hooo*!" he yelled.

"Saved his life, for sure," Homer said to Chad. "Wasn't for the birdies, Arnie'd've gone to pickin' at the sheets a month ago."

Eddie, clearly a better rider of birdies—he seemed as much a part of one of the beasts as the creature's neck—moved his mount out onto the track behind Arnie. They lined up, whooped, and took off together. The necks of the birdies stretched out, parallel to the ground, reaching, the riders bent forward to flatten against the wind. The powerful legs, striding effortlessly, carried them in a pointless but powerfully exciting contest around the half-mile track.

"All I git to do is pick lint from my belly button," Barney said morosely after he had watched them a moment. He had not been able to ride a birdie; he was awkward when his feet were off the ground. "Woe is me!" His round, button-nosed face disgruntled, he got down off the fence to wander back toward the barracks.

Chad, his eyes following the thundering progress of the riders around the track, spoke quietly to Homer. "They eat fuzzies," he said. "You know that."

"I was born on a cattle ranch," Homer said.

"You probably recognized the setup before I did," Chad agreed. "And I think Eddie knows. But I don't see any reason to scare the others, do you?"

"No."

There was a moment of silence. "Now I've got a chiller for you," Chad said. "Ready for it?"

"Try it on."

"Three nights ago I had a fuzzie in my room, sleeping on the floor beside my bed. The usual, right?"

"Yeah."

"She was a little older than the average. Maybe bigger. Anyway, about two o'clock I feel something touch my arm, waking me up. The moonlight's coming in. I can see her fine. Homer, there was somebody home behind those eyes. She was trying to tell me something."

Homer swore softly.

"She pantomimed eating," Chad said. "Meaning herself—being eaten."

"Mother of Christ," Homer whispered.

"She was asking for help."

Homer turned to give Chad a full, measuring stare. "You sure, old buddy? Makes a whole new ball game, y'know."

"I know."

"Sheep I can stand. Even if they look kind of like human beings. But *thinking* humans who know they're food animals—that's a ball-buster."

"We've had—how many?—say, four hundred run through our barracks, and I've seen one with at least a trace of intelligence. That's not a big average, but the genes are there, Homer."

"Did the lizzies mind-blank them a million years ago and they're beginning to come back? Or are they mind-blankin' 'em now at birth?"

"I'll guess with you." Chad was silent for a moment. "I marked this one, tattooed the inside of her lower lip with ink and a needle. Watch for her."

"Will do."

"Makes getting out of here even more urgent," Chad said. "We'll end up hamburger if we don't."

"Tell me how and when."

Chad's voice was quietly fierce. "I need more data," he said. "I need to know about that mind-blanker! I need to know how they can get to our world and back in a month's time! And the data will come. All this can't begin and end with us! An event as big as this can't happen by itself. There will be another event. And it will provide more data. Soon. When it happens, Homer, we've got to be ready for it."

"I'm with you," Homer said. And after a moment's thought: "Arnie's figuring a bust-out, using a birdie. Thinks if he can get in the hills he can stay loose."

"To what purpose?" Chad asked.

"He'd be his own man," he says. "Not a prisoner."

"And fair game."

"You know Arnie. Competition's his bag."

"Gotta talk him out of it," Chad said. "This competition could, literally, eat him alive."

CHAPTER 9

Tippi Calder was not the most patient thirteen-year-old alive, but she could, when put to it, control her impatience for a reasonable length of time. But on this occasion, her patience had been exhausted. She had cleaned up after Poopsalot for the last time. Returning from the bathing quarters, holding Poopsalot by the hand, she went straight to her mother's room with an ultimatum.

"Either I get diapers for this dingbat," she said, "or Poopsalot gets sent home!"

In the beginning, the three-year-old fuzzie, undeniably as cute as a creature could be, had seemed the perfect pet-companion. A girl can get awfully bored, sitting around day after day with nobody to talk to but her mother, with nothing to read, no television, no radio, no music—*nothing*! No other girls. No boys at all. And when the lizard-men had left a little fuzzie tied up at the door of the apartment—well, naturally, what else could she do but bring her in?

Weird, that's what it had been.

The fuzzie looked like a little human girl, except that she was covered with soft fur and her ears were kind of pointy. She had big brown eyes, long lashes, straight baby teeth, and all the rest. But you couldn't *teach* her anything! She had to be the dumbest kid in anybody's world. Even a puppy could be

106

housebroken! But not little Poopsalot. She *baa*ed so pitifully when you paddled her, but she went on pooping.

"Why *not* diapers?" Tippi asked her mother.

"I don't see any—reason why not," her mother said. Her mother was busy gyrating, striding, flinging her arms about to the beat of an erratic humming sound she was making. "All—you have to do—is figure out a way—to make the lizards understand—what you want—and why you want it."

"That's a lot of no help."

"I'm sorry—Tippi."

Lori knew what Tippi wanted. Tippi wanted her to do the necessary explaining to the lizard-men. But that would mean she would have to admit to them that the implant operation they had performed on her *had* been successful, and that she was able to hear in her mind what they were saying. *That* she didn't want to do.

She had refused to admit she could understand them—and that, therefore, she could communicate with them—since the operation, thinking it might gain her an advantage at some future time. Wouldn't it? If she were able to understand them, while they believed she couldn't?

After the fight in the house where Harry Borg had been killed—and she'd had some very chilling moments wondering what they had done with his body after they'd rushed it away—she had experienced the most dreadful days of her life. Only Tippi, only the child's need of her, had enabled her to hold any grip at all on her sanity. Tippi, with a child's resiliency, had recovered first, but Lori's own vision of the future, of herself, a human female, alone in a world of lizards dressed as people, had set her screaming at the top of her lungs into her pillow at night, had sucked up black tendrils of insanity out of dark pits of her mind; and she had all but surrendered to them time and again, holding on, barely, with what seemed no better a grip than fingernails scratching on panes of glass. Only a frightened Tippi, pleading, "Mommy, Mommy, please don't," had brought her back from the brink—and it had happened four times, to her everlasting discredit, she thought now.

After the fourth time, the lizard-men—and some of them were extremely intelligent, give them that—had apparently become concerned. How they knew how serious her troubles were was a question she couldn't answer. But they had known. And their answer had been, obviously, to give her the same implant they'd given Harry Borg, in the hope that being able to communicate with her captors would be a giant step toward saving her sanity. And perhaps it had. She'd had no attacks of black hysteria since; rather, she'd had, instead, many long hours in which to think about and to plan for an eventual escape.

She had gone to the door, opened it, had seen nothing, had closed the door, and had returned to the living quarters—she thought. But according to Tippi, she had gone through the door, to walk away in the company of two lizard-men, to be gone for four days, to return with a small, almost unnoticeable patch of hair gone from the back of her head, with a small, equally unnoticeable scar there on the bare spot. The missing hair, the scar on the bare spot were indisputable: They *had* fooled around inside her head, doing something or other.

But it wasn't until two days later that she'd learned exactly what they had done. Two of the lizard-men—one of them wore spectacles and what seemed a constant look of puzzlement—had come to check on the results. To her considerable shock, she had *heard* them as they came into the apartment, discussing her and the possible success of the operation. She still had been in a state of shock in the first few moments, when they had questioned her, and had been unable to answer, even if she had wanted to. Then, as she'd recovered, contrariness had at first persuaded her to act deaf and dumb. Later, of course, she had seen the advantage of continuing to play deaf and dumb, and so she had—much to the bafflement of the lizard-man who wore the glasses, who apparently had been the surgeon who had done the implant operation. The other one had been only too glad to believe the surgeon had failed, but the surgeon had found it hard to believe he could have failed, and had gone away looking very disappointed and very puzzled.

And Lori hadn't given him any help at all.

"Screw you!" she'd said at their retreating backs.

She wasn't quite sure, but she may have heard him, the one with the puzzled look, mutter, "Screw you? What could that possibly mean?" as they went out.

But Tippi thought of her own way to communicate with the

lizard-men. "I know what I'll do. I'll tear up a towel and make a diaper. Then I'll get Tillie in here and *show* her what I need."

"Way to go," her mother said.

Against the day when an escape might prove possible, Lori had begun a regimen of physical fitness for both herself and her daughter. Hers included an hour of aerobic dancing, to which effort she was exerting herself at the moment, sweat glistening on her already well conditioned body, nostrils flared from deep breathing. The exercise would have been easier if she were able to do it to something besides self-created humming. "Ever tried to hum while panting?" she'd asked her daughter. "It ain't easy."

"And it sounds terrible," Tippi told her. "Kind of like somebody dying by inches."

She was too smart for her own good, her mother often thought. But lovable.

The diaper, handcrafted from towel and certainly ill-fitting, looked cute on Poopsalot. Kind of like Baby New Year with fur, Tippi thought. She managed to get Poopsalot to wear it long enough for her to summon the female Jassan they had come to call Tillie.

"She's got to wear something," Tippi explained to Tillie with as many gestures in sign language as she could dream up— holding the nose, making a face, that sort of thing. "I can't go on following her around with a shovel and a mop."

Tillie was amused.

The way her mouth gaped, the way her long forked tongue waved, the way she gestured, had to mean she was laughing out loud. But she apparently conceded Tippi's point, because she went away, to come back a few hours later with a supply of very workable diapers, better by far than the ones Tippi had made.

Lori and Tippi had become rather fond of Tillie in the time the young female had been with them. She was not unpleasant to look at, after first revulsion had worn off; Her large yellow vertically slitted eyes seemed honestly caring, and when the gray veil covered them, she seemed shy, perhaps, or embarrassed. Her skin had a much finer look than that of the males; her features, though lizard, of course, were refined in a female way. Most of all, she seemed willing to go out of her way to do anything to please Lori and Tippi, to make them more comfortable, to make them happy—and that quality was hard to reject.

"If I'm ever going to like a lizard," Lori had said, "Tillie is going to be the first."

But, gyrating, humming, panting hard, and sweating, she was grimly sure that she would never come to like any lizard-type, male or female, except Tillie. When the chance came, and somehow she was dead sure the chance would come, she wanted to be able to kill as many lizard-men as she had to without a twinge of remorse—if that was what it would take to get herself and Tippi safely home.

"Hang in—there, baby," she told herself. "The day—wiil come."

CHAPTER 10

The first thing Harry Borg saw upon his return to what was for him, at least, the land of the living, was the closed lid of what might very well have been a coffin. Except that it was lighted, and that he was not laid out in his best dark suit, it could be a coffin. It was near the right size—no, it was bigger, he corrected himself immediately, after rolling his eyes to discover the limits of his confinement. And then, as a veil of vagueness seemed to be carried through his mind on a wave of euphoria, a wave of not caring a whistle about anything, he asked himself how the hell he could know what the inside of a closed coffin would look like.

"Be dark in there," he said.

And he discovered his voice was creaky and his throat very dry. He tried several times before he was able to clear his throat and dampen it with a few swallows of saliva. *Hey, I'm just a head! I've got no body!* And in his pleasant state of euphoria that didn't seem to be important. Just a fact of passing interest. No body. Just a head. How about that?

He soaked along for a few moments, faintly giddy, enjoying the totally unbelievable premise that he was now only a head with no body. Never have to worry about back pain again—no back. Never have to worry about getting any again—no tools. Never have to worry about staying in shape, staying sober, stay-

ing off the cigarettes, or getting caught short when he'd passed
up a chance to visit the gent's room. All right! Bodies, when he
came to think of it, could be a nuisance.

The wave of euphoria subsided gently, lowering him in the
trough toward reality, and with the reality came the first shreds
of memory. It was not a coherent, total recall, at first—just
shreds, like wisps of clouds, that floated through his consciousness.

Lori, he thought. *Tippi*.

That memory was no more than a sensation of pleasure as it
moved wisplike through his mind. And a sensation of love. Then
Lori's face appeared to him, the good gray eyes, the strong
cheekbones, the straight, dark brows, the mouth that smiled
easily or softened under the pressure of his lips with a beautiful,
engulfing warmth. And the face of Tippi emerged out of noth-
ingness. It was like the other face, though still a child's face, a
young face full of growing wisdom, questioning, unafraid of
answers.

"I love you both," he said, the words soft on his tongue.

Then, jarring, most of his memory came into focus. The
Jassan face of Guss leaped sharply into view, and with him the
others: Sos Vissir, the languid, the limp-wristed, the extremely
wealthy; Kass, the politician, string-controlled by some higher-
up; Sassan, the surgeon, faceless yet; the salivating Jassan cop.

His moment of terror on the face of the building as he had
climbed down, and his shame of it, came to him next: His
cowardice had almost killed him. Quickly then he saw a montage,
shimmering, flashing, like a sudden summer thunderstorm of
thunder and lightning, and he remembered the rest of it: the
killing of the mechanic, the flight with Lori and Tippi in the
aircraft, those moments of great personal pride in his role as a
great hero rescuing the beautiful damsel and her child from the
lair of the monsters, and, finally, his ego-crashing discovery that
he wasn't a hero after all, but a hopeless klutz who lay dying
with his leg and his arm shot clean away by monsters only a
little less klutzy than himself.

With total recall flooding into his consciousness, an anger
was born, a great, shouting, roaring anger, a black, cursing anger
that set every muscle in his body to surging and straining—and
it was at that moment that he discovered he was not a head alone,

but a head fully equipped with a normal body that had suddenly come alive and was making itself known with a thousand tingling, buzzing pains that flashed into his mind from the tips of every extremity. The discovery jolted him out of his anger, shocked him into a blazing alertness, wide-eyed, seeking answers.

What the hell is going on?

He was lying in a coffinlike container, his body floating in a fluid, weightless and, until the moment before, without life. Now his body was alive, though he found he was unable to do more than tense and relax his muscles. Try as he might, he could not curl a finger, lift a hand, or move a leg.

The topmost part of the container that held him, he saw, was transparent. Glass or some such. Above it, a mirrored ceiling showed him a reflection of the entire room and of the container in which he was lying.

The room, first: quite large, tile-walled, sparkling clean. A bank of instrument dials over there on a wall; sinks and cabinets against a different wall. Five white-smock-clad, gauze-masked Jassans. A pair of uniformed guards on either side of the entrance, both carrying arms. Closer at hand, on a recliner, wearing a gauze mask, apparently dozing, was a familiar figure: Guss.

And now his container: a tanklike affair, an oversize coffin from which hoses and cables of various sizes extruded like the arms of an octopus, going to tanks and monitoring devices— one of which apparently signaled just then that he was awake, for, at that moment, the smock-clad Jassans turned his way.

"Damn!" Harry said, struggling to move. "It was all real! It was no nightmare! It was real, real, real!"

The face of the first Jassan to look in on him was wearing spectacles, of all things, above his white gauze mask. The others were also wearing gauze masks, but their gestures, the way they gripped each other's shoulders, told they were pleased and excited, while the one with the spectacles seemed to be accepting things as if they were only as he had expected them to be.

"Please don't be alarmed."

"He's alive!"

"Oh, very much so."

"Absolutely incredible!"

"Will his limbs *really* function?"

The splatter of voices that began to materialize in Harry's

mind came dimly out of a foggy distance at first, then grew in clarity and strength until finally they took on expression—a gentle reassurance for him, and, among themselves, surprise and wonderment.

Then the lid of the coffinlike enclosure was raised and the Jassan who wore the glasses peered in at him. Behind the glasses, the large yellow vertically slitted eyes seemed to hold an expression of puzzlement, a faint suggestion that none of what was seen was wholly believed; but it might have been only Harry Borg's imagination, or the way the light caught the eye before and after the membrane moved across it.

"Please don't be alarmed," the Jassan said. "I am Sassan, and I assure you we mean you no harm."

Harry took a long moment to get his emotions in hand and his thinking straight. Sassan, of course.

"You're the surgeon," he said, his voice stumbling as he worked to regain his ability to communicate. "You worked on me before."

"Yes, that's true," Sassan said. "We're old friends, though you won't remember the other times we've spent together."

"My arm—my leg—" Harry said. "I saw them gone, shot clean off—bleeding like a fire hydrant. I was a dead turkey— I knew it."

The look of puzzlement seemed to deepen. "Turkey?"

"Slang for dead man."

"Oh. Well, you were dead to all intents and purposes when they finally got you to me. Yes, very near a turkey."

"Dead turkey."

"Whatever."

"And you saved my life?"

"As you see."

"My arm and leg?"

"As good as ever. Maybe even better, after a period of strengthening. I do keep improving my skills as times goes on."

"The last thing I thought before the curtain came down was that I was going to end up on Sos Vissir's table as the main course."

"Main course?"

"I'm a bassoe, right? You people eat bassoes, and it didn't seem like you'd waste a freshly killed one."

Sassan was upset. "A far greater waste would have been to eat you, an intelligent bassoe. And, if I may say so, a bassoe *I* had reconstructed and rejuvenated! I am the very best at what I do!"

Then he lifted his eight-fingered hands and his smock-clad shoulders in a gesture that reminded Harry of a Jewish merchant.

"Of course, if you had died . . ."

"So a perfectly good carcass shouldn't go to waste," Harry said sourly. "How long do I have to stay in this soup?"

"We'll take you out today."

"And then?"

"With hard work, you should be back to normal in two or three months."

"I can beat that."

"That's up to you." Sassan began to turn away.

"Was that Guss—I mean that sissal-player, Guss Rassan—I saw sittin' over there a minute ago?" Harry asked.

"Mr. Rassan," Sassan said, "has been waiting here with you for the past week, almost day and night. He's right—"

And before the surgeon could finish, Guss's face, wearing a gauze mask, loomed over Harry's container. "Right here, old buddy," he said. He turned toward the retreating surgeon. "How long?"

"A few minutes," came the answer.

As soon as Guss turned back, Harry said, "Lori, Tippi—the woman and the child—what about them?"

"Alive and well," Guss said.

"How well?" Harry asked.

"Back with Sos Vissir, living like royalty." And then Guss's tongue lolled and his eyes rolled in exaggerated gestures. "You exceeded all expectations," Guss said, "to use the words in the medical report."

"What the hell does that mean?"

"The female is pregnant," Guss said, lolling his tongue again.

"How—" Harry began, then gave it up. "You couldn't know for sure. It's only been, what? A couple of days?"

"Three weeks."

"Keerist!" Harry said. "I've been out that long?"

"That long," Guss said. "You can take it to the bank; you're a real stud. Sassan checked her out. Put a communicator in her head while he was at it."

"She like that?"

"Won't admit it works." Guss rested his chin on his hands as they rested on the side of Harry's container. "Human females can be stubborn as hell, it seems."

"And you can take *that* to the bank," Harry said. "And now what about those males, the football players you kidnapped? There were five of them, right?"

"Yeah, five. They're better than fine, Harry." Guss stood erect, gestured widely. "Everything they ever wanted, they've got. And more. Even a football—what d'yuh call it, gridiron?— they've got. All so healthy, you couldn't believe it."

"Happy?" Harry asked grimly.

Guss twisted his hands in a maybe-yes-maybe-no gesture.

"Seed bulls, aren't they? How do they like that?"

"They don't know, Harry. Why tell them?"

"You're a bunch of bastards, Guss. Y'know that?"

Guss looked pained. "Harry! Look at you!"

"Yeah, look at me. Shot to hell, wasn't I?"

"But now—all in one piece again. Can you say that's *all* bad?"

"That's one for you," Harry said grudgingly.

Guss came close and looked steadily at Harry, the verticle slits in his eyes quite open, giving Harry a deeper look at Guss than he'd had before. It seemed to Harry that he could see a very concerned friend looking out at him from inside that reptilian head.

"You've got to be the biggest saphead of all creation," Guss said.

"Because I tried to get loose?"

"You damned near got yourself killed," Guss said. "If it hadn't been you had the top surgeon in all creation—your world or mine—on your side, you'd be dead and gone."

"And had for dinner, right?"

"Right!"

"How come I'm not dead?" Harry asked. "I killed a couple of Jassans, as I remember it. Or don't they charge for killing Jassans in this world?"

"They charge!" Guss said vehemently. "Anybody but you,

they'd have been killed on the spot. You—you're something else."

"What d'you mean?"

"Every cop in the country knows about you, knows you're to be kept alive and unharmed at any cost. And the cost can be a dozen cops or more—not just two."

"Why'd they try to stop me, then?"

"You're not to be let out—at any cost. They've got orders to hold you until the mind-control unit can get a shot at you."

"Mind control? What the hell's that?"

"A ray, I guess you'd call it. Turns off a bassoe's mind. They use it on—never mind. Anyway, it turns you off, like. And they can turn you on again, and you'd never know you'd been turned off—except they'd have a net over you."

"Christ!" Harry said. "What next?"

"You never had a chance, you dummy," Guss said. "Not from the first minute. You could've killed yourself, climbing down the outside of that building!"

"How about that?" Harry said with some pride. "Harry Borg, the Human Fly!"

"The human klutz!"

"*You* couldn't do it!"

"*I* don't think I'm Superman," Guss told him. "I wouldn't even try. And I hope you're cured. Superman you are not, okay?"

"Yeah?" Harry's tone was challenging. "Bend a little closer, pal. I want to speak confidentially."

Guss bent closer. Harry's head was supported so that only his face was out of the water, and his hair, grown rather long now, was floating in a dark circle to frame it. He looked pale, like a ghostly face peering out of a gray, mistlike medium, but his dark blue eyes were sharply alive and intent. And the low voice Guss heard left no doubt of the resolve that burned steadily in the mind of the man who lay helpless.

"I'm not going to stay in your world a prisoner," he said. "And you can bet your reptilian ass on that. They can kill me a dozen times; I'll still keep trying."

Guss was leaning on the edge of the tank, head resting on hands that gripped the edge. His large yellow eyes studied Harry's dark blue ones a long moment. "Sounds like Harry. Sounds like he's getting well. Gotta fight something, or somebody."

"I mean it!"

"Sure you do," Guss agreed. "Now listen to me, old buddy. Keep fighting, you'll end up eaten. No question. Do like I tell you and you've got a good chance of going back—with the female and her child. A good chance, I said. Remember that. The other way, no chance at all."

Their eyes remained locked another long moment.

"What have I got to do?" Harry asked finally.

Guss's attention was caught by returning Jassans, pushing a gurney. He straightened up. "Get well!" he said cheerfully, which was either an answer or a parting wish.

Looking at the ceiling mirrors, Harry watched Guss cross the white tiled room, saw him pause to speak briefly to the white-smock-clad, gauze-masked attendants, who had turned from their duty stations at the bank of instrument dials to speak to him.

Nurses, Harry thought. *Maybe nurses' aides. Typical. Female certainly, giggly.*

Guss hadn't exaggerated when he'd said he was a Jassan Elvis Presley. The females were making a thing of what apparently was going to be a goodbye. Two of them had something to sign—and with all the fuss and giggles one of the somethings *had* to be an article of intimate apparel.

Careful, old buddy! Harry thought, amused.

He had been waiting for the Jassans with the gurney to come to his container. They hadn't come. He looked for them now and found them reflected in the ceiling mirrors near the foot of his container. They were doing something with the tanks that were connected to his container by hoses—or nothing, really.

That was it!

Harry saw that they were doing nothing, really, with the hoses, and a stirring of concern moved through him. Perhaps it was because he was so helpless, so vulnerable, that his self-preservation alarm was so sensitive that signals came at the slightest hint of danger.

"What's going on?" he breathed.

He looked for Guss and found him just as he passed between the guards at the door. The guards were saying their goodbyes, no less hearty and almost as giggly as the female attendants, to the famous sissal-player. And after Guss had passed from sight, an exchange between the guards at the door and the attendants continued to distract the guards.

Harry looked back at the Jassans with the gurney.

"Watch it!" he yelled with all the force he had.

But too late.

The Jassans at the gurney had thrown back a white covering, had caught up a pair of weapons shaped much like submachine guns, had turned them on the guards. Stripes of blue light reached out from the weapons and touched the guards, dropping them without a sound, then moved on to touch and drop the attendants, all five, one after the other, quickly, silently.

"Help! Goddamnit!"

Harry yelled that at the top of his lungs, and at the peak of his mental powers, but if any Jassan heard, there was no sign of it.

"Murderin' bastards!" Harry raved.

He was almost too furious to be afraid, but he was afraid, nonetheless. Floating in his chemical soup, able only to twitch his legs, arms, fingers, he was as helpless and defenseless as a man could be. He could only yell, only watch as the Jassans, moving with a silent, relentless purpose, set about their work.

The work of killing him.

They were assassins!

They tore connecting hoses and electrical cables from tanks and receptacles. They opened a valve on the container that held him, and Harry felt the soup he could only suppose sustained him drain away, and heard it as it gushed out onto the tile floor. He watched the two in the ceiling mirrors as they moved to the bank of dials on the wall above the fallen attendants. Stepping over the attendants, one of the assassins took up a heavy instrument and, using the instrument as a hammer, began smashing dials with a wanton, aimless destruction that was without reason or thought, that intended to destroy anything and everything that might sustain life in Harry Borg.

"Dirty bastards!" Harry yelled again, in furious, helpless frustration, struggling to move but unable to. "Where the hell is everybody?" He struggled again. He screamed. "Help! Goddammit!" And still no one came.

His screams did attract the attention of the Jassan assassins, perhaps working on nerves already stretched taut, frayed, for the assassins turned and rushed toward the container. Harry's eyes went from the ceiling mirrors to the edge of the container as the Jassan assassins appeared there. They were still wearing the white smocks and the gauze masks, but the yellow, slitted eyes were burning with the fury of creatures hell-bent on killing and destroying.

"Kill him! Kill the bassoe!"

"No! He'll die—"

"Spill him out, then."

"Yes."

Two pairs of eight-fingered hands grasped the edge of the container and began rocking it. The container was heavy and well founded and not easily overturned. But Harry finally heard the sound of breaking and tearing as the container was finally uprooted, tipped. A sudden explosion of pain ripped through him as his body was tumbled out, ripping the connecting interior tubes from arteries in his thighs, arms, and neck. The room spun and whirled as he went sprawling, naked, on the tile floor.

"Damn you to hell!" he yelled at the assassins.

Completely furious, beyond fear now, swamped with the greatest frustration of his life, Harry watched the two assassins exchange looks, and turn away from him. He didn't need the ceiling mirrors. Lying on the floor, he could watch them as they moved toward the door where the bodies of the two downed guards lay.

Harry felt himself losing consciousness again.

"Bleeding like a stuck hog!" he swore, as he saw a red geyser of his own blood spraying out on the tile floor. "Ain't gonna make it."

One of the assassins, with the apparent sudden decision that it would be better to kill Harry outright than to leave him to die by inches, stopped before reaching the door to turn his weapon in Harry's direction. His companion, framed in the doorway, uttered a Jassan curse, then screamed, "Hurry!" With that, the upper half of his body disappeared in a ball of light.

And, in the next instant, another ball of light consumed almost all of the assassin who had been about to finish Harry, the weapon he had been going to fire exploding harmlessly and clattering to the tile.

A uniformed Jassan, carrying a weapon, burst into the room,

crouched, and swept the room with the weapon, searching for any assassin who might still be alive. Finding none, he began to come out of his crouch, still wary, tense, watchful.

Suddenly a new figure burst into the room, almost knocking the uniformed Jassan from his feet. The new figure, wild-eyed, searched the wreckage of the room, found Harry, lying naked, spurting blood, dying, and charged over to kneel beside him.

"Where the hell've y'been?" Harry asked Guss.

"Had to get help!" Guss answered.

Anguish was in his yellow eyes. He was trying to stay the blood that was spurting from Harry's neck when he was thrust aside by a smock-clad Jassan, more adept, more qualified. Harry felt strong fingers pressing into his neck, his arms, his thigh.

"I'm gone . . ." he whispered as blackness came.

CHAPTER 11

The summer home of Guss Rassan, the famed sissal-player, was not as old, as extensive, or as costly as the home of Sos Vissir, the wealthy captor-owner of Lori and Tippi Calder, but it was certainly no hovel. Once the hunting lodge of a wealthy dealer in bassoe hides, it did, in fact, approach the size of a medium-class hotel.

It was located in the mountains above what would have been Santa Barbara in the world Harry Borg knew best, a place of mild temperatures, of hills covered mostly with chaparral, and of valleys where farms yielded fruits, nuts, and vegetables in reasonable abundance.

There were trails cut for the use of the original owner, a rather corpulent Jassan gone soft with easy living, that afforded easy gradients, most of them shaded by planted vines where trees were scarce, where stronger Jassans could walk, jog, or run as the need or urge arose. Guss was a runner. His pleasure usually began at first light, and it consisted of at least ten miles of running at something approaching a world-class marathon pace.

In the beginning, of course, Harry Borg's healing injuries held him to a slow walk, and he could only watch as Guss's back very quickly disappeared into the distance. That beginning did not last long, however. Either through the absolute magic of the surgeon Sassan, or because of a burning determination that he was not going to be bested by a goddamn lizard, or—most probably this was the truth of it—a combination of both, Harry progressed from a slow walk to a fast walk to a jog to a shoulder-to-shoulder run with Guss in a few short weeks. There were, to be sure, many, many hours spent with calisthenics, weight-lifting, and isometric exercising, and by the time he could run a ten-K with Guss, he was sound in all respects, as physically fit as a man could be.

And he had been in touch with Lori and Tippi.

He had been returned to the living once again by immediate and extensive repair by Sassan, who, having not yet left the premises, was brought back to demonstrate again his mastery over the final event.

Perhaps the first words that had seeped into Harry Borg's consciousness were: "If I keep doing this, I might even get to be an expert." The puzzled, bespectacled face of Sassan had drifted in and out of focus just above him. "And you might learn to like it."

"Like hell," Harry had managed before drifting away again.

Of very grave concern to Harry, when he'd gained back even a little strength, was the answer to the question of why. Why had Jassans wanted so desperately to end his life, and at such cost—the lives of two guards, the five attendants, and their own lives—when other Jassans, with official blessings, surely, were trying so hard to restore him to full and active life?

He hadn't been given an answer.

They knew the answer, but they had withheld it. And were still withholding it. Guss knew the answer, but he kept saying, "Later, Harry. All in good time. Get well first." And things like that.

It didn't seem to matter to any of them when he told them that humans didn't sleep well, eat well, or anything else knowing that at any moment, day or night, a new set of assassins might be able to breach security and spoil all of the surgeon Sassan's work.

"Later, Harry! For chrissake, quit buggin' me!"

He had even explained to them that as trying a nightmare, perhaps even worse, was the knowledge that there lurked at almost every and any hand a device called a mind-blanker that could instantly turn him into something as knowing as a tree.

Or a carrot. Not even as smart as a chicken. A dummy, like a bassoe.

"Harry, it's not going to happen to you."

"Did once."

"But not again. Okay?"

"You, I trust. How about the rest of Jassa?"

"Listen, Harry—"

Guss squirmed, picked up some kind of a small control that had been lying on a low table, put it down—stalling, Harry knew, getting ready to divert the conversation into some new channel.

"Okay," Guss said then. "You wanted to talk to the female when you had your health back. So you've got your health back. So, do you want to talk to her?"

But Harry was not to be totally diverted.

"You mean, if I quit asking questions, I get to talk to Lori and Tippi?"

"That's about it," Guss agreed.

They were in Guss's front room, a room Harry had not been let into for more than a week because of a crew of workmen doing something or other. The something or other had proven to be a new wall made of what seemed to be frosted glass.

"You going to bring them here?"

"Almost."

Harry eyed Guss a long moment. "I can lean on you, my forked-tongue friend. You know that, don't you."

"Lean on me?"

"Make you answer my questions."

"How're you going to do that?"

"I didn't say I was going to."

"If you were, how could you do it?"

A servant-type Jassan came in at that moment, as Harry had known she would, bringing a tray holding the soft drink, vassle, in a frosted container and glasses. Harry was silent as the young servant type set the tray on a low table and poured the mildly euphoric but non-habit-forming drink and served each of them. After the task was completed, she moved to stand just behind Guss.

Harry had grown used to seeing Jassans, both male and female, of almost every age, and while they all still seemed to be very much alike to him in appearance, he was beginning to distinguish small differences. This "servant-type" female had to be one of the better-looking females he'd seen yet. While he certainly did not feel qualified to say what was and what was not beautiful and sexy in the eye of male Jassans—certainly, they remained lizards to him, and therefore, if not repulsive, at least unattractive by his standard of measurement—he was willing to gamble this female might well be a Marilyn Monroe among Jassans. She was young, very young, in fact, but well and smoothly formed, her skin so refined it appeared almost without scales, the gray of it shaded into a delicate pink. Her eyes were quite large and golden rather than yellow. And her manner was provocative, even seductive, especially when she was near Guss or felt his eyes upon her.

"She's cute," Harry said to Guss, grinning. "I can't say I blame you."

"Harry!" Guss was shocked. "You don't think I'd—"

"I don't think," Harry said. "I know."

"But that would be a criminal offense! Our population control—"

"Yeah. So I could lean on you if I wanted to."

"You'd get me in trouble?"

"Not if I could help it—not if you'd answer questions."

"But the answers are top-secret, Harry! If I gave them to you, I'd be in a lot worse trouble than I'd be in for—for fooling around!"

"Why don't you marry her?"

Harry was teasing Guss now, and Guss came to realize it. He had a long drink of vassle. "You're a bastard, Harry! You know that, don't you?" He had another long drink. Then he looked rather fondly at the young female, then at Harry, his good humor returning. "Sissi, you didn't hear any of this, did you?"

Her long, pretty, forked tongue flicked toward Guss in a gesture that had to be provocative in the extreme. "I heard him," she said. "And I'm ready."

"See what you did?" Guss asked Harry.

"What *I* did?"

Guss's gaze was back on the young female, his tongue flicking toward her fondly, almost caressingly. "Get outa here," he said without anger. "You're too young to marry."

"But not too young to—"

"Git!" Guss said sharply.

She turned. And with a glance over her shoulder, a flick of her long, forked tongue, and a flirt of her behind, she went out of the room. Guss, still looking after her, sighed and then turned back to Harry.

"You'll get your answers soon enough," he said. "And from the top. The very top." His tone changed. "D'you want to talk to your female or not?"

"Of course I want to!"

"Stand by."

Guss pointed at the floor-to-ceiling wall of glass and picked up a control that had been lying on the low table. "You want to talk to her sitting down?"

"What d'you mean?"

"Stand up," Guss said. "You'll like it better."

Mystified, Harry pushed to his feet and stood facing the wall of glass, a wall that suddenly took on a warm glow, that began to flicker and then to clear, to reveal another room—and Lori Calder.

Her back was toward Harry. An almost entirely nude back, with only her bottom covered by a bikinilike pair of shorts. She was hard at aerobic dancing. Beyond her, sitting at a small table, was her daughter, Tippi, feeding, or attempting to feed, a bassoe of about three years of age. Harry was almost overwhelmed at seeing Lori and Tippi again; the flood of warmth and affection that surged through him brought a stinging to his eyes, a thickness to his throat.

"Lori," he said, tentatively. "Lori."

She did not turn. Neither did Tippi, who was holding the little bassoe's chin with one hand and attempting to spoon a pablumlike substance into the child's mouth—with very little success. Tippi's face was a study of patience and gentle anger.

"Lori!" Harry called.

Then a sudden realization hit him, and he turned angrily toward Guss. "There's no audio!"

Guss, control in hand, looked startled. "No what?"

"Audio! Sound, y'dummy!" Harry waved a hand at his ears. "Y'got a great picture, but we humans need *sound*!"

"Oh, m'gosh!" Guss was embarrassed, desolate. He punched

a button on the control and the screen went blank. "We goofed, Harry."

"Yeah, y'did!" Harry controlled his anger. "Well, give me back the picture! At least we can look at each other."

"No, no, no!"

Guss went out of the room almost running, leaving Harry to stand and stare at the blank screen, frustrated almost beyond bearing. In just a few moments Guss was back, still embarrassed, but less so.

"C'mon," he said. "Chase me a ten-K!"

"I'd rather break your head!"

"All y'gotta do is catch me," Guss said, giving him the Jassan equivalent of a grin. "Time we get back you'll have sound—all the sound you primitives need."

"Primitives! Why, you—"

Harry lunged for Guss, but Guss slipped away—out of the room, out of the building, and up the trail. He was able to remain just beyond Harry's reach a full ten kilometers, and when, showered and dressed clean, they returned to the room where the frosted glass wall was waiting, there was no longer any need to pound on Guss. Harry stood in front of the screen, feeling like a schoolboy waiting for his first date to answer a doorbell, while Guss worked the control.

"Hey, now," he whispered.

The frosted look dissolved away, and the room where Lori had been dancing, where Tippi had been feeding the child bassoe, came into view with perfect clarity, just as if it were an enlargement of the room in which Harry waited, just there, beyond his fingertips. The room was empty now. But a robe thrown over a chair, and the dishes on the low table, were reminders.

"Where'd everybody go?" Harry called.

There was a startled cry. "Who's that?"

"Harry!" he answered, his voice full of joy.

Then, at an archway on the far side of the room, he saw the face of Tippi appear, eyes round as she apparently saw Harry. "It's him!" she yelled back over her shoulder. "It's Harry! He's here!"

"Couldn't be!" It was Lori's voice, with absolute conviction and yet with a strain of hope. "Where?"

"Where the glass was!" Tippi said. "That glass wall they put in. It's gone, and Harry's there!" She kept staring from her position, not daring to advance. "Weird!" she said.

Then her mother appeared, only a head and bare shoulders, peering over her daughter's head. Apparently, since her hair and shoulders were wet, she had just gotten out of the shower. Her eyes were as wide and unbelieving as the child's.

"That you, Harry?" she asked cautiously.

"It's me."

"Tippi, get my robe," Lori said.

She gave her daughter a push. Tippi darted out, snatched up the robe, and darted back, still not willing to trust her eyes entirely.

"C'mon," Harry said. "I'm real. I'm alive."

"My gosh, my gosh."

Lori couldn't wait to get the robe entirely about her, but came rushing toward Harry while there was still an arm to get in a sleeve.

"Wait! Wait!" Harry tried to warn her.

Too late.

Lori banged into what must have been to her an invisible barrier that stood just in front of what must have been to her a living, breathing Harry Borg. And it was all so real from Harry Borg's side, he reached out to catch her and brushed his hands on the same invisible barrier. Lori yelled in pain and anger and fell on her behind to sit spraddle-legged, staring up at Harry, furious. Tippi's frightened cry echoed away as she came to her mother's aid.

"You hurt?"

"Yeah!" her mother said angrily.

She sat, staring at Harry.

"What's goin' on?" she demanded.

She couldn't help but see, now, that Harry was as upset as she was. His hands were groping at the invisible barrier, and then she saw him turn, cussing—and saw the Jassan, Guss, sprawled on the floor of the room behind Harry, pounding the carpeting in a paroxysm of what could only be mirth. She looked at Harry.

"Is that bastard laughing at me?" she asked.

"Seems like," Harry said, furious in his own right.

"I'll kill 'im!"

"With my help!" Harry promised.

They watched Guss thrashing about on the carpet a few moments, their anger diminishing. Lori began to examine her nose with tender fingers.

"Is it all right?" Harry asked, anxiously.

"I think I broke it," Lori said. "Maybe not." She got to her feet, belatedly drawing her robe about herself. "Just hurts," she decided, after one final touch.

Tippi was examining the barrier. "Hey, it's a TV screen!" she said. "A real gasser of a TV!"

Lori was more interested in Harry. "You all right?"

"Yeah. Good as new."

"They put you back together? I can't believe it!" Her wide gray eyes were examining him inch by inch. "You were in pieces! Your arm, your leg—"

"Just ran a 10-K," Harry said. "With laughing boy there." His eyes were examining her so intently that even though he knew her well she drew her robe more tightly in an unconscious gesture. "Are you all right?"

"Super," she answered.

"Tippi?"

The young girl looked up and gave him her gamin grin. "I'm fine. But Mom's fibbin'."

"Tippi!" Lori said.

"What's with your mother?" Harry said, alarmed.

"Throws up in the morning!" Her grin widened.

"Hoo-boy!" Lori said, rolling her eyes. "Big mouth!"

"It's all right," Harry said. "I heard you were—uh—in a family way."

"You heard?" Lori was suddenly aggrieved. "Who told you? I thought Tippi and I were the only ones knew."

"The doctors, you know, when they put the communicator in your—uh—head. They, well, gave you a physical, I guess."

"That thing in my head doesn't work!" Lori said with great emphasis, glancing past Harry to Guss, who had rolled to a sitting position, no longer in a paroxysm, hiccuping now. "It doesn't work!" she repeated.

Guss hiccuped solemnly.

"They know it works, honey," Harry said.

"Oh, balls!" Lori said.

"I told you they did, Mom," Tippi said.

"I had to try, didn't I?"

"It doesn't make all that much difference, Lori," Harry said. "And it can be helpful."

Lori turned her attention to other things. "Where are you, Harry? Where are you—what d'you call it, broadcasting?—from?"

"Remember where Reagan has his ranch?" Harry asked. "It's back up in those hills, back of what would be Santa Barbara, nearly as I can tell."

"That's two, three hundred miles from us."

"Something like that, if you're in the same place."

"We are."

"That guy treating you all right?"

"As good as can be, I guess," Lori said. "Except, of course, we can't leave. Can't go home."

"That's next," Harry said. "I promise you. I'm working on a deal with these—uh—Jassans. And my first priority is that you get to go home."

"What about you?"

"That's my second priority."

"You've got a new responsibility, you know."

"I know, I know!" Harry said earnestly. "I'm not going to duck out on it—I'm proud of it. I—uh—well, all right, I'll marry you. I *want* to marry you."

"Geeze!" Lori said, amused. "It's not *that* serious!"

"But it's sure romantic," Tippi said.

Lori gently batted her on the side of the head. "Will you mind your own business?" And then she held her daughter close. "When's anything going to happen?" she asked Harry. "We're not suffering at all, but we'd sure like to get out of here."

"It's going to take a little while. A week, a month—I'm not sure. But you can depend on it; I'll do everything I can as fast as I can."

"All right," Lori said. "But one thing—"

"What's that?"

"The hero bit," Lori said. "Kind of hold it down, will you? You're no good to anybody lying around in pieces."

"Okay, okay," Harry said, mildly injured. "Conan the Barbarian I'm not. Or even Arnold Schwarzenegger. But I'll give it my best shot, if that's okay."

"Your best shot—that's a buy."

She puckered her lips in a kissing gesture.

And it must be said that Guss Rassan, the entertainer, the sissal-player, knew a curtain when he encountered one, because, at that moment, he pressed a button on the control and the images on the screen faded out.

CHAPTER 12

The security measures around Harry Borg were never relaxed during the weeks needed for Harry's recovery. And the measures served two purposes: They insured Harry's safety to every degree of which the Jassans were capable; and they impressed upon Harry the fact that his life was at extreme risk every moment of every day.

Armed Jassan soldiers, wearing the regulation short sword and holstered pistol, patrolled the grounds day and night. Very often, especially at night, they were accompanied by dog-size soldier members of some species of giant ant that ranged eagerly ahead on six hardworking legs, controlled by some kind of silent command, antennae alert, quivering, searching, huge mandibles clicking eagerly. They may or may not have been as effective as German shepherd police dogs, but to Harry's way of thinking, they were a lot more frightening. The near-silent Cassal aircraft were constantly overhead. And, unless confined in the inner rooms of the main building, Harry was never out of sight of at least a pair of armed guards.

"Since you all look so damned much alike," Harry had said to Guss one evening while they were killing time playing lassippi, a game resembling chess more than any other human game, except that it was played on a three-dimensional board. "I've never been able to figure out how you knew those characters at the hospital were assassins and not attendants."

"Smell," Guss said.

"You can smell an assassin?" Harry said, disbelieving. "C'mon, now. That forked tongue's a sniffer, all right. But I can't believe it can smell an intention!"

"Didn't say it could."

"What then?"

"Cassina."

"What's cassina?"

Guss looked at Harry, his yellow, vertically slitted eyes showing resentment. "You're not helping my game any, y'know? How can I concentrate with you yapping?"

Harry grinned. "Part of my system," he said.

Guss was silent, studying the board for a long moment. "Cassina," Harry said. "What's cassina?"

Guss gave up, throwing up his eight-fingered hands, waving his forked tongue at the ceiling. "It's an oil they use on their guns. Your ordinary attendant doesn't use guns to kill patients. Neglect does the job well enough."

"All right!" Harry said. "Good smelling!" Then he was not so flattering. "You could have done something about it before they killed seven people."

"And get myself killed?"

"Well . . ."

"You're the hero," Guss said. "I went for help."

"Sensible thing to do," Harry conceded.

"Saved your life, didn't it?"

"I suppose so." He gestured at the cubelike lassippi board. "Y'want to finish this?"

"Naw."

Guss got up and went over to a circular hearth where a low flame danced among logs. Harry got up to wander aimlessly about the room. "Can't you sit down?" Guss said after watching him for a few moments.

"Got cabin fever," Harry said. "Goin' nuts."

"Be just a few more days."

"You keep saying that, old buddy. And nothin' happens."

"I'm not the man, y'know."

"Build a fire under 'im, couldn't you?"

"Not this one."

"Couple of more days, I'll go over the wall."

"That a threat?"

"A promise."

Guss turned to look at the flames. "Tell you what. You hang in for two more days, and I'll *take* you out over the wall. How does that sound?"

"Great! But—for what?"

"A concert."

A smile began to grow. "You mean *you*? The sissal-player? You're going to give a concert?"

"Along with Val Wassi," Guss said, becoming somewhat diffident. "Val's a dancer, and a very, very good one. You could enjoy what she does—hell, you can *see* her. My work, symphonic fragrances—it wouldn't do much for you."

"Sure it would!" Harry said. "Even if I couldn't smell it, I could see the others enjoying it—" and he couldn't resist a needle "—or not enjoying it, as the case may be."

"They enjoy!" Guss, the injured artist, insisted.

"All right," Harry said, grinning. "Don't sweat it. Let's let the audience decide."

Larissa by the Bay was not, Harry Borg was to discover, San Francisco by the Bay by any stretch of the imagination. But he did find many similarities. "The coldest winter I ever spent was a summer in San Francisco" was a not very complimentary saying often used by residents of Los Angeles and San Diego, and the same thing could be said about Larissa. Especially after dark. The cold sea air drifting in off the bay was the same in both worlds. Bracing, to say the very least.

But on the streets among the ancient but still enormously graceful spired buildings, with their walkways, weblike against the sky, high up and fragile, and their arched entrances and glittering facades, the city had much the same kind of after-dark excitement, the cosmopolitan flavor, the social ambiance of San Francisco or New York.

There were swift-moving if age-eroded transport vehicles discharging expensively wardrobed male and female Jassans at lighted theater marquees. This was the theater crowd of New York, San Francisco, or Los Angeles, except that—and this was Harry Borg's reaction as he and Guss were chauffeured by the lighted marquees in a very elderly limousine-type vehicle, on their way to a stage-door entrance—they were all, male and female alike, masquerading as lizard people. Lizard people who wore elaborate, feathered headgear, sparkling jewels, luxurious furs, or with contrasting severity on the males, formal black evening wear.

Harry had objected to formal, penguinlike black and white for himself, and the Jassan tailors had provided him with clothing more to the taste of a man of action: silken fabric of excellent weave for underwear and shirt; short trousers, mid-thigh length; a well-fitted jacket in a muted plaid of dark blue and dark brown; and dark, calf-high boots, rolled at the top. His gleaming white shirt was open at the throat, revealing—at Guss's insistence—a heavy gold chain; and—again at Guss's insistence—a gleaming gold band was fitted snugly to the lobe of his left ear. Carefully barbered, tightly curled hair and close-cropped beard completed what he had to admit was not a bad figure of a man, a man who seemed more to resemble a successful pirate than a gentleman concert-goer, to be sure, but Harry did not consider that a serious misfortune.

Guss Rassan, the entertainer, was, of course, more striking in appearance. An imposing figure among reptilians to begin with, taller than most, finer than most, he was absolutely spectacular in his version of a "suit of lights." The suit caught every fragment of light and somehow reflected it back in all the hues of a rainbow, none of them discomforting to the eye, all of them softly pleasing. A headpiece gave the look of a top hat, the jacket the look of tails: elegance, grace, élan, perfectly stated. And to Harry's way of thinking, such apparel had never been more correctly in place than on the trim and confident figure of Guss Rassan.

"Hard to believe," Harry muttered as they were chauffeured past a brightly lighted marquee, which announced a concert by Rassan and Val Wassi, and turned into a side street that led to a stage-door entrance.

"What is?"

"That evolution on different worlds could arrive at goals so similar. That's an opening night crowd on Broadway, except their faces are different."

"So?" Guss said. "What took you folks so long?"

"You mean you got to this point ahead of us?"

"By a few thousand years."

"Baloney!"

"Our best minds have decided we reached the peak of our—what d'you want to call it? Civilization—about twelve hundred years ago. We've been sliding downhill ever since."

"But—" Harry protested. "That television screen you had put up in our place. With Lori and me standing face to face—that had to be state-of-the-art, the very latest."

"Been around for hundreds of years," Guss said. "Our problem is finding people who still know how to make it work."

"I'll be damned!" Harry said.

They had arrived at the stage-door entrance to find the short street packed with waiting fans. An ornately uniformed Jassan, a footman, opened the door and saluted Guss with great deference. His eyes rolled at the sight of Harry Borg—a huge, beautifully clothed food animal—and the bodyguards who spilled out of a second vehicle to surround Harry and Guss with a solid wall of soldiers wearing short swords and pistols, but he lost none of his poise.

The receptor in Harry's head was ringing with the loud, confused telepathy that washed over them from the Jassans who had crowded into the street for a glimpse of Guss, the sissal-player, the Elvis Presley of his world. And Harry noted, with a certain personal pride, because Guss was his close friend and therefore something of his own, that Guss was more than equal to the moment. As the lights bathed him, as the waves of adulation rolled over him, he seemed to become a different personality, all charm, all friendship, all warmth.

"Charisma!" Harry said as they shouldered toward the doorway. "That's the name for it—in anybody's world."

Guss reached over the guards to touch extended fingertips. He signed an autograph. He threw a scarf over the guards and into the crowd, and saw it torn into several pieces for better, if not equal, division. The yellow eyes of the Jassans reflected light in the way of a cat's eyes, and so those eyes farther away seemed like a host of candlelit holes in Halloween masks, though they were not frightening in the least. And to Harry it was all very impressive, perhaps even more so because it was all done without any intentional sound at all.

Once inside the theater, the telepathy became muted, so that the silence became, to Harry, weird in the extreme. And they were backstage in a theater that differed from the ones Harry had known only in minor ways. The clutter was the same. The ropes, the lights, the flats, the curtain—all were in the expected places. Even the audience, glimpsed through a narrow opening beside the curtain, seated, row upon row, balcony upon balcony, was almost exactly as Harry Borg would have expected it to be.

"A full house," he reported to Guss with considerable pride. "You really bring 'em out!"

"Not me, really," Guss said. He was not quite *aw-shucks*! but close to it. "Val's the big draw. C'mon, I want you to meet her."

He took Harry to the star's dressing room, knocked, and pulled Harry through a crowd of wardrobe, makeup, and managerial personnel, who fell back in deference to Guss, and in utter astonishment at the sight of Harry. A bassoe, six-foot-two, one-ninety pounds, whose intense dark blue eyes absolutely glittered with intelligence. Incredible!

Harry Borg's receptor could scarcely keep up with their telepathic reactions, and finally settled by communicating the reactions to him only as a series of wolf whistles of wholehearted approbation. But the receptor was not tried to its uttermost until the beautiful eyes of Val Wassi fell upon him.

"Oh, my stars! Is this him? Rassan! He's real? He can't be real! Is he? Can I touch him? Please!"

And for the second time in recent months, Harry Borg was overwhelmed by a female. This creature was too much! A Jassan, yes, but such a beautiful Jassan! Her eyes were a translucent gold, her teeth a glistening white, her tongue a flowing, scarlet poem of motion with twin tips twirling, licking, caressing—and this was only the beginning. The most and the best of her came from within, a joy of life, of loving, of giving, that seem to Harry to engulf him in a tumbling outpouring of affection, as deep as a river, as irresistible.

She came to him to reach up and hold his face in her slender, eight-fingered hands, to turn his head slightly this way and that, then to draw his head down so that her tongue could brush his eyelids, his cheeks, his nose, his beard, his lips with the softest, most tender caress he'd ever felt.

"You're real!" Her thoughts came through Harry's receptor as a gentle whisper. "Oh, my! Oh, my—how real!"

"But—are you?" Harry whispered back.

"She's real, too," Guss said. He sounded a little impatient, perhaps put out a bit at the way the two were so immediately and forcibly attracted to each other. "She hits everybody that way," he said. "If you don't believe it, wait'll you see her dance."

Val and Harry ignored him, looking deeply into each other's eyes.

"Five minutes, Val!" another voice said.

They ignored that voice, too.

"Wonderful," she whispered.

"So marvelous," he whispered.

"C'mon, Harry!" Guss said sharply.

"Can't," Harry said.

"Why the hell not?"

"I'm in love."

He was standing before Val Wassi, gently holding her upper arms, looking down into her golden eyes, while she stroked his short beard with gentle fingertips; he was a man who had wandered into a perfumed garden by the most wonderful chance and was not of his own volition going to leave ever again.

"You can't be!" Guss protested. "She's the wrong kind!"

After a moment, without looking away from Harry, Val whispered, "What's he saying? Wrong kind?"

"I think what he means is we're in the right phylum but the wrong class."

"Is that important?"

"Only if you're a biologist."

"I'm a dancer."

"I'm a swashbuckler—"

And Harry was jerked away, back to reality, and out of Val Wassi's dressing room, by Guss. And when he had Harry, who was still looking stoned, outside the dressing room, he gave Harry a long, searching look.

"Maybe Sassan got some of your wires crossed."

Harry gave him a vacant stare. "Whaddayuh mean?"

"You sure you're *all Homo sapiens*?"

"What else?"

"I dunno." Guss twisted a hand worriedly. "The way you and

Val shot sparks, y'know? Maybe Sassan got a little snake mixed in your glands someplace?"

"How could I tell?"

"If you've been thinking you'd like to eat a live mouse, something like that..."

Harry gave Guss a sparkling, all-human grin, and an arm around his shoulder. "I'm human as can be, old buddy. I just wanted to tell you and Val what I think of her. And I think she is absolutely something else!"

"Only the greatest," Guss agreed, relieved.

Harry stopped, startled by a sudden realization.

"You folks are warm-blooded!" Harry said.

"So?"

"Pink in your flesh—almost red tongues. Hadn't realized what it meant." His eyes were going vague with inner thought. "Must be oviparous, but maybe not. Guss—"

Guss, seeing the direction Harry's inquiring mind was taking, gave his arm another hard jerk. "Later, my friend. Just now, tell me how you feel about mice. Live mice."

Harry grinned again. "I like mice," he said. "But I wouldn't eat one, dead or alive, on a bet."

"Good lad," Guss said, relieved. "Come on now."

He had arranged for a box in the first balcony, where Harry would watch the performances. There was a clear, perfectly transparent wall of something between Harry and the rest of the audience, an audience which, in the beginning, found the fact they had a live, well-dressed, and handsome—if the term could be used—bassoe sitting among them of almost as much interest as the coming performance. And there were six uniformed and armed guards to share the box with him, none of whom, he was pleased to note, salivated to any troublesome degree while they were at his side.

The house lights dimmed; the performance began.

Harry, of course, expected an orchestra and music. There was certainly an orchestra, but there was no music. There was something of which Harry received no more than a rather pleasant echo: fragrances, delicately mixed, of growing and lessening strengths, gently undulating at times, near overpowering at others, but for the most part only an overture, a preparation for what was to come.

For the Jassans, it was most satisfying. Harry saw the audience turn as one toward the stage, saw them settle back and saw their tongues begin to dance before their faces, long and supple, almost rhythmic, almost in concert, as they savored what must have been to them very pleasing stimuli.

And the curtain rose.

An orchestra of perhaps fifty instruments was grouped around the centrally located, spotlighted instrument, which was played by Guss Rassan. The sissal was a concert organ in appearance, quite large, with organlike pipes that extended upward out of sight, with a circular, many-tiered keyboard where Guss's eight-fingered hands floated, evoking a symphony of fragrances that must have been—because even to Harry's dull sense of smell they were quite pleasant—an overwhelming delight.

The audience swayed in unison at times, their hands clasped before them, their heads tipped high, as their tongues sought every small variation of scent, every vagary, every delicate blend of whatever it was they found gratifying. Was it like the fragrance of many varieties of flowers? Harry wondered. Or the smell of the sea? Or of new snow on an early morning? Or the scent of a pine forest when one walked on a bed of fallen needles? Or of a summer rain? Or perhaps their pleasure lay in something sexual, of male and female and a scent that spoke of copulation? Or did it appeal to hunger, like the smell of fresh-baked bread? No matter. Whatever it was that gave them pleasure, Rassan evoked it from the sissal in a quality and range and variation that produced, for his audience, near ecstasy.

When he had finished, the audience rose to its feet in a single, wavelike motion and the receptor in Harry Borg's mind brought him a thunderous applause that went on and on.

Harry could not believe Val Wassi could offer anything to equal the emotional and sensory gratification Guss had given the audience with the sissal. And he waited for her performance, feeling something akin to pity for her that she should be put into such an unhappy position. A subsequent act should build on the first, should surpass, if possible, the preceding act in skill, in range, in beauty, in excitement, in emotional involvement. And how was that possible with something as narrow in scope as a dance?

It was not possible, he was sure.

And he was wrong.

The curtain opened on Val Wassi alone. Alone in an amber spot, a single feminine figure, erect, a figure of consummate grace, a lithe and slender grouping of lines held in a moment's pause, waiting. Then, flowing with the unfaltering, unbroken single motion of an endless ribbon of silk, she began moving, floating, really, without seeming effort across the line of sight, circling, whirling, lifting, drifting in a poem of motion. And this Harry Borg could *see*! He needed no special sensory perception. It mattered not at all to him that she might be moving in a rhythm that followed a flow of fragrances emitted by the orchestra dimly visible through a curtain behind her. His eyes alone were enough to transport him, to take him with her into some enchanted paradise where all was beauty and gentleness, all was warmth, all was true.

Other dancers moved in to form new, undulating backgrounds from moment to moment, complimenting, accentuating, focusing, but never wholly visible, never wholly taking part. The dance was a creation of Val Wassi, hers alone, and she wove a spell with it on her audience that carried them well beyond the symphonic fragrances of Rassan, to somewhere higher, a dream of something quite unattainable, a Valhalla of all that is best.

And, at the curtain, the reaction of the audience was immense, a standing ovation that went on and on even longer than the one given Rassan, because, presently, it became an ovation for both as the curtain parted and they shared the applause.

Chapter 13

He had no idea when the creature had caught his scent. Or how. But he knew he had been discovered, and that it would be only a few moments before the confrontation would occur.

How big was it?

Anything that could snort and snuffle loud enough so he could hear it above the sound of the white-water creek that tumbled through the rocks below had to be pretty goddamn big. The size of a bull, maybe. Even bigger. The size of an elephant, a rhinoceros. But the size didn't matter as much as the fact it had to be a meat-eater. Something that ate grass or trees and bushes wouldn't care enough about him to track him by smell, would it?

A meat-eater, sure as God made little green apples.

And he was meat. One hundred and eighty pounds of it, fresh, on-the-hoof meat. He crouched back in the cul-de-sac he'd found for himself and cursed the darkness. He couldn't even see his hand in front of his face—it was *that* dark. He could feel the smooth stone face of the cliff against his back, and he could feel the smooth, rounded surfaces of the two huge boulders that formed the unscalable sides of what he had thought of as the next best thing to a cave when he'd settled in at nightfall, hours before. Protected on three sides with only a long and narrow approach to defend, he was safe.

Safe, hell!

A trap!

He had a lot to learn about this business of survival, he decided then, stiff and sweating. A hole in the ground might be a good defense against certain kinds of onslaught—an artillery shell, a bomb, something like that—but against a thinking enemy, a working, searching enemy, mobility was better. You had some options with mobility. With a hole in the ground, you had to fight, and it didn't matter a damn if you were outweighed and outgunned.

How long until daylight?

How long until there was enough light to see what the hell was out there, enough for what the hell was out there to see him? Or could it see him already? He figured that it could. A beast that was out at night hunting had to be nocturnal, and a nocturnal hunter had to have eyes like a cat or an owl, didn't it? Yeah, it did.

Then why didn't it come in after him?

Was it afraid of him? Could be. Most animals avoided anything like an even fight. And that made sense. They knew an injury, even a slight injury, could be crippling, could mean death in time. They knew it instinctively, if they couldn't reason it out. And maybe the smell of man meant more trouble than the meat was worth.

Well, this man was sure as hell going to mean trouble, he promised his adversary that, and his hands gripped the spear a little tighter. Back to basics, maybe, but he thanked God he'd had sense enough to make a spear the first thing after Ronnie Reagan had gone down. He'd sharpened one end of the eight-foot shaft into a point by scraping it on jagged rocks. Not much for looks, but hell for strong.

Hey—he was beginning to see a little.

The top of the slope on the far side of the creek was beginning to take shape, a black shoulder bulging up against the sky. A dark sky, cloudy, foggy. It had rained most of the day before, and probably would rain again soon. The lousy weather had worked for him, keeping the lizzie aircraft grounded, but it hadn't made running a bunch of fun.

"Colder'n a well-digger's ass," he remembered his grandfather saying, and he'd learned the true meaning of that expression running soaking wet most of the time.

How long had he been loose? Four days, if he counted the first night. And he counted it. Thinking back on it now, he had to admit it was maybe a damn-fool stunt, trying to get loose from the lizzies the way he'd done. But what were you going to call lying around that lizzie barracks, getting jerked off maybe once a week, without even knowing they were jerking you, without even gettin' fun out of it.

A herd bull, for chrissakes!

Not him! Not Arnie Garrett.

The sound of dislodged rocks rolling down the slopes below him brought his attention sharply back to the entrance to the cul-de-sac. Still too dark to see—no, now he was beginning to see the outline of the big boulder on the right. He thought he heard the snuffling of an animal testing scent, but he couldn't be sure, the sound of the white water was so loud. Had to be out there, though. Something had knocked those rocks loose.

He was in a steep-walled, rocky ravine, two hundred feet above a tumbling, white-water creek, just at the foot of a perpendicular rock face a hundred feet high, among fallen boulders. Across the creek, the far side was not so steep, though it went a lot higher: a mountain, really, in a range of mountains.

He'd gone into the ravine when he'd seen the lizzie aircraft hunting him, and he'd managed to stay out of sight with the help of the rain and the low-hanging clouds. Hungrier than a bitch wolf with seventeen pups, but free. Yeah! Free! No goddamn bull in a pen. Old man Garrett had never raised any of his kids to be nobody's pet bull, that was for double-damned sure.

Arnie Garrett was eighteen and, at five-ten, one-eighty, a very powerful and well-trained athlete. He had a pugnacious face, a fighter's face—short nose, blunt chin, short cropped brown hair, direct, brown eyes under heavy brows—a stubborn face. And now that the first of day's light began to find its way down into the cul-de-sac, Arnie went into a set position, a running back waiting for the snap of the ball.

He was crouched, the sharp end of his crude spear extended out ahead of him, the shaft in the grip of his left hand, the butt of the spear in his right hand, held close in at hip level.

Come on, you sonofabitch.

Another small rock slide started, as if in answer to his challenge. And this was followed by more snuffling, then the hard sneeze of a scent-hunting animal clearing its nostrils.

No birdie, that was for sure.

And he thought he could use a birdie along about now. One like Ronnie Reagan, a going sonofagun. And he remembered with fondness and fright that wild ride on the night of his bust-out. Once he'd gotten Ronnie out of the compound—those lizzies didn't know their trusted watchdog beetle had a way of sneaking out of the compound a little after midnight, on a search for a lady beetle, most likely—once that crazy beast had a clear road ahead and a chance to run, that birdie had run like he had his tail on fire! What a way to go!

And what a way to stop!

All of a sudden, total collapse. Arnie figured he had tumbled a hundred yards, ass-over-teakettle, after that birdie had gone limp in full stride, and he had the bruises to show for it.

"There it is!"

He had enough light now to see the thing that was after him, the looming bulk of it, just there beyond the mouth of the cul-de-sac. A cat! A huge cat. And the fangs, two enormous sabers extending down from the upper jaw, left no doubt at all as to what kind of a cat it was: a saber-toothed tiger.

"You ain't real," he whispered. "You been gone ten thousand years."

But that was back home. And this wasn't back home. This was lizzie-land. In the land of the lizards, you started with the impossible and went on from there.

The tiger began a slow creep forward.

Now Arnie knew how a bird felt, or a mouse, when one of them saw a cat coming his way. Scared the hell out of you. Being a mouse or a bird was no way to go.

Measuring the size of the opening to the cul-de-sac against the size of the tiger, Arnie could see the tiger would just about fit, if it decided to cover the last distance in a leap, the way all the cats Arnie had ever watched generally did. And that might be a help.

"Come on, you sucker!"

In the growing light he could see the fangs and the eyes, and the shape of the head, the ears cocked forward, the shoulders rolling slowly under the striped hide as the tiger inched closer. Beyond the head and shoulders, Arnie could see the tail held stiffly, trailing down the slope, only the tip twitching. The damned thing looked ten feet long.

"Any time . . ."

Arnie was no longer scared half to death. Being able to see what was coming at him made all the difference. Not knowing—that's what scared the hell out of a man, he'd learned. The dark. The unknown. The reality, however bad, was never as bad as the imagined, because you could measure the reality, measure your chances against it. His chances against the tiger were slim as he measured them, but they were chances, nonetheless.

The tiger stopped moving.

Its tail stopped twitching.

"Now it comes . . ."

And come it did, with a leap that lifted the powerful, striped body into the air, seeming to fill all the area of daylight above Arnie with gaping jaws, extended paws and claws. Arnie, lying almost against the foot of the cliff, the butt of the spear grounded firmly at his side, directed the point of the spear, eight feet from the butt, at the center of the chest as it dropped toward him.

"You ain't gonna like it . . ."

Arnie heard the scream of the beast as the point of the spear found its way into the chest cavity, driven by the weight of the animal as it dropped, guided neatly by the boulders on either side. The point went smoothly, inexorably through the chest and out between the shoulders beside the spine.

Arnie was crushed down as some of the weight of the tiger reached him. He felt a powerful, stunning blow as one of the sabers struck the side of his head, and then the beast was gone. It had thrown itself backward, screaming again and again, fighting the crude spear, twisting out of the cul-de-sac to tumble, writhing, down the slope toward the creek.

Arnie, too stunned, too exhausted, physically and emotionally, to move, could only lie as the tiger had left him, driven down into the earth at the foot of the cliff.

The sudden, violent movement in an otherwise quiet and deserted ravine had caught the attention of searching eyes. The crew of a Jassan aircraft, renewing the search they'd suspended with rain and darkness the night before, approached swiftly, saw the dying tiger, and found Arnie Garrett a few moments later.

Arnie saw them just as they saw him.

"Win some, lose some," he said.

CHAPTER 14

"Brazil."

"What did you say?" Guss asked.

"I said 'Brazil,'" Harry replied, staring down through the cabin window of the aircraft. "It's in what in our world would be called South America. A river that size has got to be the Amazon."

They were being flown over a jungle, though it was hard to be certain if the green carpet he could occasionally see through a cloud cover below was made of trees or not, since they were flying at an altitude in excess of fifty thousand feet. He was reasonably sure the writhing scar on the carpet was a river, a very large river—the Amazon.

"Like this," he said.

He used the back of the menu to draw a rough sketch of North and South America and indicated with an X what he thought was their location.

"You've got it," Guss said.

They were riding in the Jassan equivalent of a supersonic military personnel transport aircraft on their way, at long last, to their meeting with someone very high up in the Jassan government—*the* someone who was going to make all things clear to Harry. And he had decided that, since there had been so much secrecy involved, so much cloak-and-dagger, that *the* someone

148

had to be very high up indeed. They had begun the journey in darkness, and after several hours of hide-and-seek, they were flying into a rising sun.

"It's our capital," Guss said. "The name is Foss."

The capital city had been built on a vast plateau that had thrust up from sea-level jungle to an altitude of four thousand feet. There was no such topography in the Brazil Harry knew, and he had to remind himself this was not the Brazil he knew, this was Jassa, and that meant anything at all was possible.

The plane lost forward speed, swooped down to stop before a terminal building where ground vehicles were waiting. Harry and Guss were transferred quickly by their heavily armed escort, and, when they were under way again, Harry had the impression of riding through some ancient city—Rome, Athens, Karnak—and finding that city not a relic of the past but a functioning city still in use: the Colosseum offering games; the Parthenon, a busy temple to Athena; Karnak's Temple of Amon-Ra still a place where pharaohs came. Crowds of Jassans engaged in everyday business were moving in and out of buildings thousands of years old.

"Your ancestors built to last," Harry said.

"Couldn't do it now," Guss told him. "Haven't got the minds for it anymore, the vision. Haven't got the drive, the vigor."

"Where'd it all go?"

"No one knows." Guss sighed resignedly. "Maybe we're just worn out."

They were driven out of the central city in a buslike conveyance and transported along a stone-paved roadway that curved upward into an area of stately residences: villas with extensive gardens, pillared porticoes, artificial lakes, and sweeping areas of lawns.

"Your man—the one we're going to see—can't be hurting for money," Harry said. "He lives here, he's got it made."

"If anybody has," Guss agreed, "Moss has."

"Moss?"

"His name is Ros Moss," Guss said. "And he's our equivalent of your president."

"No!"

"Yes."

"He wants to talk to *me*?"

"You're somebody, Harry! You keep forgetting. You're a *visitor from another world*!"

"Hah!" Harry said. "I'm a reformed alcoholic from Reseda, California. Don't get me wrong—I'm somebody very big to me! But in my country I'm a nobody!"

Guss gave him what passed for a Jassan grin. "Here you're a visitor from Outer Space. Capital O, capital S. I went to a lot of trouble to make everyone believe you were someone *very* important. Try to live up to it, will you?"

"Do what I can," Harry said.

The transport had stopped at a barred gate. Guards who had been expecting them passed them right on through, up a long, curving drive, through beautifully kept grounds—artificial lakes where strange birds swam and fountains played, where all the statuary represented reptiles of one kind or another—until finally they stopped before a main residence, almost templelike in magnificence, though quite old.

The stones of the long flight of steps, Harry found, were cupped by centuries of use, worn smooth, and they led to an entranceway where huge doors of intricately carved stone— again the motif was reptilian—swung open noiselessly and effortlessly on hidden pivots. The interior was cool, the air scented with the rich perfumes of the tropics. They came at last to a door of heavy metal. It was not gold; Harry was sure of that. It was deeply and richly embossed, and it had the patina of centuries of use and care. But it was not gold. Gold would cost too much. Bronze, maybe.

"But it's not gold," Harry said.

"It's gold," Guss said.

"Imagine!" Harry breathed, impressed.

"Let me look at you," Guss said.

He stood a foot or two away from Harry and tipped his head to check Harry's appearance. Tall, hard, broad of shoulder, and lean of hip, Harry was impressive. Among average Jassans, head and shoulders taller; among bassoes, a veritable giant. And fit, even glowing with good health. The vestlike upper garment revealed a pair of very muscular arms, the shortslike lower garment, a pair of powerful legs thrust into short boots. His dark blue eyes were clear and intense under straight brows, a close-cropped beard covered a solid jaw, small ears lay tight against short, hard-curled brown hair, and a circlet of gold was clenched into the left ear.

"You'll do," Guss said.

"For what?"

"Almost anything heroic—rescue a female, slay a dragon, save a country." He gripped Harry's shoulder. "This is as far as I can go." The door was opening, the armed escort stood aside, coming rigidly to attention, and Guss leaned close to Harry to whisper, "Make nice, now, you dumb bastard!"

"Wouldn't I?" Harry said, offended.

"It's six-to-five against."

Guss gave Harry a gentle shove.

Then Harry was inside the gold doors, feeling rather than hearing them close softly behind him. The room was large and well lighted, an airy, clean, tiled place, much of the center occupied by a fountain where colored water tossed, birds glided, and fishes swam. Harry walked around the fountain slowly, his eyes drinking in the tall windows, the tapestries that hung on marble walls, the mosaic floor designs depicting jungle scenes. Tall windows at the far end opened onto a patio and a private walled garden.

"This way, please."

The voice had come from the patio, and Harry moved that way, searching. And standing near a second fountain, hand-feeding a bassoe, he found the figure of an elderly Jassan waiting for him.

"My name is Ros Moss," the elderly Jassan said.

"Harry Borg," Harry said, voice flat.

The damn Jassan was going to start out by making a point, Harry decided, a sudden wave of anger rising. Showing him how humans rated in Jassa by having a bassoe—a human—here, naked, as a pet, hand-feeding it.

The bassoe was a female, about fourteen, a budding beauty, soft gray fur and all. Her large brown eyes were empty of any meaningful expression, of course, but the appearance of Harry seemed to draw her attention and her vacant eyes remained fixed on him as she accepted tidbits from the Jassan's many-fingered hand and the gentle rubbing behind her ears.

"Does this offend you?" Moss asked.

He indicated the tidbits, the feeding of the female bassoe,

and Harry realized that the elderly Jassan had been watching for his reaction, waiting for a comment.

"Y'wanted to show me something, right?" Harry said, voice blunt, almost harsh. "Y'wanted to show me your Homo sapiens were as dumb as doorknobs."

"Homo sapiens?"

"It's the name of our species. Means 'wise man.' Means we're different from the apes."

"Oh, I see."

"But you wanted to show me we're nothing but food animals in your world. Okay, you showed me. I only hope I get a chance to show you what you are in our world."

"And what's that?" Moss asked, voice mild.

"Snakes," Harry said. "Lizards."

"And rather low-caste, I presume."

"Right there at the bottom. Zilch." But in the face of Ros Moss's continued mildness, Harry's anger began to fade, and he realized he'd run true to Guss's predicted odds of six-to-five against. "Maybe not zilch," he said gruffly. "Maybe higher."

"I hope a little higher?"

Was Moss amused? It was hard to tell.

Moss seemed taller than most Jassans, bent, thin. He wore a loose, flowing gown of silken fabric, rich gold in hue; a purple scarf wound turbanlike around his head, a single large violet stone suspended from a gold chain around his neck. His age was revealed by sagging jowls, a graying of the flesh about his mouth, a tremor in both voice and hands when not actively controlled. But his yellow, slitted eyes were sharply intelligent, and the liquid-flowing, forked tongue was as inquisitive as any. The tongue flicked steadily toward Harry, the yellow eyes held him in a close scrutiny.

"You are angry, aren't you?" Moss asked.

"Yeah, you better believe it!" Harry was getting angry again, but was unable to control it. "Every time I think of you—your kind—using us for hamburger, I blow my top."

"Blow your top?"

"Get mad, sore! Angry!"

"I see, I see." Moss's tone was placating, even apologetic. "I heard you were capable of anger—extreme anger, as a matter of fact. But I found it hard to believe. Our bassoes are not capable of intelligent thought, let alone anger. And I wanted to see for myself."

"Now you know," Harry said, still fighting for control.

Make nice! Guss had said.

"I get sore like anybody else," Harry said. "Like you, for instance."

"Not like us," Moss said quietly. "And that's the trouble."

"What trouble?"

"All in good time."

The female bassoe's attention had become more fixed on Harry. Perhaps she'd recognized one of her own kind in Harry and wanted to herd with him. Now she pushed past the hand full of tidbits Moss was holding to her mouth, letting them spill where they would, and walked toward Harry—colliding, presently, with an unseen barrier.

"I'll be damned!" Harry said. "One of those TV screens!" And then to Moss, "You're not here at all—you're a three-D image on a TV screen!"

"That's true."

"Got to hand it to you," Harry said grudgingly. "You do TV a helluva lot better than we do."

"Or did, anyway," Moss said. "Wait a moment."

Moss, the bassoe female, the room became quite suddenly a wall of what appeared to be frosted glass, and Harry found himself alone on the patio. A sound at the entrance behind him drew his attention, and he discovered Moss, escorted by two armed guards, approaching. The female bassoe was no longer with them. Moss sent the guards away, motioned toward a table and chairs.

"Suppose we sit down and start over."

"You trust me?" Harry asked as they took seats.

"In the beginning, I had to take certain security measures—" he indicated the frosted screen "—but I know you better now. I don't think you'll harm me."

"Depend on it!" Harry said emphatically.

Moss gave him a look that might have been amused. "Because you want something and need me alive and friendly to get it?"

"That's right," Harry said. "The female and her child, the five young men you kidnapped—I want to get them home. And I'd like to set up a trade between our worlds—"

Moss stopped him with an upraised hand.

"All in good time. First, we must get to know each other better."

A servant brought a tray of food and drink and placed it on the table. Moss poured steaming liquid into cups. "I was pleased to discover you, a bassoe—if you will excuse the term—could, and did, live up to what I've been told about you."

"And what was that?"

"That you were intelligent. Very intelligent. And that you were aggressive. Very aggressive. Very aggressive when you felt there was a need for being aggressive. You are capable of initiating a complex act of aggression and carrying it through to completion. And you are not at all impressed by, or daunted by, authority."

"Is that good or bad?"

"Very good, I think," Moss said. "It might be the solution to my problem."

"I don't understand."

"My subjects, the Jassans, have lost the qualities I was hoping to find in you. Have found, I am now reasonably sure."

"Qualities? What qualities?"

"Aggressiveness. The ability to be aggressive, to fight against what seem overwhelming odds, to win—or die trying."

Harry pretended great seriousness. "Is that a fact?"

"You do have those qualities," Moss said. "You demonstrated it when you climbed down from the exterior wall of Sos Vissir's place, when you stole the Cassal, when you took the human female and her child and tried to get back to your world without fear of losing your life, killing anyone who stood in your way. All of that is proof you have what we lack."

Harry sipped the drink, staring at Moss.

Becoming aware of the fixed stare, Moss said, "Something troubles you?"

"Yeah," Harry said. "I know you're putting me on. What I don't know is why."

"Putting you on?"

"Lying to me."

"No!" Moss was offended. "I don't lie!"

"C'mon, now," Harry scoffed. "I'm not a bassoe. I've got a head full of smarts—you said so yourself."

"I still don't know what you mean."

"Okay. You weren't in that hospital when three of your kind tried to kill me. They killed five of yours and got killed themselves. And you haven't seen the security I've had around me—armed guards, guard bugs, planes—around the clock. And you've got armed guards. What are they protecting you against? And me against? Somebody wants to kill us, right? That's aggression. Count the guards and I've got to say you've got aggression up to here. And you're trying to tell me you haven't got any. C'mon!"

"Oh, now I understand!"

"Glad somebody does."

"You and I are being protected against the Peacekeepers."

"Come again?"

"The Peacekeepers," Moss said, patiently. "Peacekeepers are ardent pacifists, who have become, over the past century, *militant* pacifists, if you can accept that contradiction of terms."

"Militant pacifists," Harry said slowly.

"If one takes a position," Moss said, "any position, even one of pacifism, one must defend oneself to maintain that position, and eventually one will discover that preventive action must be taken to sustain that defense, and then, finally, that measured offense is the best kind of defense." Moss sipped his drink. "You have nothing like this in your world?"

Harry found himself thinking about the mobs who demonstrated against nuclear energy plants and nuclear weapons manufacture and installation, mobs who fought police with rocks, with gasoline bombs. "Yeah, we do," he said. "Anyway, we're traveling down the road. Give us a few more years."

"Our Peacekeepers have become very militant, as you discovered in the hospital."

"Killing me is not keeping the peace."

"They think of it as neutralizing you."

"A man can't be any more neutral than when he's dead," Harry agreed. He studied the matter for a moment. "Seems like you folks in charge would neutralize these Peacekeepers."

"Oh, that would be unacceptable," Moss said. "Peace has become a holy state, a religion. The Peacekeepers are the anointed, the priests. To neutralize a Priest of Peace is to commit a sacrilege. An act against Peace, or the Priests of Peace, is an act against all things in creation that are holy."

"Like goodness and niceness," Harry said. "Like apple pie and motherhood."

"Precisely."

"So how do you deal with them?"

"We can't—not effectively," Moss said. "And as a result we find ourselves engaged in a war we are unable to end."

"A war?" Harry said, unbelieving. "You've *really* got a war? A *shooting* war?"

"Yes, we have."

"Guss said something, but I didn't take him seriously." Harry looked at Moss sharply. "Who with, for chrissake?"

"The Ussirs."

Ros Moss indicated the frosted glass wall, the 3-D television screen, and signaled a servant who brought him a small control device. Selecting a button, he pushed it, and the screen came to life.

"The face of the enemy," Moss said quietly. "An Ussir."

The 3-D representation that appeared on the screen was a lizard-man, apparently a prisoner, since he was wearing a featureless uniform and was confined in a tiled, windowless room. He faced the camera, unafraid, curious.

"He looks just like you," Harry said.

"And he is like me," Moss said. "Except for that one difference."

"Difference?"

"He's green."

"Well, so he is!" Harry said.

The Ussir was indeed green. A bright green. And not displeasing to look at, if you like bright colors, Harry decided.

"That what makes him the enemy? His color?"

"No."

"You wouldn't kid me, now, would you?" Harry insisted. "I mean, if you're a racist, a bigot, I don't want anything to do with you."

"Are you a bigot?"

"Hell, no! I just told you. I'm against bigotry!"

"Doesn't that make you a bigot? Being against all those who are bigots is a form of bigotry, isn't it?"

Harry thought about that a moment. Then he grinned. "All right," he said. "That's one for you."

"You'll have your turn."

"I've already had one," Harry said. "Militant pacifists. That's almost as good as bigoted antibigots."

"And there's more to come," Moss said.

He pushed a button on the control. The 3-D picture of the Ussir prisoner was replaced by an easily recognized map of the world—the world Harry knew, as well as, apparently, the world of Essa. North and South America were centered, with Europe on the right and Asia on the left. A line had been drawn that divided North America at about what Harry would say was the Mississippi River. All to the right of it was shaded green; all to the left was shaded gray.

"That is approximately the battle line as it stands today," Moss said, "and the occupied land. The Ussirs are the green, of course, and we are the gray."

"You winning or losing?"

"Losing badly," Moss said. "Three hundred years ago we occupied all of the Western Hemisphere and a good portion of the Eastern."

"Three hundred years!" Harry said. "You fight long wars!"

"This one's been going on over a thousand years—one thousand two hundred and twenty-five, to be exact." Moss licked his fingers. "Which brings us to the purpose of this meeting."

"And that is?"

"I want *you* to take charge of our war," Moss said. "And win."

Harry laughed. It wasn't from amusement; it was a nervous reaction to what could only be called a preposterous proposition.

"You don't take me seriously?" Moss asked.

"Not for one damned second!" Harry said.

"And why is that?"

Harry looked at him steadily for a long moment. Apparently Moss was serious. He looked serious. He talked seriously. But, for the love of Christ! Of all the ridiculous, farfetched, impossible— He leaned forward suddenly, his own face deadly serious.

"There's maybe a dozen reasons why I don't believe a word of this. But just one will do. I'm a bassoe, right? Something to eat?"

"A most unusual bassoe," Moss said.

"You're going to put *me* in charge of your war?"

"Yes."

"Who would take orders from a pot roast?"

"Pot roast?"

"Something to eat. Meat. Me."

"Everyone."

"Aw, c'mon!"

"You still haven't understood our problem," Moss said. "At least, not fully. We, as a race, have become docile. We, as a race, no longer resent, argue, fight. Our soldiers, as individuals, are no different. But you *are* different, as we said."

The old man lifted a small carved chest from the table, a chest that had the look of great age and value. He opened it slowly, and from it he took a gold chain and pendant. Holding the pendant with obvious reverence in a mottled eight-fingered hand, he extended it for Harry's inspection. Harry's breath caught. The pendant held a jewel the size of his thumb and of about the same shape. The jewel was red. But it was not a static red, a quiescent red; it was alive—a glowing, pulsating red, the red of spurting arterial blood.

"How does it do that?" Harry whispered.

"I don't know. No one knows," Moss said. "It is called the Red Flame. And it is very, very old. There is a legend that goes with it. It has been told for aeons. It's known to every child." He was looking at Harry, intently now. "Do you have a mythical hero? Yes, I find King . . . King Arthur? Sir Lancelot? Slayer of dragons. Yes." He smiled. "No, not Superman—nothing so frivolous. Your legend of King Arthur is very close."

"You're reading my mind," Harry protested.

"No. You spoke those words silently."

"But—"

"Please! Let me continue. The legend of the Red Flame lives in every Jassan's memory. He was a great warrior; this stone was his emblem. I intend that you should be his reincarnation."

"Me?" Harry whispered.

"You have the qualities of the Red Flame—reckless courage, daring, initiative, the ability to plan combat, to fight to the death—all qualities we Jassans, perhaps sadly, have lost. Given this—" he indicated the stone "—and my directive that you are the reincarnation of the Red Flame, there will be no question of whether or not you will be accepted as our military leader, or whether or not your orders will be followed."

"The Red Flame." Harry was staring at the ancient, glowing stone as if mesmerized. "Yeah, something like that could work. Given the right P.R., yeah."

"P. R.?"

"Nothing," Harry said. "Just thinking. The Red Flame Brigade—yeah. Emblem on the chest—eat your heart out, Superman. Shoulder patches. The whole bit. But not for the fun and games—for keeps!"

"I presume you're talking yourself into an agreement," Moss said.

Harry looked at him. "Something like that. But, seriously, I think it could work. If your folks feel about the Red Flame as you say they do, I can make it go."

"They will," Moss said. "Do you accept?"

"On my terms," Harry said.

"And they are?"

"I need that female and her child with me from now on," Harry said. "I need a place of my own, something like the one Guss Rassan has."

"We will make Rassan's place available to you."

"Servants, guards, transportation? Personal weapons?"

"Within reason."

"What's reason?"

"What do you want?"

"The same servants and guards Rassan has now," Harry said. "One of those little planes—Cassals, you call 'em. A sidearm and one of those short swords. I like that sword, y'know?"

"Ceremonial, isn't it?"

"Mostly. But if you need it in close—all right!"

"These can be managed."

"And those five young men," Harry said. "I want them turned over to me. They'll be my cadre, my personal bodyguards, my general staff. And I want each equipped with a communicating device, of course, so they can talk your language."

"That can be arranged."

"And when I get the job done," Harry said, "I want to be able to take my people and go back to my world."

"When you get the job done," Moss agreed.

Harry sat back, satisfied. "Then we're in business."

"If," Moss said, "you agree to the limitations—and the penalties."

Harry's eyes narrowed. "Maybe you'd better lay those out for me."

"For any abuse of your power, the penalty is death," Moss said, watching Harry carefully.

"Who's to decide if what I do is abuse or not?" Harry asked.

"I'll decide."

"You alone? I'm going to make enemies, you know."

"I know."

"They'll come to you with a bunch of lies."

"I know."

"Okay. So what else?"

"For failure to establish a pattern of winning within six months, the penalty is death."

"Hey, c'mon! You haven't been able to whip those green guys in how long? More'n a thousand years? And you want me to do it in six months?"

"I promised the Gonsilis that if I could use you as I intend, I would get results in six months or suffer death. It was the best I could do. If you fail, I fail. And we both die."

"You just told me you don't take risks!"

"As a race, we *avoid* risks. As an individual, as the leader, I have no choice. I must produce results. I must take whatever risk producing those results might cost."

"Gutsy bastard!" Harry said.

"Is that a compliment?"

"Sure as hell is!" Harry said. "But six months—that's no time at all!"

"It was the best I could do." Moss may have smiled. "You see, the Peacekeepers have seized upon this as an opportunity to neutralize me. I may be the last one to stand between them and total peace."

"Total defeat, you mean."

"I mean final destruction. Utter ruin."

"Goodlordamighty!" Harry said, beginning to sweat.

"And any attempt to cross back to your world, without my written permission, will be punished by death."

Harry looked at Moss a long moment, thoroughly alarmed.

He couldn't read anything in Moss's return gaze that suggested equivocation. The Jassan meant everything he had said.

"Death is kind of total in the way of a penalty, you know."

"Yes, it is," Moss agreed. "And don't for a moment forget that the Peacekeepers will continue to try to neutralize you. They are very determined, very ingenious. And will become more so, when they learn you have taken the position I'm offering you."

"Some position!" Harry said.

"You don't like it?"

"Not much—with those penalties."

"Consider the alternative," Moss suggested.

"All right," Harry said. "Let's give that a whack. What happens if I say no to the whole proposition?"

"There is a penalty for that, too."

"There is?" Harry didn't need to ask. "That would be?"

"Death," Moss said.

"And so good meat shouldn't go to waste, I'd be—?"

Moss's shrug was expressive.

"I'll take the job," Harry said, trying not to look ill.

What must have been a smile broke on Moss's Jassan face; his forked tongue reached out toward Harry caressingly.

"Somehow, I thought you might," he said.

CHAPTER 15

The preparations had been going on for the past three days, and from the look of them, Chad Harrison had decided that something very, very big was going to go down. And soon. Within a day or two. Could even be that afternoon.

Chad was lying on the recliner in the morning sun, naked, browning, his eyes shaded by the brim of his baseball cap, watching the lizzies working on the football field. They had taken down the goalpost and were now putting up what looked like a reviewing stand just off the field on the fifty-yard line.

"Six-to-five they're going to have a hanging," Homer said.

"I'm in for two mil," Chad said.

"You don't believe it?"

"Put up my money, didn't I?"

"Two million? That's money?"

"All I got."

"Okay," Homer said. "I've got you down for two million dollars at six-to-five. Any other suckers in the crowd?"

Homer was on another recliner near Chad; the mid-morning hour on this side of the barracks provided just the right kind of sun for tanning, and the air was still. Arnie and Eddie were close by, passing a football back and forth between them, and Sam Barnstable was away for a physical.

"Who would they hang?" Arnie inquired.

"Who they got?" Eddie asked.

"There's us and who else?"

"Wouldn't be one of them, now, would it?" Homer said.

"No way," Arnie said.

"So who's left?"

"Us." Arnie passed the football. "Homer, I'll take some of Chad's two mil."

Arnie had recovered from the near-fatal encounter with the saber-tooth with only scars to show for it. There had been no punishment by the Jassans for the attempted escape, only a return to a tightened security, to more of the same routine; but he had felt no new urge for another attempt.

"All there is out there," he'd said, "is more of the same and some worse. A lot worse."

He had decided to accept Chad's reasoning that they could not possibly be victims of a single, isolated incident, that there had to be, would inevitably be, more that would occur. And he shared now, with Chad and the others, the feeling that the more that was going to occur was going to occur within hours possibly, within a day or two at the very outside.

And with good reason.

Everything had been double-scrubbed for openers. And that included themselves. They had each been given physicals—which had included, for some damned reason, a shaved spot on the back of each of their heads—and fitness checks that couldn't have been tougher if they'd been trying out for the L.A. Raiders. New threads. And *get this*: the new threads were like combat fatigues with insignia! A red flame on a blue field, and such a red flame! It seemed to glow! But why a uniform? There was no army!

And now the Jassans were fixing up the football field they'd only finished a short while back, changing it into something they could use for a hanging—or whatever.

"Hey, Eddie," Arnie said. "How about this? They're gonna sell us, that's what they're gonna do. Gonna hold a slave auction, like they did with your great-great. Sell us for toy soldiers, okay?"

Eddie, who was black, grinned. "Right on!"

"Feedin' us up? Shinin' us up?" Arnie said. "Fits, don't it? We bein' studs and all."

"Like a glove," Eddie said. "You buy that, quarterback?"

Chad Harrison laughed. "Y'know, knucklehead might have something there at that."

"Naw," Homer said, scoffing. "Not knucklehead!"

"Watch it, cowboy!" Arnie bristled.

"Why couldn't he get an idea?" Eddie asked, grinning.

"Just ain't possible!"

Arnie charged the bigger young man with a ferocious roar that was all pretense and no bite and knocked him out of the recliner with the force of his attack; they rolled on the ground in what looked and sounded like mortal combat but was really only an excuse for physical exertion. But it brought the Jassans running.

There were two of them. The Jassans served as servant-valets as well as custodians, and they were very able at their assignment. They were both young, both large for their kind. They wore white germ-proof masks at all times, white smocks, white boots and gloves, apparently in fear of infecting their charges, and now, as they struggled to separate the two mock-combatants, their principle concern was obviously that one or both might be hurt or bruised.

"Knock it off!" Chad said to Homer and Arnie.

They broke free, giving in to the hands of the Jassans, who were frantic in their efforts to get them apart. Once apart, they were examined minutely for signs of injury, attention Arnie took to be proof of his contention they were going to be auctioned off.

"They don't want their merchandise damaged," he said. "Y'see, you cowjockey, I was right!"

"You haven't been right since you quit suckin' your thumb," Homer answered mildly. "And when was that? A month ago?"

And the Jassans got between them again. Now it became apparent they wanted all four to go inside the barracks. There they found their clothes laid out, ready to wear. But first they had to shower again.

"Slave auction, sure as hell!"

Sam Barnstable was brought back from his physical. Enormous, grumpy, but scrubbed clean, Sam could remember nothing of what had happened to him the past three days, as was usually the case, except a dream: "I could hear those lizzies talkin'. It was real as hell." He, too, had the shaved spot on the back of his head.

When they were dressed, they looked sharp. Very sharp. Five young athletes, seventeen to twenty, in perfect physical condition, they were an obvious source of pride to themselves as well as to their Jassan custodian-valets. They stood, good-humoredly submissive, while the Jassans gave them a final last-minute inspection, a cooperative attitude they'd assumed once they had discovered the Jassan attendants' only purpose, ever, was to insure their comfort, health, and happiness. And then, in deference to the fact that they were wearing uniforms, they marched through the doorway that led toward the football field—in step, in file, to a cadence called by Chad.

"Hup, two, three, four . . ."

To find—

"Good grief, Charlie Brown!" Eddie breathed.

While they'd been held away, occupied with getting clean and sharp and dressed, the preparations at the football field had been completed. Land vehicles had brought Jassan luminaries—military, for the most part, to judge by the fact most were wearing uniforms, some of which were very elaborate—who had taken or were taking places in the reviewing stand, while others, dressed in the uniforms of honor guards, were standing in ranks, ready to perform, and still others, heavily armed and in combat uniforms, were stationed on a distant perimeter, alertly guarding against something or other. Brightly colored flags, some of them with the Red Flame insignia, were flying.

"Hey!" Arnie whispered. "Ain't that our outfit—the Red Flame?"

"Sure as hell," Eddie whispered back.

One would expect such preparations to include a military band playing martial airs, but there was none, since sound was of no great consequence in the lives of the Jassans. But there was a group of uniformed Jassans holding instruments of some kind from which emanated odors varying between acrid, nose-tingling, sweet, and eye-smarting in turn, and which seemed to please the Jassans, whose forked tongues waved constantly, tasting the drifting scents, but which caused the humans to sniffle and sneeze and snort and their eyes to water.

Most striking of all was the assemblage of aircraft.

"I don't get it," Arnie kept saying. "I'm seeing that flame everywhere."

The blood-red flame was, indeed, on planes, on flags, on uniforms at every hand. Something approaching a hundred craft of varying sizes and purposes hovered directly overhead or circled nearby. The farthest were light military aircraft in support of the ground troops, obviously guarding against some unknown enemy. Those nearer and directly overhead were transport craft, some capable of holding as many as fifty or more. A most astonishing display, and it was set against a dark blue sky decorated by magnificent cumulus clouds that had been set out, one could almost be persuaded to think, especially for this occasion. And most remarkable of all was the total lack of the continuing thunderous roar that would naturally accompany such an air armada of human craft. Here there was only a deep and not unpleasant buzzing-humming, as if from a very large swarm of bees.

Sam Barnstable's mouth was open in wonderment. "What keeps 'em up there?"

"Magic," Chad told him. "What else?"

The five humans were shepherded onto the football field before the reviewing stand where without persuasion they formed into a rank, facing one of the larger aircraft—this one emblazoned with the largest of the Red Flame insignia—as it settled gently to the ground in the center of the field. Very quickly, two lines of the Jassan honor guard formed up, creating an aisle from the aircraft door to the reviewing stand and the five young humans waiting before it.

And the five were impressed. Very.

"Gotta be the High Poobah himself," Homer said.

"*The* Man!" Eddie agreed.

"Somebitch!" Arnie said, marveling.

Sam Barnstable resisted an urge to belch.

Chad gave a quick scan down the line. "Snap to!" he said. "Let's show whoever it is who *we* are."

"Americans, by damn!" Homer said.

Though none of them had done time in any service, there was nothing about their rank that would have been found unacceptable by any branch of the military—shoulders square, guts in, chins up, thumbs on seams. They were only a few, but they looked good.

The door of the plane was opening.

"Ten-*hut*!" Chad said quietly.

Later he said that he had expected, after all this preparation, a lizard-man at least ten feet tall to show up in the doorway. Eddie said he had expected a lizzie wearing a gold crown. Arnie said one with fangs. Sam said maybe a queen, male or female; he didn't know. What they got was an absolute astonishment.

Six-foot-two of dazzle. An eyeball-cracking stack of bone and muscle. Short beard and gold earring. Sidearm and short sword. Goddamn! Fierce dark blue eyes, hard, white teeth, and a merry grin. A swashbuckling son-of-a-bitch. He was wearing a uniform bearing the insignia of the Red Flame, but it was a dress uniform: boots, shorts, and a white knit silk shirt, tight across a massive chest, on which lay a gleaming red stone suspended by a gold chain about his thick neck. He came out of the plane with the stride of a tiger stalking prey.

"It's a man," Arnie muttered. "Ain't it?"

"Not real," Homer whispered. "Can't be."

"Cool it!" Chad hissed.

Chad knew every yellow, vertically slitted Jassan eye was on them, watching for their reaction. And that reaction could have enormous consequences, either good or bad. Here was that data he had been waiting for: that next occurrence. But was what he was seeing true? Or was this cockamamy, buccaneer cowboy only an illusion concocted by the Jassans as some kind of a test? He hissed an additional order from the side of his mouth as the apparition approached.

"Follow my lead!"

"On the count of one," Homer promised.

The others stood tense.

The apparition that looked like somebody's idea of a cross between Mr. America and John Wayne went to a braced leg stance just in front of them and stared at them with hard blue eyes. Eyes that found doubt, even disbelief, staring back at him.

"The Anaheim Rams are bush," the apparition said softly. "I'll take the L.A. Raiders anytime."

He saw the doubt go away and gladness come. Quickly, he said, "I'm your C.O.—and I need your support."

Chad snapped, instantly, "Hand—sa-*lute*!"

And the five of them threw him their best highballs.

And he threw his best right back.

And it was fine!

"Name's Harry Borg," Harry said. "And I've got to be the proudest human being in this world—or any other." He grinned. "At ease."

"You're for real?" Arnie had to ask.

"I'm for real," Harry said. "From Reseda, California, 91335."

"Where are we?" Chad asked.

"Take hours to tell," Harry said. "Now, we've got a thing to do to stay alive. Trust me?"

"Till we learn different."

"Turn and face the stand like the damn-fine soldiers you turned out to be. I've got to make a thank-you speech, and then we'll depart this post and station. Okay?"

Chad snapped them to attention, gave them an about-face.

The Jassan luminaries were impressed. Now they sat in respectful silence, their long forked tongues fluttering, their yellow eyes partially hidden by the inner lids, while Harry went into his speech, voicing his words through his speech communicater as well as with sound.

He was there, he said, acting on the authority given him by their president, Ros Moss, representing the military high command and, not incidentally, the adjoining planet Earth, and the four billion human beings who populated that planet.

He understood, he said, that to the civilians here present, the respected members of the College of Genetic Sciences, the five human beings here at his side were a most valuable scientific acquisition, and that their transfer from the relative safety of the college to the possibly hazardous duty in their service to this country was a sacrifice few would be called upon to make.

After a good bit more in the same vein, all worked up by Ros Moss and himself with an eye to buttering up the scientific community, he said he wanted to thank them for their patriotic sacrifices, that he, personally, would guarantee their studies would lose nothing because of it. There would be a great deal of even more unique data made available to them in the very near future.

He was going down the list of names Ros Moss had wanted

him to thank specifically for their generosity, nearing his closing remarks, when the shooting started.

One of the hovering craft took an incoming round apparently intended for the viewing stand and blew apart almost immediately overhead with a loud bang, sending a shower of small parts over most of the area.

"Take cover!"

It was Harry's voice, a roaring command almost as loud, it seemed, as the explosion in the ears of the humans and in the minds of the Jassans, and it sent the elderly dignitaries tumbling out of the stands, and the humans into the deep, three-point sets they had learned would defense them against almost any attack. Their eyes followed Harry, who, sidearm and sword drawn, bounded into the reviewing stand to a high point, a powerful, vital figure who with commanding voice and gesture directed the Jassans to the relative safety of the dry creek bed that threaded through the property, and then scanned the perimeter for the source of the attack.

He found the source as a flash bounced off the side of a university building a thousand yards distant, outside the fence-enclosed grounds, beyond a tall hedge of ornamental trees. The armed Jassan soldiers on the perimeter were broken and dislocated, running into groups. And now Harry saw armed civilian Jassans coming through the passage between the buildings. Harry leaped off the reviewing stand and landed running and yelling.

"Get in the ditch!"

He meant that for the young humans, still in the instinctive set positions of defensive linemen, though words might have been lost in the blast of the second incoming round as it tore a hole in the barracks beyond the football field. The third round sent a geyser of earth and rock skyward on the far side of the field. Harry had reached the road and gateway in the fence between the impoundment and the university buildings when the small-arms automatic fire began. Like a scythe cutting grain, the first burst cut down a group of the uniformed perimeter guards who had panicked into a tight group at the bank of the dry creek, then went on to crackle above a second group that had hit the ground in response to a command that Harry had sent screaming through their minds as he drove himself, running, crouched and weaving, into the ditch where the first group had fallen.

"Damn!" he heard a voice pant behind him. "You're some kind of a runner!"

He turned and saw Eddie picking himself up off the bottom of the dry creek bed, and then in quick succession, as small arms fire cracked above them, Arnie, Homer, and, after an interval, Sam, with Chad pushing and cussing behind him.

"—run like a slow freight!" Chad complained.

"Y'expect a goddamn gazelle?"

Chad found Harry's hot blue eyes.

"Sir!"

"I told you to take cover!"

"Didn't say we would—sir!" Then, flatly, coldly, brooking no nonsense, Chad said, "Where you go, we go, and you can stick that in your ear—sir!"

They had a moment of eyeball to eyeball staring.

"You're a fiesty bastard," Harry said.

"There's five of us," Chad said. "We can clean you."

Harry took another moment. He found them all the same, hot-eyed, savage, flatly resolved. He laughed suddenly, a joyful bark.

"Like hell!" he said. "But there's work now! C'mon! Move it!"

He turned and, bent low, ran on down the ditch with them following. He found the fallen Jassan perimeter guards, stripped them of their weapons—medium-range, automatic-firing laser-like guns—and armed the five young humans.

"Trigger here, safety here," he said. "Sights like a rifle, kills like a fifty caliber. Any armed civilian is enemy. Kill him—or he'll kill you."

At the ditch edge, he sorted out the field problem. There was a grenade-thrower of some kind behind the squat, two-storied university building on the left; there were armed civilians, pinned down for the moment by the fire of the uniformed guards.

"Give me three minutes," he said to Chad, "then open fire on the civilians in the trees. The uniforms are friendlies."

He took the two fastest, Eddie and Arnie, leaving Chad, Homer, and Sam bunkered into the side of the creek bank. Moving at a dead run, he led the way down the creek bed until they were below the squat two-storied building. They moved up the bank at a bridge crossing, saw the way was clear, and ran for the back of the next building. But when they burst around the corner, weapons ready, they found they'd been expected.

"Scatter!" Harry yelled.

Three armed civilian Jassans hid behind a decorative revetment, manning the grenade-thrower—and the thrower was triggered by an excited hand. The projectile whooshed over their heads and detonated against the building behind them. Powered by the blast, Eddie and Arnie went down, rolling hard. Harry, who had dropped to a hard squat, his sidearm leveled before the grenade thrower had fired, remained firm and was able to pick off the third Jassan as the lizard-man attempted to bring his piece to bear. The two with the launcher threw that weapon aside and dropped behind the protective revetment, drawing their sidearms.

"Yahhh-whooo!"

It was half roar and half scream, uttered by Harry, a man now caught up in the insane joy of mortal combat, and it served to distract and terrify the enemy as he lunged upward, throwing himself at the revetment, leaping high over the top of the wall to land with the two Jassans. They tried their best to bring their weapons to bear, to kill.

"Bassoe—die!"

The mental screech was uttered by a burning-eyed Jassan an instant before Harry's short sword ran him through. The dying Jassan's sidearm discharged, scorching the side of Harry's neck in a near miss. Harry had turned to the last Jassan, blocking away his sidearm. He caught the Jassan's arm, broke it, sending the weapon flying, then caught up the Jassan to hold him in the grip of both hands at arm's length above his head, then hurled him, writhing and silently screaming, against a nearby wall where he crumpled, dying.

Just then Eddie and Arnie reached the revetment, gape-mouthed and bug-eyed at what they had seen.

"Wild somebitch!" Arnie said, awed.

"Killin' machine!" Eddie agreed.

"More to do!" Harry said. His cocked ear had caught the hard rattle of fire from the front of the buildings. "That's friendly fire—your buddies."

"Chad, Homer, and Sam," Arnie said.

"Kickin' ass," Eddie said. "On time."

"Let's give 'em a hand," Harry said.

He leaped back over the revetment and, with the two younger men behind him, moved quickly to the front of the building. The remaining civilian attackers were pinned down in dense ornamental shrubbery across fifty yards of lawn. They were exchanging heated fire with both the humans and the guards prone in the fields before them.

"Pick your shots," Harry told Eddie and Arnie.

With their first shots they came under fire, and again Harry had reason for pride. The two young men, who had never before been in a firefight, proved to be true fighting men, able to muster that cool, quiet desperation needed when men have to kill to stay alive. They had found cover, prone behind a low wall; they ignored the explosions that tore masonry to fragments within arm's length; they chose targets carefully and killed with precision.

"Hold your fire," Harry called finally.

The armed civilians had stopped fighting. A riflelike weapon had sailed out of the undergrowth to land in the open, a gesture of surrender.

"I think they want to quit," Harry said.

"Looks like."

Harry stood up in the open, erect, a clear target. Then, with Eddie and Arnie kneeling beside him, weapons leveled, Harry sent his voice, both vocal and mental, to the Jassans across the way. They could throw down their weapons, he told them, and come out with their hands on top of their heads. Or they could die. It was their choice, but they had to make it on the count of three.

"One."

Nothing.

"Two."

Nothing.

And then, suddenly, there was a scream—a silent, mental scream—as a civilian Jassan, a mindless radical, to be sure, rose up and charged at Harry, firing with a hip-level weapon. He was able to get off several shots before Eddie and Arnie, firing together, blew him away, but his closest shot missed Harry by at least two inches.

"Three!" Harry yelled.

The eight remaining civilian assassins came out with their

hands on top of their heads. Eddie and Arnie watched them with great care as they filed in and began to stretch out on the pavement, face down, before Harry.

"Who the hell *are* they?" Arnie asked.

"Why'd they want to kill us?" Eddie added.

"They're Peacekeepers," Harry said. "Sworn to bring peace to their world."

"Killing *us* is keepin' peace?"

"They were after me," Harry said. "I'm Commander-in-Chief of the Jassan Armed Forces. You're my staff now. We're fighting a war. The Peacekeepers'll kill anybody fighting a war. So now they want to kill you along with me—to keep the peace."

Arnie's mouth dropped open. He turned to stare at Eddie.

"You hear what the man said?"

"I heard him."

"He's a Commander-in-Chief of somebody's *army*?"

"What I heard."

"We're his *staff*?"

"What he said."

"The Peacekeepers *kill* to keep peace?"

"You got it."

Arnie gave Harry another long, hard stare.

Then, to Eddie: "You believe any of this?"

"Not a single word," Eddie said.

CHAPTER 16

Lori Calder awakened slowly. But it was not a usual kind of an awakening; of that she was sure. She had not awakened from sleep. She had awakened from a void, an emptiness, from a part of her life that was missing, gone. Not sleep. It was easy to know the difference, she reasoned carefully. She was being careful because she didn't want to frighten herself more than she was already frightened. More fright, she was sure, would certainly drive her mad. Her careful reasoning had concluded that when one awakened from normal sleep, one remembered what one had been doing immediately before falling asleep. But that part of her memory was blank.

Blank!

It was scaring the holy hell out of her!

There was a fine film of sweat on her body, the sweat of fear. And it didn't scare her less to see that the sweat covered her entire body—her breasts, her belly, her thighs. It didn't scare her less to see that she was naked.

Naked!

She held herself rigid.

Had they—

Was her baby—

With great effort, moving only a little, she forced her right

174

hand to her pubic area, touching. Nothing sore, nothing bruised. Thank God.

She brought her hand back to clasp her other hand tightly just below her breasts, to lie rigidly again. Then her eyes traveled about slowly to discover what she could of where she was.

She was lying on her back on a soft pallet, fully exposed, unfettered, on the floor in a room that was like a well ten feet square and fifty feet deep. Light came down to her from a row of windows at the top, glistening on smooth walls. The smooth wall on the right was marked at the bottom by a line drawn in a rectangle that could mean a door.

Tippi! It was a sudden, shattering remembrance.

"Tippi!" she cried out.

There was no answer.

Then, lifting her head in panic, she found her young daughter lying, as she was, naked, motionless, apparently sleeping, apparently unharmed, on a pallet below her feet. She dropped her head back to stare upward again, reassured by that tiny bit.

Tippi was all right.

She was all right.

But where the hell—

How the hell—

Her mind fought for stability, floundering like a panicked swimmer unable to find firm footing in what was, for her, a churning sea of fear. It was a desperate fight, but gradually, bit by bit, she found a measure of stability. She was Lori. She was a woman. She could cope.

"Think!" she commanded herself. "Think it through!"

She thought back to the last remembered moments, then beyond that to the events that had led up to that instant when knowing had stopped.

"I'm coming after you!" Harry had said.

She thought back that far.

The 3-D television screen in her apartment had suddenly come to life, startling her out of an idle daydream, evoking a happy yip from Tippi, who had been trying to persuade the willing but senseless Poopsalot into eating with a spoon—and there was Harry Borg.

Harry, the swashbuckling buccaneer, the Errol Flynn-Arnold Schwarzenegger-John Wayne-Superman mixture, everyman's dream of his own heroic self, complete with short beard, flashing teeth, devil-may-care grin, gold earring, and all.

"I'm coming after you," he said. "How d'you like that?"

"I like it fine!" she told him. "Only it can't be true."

"Why not?" His teeth flashed; his eyes gleamed.

"Harry!" she protested. "You tried that once, remember? You got shot to pieces!"

"Different now," Harry said confidently.

"How different? I'm still the bird in the gilded cage, pride of Sos Vissir, the richest Jassan in the land. And who are you, besides a poor man's Errol Flynn?"

"The man in charge," Harry said. "The Commander-in-Chief of the Armed Forces of Jassa!"

"Oh, you poor man!" Lori wailed.

"What's up, Mom?" Tippi asked.

"Our Harry's gone bonkers," Lori said to her daughter. "He's lost an oar." She turned back to Harry. "You been drinking, Harry? Smoking something funny, maybe?"

"Nope."

Harry didn't seem to be perturbed by the good-natured but unflattering remarks she'd made about him to her daughter. He drew the short sword from the sheath at his belt, tested its edge with his thumb, resheathed it; drew his pistollike sidearm from the holster on his other hip, aimed, and snapped off an imaginary shot at an imaginary target—all to call attention to the fact he was armed, to suggest that if he was privileged to carry arms, he was privileged indeed.

"How corny can you get?" Tippi asked, marveling.

"About like that," Lori said.

Harry grinned at both of them, showing those great white teeth that gleamed in the short, curled brown beard. "That's my girls—a couple of smart-asses." He turned his head. "Guss," he called. "Can you spare a moment? I've got a couple of unbelievers here."

"You mean, you really—" Lori began.

And then Guss appeared beside Harry. The same old Guss, about the best-looking lizard-man yet: kind of tall, for a Jassan; his friendly yellow vertically slitted eyes a shade toward gold;

his long, forked tongue gracefully flicking, almost caressing. And he was dressed casually in silks and fine leathers, as only the very well-to-do in Jassa could afford to dress. When he put an eight-fingered hand on Harry's arm and tipped his pleasantly tapered muzzle up to look at Harry, then at Lori, it had to be with pride.

"It's true," he said.

"What'd he say?" Tippi had to ask, since she had only recently been given a receptor implant and still did not believe it.

"He said it's true," Lori said with growing awe. "Our Harry's somebody. Somebody big."

"Commander-in-Chief," Harry said soberly, the comic-book hero role gone. "Of the Armed Forces. I know it's hard to believe. But it's true. And it means I outrank Sos Vissir where you are concerned."

"Oh, boy!" Tippi said. "Come and get us!"

"Shush!" Lori said to her, now all hot and confused.

"I'll be there in an hour," Harry said. "Get packed. Get ready."

"We goin' home?" Tippi asked.

"You're comin' here."

"Can I bring Poopsalot?"

"Tippi—damn it!" Lori grabbed her daughter and clamped a hand over her mouth. "Harry—this squirt! I can't get a word in. Is it—yeah, I guess it is. It's true. All right. We'll be ready. I want to bring Tillie. And—let me think—my good shoes, my blue wrap . . ." She had gone scatter-witted with happiness.

"Sakes alive!"

They waited more than an hour. Didn't everything always take longer than it was supposed to? It took two and a half hours! Two and a half hours of finger-gnawing, nail-biting uncertainty. Had they only dreamed they were going to be rescued? That Harry, the poor man's hero, was all of a sudden somebody important? And then, quite suddenly, the sky seemed to fill with aircraft.

"Mom!" Tippi, watching at the window, yelled. "Come look at this!"

Looking down, Lori saw the flight of aircraft settling down on the land below the high window, saw the door of the largest aircraft open and Harry emerge. Suffering Sassafras! The poor man's Errol Flynn was for *real*! He paused dramatically at the top of the steps, arms akimbo, grin flashing, then leaped to the ground. Uniformed Jassan soldiers formed up around him and escorted him to a ground vehicle; he was a personage of great importance—you could take it to the bank!

"Sheez!" Tippi whispered. "Would you look at him!"

"I don't believe it," Lori whispered back.

But they had to believe it. After Harry and several others had signed papers, after the very unhappy Sos Vissir had folded the signed papers and stowed them away, Harry Borg took them—Lori and Tippi; Tillie, the Jassan maid; Poopsalot, the child-pet bassoe—aboard the biggest aircraft and took them away to Guss's place.

"Y'got a nice little pad here," Lori said when they were brought in, trying to hide her awe behind a tone of hip jocularity. "Do for the king and queen of something."

"He *is* the king—of—of fragrances," Harry said, fumbling for the right words, taking pride in his friendship with a VIP Jassan.

"It's Harry's now," Guss said to Lori.

"Geez!" Tippi said when Lori told her.

"On loan to the government," Harry corrected. "Who loaned it to me for our use while I'm working for them."

"Whatever," Lori said.

She was looking about, if not with awe now, certainly with appreciation: the many tall and spacious rooms, the graceful drapes, moved gently by scented airs, the softness underfoot, the clear windows, the doors that operated, it seemed, on whim alone, the welcoming flames in hearths, the inviting recliners at every hand, and the colors everywhere translucent, warm, always pleasing, that seemed to change with every glance.

And there was a shy Jassan, a female, who came forward timidly.

"This is Sissi," Guss said, introducing her to Lori and Tippi. "She is the head of my household—and also my very good friend." He looked lamely at Harry.

"Very good friend," Harry said, straight-faced.

"I'm his mistress," Sissi said.

And Lori knew, when she saw both Harry and Guss wince dramatically, that she was going to like Sissi very much.

"My pleasure," she said, meaning it.

* * *

There followed two weeks of exciting living.

In the security of Harry's arms, living with the fear totally gone, life became new, a voyage to a distant land with much that was different and exotic to see and enjoy. A land in which reptiles remained dominant! Imagine that! How unique! And in so many ways—how enchanting! A very, very old civilization, she discovered, that had peaked centuries ago, that was now near to the bottom of a long, long decline: incredible architectural beauty, crumbling into decay, amazing scientific and industrial achievements fading into the darkness of lost memory—the very end of this once marvelous civilization could not be far removed.

The Jassans were not, Lori had come to know, an unkind or cruel race. Rather the opposite was the truth. And that truth was, in fact, the source of their great peril.

They had become so unantagonistic that they were now unable to protect themselves from those who were antagonistic.

That was the reason—actually, it was a desperate need—for putting Harry at the head of their armed forces. Harry was a human being and was, therefore—by nature, by heritage, by instinct—antagonistic. The Jassans needed his antagonism, his willingness to fight, his easily triggered eagerness to fight. They needed it to awaken in themselves their ability to defend themselves against an implacable and capable aggressor, whose single purpose, however they obscured it with rhetoric, was, quite simply, to destroy them.

"And you've got these—whaddayuhcall'ems, Peacekeepers? You got to fight them, too?" Lori had asked, when Harry and Guss had taken a few hours to explain his mission to her. "You tryin' to tell me they're not what you call 'antagonistic'?"

"No, they're not," Guss said.

"Tryin' to kill you is *friendly*?" Lori asked, belaboring the paradox with deliberate sarcasm.

"They are willing to kill to stop the fighting—all fighting."

Lori stared at Harry for a moment. "These what you call Peacekeepers have got to be flat-out idiots."

"Now you've got it," Harry said.

And then there were the young men.

While she didn't get to see much of the young men who

served as Harry's staff, each time she did was like a little bit of home. They were so big! So damned physically capable! They didn't seem like kids just out of high school; they were fresh, unspoiled, unused examples of males of the human race at the beginning of their manhood. They were so polite when they talked to her. They were so careful without any suggestion of a sexual overture. And yet with their amused eyes so knowing, they made her female nerves hum when they were near. And poor Tippi!—she fell in love with them, each and every one in turn.

How quickly they had become soldiers!

"Born to it," Harry could not help saying with great pride. "Professionals, almost from day one."

She found herself taking the same pride. She would trust her life to them, to any one of them, at any time, without a moment's question: Chad, the no-nonsense, always-in-control leader; Homer, the quiet adjutant, fully capable; Eddie, smooth and graceful, coiled power; Arnie, the tough and undauntable; and finally Sam, the behemoth, amiable and unstoppable. They were fine, charming company, all of them, but, alas, they had little time away from the tasks Harry set for them.

"We've got a war to win," Harry said very seriously, "and six thin months to win it. If we lose it, we don't just get fired. We get slaughtered, stuffed, roasted, sliced, and eaten."

"What a way to go!" Arnie said.

"Bon appétit!" Eddie said.

"I get an apple in my mouth?" Sam asked.

"You get served as steak," Homer told him.

"We don't lose," Chad said quietly.

And then one night, when Harry, Guss, and the young men were all away, the kidnappers came. They claimed they had orders from Sos Vissir—and they had papers to prove it—to see for themselves that Sos Vissir's prize, museum-quality bassoes were being properly cared for—which was a right guaranteed to Sos Vissir in the fine print of the agreement by which she and Tippi had been taken from him.

She remembered that argument now, as she lay still and naked and sweating and afraid in the well-like room. Sissi, the shy young head of Guss's household—his mistress, for god's sake!—had proved not shy at all in her efforts to keep the lizard-men

away. Had she survived the clubbing? She remembered the two
lizard-men stepping over Sissi's inert body, aiming a yellow tube
at her—

And that was all of the "before" she could recall.

She heard, faintly, distant voices of the lizard-men in her
mind, coming through the implanted receptor, then a pneumatic
hiss as the rectangular line on the wall at floor level on her right
became the expected door, opening to admit two lizard-men,
one wearing the blue which she had come to know designated
someone in authority, the other the white of the working class.

". . . every hour!" the Blue said, finishing his sentence with
a sharp, reprimanding tone.

"But they will not awaken for another day—or recover their
intelligence in less than two." It was a mild defense.

"These are not our kind of bassoes, Issi! They may react
differently to the mind control!"

Lori had closed her eyes and was holding herself in rigid
control, trying desperately to appear unconscious, mindless. A
Jassan hand, cool and dry, gripped her ankle, lifted her leg
roughly, and let it drop in a testing routine.

"Seems to be still under control."

The Blue's remark was grudging, and it was followed, from
a little distance by, "Her pup is deeply controlled."

"They must be inspected every hour without fail, Issi! Is that
clear?" Blue insisted.

"Every hour, sir!"

Lori, holding her eyes carefully closed and motionless and
her body still, felt the eyes of the Jassan inspecting her naked
body inch by inch.

"Fine animals—both of them."

"Exceptional."

"Strange the only fur on them is that patch at their sexual
organs. I rather like the appearance of our bassoes better."

"Yes. So do I. But I think we'd get a better quality of hide
from these. It would be easier to tan, that's certain."

"Well fleshed. Not too fat."

"Choice, I would say, sir."

"A herd of them—think of that."

"You'd be the wealthiest citizen in Jassa."

"I wonder about the quality, the flavor."

"So do I. I've wondered why we haven't been able to test the meat. For taste, tenderness, cooking. One or two animals, at least."

"Haven't had any to spare from the breeding program. And that, by the way, is very successful, I understand. The young males have proved to be excellent progenitors."

"Look at this one, sir. Young. Choice, indeed!"

"Ah, yes! I can almost taste that thigh!"

"Say the word and she'll be ready for your table by tomorrow night." A dry, mirthful sound. "You might say I have the equipment close at hand."

"Right here in the country's largest packing plant—I should think you have the equipment. But no, thanks. Sos Vissir would have me up on one of those hooks!" There was a moment of silence. "Did you know he has a wardrobe designed using these hides?"

"No, I didn't."

"Well, he has. Female garments. Beaded, I think."

"Lavender, I'm sure."

"Ah, yes!"

"But sir, after they have served the cause of the Peace-keepers—accidents do occur, substitutions are sometimes inadvertently made."

"Issi, you are on dangerous ground!" Blue's tone was low, amused.

"Treading very carefully, sir." A long pause. "Shall we expect an accident tomorrow? There would be time to send invitations for a very select few. A gastronomical triumph."

"Issi!" Blue said sternly.

"Sir!"

Lori, seething with fear and fury, could only guess at what unspoken understanding passed between them. She heard then the soft scuffling of leather on the floor as the Jassans turned away. Opening one eye just a slit, she saw them as they reached the door, saw where the Jassan in white pressed to cause the door to open.

". . . every hour without fail," Blue was saying as they passed through and the door began closing.

"Depend on it," White answered.

And the door closed tightly behind them.

Lori remained still for a long moment, the deep fury boiling inside her, fury that turned her fear into usable fuel.

"You bastards!" she screamed after them.

They had talked about Tippi as if she were a calf they were going to turn into veal parmigiana. And herself, too. What was she going to be? Pot roast?

She whipped her hands over her head, then brought them down with a hard swing that rolled her to her feet. She stood erect, stretching, a beautifully formed, perfectly conditioned, completely naked female. A few simple stretches told her she was unharmed. Then she went to kneel beside her child.

"Tippi," she whispered.

There was no reply. Tippi lay as if sleeping, on her back, breathing quickly. Thirteen. Budding breasts, swelling hips, the beginnings of shapeliness coming to still-too-slender legs. The young face was already showing signs of the woman she was going to be, with a broad forehead, slightly heavy brows, strong cheekbones, a generous mouth. Strength and intelligence were written there, even in sleep.

"Tippi, wake up."

The Jassan had said they were not supposed to awaken for another day, but being a human being and not a bassoe, she had awakened a day early. "Tippi!" she whispered. She shook her child's shoulder with a gentle hand. Nothing. Then she cupped her child's face in both her hands.

"Tippi," she pleaded. "Tippi—for godsake, wake up!"

And then, at last—

"Mom—Mom—" The brown eyes cleared rapidly as intelligence came with the return to wakefulness. "What's goin' on?" Then, sharply: "You're naked! Where are your clothes?"

"I haven't any. Neither have you."

Tippi sat up, alarmed. "Hey!" Her eyes flashed down at her naked body, then quickly at her surroundings. "Where are we? Why are we naked?"

"We've been kidnapped," Lori said.

"Yeah, but—naked?"

"Our nakedness doesn't mean anything to Jassans," Lori said. "We're like bassoes to them—animals."

"They got a nerve!"

"All right!" Lori was firm. She pulled Tippi to her feet.

"You're naked, I'm naked. We've got to live with it. We *can* live with it. Are you all right—otherwise, I mean?"

Tippi tried herself. "Good as ever."

"Fine. C'mon, we've gotta get out of here."

"Like this? Bare-ass?"

"Yes, bare-ass!" her mother said. "We'll get decent when we can. Just now, the trick is going to be getting out! I know how to open the door. Stand to the side."

Tippi waited, back against the wall, while her mother pressed the wall where the white-clad Jassan had pressed it. The door hissed open. Beyond the open door was a corridor, a few closed doors, a right-angle turn.

"Where *are* we?" Tippi asked, whispering.

Lori peered cautiously up and down the corridor. She thought she knew where they were from the conversation she'd heard between the two Jassans. They were in a packing plant where bassoe meat was readied for market—but she didn't see the need to tell Tippi that.

"Doesn't matter," she said. "It's just no place for us!"

They moved into the corridor, their bare feet soundless on the smooth, tiled floor. Going naked gave them a feeling of being even more defenseless than they might otherwise have felt. Tippi giggled nervously. Lori felt goosebumps. And having no known destination, no pathway to escape, she had to fight panic with every step. Every step might be leading them into an even more dangerous predicament.

At the turn, Lori paused to peer around the corner. Another short corridor led to a transparent door that revealed factory buildings, walkways, towers, and tanks beyond. There was a closed door in the short corridor wall on the right, a large window on the left.

"I have to go to the bathroom," Tippi said.

"Can't now!" Lori said.

"But Mom—"

"I said hold it," Lori told her. "I want to peek through those windows." She began a cautious approach.

"I can't."

"Can't what?" Lori had reached the windows.

"Hold it."

There was a soft, pneumatic hiss behind Lori, but she didn't heed it. She had reached the windows, and what she saw through them had grabbed her full attention. With caught breath, wide-eyed, she stared in shock and sick dismay.

The area below was two stories down, a wide area opening to the outside, and filing in from the outside was a line of bassoes, clad only in their soft, gray fur, moving slowly but without resistance into a tiled area filled with gleaming equipment, where Jassans clad in white, liquid-proof garments worked with practiced efficiency to stun them, cut their throats, eviscerate them, and hang their carcasses on traveling overhead hooks to be carried away.

Lori, choking back vomit, turned to hold Tippi away, to protect her from the sight, only to discover that she had vanished. And then the door hissed open and Tippi appeared, smiling. The door closed behind her.

"Was that a restroom?" Lori asked.

"No."

"Then you—didn't—"

"Yeah, I did."

"Tippi! How could you?"

"There was a kind of a wastebasket."

"I didn't mean where! I meant—"

"Mom, if you gotta, you gotta."

"Never mind!"

Lori grabbed Tippi to hold her away from the window. "Come on, come on," she said, and pushed Tippi to the outer door, and through it, when she had it opened.

"Come *on!*"

"But—naked, Mom! Geez!"

They found themselves on an outer landing, three floors above the ground, in what was probably the administration building of the large meat-packing plant. An outer stairway led to upper floors and eventually to ground level. Lori saw a distant gate, where a guard paced. Several freight vehicles moved between the buildings. A white-clad Jassan carrying a clipboard moved along a lower walkway. Lori was trying to decide which way to go when the alarm suddenly began honking through the receptor in her head. Tippi heard it too.

"Mom! They know!"

Activity burst out all over the place. Lizard-men came running out of buildings into the street below, some armed, some not, hunting, looking. Several had the huge mastiff-size beetles that were used to herd and guard. Now the beetles were turned loose. They ran, scurrying about on their many rickety legs, long, clawlike mandibles clicking open and shut, antennae waving, searching. Lori, terrified, turned back to the door and tried to open it.

"Locked! Damn it!"

There was nothing left but to run higher, and they did, climbing the stairs that led upward. They were seen as they climbed. The silent shouts of the Jassans came clearly through Lori's and Tippi's receptors, adding speed to their racing feet. They reached the top of the flight, breath tearing in their lungs, to find themselves on a flat roof studded with shedlike buildings. Lori saw a door in an alcove of one of the buildings. She urged Tippi that way, running through scattered refuse that had been left, unwanted and forgotten, on the rooftop. Along the way, Lori found a length of metal she could use as a club.

The door was locked.

They were trapped in the alcove. Tippi found a club and they crowded shoulder to shoulder, backs to the wall, to face the first guard beetle as it came off the stairway and onto the roof. The sunlight struck gold lights from the beetle's hard shell, from its bulbous, many-faceted eyes. Its antennae were erect, quivering; the long and powerful mandibles with their serrated inner edges were clacking eagerly. The huge insect came to a sliding halt just in front of the naked woman. A second and third insect followed to range beside the first, blocking all escape. But they were held at bay, at least for a moment, by the upraised clubs in the hands of Lori and Tippi, by the desperate, snarling courage on their faces and in their eyes.

The first and nearest beetle elevated itself on its six legs until its height was equal to Lori's; now she could see the mouth parts of the beetle working like meshing knives. It seemed to Lori those knifelike parts would cut through steel as easily as naked flesh. The other beetles shuffled, then elevated, mandibles clacking, antennae waving, eyes glittering.

"Get back of me!" Lori cried.

The nearest beetle attacked. The wide-open mandible was thrust at Lori, a serrated jaw scraping either side of her waist.

She had the club raised high, and she brought it down with all her strength on the nearest of the giant insect's eyes, blinding it, causing it to snap the mandible tightly around her. The giant insect lifted her, wheeling away. She screamed with pain and fury, struggling, beating at the insect, flesh torn, bleeding. A second insect lunged in and caught Tippi, held her high, and wheeled.

Tippi screamed in pain.

Lori knew she was being eaten.

Killed by bugs! her mind screamed in anguish.

As she was spun in the mandible of the giant beetle, she had a fleeting glimpse of a Jassan. He was one of the guards, standing at the rooftop edge. He seemed untroubled as he pointed a yellow tube—

A Jassan voice drifted into Lori's awareness.

"You're sure about that?"

"Absolutely."

"But to excise only a very small amount of memory—this particular amount of memory—it doesn't seem possible."

"It's been done, I assure you. They will remember being kidnapped. They will remember getting out of the storage room, running up the stairs, and finding the aircraft on the roof and flying it to safety. That's all they will remember."

"But the program in the adult?"

"Planted securely."

And the voices drifted away.

After looking down at the gate and the Jassan guarding it, and at the white-clad Jassan with the clipboard—and this was the way Lori and Tippi were to remember it all—Lori decided their only way to go was up the stairs. On reaching the roof, they found a two-seater aircraft sitting on a landing pad, almost as if waiting for them.

"Would you look at that, baby!" Lori cried to Tippi. "We got lucky for a change!"

"Can you fly it?" Tippi asked eagerly.

"Betcher damn life I can fly it!"

They raced to the aircraft and piled in. The key was in the switch, and it was only a moment before Lori had the craft airborne. Looking down, they saw no pursuit, and in the flight that followed, there was none.

"How come?" Tippi wanted to know.

"Kidnappers, honey," Lori told her. "They won't admit even *knowing* their victims, once the victims get loose."

It made some kind of sense.

And after only a few wrong turns, Lori was able to find their way back to Guss's place. She brought the craft in for a landing near an entrance to their sleeping quarters. Once they were on firm ground, they collapsed into each other's arms, great waves of relief washing away the terror.

"Mom," Tippi said finally. "You're absolutely *it*!"

"What's an 'it'?"

"A champion. I'm going to see you get a medal."

Lori gave her a hug. "Right now, I'd rather have my panties. I've been bare-ass long enough. How about you?"

"Aaaaah! I dunno. Gettin' so I kind of like it."

Lori batted her lovingly, and they ran for the house.

CHAPTER 17

The War Room was deep underground.

It was very deep, Harry Borg was sure, because to reach the area from the surface had taken five minutes of plunging after a stomach-lifting first moment of drop to gain near free-fall velocity. They were under what he would have called the Rocky Mountains had he been in his own world. Somewhere around Denver.

"We've got a War Room in our Rocky Mountains," he told Guss, who, along with Chad Harrison and assorted military brass, was traveling with him. "Never been inside it, of course, but I've seen pictures. Strategic air, submarine, intercontinental ballistic missiles—all controlled from that one center with electronics you wouldn't believe."

His tone may have been a little smug.

"Good for you," Guss said.

And Harry knew his tone had been smug. When Guss talked like that—patronizing, sort of—there was generally a comedown just beyond the bend. This time was no exception.

When their pneumatic-tube conveyance had opened its doors to no obvious command, Harry found himself in an underground cavern so vast it could have housed a city of considerable size. Pillars of gleaming metal a thousand feet high supported a sky of solid rock arched above tall buildings, wide thoroughfares, park areas, and even a lake. Harry could discover no apparent source for the light. It was just there, a soft, comfortable glow, everywhere the same, so that shadows were almost nonexistent.

But it was not any of this that held Harry in genuine awe.

"It's all *empty*," he said. "Nobody here!"

"Been unused for centuries," Guss said.

The streets were silent, still. There was ancient refuse on the pavements; there were broken windows, like blinded eyes, staring; there were great, dripping ropes of webbing left by some giant insects; there was a stalagmite in the center of a boulevard reaching up toward a stalagmite somewhere in the rock ceiling where limewater dripped.

"Once a great nation," Chad Harrison whispered. "Gone now."

"Like Egypt. Could be the tomb of Ramses the Second."

"Has that look, that feel, that smell."

"Gentlemen," Guss spoke the quiet reminder.

The military brass were waiting impatiently beside a buslike vehicle. Harry and Chad followed Guss to join them. They were transported swiftly along a roadway that entered solid rock again through great doors of metal. The doors closed behind them with a deep, vaultlike sound that perhaps only Harry and Chad could hear, and they found themselves in the War Room at last.

Large enough to house the Superdome, the War Room was cut in many levels, so that a viewer could look down on screens displaying land surfaces and up to see the skies on other screens in most realistic perspectives. Everywhere there was what Harry would call high-tech gear. The huge room was solidly packed from one far reach to the other, but only a relatively small corner—an area the size of a high school gymnasium—was lighted and being used. The rest stood dark and silent, dust-layered, crumbling.

The tenth of the room that was being used, that was lighted and operative, was filled with equipment technically far superior to any the two men had seen or imagined to be in use by their own government. Most spectacular were huge 3-D television screens showing live pictures being taken by cameras equipped with incredible lenses.

Harry was staggered by the wizardry of it all. "Absolutely flabber-damn-gasted!" was the way he was to describe his feelings later. But, since he was Commander-in-Chief, he felt he had to act like he'd been using equipment even more advanced than this for years.

"Adequate," he said. "Rather good, in fact."

"Gee, thanks," Guss whispered sarcastically.

He couldn't fool Guss.

Chad could afford to be impressed. "With stuff like this, they're losing?"

"It takes more than stuff," Harry said portentously.

"A great deal more," Guss agreed.

Then Harry was introduced to the very top military brass of the Jassan Armed Forces. The Chairman of the Joint Chiefs, General Mass, reminded Harry of Kaiser Wilhelm of Germany without the mustache: excessively military, bemedaled, ribboned, braided, helmeted, aged, and portly. And, Harry was to learn, just as ineffective. The others were: General of the Army Luss; General of the Air Force Hoss; Admiral of the Navy Biss. They were all richly uniformed, all elderly, some thin and rickety, others, like Mass, gone round with easy living.

Harry made a little speech, keeping it as short as possible, ending with: "I'm sure we'll work very well together."

There was no outward indication of resentment at giving over their authority to Harry Borg, though Harry's voice receptor picked up a muttered reaction that, when translated into his kind of language, went, "A damned bassoe telling *me* how to fight a war? I've *eaten* a thousand of his kind!" Harry decided to let the comment go unremarked.

He could afford to.

Among them, physically at least, he was a Goliath. He stood head and shoulders above them, a great figure of a man. Wide of shoulder, slim of hip, long of leg, shirt open on a hairy chest, sleeves rolled on bulging biceps. At his waist, belted, the short sword on one hip, pistol on the other.

And standing beside him was Chad Harrison—smaller, younger, still growing—an equally impressive specimen. His sun-bleached hair was almost white now, contrasting with the deep tan of his face; a good face with gray eyes, a quick smile, a cleft chin. At nineteen and six-two, he had the body of an athlete in his prime, lean, muscled, powerful. He wore the same weapons Harry wore—short sword and pistol—and the same air of confidence in his ability to use them.

Together they were a pair of the best examples the human race had to offer, and they were, the way Harry made the comparison, far and away better than any damned Jassan, that was for sure! Maybe not smarter, in certain ways, but, by God, all-around better!

The fact that he and Chad and the other Homo sapiens were actually repulsive—except when cooked—in the eyes of most Jassans didn't matter at all. That was their problem.

His problem was to win their goddamn war!

Within six months!

Or they all would lose their asses.

And, oh, yes—he never lost sight of this—his long-term problem was to open up commerce between his world and theirs. The rejuvenation skills of the surgeon Sassan, once he was able to get them into a bottle with a nice label, so to say, was going to make Harry the richest man between the North and South poles.

But right now . . .

"Show me the situation," he said sharply, all direct, forceful energy, so much in contrast to their laid-back way. "The enemy lines, our lines, the comparative strengths, the weaponry in use and in reserve, our plans and what we know of theirs."

It took three days of hard study. Three days of studying aerial photographs, wide-angled enough to encompass a three-state area, or close up enough to read the fine print on a bank-loan contract. Three days of reading translated intelligence reports and reports on their known weaponry and strengths and resources. And when he had assimilated all this, sorted it carefully in his head, and was ready to make a final, intelligent, carefully weighed assessment of their chances, he made it in the seclusion of the quarters he shared with Chad and Guss.

"We're dead," he said with absolute conviction.

"And buried," Chad agreed.

Guss moved the gray film across his large yellow eyes, an action that registered a patient willingness to endure their human, and therefore unexplainable, eccentricities for as long as he thought it polite—about three seconds, in this case—then cleared it back. He flicked his long, supple, forked tongue at each in turn and folded his eight-fingered hands before him.

"Bullshit!" he said.

"Guss!" Harry pretended shock. To Chad: "He talks dirty!"

"I heard," Chad said. "And it's just awful!"

"The words are yours," Guss said, "but the thought is mine, and there is nothing dirty about it. I know you're putting me on—that you have no intention of admitting defeat. So, to use your expression, let's take the problem by the face."

And this, when "taken by the face," was the problem: The Ussir Armed Forces, the Green Guys for short, had after centuries of desultory fighting won everything east of what Harry and Chad knew as the Mississippi River. And that area extended all the way around the globe to about the western border of what would be China.

A fair piece of real estate.

The western headquarters of the Green Guys was a huge military complex that had once been the city of Usso. It was situated at the tip of one of four great lakes. "Looks like Lake Michigan and the city of Chicago," Chad had said. "And there's Lake Erie and Lake Ontario run together so it's one lake."

Harry agreed. "Somebody up there didn't read his geography," he said. What concerned Harry most was a buildup in arms and equipment he had discovered in the Usso/Chicago military complex. It far exceeded any requirement of a "conventional arms" war intended to maintain a status quo, as Chairman of the Joint Chiefs Mass had insisted.

"They are as unwilling as we are," General Mass had said, "to escalate this engagement into a serious conflagration."

"Unwilling," Harry had said. "That's it!"

"What?"

"The operative word," Harry had said with considerable vehemence. "Unwillingness. You people, the Jassans, have been and are now unwilling to face up to the fact you have problems, to seek out your problems, to recognize your problems when you find them, to actively hunt for solutions to your problems, to actively implement those solutions, if and when you stumble on them. Apathy is another name for it—don't get involved, don't feed it, and maybe it'll go away. That's not a dangerous attitude, old man. That's a *lethal* attitude. It will kill you!"

General Mass had been huffily offended. "I have always felt that certain restraint is commendable."

"In a war," Harry had said, "restraint will get your ass busted!"

Now, in the apartment with Chad and Guss, he said, "I want an overflight of that complex, Guss, a see-it-with-my-own-eyes. They may be tricking those cameras—I got a feeling they are."

"It would be very dangerous," Guss cautioned.

Harry snorted. "There you go! Unwillingness, restraint, caution—all your kind have the same disease. It's gonna kill you if I can't cure it." He gave Guss a hard grin.

"I'm going on that flight, you hear?"

"Then you'll have to go within two weeks."

"Why's that?"

"Truce Time."

"Come again?"

"The first twelve-day period after Bissis, which would come"—he thought a moment—"in mid-October, your time. That was designated truce time at the Convention of All Powers a hundred and sixty-five years ago. Truce Time is a time of universal peace. A sacred covenant. No fighting is permitted."

"You're jerking me!"

"I couldn't be more serious," Guss insisted quietly. "During that twelve-day period, instead of fighting, both sides meet on neutral ground and engage in various contests of strength and skill—games, I think you call them."

Harry and Chad were incredulous.

"Games?" Harry's voice was shrill with disbelief. "Both sides? Together? Feats of strength? Contests of skill? Why ever in the hell would they think up a dumb thing like that?"

"Purposes of morale, as I understand it," Guss said. "It breaks the monotony of fighting, the boredom. The lot of a common soldier is a tedious one, you know? And it was generally accepted that truce time would give them something to look forward to." Guss examined the eight fingernails of his left hand in an offhand way. "I have given concerts at the last two—and was very well received, if I may say so."

Harry and Chad were exchanging looks of utter bafflement.

"He's gonna tell us next they stop around four o'clock every day and have tea together," Harry said.

"They often, in very hot weather—" Guss said seriously.

"That's enough!" Harry shouted.

At that moment, perhaps fortuitously, a servant came in with the information that there was a message for Harry on the big screen in the main lounge of their quarters. "A female bassoe."

"Lori!" Harry shouted, up and running.

He had given up Lori and Tippi as gone forever when he'd learned they had been abducted by the Peacekeepers in his absence. Sos Vissir had professed to know nothing of their abduction; had, in fact, been furious that it should have happened, that his precious museum pieces had been stolen, perhaps damaged, even eaten.

Harry skidded around a corner into the lounge—and there she was! Not live, but seemingly so, on the life-size 3-D screen with Tippi beside her. Radiantly beautiful, she was wearing a near-transparent gown of silk. Her hair, soft about her shoulders, gleamed golden brown, her gray eyes, beneath the strong brows were both very angry and very concerned. Tippi, a gaminelike copy of her mother, grinning her usual mischievous grin, was only very happy to see Harry again, no strings attached.

"Harry!" Lori exclaimed. "Where the hell have you been?"

"Lori, I—"

"I've been trying for days!" Lori's torrent went on. "No one would tell me where you were. I've worried myself sick. Were you dead? Were you alive? Were you eaten? Harry, you shouldn't *do* that to me! I just—"

"Hey!" Harry interrupted.

"Well?" she demanded.

"I'm okay! I've been busy is all. I—"

"*You've* been busy!" Lori, hurt, rushed on, voice climbing with indignation. "What about Tippi and me? Didn't you care that we'd—we'd been kidnapped? Perhaps eaten? If you knew how close we came—"

"C'mon, sweetheart! Of course I cared!"

"You didn't come after us!"

"I tried!" Harry was getting a little desperate. "There was a ransom demand. We were trying to negotiate—" Sudden realization came to him. "Where *are* you? You still a prisoner?"

"We're home—at Guss's place."

"But the Peacekeepers—how'd you get loose?"

"We escaped!" Tippi broke in proudly. "Mom swiped an airplane and flew us home!"

"No kidding!"

"Naked," Tippi said. "Bare-ass!"

"Tippi!" her mother yelled at her.

"Well, it's true—"

Lori grabbed her daughter and clamped a hand over her mouth. "They took our clothes," Lori said defensively. "We didn't have any choice but to run naked. And the Jassans don't care, Harry. No human saw us."

"Lori, it's all right. Just so you're home safe!"

Chad and Guss had come into the lounge, and Harry turned to glance at them, so proud he could hardly stand it. "Y'hear that? Lori and Tippi got loose and got home! Stole a plane and flew it home! Talk about guts!"

He turned back, glowing. "I'm proud of you! Proud of you both!"

"It couldn't have been easy," Guss said.

"How'd you do it, Mrs. Calder?" Chad asked.

"They'd zapped us with one of those—what d'you call 'ems?— mind-blankers. They thought we'd be out for another day or so. I peeked and saw how they opened the door. We sneaked out, went up on the roof, and there was the Cassal with the keys in it. We swiped it and flew home."

"They were going to eat me," Tippi said. "Mom heard 'em."

"We were in a meat-packing plant, Harry," Lori said. "Sos Vissir's meat plant where they slaughter bassoes. They were going to fake an accident and serve Tippi up for the plant manager's dinner. A gourmet repast—I heard 'em, Harry. I swear to God—"

"Hey!" Harry said hurriedly. "You're safe now, and I'm coming right home. Be there in an hour or so. Okay? I've got a couple of things to do."

Harry took up the TV remote control.

"Listen, Harry," Lori began.

"An hour, honey. Okay?"

He pushed the button, and the screen went back to frosted glass. He turned to the others, a little sheepish about the scolding he'd taken, but still very, very proud that Lori, a human female, had had the courage, the wit, and the skill to get away from her Jassan captors.

"Some kind of a gal!" he said to Guss and Chad. "How about

that! Didn't even have a stitch of clothes, and she still got loose?
What I call gutsy! All the way!"

Chad agreed with him wholeheartedly. He, too, took immense
pride in the fact that two naked human females could defeat the
best the Jassans had to offer.

"Got to hand it to her," he said. "She's super."

Guss was not so pleased.

He was very distressed, in fact.

"Harry," he said, after Harry and Chad had basked in the
glow of Lori's accomplishment until it seemed they both must
aquire a deep tan. "Can I speak truthfully?"

"Sure!" Harry said. "Go right ahead!"

They'd had several glasses of vassle, the euphoria-inducing
drink, in celebration of Lori's escape and return home, and that,
together with the genuine relief at having Lori and Tippi safe,
had lifted him to a very considerable high.

"You're not going to like it," Guss said.

"C'mon now, old buddy!" Harry said.

"I mean it," Guss said.

And apparently he did. His long, forked tongue was almost
a blur, flicking toward Harry; he kept lifting his muzzle the way
Harry had learned he did when upset. Harry sobered out of
consideration for his friend.

"Try me, Guss," he said.

Then Guss said quickly, bluntly, "You've got to kill her."

Harry felt a sudden sinking feeling, as if the bottom was
dropping out of everything. He looked quickly at Chad, and saw
that the young man was feeling the same thing: stunned.

"Did I hear you right?" Harry asked.

"You've got to kill her, Harry," Guss said.

Harry took another moment, staring at Guss, his face gone
white, stricken silent. It wasn't entirely what Guss had said; it
was nearly as much that Guss, his most trusted friend, had said
it. He didn't believe it. He didn't *want* to believe it. But he had
to believe it, because now Guss was saying, "You couldn't kill
her, I know. But I can have it done for you, Harry. You won't
need to know a thing about it—just that she and the young
one are gone. It will be painless. And they wouldn't be
eaten."

"Good Christ Almighty!" Harry suddenly roared. "Have you

lost your mind? Why in the name of all that's holy would I let anybody kill Lori and Tippi?"

"If you don't kill her, she'll kill you."

"Goddamn it!" he yelled. "You're outa your stupid head!"

Harry was on his feet now, face red with fury, the cords of his neck rigid. Guss got to his feet to stand facing him, plainly afraid, but giving not an inch. Chad, very alert, deeply concerned, got between them, facing Harry.

"Listen to him, sir!" Chad said. "You've got to do that!"

"I'll wring his—"

"Listen, first!"

Harry and Chad locked eyes, chest to chest. The moment was very tense, with Harry on the brink of violence, and Chad determined to be the first casualty—and then it was Harry who gave ground as sanity and reason overcame his blind fury.

"Yeah, yeah," he said.

"He's trying to tell you something."

"Yeah."

"Something we don't know."

"All right." Harry swelled his chest in a deep breath and exhaled it slowly. "Sorry, Guss. You wouldn't say a thing like that if—if you didn't have a reason. I know you wouldn't."

"You're right—I know what she means to you," Guss said.

That deflated Harry. He poured himself a large glass of vassle, took it to a recliner, and slumped there. He looked at Guss a long moment.

"So tell me," he said.

Chad poured a glass of vassle for himself and one for Guss. He dropped the straw in Guss's, gave it to him, and they both sat down. After they'd all taken a drink and Guss was sure that Harry was calm, he spoke quickly and quietly.

"Lori couldn't have escaped from the Peacekeepers," he said. "It's not possible. I know you'd like to think that a human could do it, especially a human female, that two naked human females could do it. But, no, Harry. As you say, 'No way!'"

"Damn it, Guss! They did!"

Guss held up an eight-fingered hand. "Not possible, Harry."

"They're loose, ain't they? They—"

He broke off what was going to be another angry outburst,

clamping his jaws, staring at Guss, his dark blue eyes burning beneath his scowling brows. Guss spoke almost gently.

"They let her go, Harry. If she found a Cassal with the keys in it, ready to fly, it was because they left it there for her to use."

After a long fight, Harry had to recognize the probability of that being true. Either that, or Lori and Tippi had been impossibly lucky, and a sensible man didn't believe in that kind of luck. He searched for an acceptable answer and finally found one.

"Well, all right," he said with relief. "So they let her go. It figures they would, after they'd thought it over for a while. They came to realize I'd make them pay, and pay big! And the first one to pay would be that damned Sos Vissir!" He was on his feet now, planning vengeance. "It was his meat-packing plant. I'm still going to have that bastard's head on a platter—"

He broke it off when he realized that Guss was sitting quietly, gray inner lids covering his golden eyes, waiting patiently for him to settle down. Harry drew an uncertain breath.

"There's more?"

The golden, vertically slitted eyes cleared, and the long tongue flicked out toward Chad, whom he recognized as a cool, clear head.

"This is the hard part," he said to Chad.

"Give it to him," Chad said. He got to his feet.

"Why would they let her go?" Guss asked Harry.

"Scared?" Harry asked tentatively. "Worried what I would do?"

"No."

"Then why?"

"To kill you," Guss said.

"How in the hell—"

"Hypnosis!" Chad said. "They programmed her!"

"Something like that," Guss said. "I'm sure she doesn't even know it has been done to her. But it has been done. Take my word for it. Unless they could get what they wanted most by letting her go, they would give a thousand lives to keep her. And what do they want most?"

Harry didn't answer.

Chad said, "To kill the Commander-in-Chief of the Jassan Armed Forces: Harry Borg."

"Right!" Guss said.

Harry sat quite still, rigid, hands gripping his bare knees, his hot blue eyes staring, the muscles in his jaw working, as his mind attacked the problem, searching for an answer he could live with. And finally he found it. His mind held it, turned it, and felt a growing, burning triumph. Then he spoke slowly, with great emphasis.

"It—won't—work."

Guss looked at Chad and lifted his shoulders helplessly.

Chad looked at Harry, waiting.

"They might try!" Harry said. "All right, I'll give you that. They *did* try! But it won't work. Not with humans! You can't hypnotize, program—whatever—a human being to do something that goes against his or her nature. That I know! I'm talking about *human* beings, now. Not Jassans. Maybe you could do it with Jassans; I wouldn't know. But I do know you can't do it with humans!" He looked at Chad. "Isn't that right, son? You've read that, surely?"

Chad felt a growing relief. "By God, I have!"

"There y'go!" Harry said to Guss.

"Harry—" Guss tried.

But Harry was on a roll, picking up authority, and he plunged on. "Have you ever done it to a human before?"

"No, of course not."

"Then you don't *know* that you can!" He was triumphant now. "I think I can say I know humans better than you do. Oh, you Jassans could have tried, all right. And I expect you did. But it won't work. Absolutely not. And I'll stake my life on that!"

"You're determined?" Guss asked.

"I am!"

Guss lifted his glass of vassle and turned it slowly in his many-fingered hand so that the liquid glowed softly purple. His long, supple tongue flicked slowly, caressingly, tiredly. Then he gestured with the glass toward Harry, a salute.

"My friend," he said.

"Yeah?"

Guss spoke softly. "Been nice knowin' yuh."

CHAPTER 18

It was not an ordinary homecoming.

It was not a meeting of two people, deeply in love, who had been separated for a brief while for whatever reason. This was a meeting between two people, one of whom had died, as far as the other knew, who had been given up by that other person as gone forever, who had been grieved over brokenheartedly, and who had then been put away as a treasured memory—but who was now, somehow, miraculously restored to wonderful, radiant life.

"It's—it's like a second chance," Harry whispered, holding her close, breathing the warm perfume of her hair, trying to find the words. "A new beginning."

Lori tipped her head back to look at him. "D'you really love me, Harry?" she asked. "I mean *that* much?"

They were standing in the front hallway, the door still open from Harry's entrance, his bags fallen where he'd dropped them when he'd opened his arms to catch her rush. Tippi had followed her mother, and she was standing near them, her nose a bit wrinkled.

"More than you know," Harry said to Lori with the greatest sincerity. "More than I could possibly tell you."

"Harry."

"Lori."

"How yucky can two people get?" Tippi asked.

Then she ran, as Harry chased her, whooping a threat to paddle her behind.

Guss made his presence known, expressed his happiness that Lori and Tippi were home safe, gave Harry a look that may have been sweet sorrow—with Jassans, Harry had found, it was hard to be sure—and said something to the effect that they must surely want to share their happiness without a fourth person getting in the way. Harry gave him a hearty thump on the back.

"Nonsense!" he said. "You're more than welcome!"

It was getting so he lied a lot.

But about his lack of fear that Lori might have been hypnotized—programmed, whatever—to do him in, he was absolutely straight-arrow. She couldn't be hypnotized to kill the man she so deeply loved. He knew that absolutely. He was so sure of it, in fact, that he almost told Lori all about it, to show her how ridiculous he thought it was, so they could both have a laugh. Then he decided not to tell her. Why frighten her with the thought that lurking somewhere deep in her subconscious there might be an order to murder him, an order she would have to obey, wanting to or not? Why, a thought like that could very well drive her bats!

Kill him? Naw!

He kept saying it.

She couldn't be hypnotized into doing a thing like that. No way! And even if she could—and he was damned proud of this—she would find he was a very hard man to kill! Kill him? A woman? Never! He didn't even need to take any precautions— he was that absolutely sure. Well, maybe a little one? A little one couldn't hurt.

"C'mon!" he scoffed at himself. "What am I? A damned coward?"

Naw!

And he took that faith, that staunch masculine confidence, with only a little crack in it—in the back of his mind there lurked the knowledge that Guss was a pretty smart turkey when it came right down to the nuts and bolts of it—to bed when it was time to get on to other things of a more pleasurable nature.

A woman kill me? were his final thoughts. *No way!*

It had been a beautiful evening, replete with good food and

good, euphoria-inducing wine. A warm retelling of her adventures of the past few days had given Tippi a chance to enjoy center stage, and a witty, sparkling, mischievous, and, to her mother's despair, sometimes salty-talking tale-teller she had proved to be.

"She's not my kid," Lori had said. "I'd be ashamed."

"Oh, poop!" Tippi had responded, grinning impishly.

"See!" her mother had yelled, and gave her a hit.

When it had come time to separate for the night, Tippi had gone disconsolately to her room, the doll-like Poopsalot—whom she had managed to potty-train—chirping along at her side. "Grown-ups have all the fun," she had said to Poopsalot.

The little bassoe had *baa*ed agreement to that.

And fun it proved to be.

But it was not alone fun and games. There was a deep, emotional communication far more important to both than the sexual exercise that was deeply rewarding. They fell asleep in each other's arms, completely happy, warmly secure. Harry slept on his back, his right arm hanging beside the bed. Lori slept curled inside his left arm, her head resting on his shoulder and chest. Harry's sleep was very deep and dreamless.

Lori awakened after about an hour.

CHAPTER 19

Her name was Illia, though she was not born with that name. Bassoes, unless raised as pets, were never given names; they were raised as herd animals, and there was never any need to identify them as individuals.

Chad Harrison had given her the name, the same night he had given her the tattoo on the inside of her lower lip. *I*s and *L*s were easier to inscribe with dots in the tender inner tissue than letters or numbers with curves. Thus, Illia. And the name had a pleasant feel on his tongue, a lilt that he liked, even when whispered.

She liked it.

She had liked it when he had first given the name to her, though it must have pained her severely. Her eyes had teared, but she had held perfectly still, almost unwincing as he worked with the sharpened penpoint and ink in kind of a cold, desperate fury to mark a bassoe—*a meat animal*—he'd found to be intelligent. And when he'd spoken the name to her in a kind of "Me Tarzan, you Jane" routine, she'd shown something far more than pleasure, far more than delight: a deep, shuddering gratitude that brought a flood of tears, that made her clasp his hands and press them to her lips in what had to be her first kiss, given or received. The Cowardly Lion couldn't have felt more when he had been given courage, the Tin Woodsman more when he'd been given a heart, or the Scarecrow more when he'd been given wit.

She had been given identity.

How much that mattered! To be somebody. To be one of a kind: *me*!

When Chad had decided to give her the mark, it had been only so that he would be able to recognize her should they meet again. But when it was brought clearly to the front of his mind how much being an individual could mean, he couldn't risk her losing it; though her individuality was, to be sure, the smallest part of what she was scheduled to lose—and that was her life to the butcher's knife.

Her eyes had never been like the eyes of other bassoes, lighted windows behind which no one lived. From the first, hers had held an inquiring spark, but now they had become warm and luminous and live. Her eyes were large and iridescent brown, long-lashed, in a face as finely formed as any girl Chad had ever known; quite beautiful, even though covered for the most part, as was the rest of her, with soft, gray fur.

After that first dispute over whether he could keep her or not, with all five humans standing between her and the lizzie keepers— a fight to the death plainly the issue—Chad had had no trouble keeping her. If they thought he wanted her only for sexual purposes, that was fine with him; he was willing to accept any rationalization on their part so long as it achieved his purpose, which was to keep her alive, first of all, and then to learn the answer to three most mind-chilling questions:

Were bassoes normally without intelligence?

Was there only an occasional bassoe with intelligence?

Were all bassoes normally intelligent, but kept mindless from birth by some artificial means to keep them docile and blankly submissive for slaughtering as food animals?

Illia had had no knowledge of language in the beginning, and so in the short span of time between finding her and the appearance of Harry Borg he had not been able to establish any indepth communication with her. Once in his own residence, guarded by two of his own dedicated soldier lizard-men, however, and certain she would not be taken for a "booster" treatment of some sort, he had set up a crash program to establish a line of communication that would tap her store of knowledge.

Homer, Arnie, Eddie, and Sam—the five young men lived in a closely guarded, very plush apartment complex ten minutes by air from Guss's place, and all of them joined in the effort, working in relays, for her hunger to learn could exhaust a single teacher in a few hours. Together they had transformed her from a near-vacuum to an active, thinking, participating member of their group.

Chad's female, to be sure, by mutual consent.

That they had succeeded in even a limited way in so short a time was remarkable. And something to contemplate. The brain was there, in a bassoe, fully capable. Intelligent? How intelligent? She was quick, she was sharp, she was eager. She had an intelligence quotient of about 110, Chad thought, possibly 115, though he could not rate her against any known norm.

"You're a smart cookie!" was the way he rated her.

That, for him, said it all, and never mind that the rating was not recognized by the faculty of any college. It said it all for her, too, for a gorgeous smile lighted her face and eyes. She had such beautiful, expressive eyes, and her smile revealed teeth no Hollywood caps could match.

"I—like—you!" she responded to his compliment.

"Atta girl!"

Stroking her gently curving side, her swelling hip, as they lay together, he thought again she had a figure any Miss America would envy: all things perfectly proportioned, perfectly balanced, exactly in place. He teased her and he smiled at her immediate, almost eager excitement.

"Fur's not the only thing you've got like a mink," he said.

"Is bad?" she asked, concerned.

"Is good!" he said, and embraced her warmly.

Later, as they lay relaxed, he stroked the soft fur on her cheek with a fingertip. The fur, shaped nicely about her eyes, nose, and mouth, leaving them bare, was quite short and as smooth as the finest mink, a gray with a shine to it. He had become used to it easily, accepting it with not more difficulty than the women of his world accepted men with beards. And the fur that covered the rest of her body, while a bit longer and more dense, was still mink-soft and could be thought of, at least by him, as a body stocking of a quality and fit beyond skill and any price.

"When the women in my world see you in a bikini," he told her, "they're gonna go stark, raving kelly green with envy."

She knew it was a compliment and kissed him.

He moved his face against the hair of her head, hair that grew into a pleasing ruff before it fell, manelike, thick and luxurious below her shoulders.

"Besides," he whispered, "you smell great!"

But there were other things besides teaching her and making love, things that were deeply, frighteningly, starkly important, to come crashing back upon Chad and Illia, and Homer, Eddie, Arnie, and Sam as well.

A war to win in six months.

Or die.

And get eaten.

You want a chiller to wake up in the middle of the night? Try that one on for size! They'd put it to each other in just that way a dozen times:

"Shee-ucks!" Eddie would say. "Be worse'n flunkin' algebra!"

"Flippin' clown," Arnie would groan in pain.

"A black comic," Sam would agree. "The very worst kind!"

They—Eddie, Arnie, and Sam—had been given by Harry Borg, the Commander-in-Chief, the task of training a cadre, of turning basically pacifistic Jassan officers into killing machines.

"Don't know how you're gonna do it," Harry had said.

"Kick ass," Sam had said. "How else?"

"Go!" Harry had told them.

Three young men, not long out of high school, with almost no military training of their own, facing a line of complaisant but very tentative Jassan officers in the cold light of early morning on a parade ground—what do you do? You overpower, you dominate, you scare the steaming piss out of them.

"Kill or die!"

That was the voice of Sam Barnstable, really a giant of a man, bigger than any three Jassans, roaring at them like the blast of a hurricane wind from his implanted communicator, louder and with a greater fury than any Jassan had heard in a thousand years.

"Kill! Kill! Kill!"

Arnie and Eddie drove the words into them, their voices

cutting like the swords and bayonets they had decided to use in
the training in the hope that the basic savagery of those weapons
would awaken blood lust faster than would long-distance killers.

"Is it gonna work?" Homer asked.

Sometimes they thought maybe.

Sometimes they were not so sure.

CHAPTER 20

After awakening, Lori Calder lay quietly, rigid, almost unbreathing. She knew she was awake, yet it was a wakefulness like none she had ever experienced. Even the awakening in the meat-processing plant of Sos Vissir had not been like this. This time she remembered all the "before": the evening with Harry and Tippi, the going to bed, the making love, and the slipping away into euphoric sleep.

With *this* awakening, Lori felt as if she—or her mind—were somehow enclosed, as if in a sphere of glass, as if she were no more than a disinterested spectator, viewing and experiencing the life in the room—the soft hum of the air conditioning, the moonlight shadows on the wall, the beautiful draperies, the comfortable furniture, the deep-pile rugs—from a distance. She was perfectly aware of Harry, lying beside her, breathing in the slow, regular cadence that told of deep, relaxed sleep; but he had no presence: he was nothing, he meant nothing.

She raised herself to a sitting position, swung her legs to the side of the bed, and rose to her feet in one quiet, flowing motion that did not disturb Harry at all.

Standing, she was nude and beautiful. She was all that a mature woman could want to be, unmarked by childbirth or years, breasts firm and delicately nippled, waist slender, hips generous, and thighs that were fit and lean.

She combed her fingers up through her shining wheat-colored hair, letting it fall below her shoulders again as she extended her arms fully above her head. She held the position—arms extended upward, backs of wrists together, fingers gracefully aloft—a long moment, a beauty poised, before she let her hands flutter softly to her sides. Quietly then she moved toward the hall and the bedroom where Tippi lay sleeping.

Even walking she was, as she perceived herself, still a remote, distant figure for whom she felt no interest, really, other than a vague, fleeting curiosity. At the doorway of Tippi's bedroom, she was able to see Tippi lying quietly asleep in the light of a lamp the girl had left on, sprawled in that totally relaxed comfort only the very young are able to achieve.

Pretty child—but of no concern.

The naked woman turned from the doorway and made her silent way back to the bedroom where Harry was lying. He was sleeping as before, naked, lightly half covered by a sheet of silk, flat on his back. His right arm had fallen off the bed on the far side; his left arm was lying at his side, palm up, fingers curled. His head was back on the pillow, bearded chin jutting upward, his mouth, barely visible, open to slow breathing.

And he was nothing.

She went to the glass sliding doors. They were closed, locked. Outside them, a wide balcony hung over a precipitous drop to a valley, and above the balcony there was bare wall reaching fifty feet up to a tile roof. Lori knew of no reason for the naked woman to go to the glass door, no reason for her to stand inside it. While her eyes could see through the glass, there was nothing but black sky out there and the dim outline of the balcony. And yet the naked woman stood there.

Uninterested, uncaring.

That this room had been chosen by Harry for sleeping quarters because it was inaccessible from the outside, that a twenty-four-hour guard was maintained outside the room in the corridors, did not enter the mind of the naked woman. Those were factual matters, and the naked woman at the door, the woman Lori Calder was seeing from a distance, was impelled by some other force, unheard, unseen.

The naked woman moved to the door, unlocked it, and rolled it open silently. Only the soft current of air that moved the draperies and caressed Lori's own skin told of its opening. And the naked woman then stood in the open doorway in an attitude of waiting.

Waiting for what?

Of course! She was waiting for Bissi!

Bissi?

Bissi dropped, seemingly from the sky, but in truth from the rooftop above, spinning its own strand of web—for Bissi was a spider, an enormous spider.

Lori saw the naked woman bend in a curtsy of welcome, heard her whisper a soft "Bissi . . . Bissi" as she moved out of the way.

It was only of slight interest to Lori how that naked woman could have known the spider would come, and what the spider's name would be. But she found herself accepting both facts as being as they should be.

And she accepted the hugeness of the spider.

The spider came into the room to stand on eight hairy legs that spread much wider than the doorway. Its head was on a level with the woman's head, so that its four eyes were able to stare directly into the eyes of the woman. Even though she was remote from it all, Lori felt the power and strength that beamed from the two lower eyes, half-buried bulging eyes the size of basketballs that peered out of the hairy face. To look into them was to look into the open door of a furnace where fires lay banked, red, glowing. The upper pair of eyes, set wider, were sharply alert, watchful, adding outer vision, and Lori knew nothing could escape them. Extending forward on either side of the spider's head were shorter leglike appendages, hair-covered, meant for grasping, and between those were mouthparts from which protruded two black, curved, sharply pointed fangs, each a foot long—each, Lori knew without wondering, loaded with poison.

All was as it should be.

Bissi had come.

Lori watched the naked woman stand aside, calmly and untroubled, as the monstrous spider, trailing a strand of webbing larger than her small finger, crossed the room on those silent, claw-tipped legs. It went straight to the bed, where it paused to examine the still-sleeping man. Then, balancing artfully, careful not to awaken the man, the spider lifted itself over the bed, several legs against the far wall, so that its head and body were over the sleeping man, its needle-sharp fangs just above the exposed throat.

Still at a distance, still remote, still calmly detached, Lori watched the naked woman she knew to be herself stand idly by, her head bowed in reverence. For Bissi was of Holiness. Bissi was All. She, Lori, and the naked woman, somehow knew that.

And it was right.

She knew the poison, when injected, would liquify the internal organs of the man she knew to be Harry Borg. She knew that liquid would be sucked up and consumed by Bissi, leaving the man only a husk, making Bissi rich and full and even more powerful.

And that, too, was right.

Then Tippi screamed.

It was a mind-tearing scream of absolute terror. It came with such power, both vocally and mentally, that the giant spider was held, startled, for a brief instant—and a brief instant was enough for the awakened Harry to see those hideous, fang-armed mouth-parts poised above him, enough for him to coil his legs and kick with a force that sent the monster flying off him and across the room. The hand that had been out of sight beside the bed came up with a short sword fisted tightly, and Harry rolled from the bed to land on his feet, a blazing-eyed savage, roaring with fury.

Tippi, standing in the entrance to the hallway, clad in a thin, transparent gown, her face a tormented mask of fear, screamed again and again, holding the eight-legged, four-eyed, poison-fanged monster momentarily distracted.

Catching her breath in a ragged gasp, Tippi ran to the naked woman she thought to be her mother, wanting protection, wanting to give protection, only to find in the blank, unseeing eyes a total, uncaring stranger. And she was instantly repulsed and screamed again.

Harry Borg, naked, fully awake, every nerve on fire, every muscle convulsed into full readiness, stood in the center of the room, planted on widespread legs. He had never been more terrified. To awaken suddenly to a piercing scream, to find the hideous mouthparts, the great fangs of an enormous spider looming just above his face was the stuff of a nightmare beyond imagining.

But even as he had kicked out, then leaped to save his life, he had seen Lori standing naked and unharmed beside the open balcony door—a door that had been *locked*—and knew she had betrayed him. She *had* been programmed! Guss had been right: *He should have killed her! And there was that still to do!* And his fury had become a fire-storm that washed away his initial terror. He had a beast to fight, to kill.

Seconds to live.

Stupid fool to keep the sword! The thought raged through his mind as he watched the spider crouch to spring. *A handgun could blow him away!* The spider's fangs came up like lance points, aimed at Harry, the spider leaped—

God! How quick the damn thing could move!

Harry threw himself to the side in a powerful leap of his own, whipping the sword in a flashing arc that severed two of the spider's legs at the first joint, saving himself from the lancing fangs by scant inches. He was struck by the spider's bulbous abdomen as it passed, and he fell, trying for a thrust, missing. The sticky strand of web, extruding from the spinnerets at the spider's rear end, draped across Harry's legs and trapped him for precious seconds as the spider raced to climb the far wall.

Harry, struggling to cut himself free, saw the door of the apartment burst open. Three members of his Jassan guard, brought by Tippi's screams and his own mental roaring, rushed in, weapons drawn. A fervent "Thank God!" flashed into Harry's mind— and died there.

Instead of firing when they saw the giant spider, the three guards threw down their weapons and prostrated themselves, face down, arms spread in total obeisance.

"You bastards!" Harry screamed in rage. "Get up!"

They shivered, but they did not rise.

And Harry was left to do it alone.

Before he could reach the weapons of the guards, the giant spider raced across the wall to get above the guards, to pierce each guard quickly with a thrust of fangs that caused their bodies to leap convulsively and then lie still. And again the spider crouched, facing Harry, fangs lifted.

"You black crud!" Harry yelled hoarsely.

He crouched, his great, naked, powerfully muscled body gleaming with an oil of sweat, every muscle tense, the short sword ready. That shining blade of steel was a fang in its own right, a different kind, surely, but one the spider with two less legs than it had had before must have recognized as being as lethal as its own—for now its tactics changed.

A spider's first weapon is the web: Ensare, then kill. And now the spider began that effort in deadly earnest.

The creature could move with lightning speed, Harry discovered, traveling the walls and the ceiling, trailing thin, powerful cables of sticky excrescence, always trying to keep its body just out of reach of Harry's thrusting, slashing blade, trying to loop strands of sticky, entangling web across Harry's arms and shoulders.

Harry dived under a looping strand, whirled, cut it with a stroke, lunged on, leaped, and felt his blade bite through another leg. Near blinded with streaming sweat now, he counted three gone on one side. There was hope! Get one more on the same side and the beast was done for; the fourth that was left could barely hold it now—and then a looping strand of web fell on Harry, entangling him—and the hope was gone.

He couldn't swing the sword to cut the strand.

Roaring like an enraged bear, he dragged himself forward, dragging the sticky web, and, falling, lunged with his final strength and reach—

The blade sank cleanly, smoothly to the hilt.

Into the spider's abdomen!

Instantly, as if under great pressure, a gout of nastiness burst across his hand and forearm, and he whipped the blade hard, searching for more.

A scream of rage and agony seared in Harry's mind—it was the voice of Bissi.

The spider's legs began thrashing wildly, senselessly. It sank to the floor, screaming once more, the sound ripping through Harry's mind, then fading to a whimper, to nothing.

"Got you!" Harry's voice held savage triumph.

He pulled his sword free and cut away the web strands that hindered him. Then, with one last roar of rage, he lifted the sword high and with a full, overhand cut, struck through the stem that joined thorax and abdomen, cleaving the great spider in two.

He stood over the spurting pieces, his great chest heaving

with exertion, still filled with rage, watching the death throes of the giant spider, a triumphant savage.

"Die! Damn you!" he roared.

He heard then, "Oh, God! Harry!"

It was the voice of Lori Calder, sounding in an agonized wail of fear and realization. He turned, saw her naked, her hands pressed to her face. The death of the spider had somehow set her mind free. She was staring at him and at the dying spider with the kind of horror only a clear mind can feel. But Harry's rage at his betrayal blinded him. He went to her in long strides, sank his fingers, clawlike, into her hair, and jerked her head up, exposing her throat to the point of his blade.

"You traitor!" he yelled at her. "You filthy traitor!"

He was going to kill her!

He was going to kill her in a particularly bloody fashion, ripping her up the middle to spill her viscera onto the floor while she was still living, or he was going to behead her with a powerful stroke of the sword, leaving her head gripped by the hair in one hand, and her blood-spurting body lying on the floor—he was going to do one of these, or something even more terrible, in another moment, so great was the seething flame of fear and anger and revulsion that stormed in his mind.

And then a small yet wildly, desperately, insanely determined fury enveloped him, literally climbing his huge frame to beat at his face with small fists, to scream: "Stop it! Stop it! Let her go! Let her go!"

He released Lori's hair to protect his face from Tippi's battering, clawing hands; then he had to use the grip of his left arm to hold the child from falling—and in that moment Lori's life was saved.

He would have killed Lori, had it not been for Tippi's raging defense—he was sure of that later, to his everlasting shame—but the child's attack, distracting him, had given the red storm thundering in his mind a chance to break, for sanity to return. With sanity came the realization that Lori had not run from him when he'd let her go, but was, instead, clinging to him, her gray eyes enormous, frightened, pleading.

"Harry—dear God, what have I done?"

And he knew then that she was not at fault.

He threw the sword from him with a new kind of anger, an

anger at himself for the false accusation that had almost caused him to murder the woman he loved so desperately, who so desperately loved him. It was anger and anguish. He caught her to him, to hold both her and the child in his powerful arms.

"You didn't do anything. You were programmed by those damned Jassans! When they kidnapped you, they programmed you and turned you loose—to kill me."

"Harry!" She stared up at him, eyes wide. "I—let that monster in to—*kill* you?"

"It's all right. It didn't work, did it?"

"But, Harry, I must be still—"

"Mamma, no!" Tippi shrieked. "You're not! You're not!"

"C'mon, now! Cut it out!" Harry said, still holding them both. He tried to break through the terror that was creeping rapidly into Lori's tormented face. "I can handle it! I showed you. Even if you are still programmed, I can take care of it—of both of us!"

"How can I know, Harry?" The fear in her eyes was total. "How can I trust myself now?"

"Lori!" Harry said desperately. "I said I'd think of something!"

"He will, Mom! He can! I know he can!" Tippi said.

But Lori, staring at Harry, was not so sure.

CHAPTER 21

The building could not be entered.

That was what had been intended when it had been built, perhaps a thousand, perhaps two thousand years ago. There were no doors, no windows. A huge rectangular block of some obsidian material, glasslike in smoothness, at least a hundred feet in height, it covered an area of at least a hundred acres—an ominous and, though silent and unmoving, a somehow threatening presence.

Chad Harrison, standing in near total darkness, could feel the threat, like the radiation of a powerful heat, washing over him. The threat was not simply against him, a single individual; it was something larger, something much more sinister: It was what the building held, what the building represented, that caused his flesh to crawl.

"Goddamn it, it's got to be!" he whispered.

He had flown over it in the course of his duties as Chief-of-Staff for Commander-in-Chief Harry Borg, and he'd asked about it then, and many times since, at every level, from generals to private soldiers, from high political officials to private citizens, and not one of those he had asked admitted the giant building existed, let alone admitted knowing what its purpose was. They covered their yellow eyes with gray film, they looked blank, they turned away, they ignored the questions, they talked of other things as if the question had never been asked. And there was in this total denial of the building's existence an answer: If it were nothing else, it had to be the one thing left.

Evidence to support the "one thing left" reasoning had been easily found, once the premise had been accepted. Flying alone at a very high altitude, Chad Harrison had been able to establish that the building was centrally located in an area where the bassoe farms, when encountered on the ground or viewed from the highways, seemed randomly scattered but were actually on the rim of a wheel ten miles in diameter, with the huge black building at the hub. An infrared scanner, used on later flights, had revealed that the farms were connected to the building by underground passageways, which were like spokes of the wheel.

"Got to be!" he said fiercely. "Got to be."

He had come in almost total darkness, flying the Cassal low to avoid detection, depending on the craft's safety devices to keep him clear of obstacles. He'd landed near a very slight, almost indiscernible pathway through the grass, a pathway that extended from an apparently blank wall of the building across a field to a riverbank and what had to be a secret rendezvous. A lovers' meeting place? A place where drugs were traded? Where crimes were planned? Chad did not know, or care.

What he cared about was finding a way into the building. And when the Jassan who had made that path came out again, he was going to go right back in—with company this time.

This was the fourth night Chad had waited.

He stood against the wall, a lean and powerful figure in battle dress, the sinister ruby glow of the Red Flame alive on his chest, sword and handgun at his belt, his near-white hair concealed with a ski-mask covering, a sinister, frightening figure. And he waited with that rigid, unyielding patience only the implacably determined can achieve.

An hour.

And another.

And then, finally, the door opened.

The sudden spill of dim light was the only indication that there was a door, or that it had opened, for there was no sound. Then the light was blocked by the emerging Jassan. He had taken two steps outside and was turning to aim a hand-held control at the door opening when Chad caught him by the throat in the grip of his left hand and brought the tip of the sword to bear on his chest.

"Silence!"

The command was heeded—not a whimper came through Chad's receptor—but stark terror leaped out of the thin, almost fragile, Jassan's yellow eyes as they became fixed on the Red Flame burning on Chad's chest. The slits widened until the yellow was a barely visible gold rim around a black pupil; the forked tongue was a frantic blur. The door closed silently, shutting out the light.

Chad brought his face close. "Be very quiet."

"Y-yes," the Jassan answered. "Who are you—what are you?" His voice held disbelief, a terrified wonderment.

"A bassoe," Chad said.

"You can't be!"

"But I am," Chad said. "And I'm going inside."

The Jassan squirmed, suddenly alive with even more terror. "You can't! It's forbidden!"

"Why is it forbidden?"

"Sacred—holy—of Rissi."

The meanings struggled for equivalents in Chad's receptor; apparently none quite accurate existed. But the meaning, at least to the Jassan, clearly had the importance of towering and consuming flame.

"I'm going in," Chad hissed.

"You'll die!"

"You were alive in there."

"But to admit you—anyone—is death!"

"To the Red Flame?"

"Yes. I—" Uncertainty widened the yellow eyes even further. "I don't know. But—almost surely."

"Means we'll have to be very careful." Chad put pressure on the sword, puncturing clothing and hide enough to cause pain. "Open the door."

"We'll be seen!"

Chad added pressure to the sword point. "You've been sneaking out and sneaking back in without being seen. You'll have to do it again—or die here, now."

"I'll die if I do!" The plea was anguished.

"Inside it will be quick and painless," Chad said, his masked face inches from the terrified eyes. "Out here it will be very painful, very slow."

He added more pressure, held the writhing Jassan in a locked grip, and finally felt a collapse of muscular strength and of will.

"Be very quiet," the Jassan begged. "Do just as I say."

"Open the door."

The Jassan, breathing raggedly with what had to be sheer, barely controlled terror, turned and aimed the control. The door opened silently. Chad shifted his grip so that he held the Jassan from behind, then urged him through the door and inside the building.

They were in a very narrow corridor, scarcely more than a tunnel, dimly lit by a fluorescence that seemed built into the smooth walls. The corridor was seldom used, to judge by the litter, dust, and insect webbing.

"What do you want in here?" The Jassan's question was a tremulous plea.

"To see what goes on," Chad answered. "I think I know, but I want to see it with my own eyes."

The tunnel had taken them to an ancient, long unused storeroom, huge, filled with long-forgotten equipment—great drums, tanks, spools of wire, crates, capacious bins, laden shelves— all bearing the stale patina of discard. They went through the storeroom, still following a narrow track through the dust. Then, at another door, the Jassan stopped again.

He tried to speak—to communicate—but could not, because of mind-bending fear, Chad knew. The Jassan was frail, almost albino; he wore the dark green smock Chad had seen on the highly educated, the scientists, the doctors.

"You got a name?" Chad asked, not unkindly.

"Toss," the Jassan managed. "Dactician, Level Two."

"Doctor? Something like that?"

"Yes. Genetics."

"Listen up, Toss. We're goin' in. And if I live, you live— that's a promise. So move it."

Still Toss hesitated. "But no one is allowed to know!"

"*You* know," Chad said. "And all the others like you in here know."

"But—we were born here, raised here. Our lives are dedicated to—to this task. We die here. And others follow. It has been like that for centuries."

"Why?"

"I don't know why."

"You've got to know a lot more than you say you do. You wanted out, you found a way."

"I found that door." The Jassan was pleading. "I saw there was—an outside. I wanted to see, to feel. All I ever knew was this—inside."

"That's why you're pale and frail," Chad said. "Sorry about that. But we're going in just the same. Once more—move it!"

The Jassan made a final plea, turning so his eight-fingered hand could pluck imploringly at Chad's uniform. "If you see— will you go then?"

"If we're still alive."

Beyond the door, there was another, more obviously traveled corridor, then a steep flight of stairs that turned around a central column and brought them to what Chad was sure must be near the top of the building. A suspended walkway took them out along the edge of a large central room. Being careful not to be seen, Chad peered down to stare at the activity below.

"My God," he whispered.

A slow-moving conveyor belt carried female bassoes into the room. They were lying on their backs, bellies hugely distended, their heels fixed into stirrups, knees spread wide. They were obviously in their last moments of pregnancy, about to give birth, but clearly unaware of anything, perhaps not even the pain.

"Where do they come from?" Chad whispered.

"I don't know," Toss answered. "The conveyor brings them— sometimes a few, sometimes a hundred. The infants are kept here until the age of two years. The females are sent back by conveyor—and that is all I know."

As Chad watched, white-clad, masked Jassans delivered the new infants with a drug-induced, machinelike regularity. Then a belt took the infants under a towering lamp that delivered an intense yellow beam, under which they were held for what was, to Chad Harrison, a significant period of time.

"What does that yellow light do?" He really didn't need to ask.

"It cleanses—their minds."

"I knew it," Chad said softly. "I knew it!"

"But it doesn't harm them," his frightened guide whispered through Chad's receptor.

"Just turns them into zeros," Chad said. "Now let's get out of here."

He turned, expecting Toss to turn with him. The Jassan remained where he was, and when Chad turned back he saw that the Jassan was crumbling in fear, his eyes fixed on a point farther down the walkway.

"There—" Toss hissed, his terror, multiplied, returning.

Chad looked and saw the long mandibles of a giant termite probing onto the walkway from a side entrance. The insect was a hundred yards away. There was still time.

"C'mon—c'mon!"

But the strength was gone from Toss. He had given up. His mouth had dropped open, his long forked tongue was lolling, the gray lid had covered his yellow eyes—he had fainted. A glance told Chad the huge insect had made the turn and was approaching, antennae searching. Chad bent and with a swift, powerful heave, lifted the crumpled Toss, slinging him over his shoulder, then turned and made for the stairway. He ran easily, despite the dead weight of the Jassan, sidearm drawn and gripped in his right hand, ready.

An alarm must have been tripped for, on reaching the landing below, he found another giant termite waiting, blocking the corridor that led to the storeroom. The Red Flame meant nothing to insects—that was clear. This one had erected itself on its six legs to the height of Chad's shoulders, its mandibles open wide, waiting.

"Sonofabitchin' bug!" Chad cursed.

The hot, vivid ray of his gun caught the huge insect at the joint of the gaping mandibles, exploding. The insect's head blew away, leaving a barricade of legs and thorax and abdomen, quivering in aimless death throes. Chad holstered his gun. Then, using his sword as a machete, he chopped his way through the brush heap of dying insect parts to the door to the ancient storeroom. He ran down the aisle that led through the towering, crumbling heaps of aeons-old dreams to the outer door and then to his hidden aircraft.

"Okay, hero," he said to the still-unconscious Toss as he

stuffed the Jassan into the passenger side of his craft. "You made it—gonna live to fight another day."

Toss did not recover consciousness until they had been in flight for several minutes, safely away from the huge black building, with no longer any need for concealment. The frail, pale Jassan awoke, struggling against his safety belt, a residue of his terror still clouding his mind. Chad laid a strong hand on him.

"Easy does it!" he said. "You're safe!"

The terror was replaced with stunned amazement. Meanings tumbled through Chad's receptor. "I'm alive—didn't leave me! Outside! Free!" Then he looked at Chad, his yellow eyes glowing with light reflected from the instrument panel.

"You didn't leave me!"

"Hell, no," Chad said.

He'd torn the ski mask from his head, revealing almost-white hair that seemed to glow; his tanned face was like a dark mask from which his gray eyes seemed to burn with accusation. He had been made deeply furious and implacably determined by what he had seen and learned. But his fury was not directed at Toss, who was obviously a single cog in a giant gear, unable to direct or alter the course of the machine of which he was so small a part. And Toss had been searching, however blindly, for freedom—his pathway toward it had made possible Chad's entrance to the building.

"But—why?" Toss asked, honestly puzzled.

"I said if I lived, you'd live," Chad reminded him. "I don't know how it is with you reptiles, but with us, a deal's a deal."

Toss's eyes became fixed on Chad, and in the whispered words that followed, Chad could sense something close to reverence.

"I can't believe it."

"Believe it!" Chad said almost angrily. "It's true. You wanted out. Okay? You're out. Stay close to me and you'll stay alive— that's a promise." His fist struck the steering lever as his attention focused again.

"Bassoes are born intelligent, right?" It was a demand for correct information, rather than a question.

"It—it may be so," Toss stammered.

"Why *may* be?"

"I've never seen an intelligent bassoe——" He corrected himself hurriedly. "Until you, I mean. You *are* a bassoe?"

"I am! First cousin, anyway."

"All I have seen are mindless," Toss said. "And the infants."

"You mind-blank them permanently with that yellow ray! Right?"

"It cleanses their minds——for their own good."

"For their own good!" Chad's voice was harsh. "That what you think?"

"It's what we are told." Toss was puzzled. "What other reason could there be?"

"I'll be go to hell!" Chad hit the steering lever again.

"What is it?" Toss said, alarmed.

"You really *don't* know?"

"I told you, I——"

"I'll tell you!" Chad said, his voice low and furious. "You mind-blank the bassoes so they're docile. Like sheep. Like cattle. So you can slaughter them for food! You use bassoes as food animals!"

There was no response.

A long moment passed, and then Chad realized that the reason for Toss's blankness was shock. Stunned shock. And then, finally, a trickle of meanings came through.

"Is——is that possible? Intelligent creatures? Kept mindless to slaughter? For *food*? We *eat* them?"

He was so incredulous, so shocked, Chad had to believe him.

"*You've* been blanked," he said. "Mind-controlled, at least."

"For centuries!" Toss whispered. "And more."

"But why the secrecy?" Chad asked. "If you're going to use them for hamburger, why hide it? Been eating them forever. Public knowledge, isn't it?"

"I——I don't know."

That question was still unanswered when Chad landed the Cassal on the roof of the apartment complex as dawn streaked the sky. Other questions had been answered, though. And with those answers had come a resolve. He was going to put an end to the mind-blanking of infant bassoes, and the using of bassoes as food, before he left Jassa. Even if it cost him his life!

But now his mind filled with Illia.

She was a living example of what Homo sapiens could be on this planet if left to develop naturally. Somehow she had escaped the yellow beam, or had been imperfectly blanked. At least she was one bassoe who was living proof that bassoes were not born mindless.

The thought of her was vivid and warm as he ran down the curving walkway that led to the floor below and his apartment. He heard the quick patter of Toss's feet following close at his heels, but his mind was on Illia. He knew she would be waiting for him anxiously, with warmth in her smile, with welcome in her eyes.

"I think I must be in love."

Inside the apartment, he called, "Sweetheart! I'm home!"

There was no answer.

Then she appeared, beautiful, as he'd known she would be, wearing a thin, transparent nightdress, her soft fur shining like a coat of silver, her hair lustrous, falling around her shoulders. His heart leaped at the sight of her—

Then fell as if shot.

He had realized the apartment was a shambles, and she usually kept it sparkling clean. There was the smell of feces and urine. And she was looking at him with vacant, unknowing eyes.

"Illia!" he yelled in sudden fear.

She didn't look at him; she looked through him.

Her voice was soft, untroubled, meaningless.

She went, *"Naaaaa . . ."*

CHAPTER 22

From the beginning Harry Borg had found it difficult to fully understand, let alone believe, that a nation the size of Jassa, with the levels of scientific and mechanical development Jassa had achieved centuries before his own civilization, could have crumbled and withered, like an overripe fruit, to a state of near helplessness.

And it was not the achievements that had disintegrated, he learned; it was their state of mind. They had lost their ability to see problems clearly, to see the measures necessary to solve those problems, and to execute those measures with force and precision. They had become a nation of inhibited, lazy, uncertain, disputatious, wary, even fearful individuals, none of whom was willing to accept responsibility or risk failure.

"A collection of buck-passers," Harry had growled at Ros Moss on one of his frequent visits to the head of the Jassan government, who had given him the impossible assignment of winning a centuries-old war with the Ussirs. "'I didn't do it; it was *him*!' Or 'Give it to *him*, that's *his* department!'"

"Very true," Moss had agreed.

"There isn't a damn one of 'em wants to do anything! What they want is the other guy to do it, so they can jump on him and holler he did it wrong!"

"Exactly!" Moss had agreed again, and if it were possible for him to smile, he had been smiling then. "The first step in the solution of a problem is to describe the problem exactly. Now that you have accomplished that very vital first step, how do you propose to solve the problem?"

"Kick ass!" Harry had yelled, and stomped out.

Strangely enough, and to Harry's considerable surprise, the tactic proved effective. He did not use his booted foot, or their behinds, needless to say; what he did use was a blast of mental strength that struck them with a hurricane force, unyielding, implacable, driving; he accepted no arguments, no excuses, no failures; he required immediate, willing, unquestioning, if not cheerful, obedience; he demanded the impossible and would only agree that the impossible sometimes took a little longer.

And they liked it!

Not at first, to be sure, even though the Red Flame held them in awe; but within days the new way of doing things began to take hold of the Jassans in the military like a powerful narcotic, stimulating the officer class, exhilarating them with newfound, or newly remembered, abilities, a narcotic that seemed to grow more powerful each day. Perhaps they had forgotten how good, hard living was done, and, once reminded, engaged in it with a vigor and enthusiasm that had been sleeping for centuries.

The noncommissioned class, and the private soldiers, were affected differently but even more so. To them Harry Borg was a giant, a blazing, blue-eyed bassoe from some distant universe—the Red Flame reincarnated, wearer of the Red Stone, a god, surely—come to lead them out of a swamp of failure and despair that had been their lot for as long as any could remember, to lead them to the glory and richness their ancestors had once known. Such a god-legend had been storied for thousands of years, and, as they saw it now, it was their good fortune that the great god, the Red Flame, had arrived in their time.

"I'll buy it," Harry had said to his staff—Chad, Ernie, Arnie, Sam, and Homer. "I'll buy any kind of a story they care to dream up, so long as it works!"

"It's working," Homer told him.

Homer, the wide-shouldered, quiet, straight-thinking son of a cattle rancher, had been given the task of searching the past of the Jassan civilization. "Find their equivalent of our Smithsonian—they've got to have one—and give me a step-by-step of what they did, and when they did it, to get where they got to before they started downhill," Harry had said. "Steam engines, internal combustion engines, weaponry, electric current, flight, and all the things they know that we don't. Okay?"

"You want an encyclopedia?"

"I want a dozen pages, you big clown!"

"The fifty-thousand-year history of Jassa in a dozen pages," Homer said with a straight face. "Sir!"

Harry had broken up. "Another wise-ass!"

But they both had known what was needed.

And Harry knew he would get it.

Even so, because of its size and scope, the problem they faced had been beyond any reasonable hope of solution from the very beginning. The armed forces numbered less than half a million males, of whom no more than a hundred thousand could be considered combat troops, and those were badly trained and badly equipped. The small arms and artillery being used in the "conventional weapons" war that was being fought were old, rusted, and badly in need of replacement, and no new materiel was being made. Only a few of the military aircraft were airworthy. The ground transport was a joke. Supply was hit or miss. And intelligence was largely rumor—he had no certain knowledge of the enemy strength, placement, or intentions.

All this Harry Borg had discovered early on, and his efforts to remedy the ills, together with the need to reawaken an effective mental attitude in the Jassan high command and then to delegate authority, kept Harry busy, quite literally night and day, with only moments to eat and sleep.

He had found time to give Lori Calder into the care of the surgeon Sassan, who had promised to return Lori to a safe condition within a week or two, but who had been less confident than Harry would have liked when he had made the promise.

"They were very clever," Sassan had said after making his examination. "It's hard to know exactly where in her brain they planted the seed of your destruction. But with a little luck . . ."

Not all that Harry had hoped for, but the best he was going to get. In Harry's view, if Sassan couldn't do it for Lori, nobody could. And if he failed?

"I'll take care of eliminating her, when it becomes necessary," Guss had told him. "If that's any comfort to you."

Some comfort!

Chad's problem with Illia had been more difficult. It had come as a complete surprise to Sassan—so he had said—that infant bassoes were born intelligent and were mind-blanked. "So that's what goes on in that building! I've often wondered," he'd said. He would have to do extensive research to find if there was a way to reconstitute Illia's mind.

That Chad's apartment had been invaded in his absence and that Illia had been subjected to a powerful dose of the dreadful yellow beam had been quickly discovered. The invaders, masquerading as government officials, had been either Peacekeepers or members of the secret organization that had perpetuated for centuries the lies that all bassoes were born mindless, and, on learning one of their own bassoes was intelligent and running free, had broken in to correct the oversight.

Even if it had not yet been established whether or not Illia's mind had been permanently destroyed, it had been established with absolute certainty that the perpetrator had made mortal enemies of the men from Earth. The men from Earth swore a solemn oath that they would not leave Jassa, even if they were able, before the black building and all others like it were destroyed.

But first they had a war to win.

A war against the Ussirs.

And time was short and growing shorter.

Hardly a day had gone by without an attempt from the Peacekeepers to eliminate one or all of them. And never a day went by when they weren't aware of the awful danger of the yellow ray: A short blast could render them incapable, mindless, and unremembering, for a day or two or three, as they had learned in their lives as seed bulls; a long blast could render them as mindless as Illia.

Just as ominous, just as bone-chilling, were the "religious cults," for the lack of a better name, particularly the Cult of Bissi, the worshipers of the great black spiders. The size, the intelligence, the lethal poison, the frightening aspect of the spiders had evoked a predictable reaction in Jassans, as it had in primitive man:

If you don't understand it, worship it, and it may not harm you!

And for many—as it had been for the men who were to have

guarded Harry Borg—obeisance to the giant spider took precedence over all other allegiances, even to their oath to the Red Flame.

The Cult of Bissi was not unique, Harry and his young men soon learned. It came to them that there would be a religious cult that forbade, separately, almost every task that had to be done, because of a holy day, a holiday, or because the act was expressly forbidden by some religious law.

"Cults begun for fun or profit centuries ago," Moss had told Harry Borg on one occasion, "become to following generations the absolute holy writ, all-pervading, all-consuming, because they have forgotten, or never knew, the triviality of their beginning."

"We've got a few like that," Harry answered. "More than a few. New ones sprouting up all the time."

And then Moss had seemed to smile. "The cult of the Red Flame is growing," he said. "I hope it becomes large enough to be the salvation of my country. And soon."

Harry held the gold pendant in his fingers. It seemed to him he could feel the pulsing of the bright blood-red stone. His face became very serious.

"I joked about it at first," he said quietly. "But I dunno."

"You feel a life there?"

"Feel something—that's for damned sure!"

"It is life. It is a living stone," Moss said softly.

CHAPTER 23

It was the tenth of October, as Harry computed it, a cold, blustering night three days before truce time, and he was sitting in the cockpit of the best high-flying reconnaissance aircraft the Jassan military had been able to provide, cleared for takeoff but refusing to give the order to go.

Beside him, Guss was waiting at the controls, more puzzled than impatient. "Five minutes ago, it was hurry, hurry. Now it's wait, wait." He looked at Harry, his supple, forked tongue flicking. "You don't have to give me a reason. I couldn't care less."

Harry, a finger pressed to an earphone, ignored Guss. A moment went by, then another. Then Ernie's voice came through the earphone:

"Loud and clear, sir!"

"Good lad," Harry said. Then to Guss: "Go!"

Guss took the aircraft aloft with a stomach-dropping G-force, squirting them up through the cloud deck in a matter of seconds, reaching for a flight level above a hundred thousand meters.

"What was that all about?" Guss asked.

They had reached altitude and were on a course that would take them over the Ussir western command, an area that, in Harry's world, would be the lower half of Lake Michigan and the Chicago area and a five-hundred-kilometer-wide strip of land east of the Mississippi as far south as Memphis, Tennessee.

"I was waiting for a message from one of my lads," Harry said. "A *sound* message on a radio wave. Audio. Remember? The way we humans communicate."

"Oh," Guss said. After thinking about it, he became mildly miffed. "You're nothing but a damned reactionary."

"Why is that?"

"Our thought communication is better, faster, more efficient. Your way is strictly horse-and-buggy." He looked at Harry, amused. "I thought you had upgraded."

"So it's old-fashioned," Harry said grumpily. "But we're used to it. Reminds us of home. Okay?"

"All right, all right!" Guss said soothingly.

"And while we're about it," he grouched further, "a ten-G takeoff is not my style. I don't know why all you Jassans have got to hotdog takeoffs and landings."

"Military tradition," Guss told him. "I learned it in flight school. Put me in a uniform and it all comes back."

The cameras in the craft were scanning the ground below using rays normally beyond vision—X rays on the high end and infrared on the low end—and what they saw was being translated onto a screen set before Harry, as well as being sent to the War Room on the ground. The translation was highly sophisticated. Harry had key controls that enabled him to spot-enlarge areas of interest until he was able to distinguish objects as small as ground cars; he could recognize high concentrations of metal and identify the kind of metal; he could measure troop concentrations by body heat.

"Warm-blooded reptiles," he muttered as he stared at the screen. "How about that?"

"You don't like it?"

"Love it. How would I know how many of the enemy were down there without it?" He fingered the key controls with great delicacy as he talked. "In my country, reptiles are cold-blooded. Warm blood was the fork in the evolutionary road that led you to the smarts, I guess."

"Could be," Guss said.

He was just as intent on his instruments as Harry was on his screen. Guss had agreed to this flight most reluctantly, calling it unnecessary. The Ussirs, to his certain knowledge, based on historical fact and on their conduct during the last century, were— like the Jassans—dedicated to fair play. They fought hard, when they fought, but they fought fair. There would be nothing new to be discovered. All the troops, all the troop placements, all the equipment, and most importantly all the plans of the Ussirs had been known by the Jassan high command for years.

There was danger in making this flight, however. Extreme danger.

It was a very serious violation of the war ethic to distrust the opponent so much that a spy flight was felt to be necessary. By implication, such distrust reduced war from clean, wholesome killing to mad savagery and, again by implication, described the adversary not as civilized, intelligent, right-thinking beings who engaged in carefully moderated eugenic genocide but as savages capable of the most despicable bloody lusts.

And the penalty prescribed by a law hundreds of years old was death. But not immediate death. Immediate death was too merciful, and was certainly not suited to a crime as heinous as this. Translated into human terms, as Guss had translated it for Harry, it was death by overstimulation. Every sensation the body was able to experience was carefully overstimulated with slowly increasing strengths over a period of time—some had been able to endure as long as several months—until the nervous system burned out, the mind blew up, and the body died. Included in the sensations were hunger, thirst, bitter taste, sweet taste, pain, elation, pleasure—most especially sexual pleasure—fear of heights, and all similar phobias.

"Don't know about you," Guss had said, after telling Harry what would be in store for them if captured, "but it scares the hell out of me."

"Stay home, then," Harry had said.

"And admit I'm a dirty coward?"

So here he was, a dirty coward, flying Harry, who didn't have sense enough to be frightened, over enemy-held territory, trying to keep an exact course so that Harry and the generals back at the War Room would have an accurate plot of the Ussir position.

Harry was intent on his screens. "You've got an island a hundred kilometers offshore in what we call Lake Michigan. A kilometer square. How about that?"

"Must be Rassmod. What about it?"

"We don't have it in our Lake Michigan."

"You're not missing anything. Nothing there. Used as a prison, abandoned centuries ago. Just rock."

"Alcatraz," Harry muttered.

"What's an 'Alcatraz'?"

"A boil that festered on our public conscience. It was never cured. It was just broken up and scattered."

And so it went, for an hour and then another, with Guss flying the precise pattern back and forth over the Ussir-held territory, while Harry sought out and identified weapon and troop concentrations, sending the information to computers for analysis and summation.

They were approaching the Mississippi River from the east on a leg that would take them just north of Memphis—Harry could not help relating the geography below to the geography he had known in his own world—when the onboard computer came up with a final summation. Harry's reaction was one of dismay but not surprise.

"We've got a problem," he said to Guss.

"A serious problem?" Guss asked.

"They're going to kill us inside three months," Harry said. "If you call that serious."

"Ahhhh!" Guss said, not believing him. "You keep saying that."

"The *computer* says it this time." He tapped the computer readout. "The Green Guys've got four times the manpower, four times the firepower, and they're ready to go. If you believe they've stacked it up like that for exercise, you've got to be big on the Tooth Fairy, the Easter Bunny, and Santa Claus."

"Whatever they are."

At that moment, the first enemy round, a streak of fire, whistled across the sky ahead of them. "Keerist!" Harry had time to say before Guss drove the breath out of him with the first evasive tactic, a hard left turn—ninety degrees? at close to a thousand knots?—then hard down, then hard right.

"Good Godalmighty!" Harry groaned.

The enemy was good!

He had reactions like greased lightning. Worse, he seemed to be able to anticipate what Guss's next move would be. That blazing streak of lightning, that sudden bolt of death, had a way of zipping across the night sky ahead of them, as if it knew where they were going to be next, needing only a few more tries before being able to lay it on them a second before they got there.

But Guss was good too.

He never did the same thing twice, leaving the enemy to anticipate a new move each time. The tactic bought them time, but not escape, even though Guss used all the sky, it seemed, between the stars and the ground. Other marksmen joined the hunt, other bolts of eye-blinding rays sought them out.

"Got us!" Harry roared furiously.

A ray had scorched by as near as a hundred yards, leaving a hole in the sky, a turbulence that sent the craft tumbling out of control. Guss was stunned, blinded. Harry reached over in a desperate effort, got hold of the controls—there were none on his side in this craft, because of the reconnaissance gear—and fought to right the ship. Still they tumbled, wobbling across the sky, losing altitude like a falling piano.

"Guss! For chrissake! Come back!"

But Guss was still stunned. His head rolled loosely; his long, forked tongue flopped out of his gaping mouth like a necktie; the gray inner lid blinded his eyes. Harry loosed his seat belt. Then, still reaching over Guss's helpless body, he struggled with the wheel as the horizon vanished upward, reappeared, vanished downward, then held and pinwheeled wildly.

"Great sufferin' jehosophat!"

Harry fumed, stormed, and raged—and fought the craft as if it were a living thing out to destroy him. The power went out when the altimeter read less than a thousand kilometers, and the craft wanted to stop in midair. With the beams still searing and snapping in search of them? Good Godfrey, no! He found the safety release, and again he was riding a falling piano.

"Come out of it!" he roared.

And then, as if in answer, the craft leveled off with still a little air under its bow, sheared off treetops that whipped out of the darkness, slowed, settled, crashing, crumpling, and finally stopped.

"What happened?" Guss asked weakly.

"We landed," Harry said succinctly.

Recovering rapidly now, Guss looked about, then looked at Harry with shock and growing anger.

"You wrecked our plane!"

Harry looked heavenward. "You believe it?" he asked.

Suddenly he kicked the door open and jumped to the ground. He looked about. The night was about gone; light was coming. And they were on enemy land.

"Get your ass outa there!" he said.

Becoming alert, Guss jumped down from the plane. "Where are we?"

"Ussir country. The next face you see is gonna be green!"

They stripped out of their high-altitude clothing, and, clad as they usually were, armed with their usual weapons, they raced away from the downed aircraft. Both could run very well, and in Harry's opinion they could have reached the Mississippi, given a little luck. But—

"Damnation!" Harry said.

A two-man military search ground vehicle had picked up their trail, and the fact that Harry could hear it had saved them. Unnoticed by the earless Essans, the power unit of the vehicle emitted a shrill whine as it traveled a foot or two off the ground, supported by energy units.

"You or me?" Harry asked.

"Me," Guss said.

Guss staked himself out as bait, and when the two Ussirs moved to take him, Harry came down on them like an avenging angel. And while Guss wanted to tie them, take their ground car, and go, Harry wanted something else. And he got it.

"Still believe in Santa Claus?" he asked Guss afterward.

"But Harry!" Guss had never been so distraught in his entire life. "Truce time is holy! It has been observed, inviolate, for over a hundred years! I can't believe they would attack us then!"

"You heard 'em," Harry said. "Believe it."

"But we will have set aside our weapons. We'll be utterly defenseless! They'll *slaughter* us!"

"That's the idea, son," Harry said.

"It's only three days from now!"

"Means we better move."

"Harry, I—"

"I hear another car!" Harry said sharply.

Even as they boarded the vehicle they'd taken, another car appeared on the far side of an open field, and a wild chase began.

This one followed the terrain only a foot or two above the ground. Harry, at the controls, found the little vehicle capable of astonishing speed and mind-boggling turns. They ducked into a woodland, whipping through trees, dropped into a ravine to follow a winding creek bed, then up into and across an open field. The car behind them followed relentlessly, tenaciously, and soon it was joined by two more.

"It's no use, Harry."

"The hell it isn't!" Harry answered.

He was searching now, not just fleeing.

"There y'go!" he said.

He whipped the agile little car in a sharp turn that carried them toward a small stone building, apparently abandoned long ago. Reaching it, he stopped the car and jumped out. "Come on!" he yelled.

Guss, totally confused, near panic, followed. "Harry, for your God's sake—"

Inside the building, Harry drew his sidearm and with careful aim picked off the first of the approaching cars. That stopped the others. He wheeled away from the windowlike opening and swelled his chest with a deep breath. He gave Guss a hard grin.

"How ya doin', buddy?"

Guss put his back to the wall and slid down to a sitting position. His yellow eyes were dull with the gray inner film, his long, forked tongue limp.

"In a few days my people are going to be destroyed, our nation reduced to slavery," he said. "Just out there, in a very little while, there is going to be a lot of Ussirs, not just a few, and they will, at their pleasure, wipe us out." He looked at Harry briefly. "How d'you think I'm doing?"

Harry gave him another hard grin. "Hang in!"

Then he looked out of the window, and what he saw made him whistle softly. Still looking, he spoke over his shoulder to Guss. "You know what Custer's last words were?"

"No. But you're going to tell me."

"I've got it on good authority," Harry said. "The last words of General George Custer at the Battle of the Little Big Horn when he saw what I'm seein' now were, and I quote: *'Would you look at all them goddamn Indians!'*"

CHAPTER 24

At the age of twelve, Homer Benson had been left at the Smithsonian while his father had attended a series of meetings at the Department of Agriculture; and while the venerable institution had been a convenient baby-sitter from his father's point of view, to the twelve-year-old it had been an archway opening on a vista glorious to behold. From the "now" experienced at the threshold, there extended away as far as his eye could see or his mind perceive the story of life back to the very instant life had begun, including mankind and all that mankind had achieved using only the most recent few moments in the long passage of time.

Now, this time as a grown man, Homer had been given a chance to relive that experience. A walk through the great National Museum of Osis, like a walk through the Smithsonian, was a walk down the corridors of time. A very long time.

While Homer Benson understood perfectly that he was on a mission of life-or-death significance, he had become completely enthralled the moment he walked through the giant and very ancient archway, the moment the clicking of his heels echoed back to him from dim and distant walls across uncountable exhibits standing silent, as they had for centuries, blindly enduring the slow passage of time, dust-laden, largely forgotten.

As with everything else Jassan, the museum, the interest in

things past, the importance of things past, of heritage, had suffered a slow but persistent decay. Homer had come to believe a "loss of interest" was responsible. Just as a child wanders away from a toy, the Jassans had wandered away from their moments of glory, their great achievements, as their interests gradually turned to pursuits that required less effort, less expenditure, less risk, less time.

"Less and less and less," he said to himself. "Kind of like a creeping disease."

He spent the first days searching the most recent time eras for the object—whatever it might be—that would best suit Harry Borg's need, a need shared by all the Homo sapiens in Jassa. Not finding it, he began going back, using first the National Museum at Osis and then lesser or more remote museums as vehicles for his search through time.

He went alone.

Because of his size—he was six-two, weighed one hundred and ninety, and was very broad of shoulder, with long and powerful arms and big, square hands—he was a giant among the Jassans, inspiring awe and even fear. A long, thin face held thoughtful, watchful, gray eyes set under heavy brows on either side of a strong nose. His mouth was wide, straight, and flat, his chin almost hooked under it, a statement of determination that was almost belligerent. The uniform he wore, identifying him as a member of the Red Flame Brigade, was recognized and respected, even revered, by all Jassans except the Peacekeepers, and the weapons he wore discouraged all but the most dedicated of those fanatics. So far he had been forced to kill only one Peacekeeper while injuring three others in two separate skirmishes.

He walked where he wanted to go, and no Jassan chose to deny him entry or passage—until he came to a museum of military weapons. There the way was barred.

Originally an arsenal, located deep inside the mountain range he knew as the Rocky Mountains, the museum had always been, and still was, kept under high security.

"It's like a temple," he had told Chad Harrison, who was in command during any absence of Harry. "The guards are like priests. I don't think they know what they're guarding, or why they're guarding it. It's a sacred mission handed down through centuries, and they go on doing it. Wearin' their funny robes, doin' their funny rites."

"What about the Red Flame? Won't that get you in?"

"They put their religion first."

"And they're dead serious?" Chad had asked.

"Right. I'll have to kill a few. Maybe a lot."

"There isn't time to go through channels."

Homer had been very sober. "I've got to get in there, Chad."

"You want help?"

"I can burn my way in," Homer had told him. "Getting out might be a problem."

"How long will you need?"

"Give me two days."

"You've got 'em," Chad said. "Call in, y'hear?"

"Will do."

Homer had spent the first day trying again to reason his way past the Jassans guarding the entrance, a towering gateway of some glittering metal set into a sheer cliff face. The Jassans wore robes of scarlet and plumed crowns, and performed a sacred rite of some sort continuously before the gateway, night and day. Homer supposed the ceremony had at one time been a simple changing of the guard, and that with the passage of time it had somehow evolved into a religious ceremony. But, while the priest-guards were polite and respectful, they were nevertheless adamant: No one passed.

And they had weapons.

By the second day, Homer had learned the secret of how the glittering gateway was opened, and he had learned what priests and what weapons had to be destroyed if he were to gain entrance. As he walked along the ancient road toward the gateway, a relatively tiny figure in enormous surroundings, he had time to think about what he was doing and what he was going to do, about the cruel necessities of fighting, and winning, a war—and to wonder how any creature, given that most miraculous, most precious of all gifts, the gift of life, could be brought to destroy that gift at any time for any reason.

He killed the first three priest-guards before they knew he would. Three bursts from his handgun, carefully placed, blew them away quickly and painlessly. The emplaced rapid-fire cannon and the priest-guards who manned them took longer, but they were only able to get off a single panic-wild burst that missed Homer by yards before they too were made to vanish.

And then there was silence. Replacements for the dead priests were an hour away: Their living quarters, a small, cliff-hanging community high on a granite face, was that far off.

Homer stood before the great, glittering gateway, the cold morning sun shining down on his bowed head. He had no religion of his own, or any belief; yet killing, however mercifully done, was to him a crime beyond forgiveness, a crime for which he had to make this gesture—an honest, unflinching acceptance of guilt—to whatever, whoever, had given the lives he had taken.

Then he was inside the huge armory, with the gateway closed behind him. He walked forward, going backward in time: from weaponry that had been modern a century before to older and older weapons, stored and forgotten, weapons whose functions and purposes he could only guess at, weapons as yet undiscovered by his own civilization. Finally, far back, he found familiar weapons: missiles, aerial bombs, cannon, machine guns, rifles, blunderbusses, crossbows, longbows, swords, spears, then clubs with heads of stone.

"It started here," he said, his voice echoing.

Certain now that he knew it all, he turned back along the corridors of time to a period when the weapons matched those his own civilization had learned to use in the century in which he had been born. There he searched again with great care, through long passageways filled with old cannon, tanks, bomber aircraft—and found what he'd been sent to find.

"There y'go!" he said. "Canned insanity."

He turned and headed back at a run. Reaching the great outer door, opening it, he went through, only to slow to a walk and then to a stop.

He had been too long inside.

The Jassan priest-guards formed a line across the ancient roadway. They had obviously been waiting for him, all armed, a silent line of accusers. They began moving toward him.

"Time to call home."

He lifted a communicator from his belt and spoke into it as he watched the approaching cordon of priest-guards.

"Read you, baby. Loud and clear," Ernie's voice replied.

"Mission accomplished," Homer said. "It's here."

"You home free?"

"Negative."

CHAPTER 25

"Indians? What Indians?" Guss asked.

Guss stood by Harry Borg's side, looking past him through the opening that had once been a window in the ancient, crumbling stone building. Other ground-search vehicles had joined the first, and he could see their insignia.

"Those are Ussirs!" he said. "*Sos* Ussirs!"

The vehicles had emerged from the woods to drop in a ravine and out of sight, using the rise before them as a protective bulwark. Harry shouldered Guss out of the way.

"What's a Sos Ussir?" he asked.

Guss was a moment finding the human equivalent. "A storm trooper?"

"The very worst kind!" Harry said emphatically.

He had drawn his sidearm, and now, holding it in a two-handed grip, he triggered a careful string of shots traversing his field with spectacular results. Each shot exploded with shocking force, sending a huge column of earth and rock into the sky, filling the gray dawn with a sound like cannon fire.

"Harry!" Guss was stunned. "You're using a kol!"

"Better believe it," Harry said, reloading.

"But they've been outlawed!"

"I know it."

"They're—they're illegal!"

243

"Killin' me—*that's* illegal," Harry said. "According to the law of Harry Borg, anyway."

Guss was staring through the opening. The rise across the way was heaped with piles of smoking earth, cratered with deep holes. There was no life, no movement.

"You killed them all!"

"Not even one."

Harry had left the window. He was striding from opening to opening, scanning the perimeter. "They're gonna circle us, sure as hell." He edged carefully along a passageway that led through the thick wall, placed his back hard against the stone, and laid down another careful barrage that tore up the peaceful meadow, ripping it, shattering the early morning stillness with another blasphemy of sound. Even though the Essans couldn't hear what happened, they could certainly feel the concussion and see and smell the result. He picked a tall tree at a distance of about a hundred meters, put a shot into the thick trunk, and brought the tree down with a crash.

"Harry! What're you doing?"

"Buyin' time!" Harry said.

There was an intensity about him, a fierceness that almost made him glow. His dark blue eyes, the glint of gold on his earlobe, his strong, bearded face, his corded neck, his wide chest and powerful arms, his lithe movements on legs that seemed able to send him leaping to any needed height—all of it together transformed him in Guss's eyes into a super-being, capable of performing feats beyond imagining. Now, watching Harry Borg climb the interior wall to a broken roof truss, leap a void, and catch and swing up to a broken timber that gave him a view over the open country, he was sure of it. "Super" was the word. He saw Harry take a small metal disk from a pouch at his belt, place it on top of the broken wall, then turn and come down again.

"Your Sos Ussirs have pulled back," he told Guss with a hard grin. "They don't like that heavy fire."

Guss was stricken. "Harry, kols have been outlawed for fifty years! They're too barbaric!"

"Killin' sonsabitches!" Harry agreed.

"And you killed them—horribly!"

"Nope. Just scared the piss out of 'em."

Harry had gone to the window to stare intently. "Guss, I love your delicacy," he said over his shoulder. "It's all right to kill, but you gotta kill nice."

An incoming round screamed overhead.

"You watch out that side, y'hear?"

Guss ran for the short corridor and looked hard. "Nothing out there."

"Just wait awhile."

They heard the incoming round that had passed overhead strike ground and explode in the distance. At the window, his handgun again loaded with the illegal rounds, Harry waited and tried to guess the Ussirs' intentions. The use of the kols had told them it was going to cost a lot of lives to take Harry and Guss alive, and for that reason he might have been wrong using the powerful loads. They might decide to hell with capture and kill them with rocket fire. A gamble, however you sliced it. But whatever the final answer, he wouldn't have gained this much time if he hadn't used the kols and scared them into a debate. And time was what he needed.

The sun broke above the horizon and started climbing. There was little heat, because it was autumn in what would be Tennessee at home; there was frost on the ground. And there was little comfort in the brightness. Harry was sure the Ussirs would use the blinding brilliance as a shield to come at them out of the sun. And soon. Before the sun got too high. Twenty minutes went by, twenty minutes of tense watching and waiting.

"Harry, I can see Ussirs."

"Good eye, baby," Harry said. "And I've got a platoon."

The Ussirs had done their thinking and made their decision. And now they were going to act. But, as was almost always the case with the Essans, green or gray, they had argued too long.

For now four aircraft appeared, coming in low, splitting apart, three to carve a beautiful circle above the heads of the Sos Ussirs and their ground vehicles, to circle again, hosing a steady stream of fire into the ground between the Sos Ussirs and Harry and Guss in the stone fortress. The fourth craft came directly toward the fortress, stopped immediately above it, and then landed very close by the short stone corridor where Guss was standing open-mouthed.

A port opened. Chad Harrison appeared there, white hair shining, a broad grin on his deeply tanned face.

"Will you come aboard, sir?"

"Hell, yes!" Harry answered, roaring. He came up from behind the befuddled Guss, caught him by the arm, and all but threw him into the ship. Both aboard, the port closed, and the ship reached for the sky, driving all three into a heap on the deck, breathless, groaning.

When he was able to stand, Harry glared fiercely at Chad Harrison. "Took you long enough!" he snarled.

"Had a ways to come," Chad said, unimpressed.

Then Harry grabbed Chad in a bear hug. "Goddamn, you're a winner!" he yelled, dropping all pretense. "Saved our asses is what you did! Another three minutes we'd been wiped out!"

Chad grinned. "Glad to help."

Guss had been looking at the two humans, baffled, his forked tongue flicking, seeking answers, finding none, his yellow eyes wide.

"How did he *know*?" he asked Harry. "Where we were, I mean. I—I didn't even know—that close!"

Harry guided Guss toward a seat. "A little old-fashioned Homo sapiens communication," he said. "What you folks have been thinking was static on the airwaves has been a radio we can convert to sound. Sound. Audio. The old-fashioned way of communicating? Remember?"

"But, how—"

"My boy Eddie grew up in a radio shop," Harry said as they settled in. "No trick for him to build a beeper I could carry. They've been trackin' us all night from our side of the river. They knew when we went down. They've been hunting ever since. Right, son?"

"Like bird dogs," Chad said.

"And that thing you put on the roof?"

"Beamed 'em right in," Harry said. He was taking an almost childish delight in the fact they'd done something the Essans hadn't done five hundred years before. For a change. "Thanks to the advanced scientific achievements of the Homo sapiens society, here we are, you and I, still alive, still kicking."

Guss got the dig all right. "And I understand you've even mastered the bow and arrow," he said with only barely noticeable sarcasm.

"Guss, by all that's holy, I'm gonna—"

"Sir!" It was Chad, and he was dead serious.

"Yeah?"

"Homer's in trouble," Chad said. "Bad trouble. Eddie's been tracking him, got the word a half hour ago, gave it to me."

"You didn't go after him!"

"You were first priority."

"Oh—right."

"We're going now—with your permission."

"You got it! Where is he? And what's the problem?"

Chad told him. "He threw down his weapons so they would take him prisoner. And they did. They're going to kill him, sure, but they've got to do it with ceremony, y'know? And ceremony takes time. They don't know he's talking to us."

"Y'see?" Harry said to Guss, digging him. "Old-fashioned communication again. Radio. Audio. They can't hear. So we don't even need code."

"Very clever," Guss said. But he was honestly concerned for Homer. "Where do they have him prisoner?"

"Some kind of a—he called it a bat roost on the side of a cliff."

"That would be the Dossoes," Guss said. His yellow slitted eyes covered with the gray film, a sure indication that he was thinking hard. His forked tongue flicked. "Guardians of the Past." His eyes cleared, and they held anxiety. "Harry, you can't get in there."

"Why not?"

"They're reclusive. Their dwellings are high up on a cliff."

"Damn!" Harry said.

"Sir," Chad said. "Homer wants you to know—in case they get him before we do—he's found what you were looking for, and it was right where you thought it would be."

Harry's face lighted. "Great!"

Guss noticed Harry's reaction. "What's this? What were you looking for that Homer found?"

"Top secret!" Harry told him.

"Harry!" Guss was suddenly anxious. "Don't do that to me!"

Harry put an arm around Guss's shoulders. "Trust me, old buddy."

"But Harry, you scare me. When you start keeping secrets,

I start getting in trouble. Like the kols? How am I going to explain them to Ros Moss?"

"You a spy for old Moss?"

"Don't change the subject!"

"Well, are you?"

"You *know* I am! Why do you keep asking?"

"I want you to keep answering. So you'll feel guilty."

"I feel guilty! Okay? Now tell me—"

But Harry's attention had gone away. His face had begun to glow with that intensity Guss had learned meant a drive was generating, a drive that would not stop until—the words he heard Harry muttering described it best: "Gonna get that boy outa there some-goddamn-how or other!"

Homer had a view. From a height of over three hundred meters, he could see ten kilometers down the valley and five across the valley to the next range of mountains. The priest-guards, who were working in the courtyard immediately below, appeared as small sticks casting slim shadows in the early morning sunlight as they moved about an open pit where a fire was being prepared. And Homer was struck, in a macabre kind of way, at how parallel the development of two civilizations had been: a barbecue pit was a barbecue pit, whether on his father's cattle ranch or in a stone-paved courtyard on Essa.

"The thing is," he said, speaking into the small microphone as he looked down at the work going on below, "when we get a hog or a steer ready for a barbecue, we kill 'im first, see. Then we dress 'im out—all the guts, but maybe save the liver and heart; skin 'im—hide's valuable, y'know; cut the legs off at the first joint—those'll go to the glue factory; all this *before* we put 'im on the spit."

"Homer, for chrissakes!" The voice was Eddie's, a sick wail. "Will you cut it the hell out?"

"Hey, baby!" Homer was concerned. "What's-a matter?"

"You're gonna make me throw up!"

"A barbecue makes you throw up?"

"It ain't funny, you big cow flop!"

"I'm just tellin' you what they're doin', Eddie. Kind of a runnin' commentary. Y'know? Like a newscaster?"

"My ass! You're buggin' me!"

"You aren't even interested if they're gonna kill me and dress me out before they put me on the spit?"

There was a gagging sound.

"Eddie? You there?"

More gagging.

"Goddamn, Eddie. You better see a doctor, hear?"

Silence. A sniffling, snuffling sound.

Then Eddie's voice, weak but determined, came through. "Homer, I don't give a damn how big you are. When we get you back here, you're never gonna be safe. I'm gonna be sneakin' up behind you with a two-by-four and I'm gonna make you pay for what you just did to me. I'm gonna beat your goddamned brains out!"

Homer, mildly shocked, said accusingly, "You're talkin' dirty, Eddie!"

"Homer—goddamn!"

Then silence.

Homer waited, looking down at the activity below.

The priest-guards had not hurt him at all. Since he had offered no resistance, they had used no violence when they had taken him several hours before. They had tied his hands, bound his arms, and brought him to this cell-like cubicle, one of many fixed to the vertical face of the granite cliff. Beyond the heavy door that sealed him in there were armed priest-guards, and beyond them corridors that honeycombed the rock, centuries old, filled with the dry-dirt smell of the Essans, stale, gravelike.

A single vertical shaft, with a small and creaking elevator—the way they had brought him in—was the only means of access, he was sure. The cubicle, a very austere living space for a priest-guard when in everyday use, did sport a tiny balcony, on which Homer was standing now, and the railing held his uniform shirt displayed so that the particular cubicle that held him could be identified through binoculars; but Homer could not at the moment see any possible avenue of rescue.

"You there, cow flop?" Eddie asked.

"Bright-eyed and bushy-tailed."

"Now hear this—"

Then the voice of Harry Borg: "How y'doin', son?"

"Hangin' in, sir!"

"Good lad! We're gonna take you out of there."

"I'm willin'. But I don't see how."

"Turn around."

"I'm turning—hey!" Homer's voice rose in a sharp note of delight. "Where the hell did that come from?"

His eyes had found a thin, almost invisible line, weighted with a small sinker, then ran up the cliff face to disappear in the direction of the top, five hundred meters above.

"A gift from Arnie," Harry said. "He says it'll hold a ton."

"Damn whistlin'!" Arnie said. "I was stealin' that line to take home."

"You thief!" Homer said happily.

"Can you tie a bowline?" Harry asked.

"Can a bear crap in the woods?"

"Make it a good one, because you're goin' for one helluva ride."

Homer had the line wrapped in his shirt, looped around his chest and under his arms, and tied in a secure bowline in a matter of moments. "I'm tied and ready."

"Stand on the railing, like you were gonna fly."

"Am I gonna fly?"

"Like a bird, son. Like a big-ass bird."

Homer climbed to the railing of the small balcony and balanced there precariously. He looked down at the small sticklike figures of the Jassan priest-guards, busy with their preparations for the barbecue, and felt no regret at all that they were going to be disappointed. As he felt the line tighten, he could not help but holler: "Ya—hooo!"

An aircraft that had been hidden somewhere back of the top of the cliff face had appeared, moving carefully to take a smooth, even strain on the thin line and to pick Homer off the balcony rail as if he were taking flight.

And indeed, to the startled priest-guards below, who could not possibly have seen the line, it must have seemed as if the giant bassoe, remarkable enough in all respects from the beginning, could even fly. His strange call echoed back as he grew smaller in the distance. "Ya—hooo! Ya—hooo! Ya—hooo!"

But of course they couldn't hear it.

CHAPTER 26

As Harry Borg started down from fifty thousand meters in a corkscrew dive that lost altitude like a spinning, out-of-control rocket shot at the ground, he wondered if hot-dogging one of these one-man pursuit aircraft was an infectious disease or just a need born in every man to show off. Whatever it was, it had gotten so he couldn't fly square anymore.

"Damn showboater!" he said glumly. "Feels good, too."

The ancient city of Foss, the capital city of the Jassans, was growing before him as he screamed down toward the scattered cloud deck on his way to pay yet another visit to Ros Moss, the head of the Jassan government. While he didn't want to admit it even to himself, perhaps the principal reason for his show-off flying was that it afforded some kind of release from building inner tension that had gone beyond wire-tight to a point somewhere close to popping.

Time was so goddamned short!

He had left behind him tasks delegated to others which he would much rather have done himself: Homer and Arnie to perhaps the most important task; the big, amiable, but devastatingly effective Sam Barnstable to another; Guss to still another; and Chad and Eddie to the biggest and most difficult task of all. 'And me, I'm the ass-kisser."

He had to do whatever it was going to take to get Ros Moss

to believe what he had to say, and to get the full cooperation o the Jassan government in doing what had to be done.

Right now!

If they were going to stay alive longer than two days.

The old Jassan was waiting for him beside the fountain an pool in the outer garden. He was wearing his formal attire, th flowing gown of gold fabric, the purple turban, the violet ston that spoke of his authority suspended about his neck on the gol chain. He was most cordial. Was he ever anything else?

He heard Harry out, listening with his age-grayed muzzle tipped up attentively, his tongue playing about in Harry's direc tion, his large, golden eyes quite interested as Harry made th most impassioned pitch of his life. But he didn't believe a wor of it.

"But, sir!" Harry protested. "It's true! I double-damn-we guarantee it!"

"You've been misled," Moss said gently.

"No way!"

"Calm down, now, Mr. Borg," Moss said, still gently. "Liste to me for a few moments."

Harry took a deep breath. "I'm listening!"

Moss seemed to smile. "I trust you won't explode before I'm finished." He held up an eight-fingered hand quickly to foresta the outburst on Harry's lips. "Your mistake is understandable You don't fully comprehend the importance of our Essan—Jassa and Ussir alike—traditions."

"Bull!" Harry said under his breath.

"A tradition as important as Truce Time, and as old, one tha has been observed for so many years, is inviolate. Neither side under any circumstances, despite any provocation or any hop of gain, would give the thought of breaking truce time even moment's consideration. In your civilization, with your complet disregard for the important amenities, those decencies that mak life worth living, such a desecration could very well occur. Bu not in our civilization, not in our society."

Harry hit himself a hard crack on the side of his head. "My god!"

"What is it?" Moss said, alarmed.

"I think my communicator must be busted!" Harry said, hi

voice choked by a blue rage. "That crap I hear coming through can't be right! It can't be!"

Moss seemed mildly offended. "Are you doubting me?"

"Doubting you?" Harry said, fighting for control. "I'm tellin' you you're off your blasted rocker! The Ussirs are going to mount a full-scale attack during Truce Time—and you can take it to the bank! They're going to kill us! Believe it!"

"Not so," Moss said, quietly, adamantly. "You've been misled. Why? I don't know. Perhaps in jest. Perhaps, because you're from another world, to frighten you."

Harry threw his hands in the air. "Geez!"

He turned and began striding around the inner fountain in a fury. Behind him, Moss rose from the table and began feeding pellets of food to the large aquatic insects in the outer fountain, content to wait until Harry had stabilized again. This had happened before. Homo sapiens, Ros Moss had discovered, were inclined to rages that verged on insanity and from which they recovered, given time. Usually. To some extent, at least.

"All right!" Harry said, striding back, his voice under some kind of control. "I've got to tell you that I know with absolute certainty after that overflight I made yesterday—and your own General Staff will tell you the same thing—we can't beat those Green Guys! Not with our personnel! Not with our equipment! Not fighting the silly kind of war you've been fighting for a hundred years!"

"You're positive about that?"

"Dead positive!"

"Then what do you propose? I know you don't intend surrendering."

"How about letting *me* attack *them* during Truce Time?"

"Ah! Now I understand. Why didn't you ask this first, instead of lying to me about their intentions?"

"Goddamn it! I didn't lie to you!" Harry roared. "They're going to attack. But if I can get you to okay my attacking them, I've got the same result, haven't I?"

Moss conceded the point with an amused wave of his hand. "Yes, I suppose you have." Then he looked straight at Harry, so there would be no possibility of misunderstanding the thoughts he was communicating. "No. I will *not* give you permission to violate Truce Time. Do not ask again!"

But Harry kept trying. "It's about our only chance for a win in this comic-opera war of yours! It's about the only chance there is for you and me to stay alive another week!"

"Another week?" Moss asked. "We have six months!"

"To *win*, for chrissakes!" Harry's voice had climbed again. "We can lose it in the next three days! And that's *not winning* in block letters a mile high! You won't have to wait six months!"

Again, Moss held up a restraining hand. "Calm yourself, Mr. Borg. You can make your points without creating all that thunder and lightning in my head."

He turned to the insects again for a moment, to feed them and to think while Harry seethed. Then he turned back. His golden eyes, glowing now, became fixed on Harry. "You said 'about the only chance,' and that suggests you may possibly have still another alternative in mind."

Harry's dark blue eyes, never more furious, met and held Ros Moss's gold vertically slitted eyes. They both knew it was a confrontation. A contest of wills. And Moss's eyes gave first, the gray veil moving protectively across the shining orbs. Harry accepted it as a win.

"I'll tell you this much," he said. "I never give up—you know that."

"I know that."

"And if I have anything else in mind—and you don't know what it is—you can't be held accountable for it. Can you?"

"I suppose not."

"And you can't say no to something you're not asked?"

"Hardly."

"Okay," Harry said. He could feel sweat, suddenly, coldly, on his back, for his mind had been made up on a course of action that had until this moment been only a possibility, but that had now become a certainty sealed in the concrete of necessity. "Gonna leave it there, then," he said. "You've got until—" he looked at his watch "—eighteen hundred hours tomorrow to change your mind about attacking them first a day *before* Truce Time. If I don't hear from you—"

He didn't finish the sentence.

"Eighteen hundred hours?" Moss said after a long moment.

"Right!"

"Agreed," Moss said. "And, for the record, I'm telling you

that you are not to do anything of importance without consulting me first."

"For the record," Harry said.

"Now, is there anything else?"

"You damn well know it!" Harry said. "I told you my man had discovered you people are mind-blanking bassoes at birth. You said you couldn't believe it, but you would look into it. Have you?"

"Oh, that." Moss became indecisive, even evasive. He went back to his table and summoned a servant as he talked. "I haven't forgotten it. But I must say, in light of all else that needs my attention, I haven't given it first priority."

"It figures," Harry said. "And I know why."

"Suppose you tell me."

"Number one, while bassoe meat and bassoe hides are *not* necessities, bassoe meat is a delicacy and clothing made out of bassoe hides is a luxury no one is going to give up willingly. No one who can afford them, that is—the rich, the ones who run this country. Okay?"

"Number two?" Moss asked as a servant appeared with a tray laden with the usual light food and hot drink. "Have something?" he offered, helping himself.

"Number two," Harry said, the cords of his neck beginning to show the strain of inner pressure. "The fact the bassoes are born intelligent and are mind-blanked has been kept a deep, dark secret for a thousand years. Why? Why a secret? Because your *citizens*, your *average* citizens—and I'm not talking about the rich elite—would never for a moment stand for using intelligent creatures for food! Now would they?"

"I think not!"

"So you don't want to know it's done."

"If it *is* done." Moss took a candied fruit and put it in his mouth. He waved his hand. "I have no real proof. The whole idea is so very farfetched, Mr. Borg. Really."

"Damn it!" Harry said. "My man saw it being done!"

"So you say. So he says."

"You're not going to make an investigation of your own?"

"Of course, I will."

"When?" Harry demanded.

"Soon." He picked up another morsel. "These are really very good."

"Damn!" Harry said.

He turned and strode away. Ros Moss's gentle voice came to him as he reached the inner fountain. "Mr. Borg."

"Yeah?" he replied without turning.

"I'm not clear on what you intend next."

Harry turned. "I'm gonna wait until eighteen hundred hours tomorrow to hear from you. If I don't hear, I'm gonna do whatever I have to do to save your country's ass! And your ass! And my ass! And I'll do it or die trying!"

Ros Moss's voice was gentle again, remote. "I expect you will."

"Will what?"

"Die trying."

CHAPTER 27

The building that had been used as a gymnasium by the former owner of the estate Harry knew as Guss's place had been converted into a satellite War Room, which now contained all the necessary equipment—the giant video screens, the thought communicators, the receptors for the satellite cameras, and much else. The "old-fashioned" radio Eddie Cole had installed used only a small space in one corner, but it was to this that Harry went directly after landing.

Chad Harrison, Eddie Cole, and Guss were waiting for him there. The Jassan technicians at the main screens and instruments kept their attention fixed on their work and away from the humans. Harry's first question was for Eddie. "What d'you hear from Homer?"

The forehead of the young black gleamed with a shine of sweat, and his almond-shaped eyes were distressed. "Nothing, sir—in the last two hours."

"You got a problem?"

"Not with the equipment, sir," Eddie said. "I'm sure not." His tone suggested he was wishing he was more certain than only sure. "I don't think he's got his receiver open."

"Homer's like that," Chad said, trying to take the weight off Eddie. "Won't report until he's got good news."

"Damn!" Harry said. "I could use a progress report, you know!"

"I'll keep trying, sir!" Eddie said.

"What about Sam?"

"Same thing, sir. No word."

"Balls!"

"I'm sure it's not the equipment, sir. I—"

Harry dropped a hand on Eddie's shoulder. "And so am I, son. Listen to me. That locater saved my ass this morning. You're my man, win or lose. Just hang in."

A relieved smile broke on Eddie's face. "Sir!"

Harry turned to Chad and Guss. "You been in touch with the General Staff?"

"All day," Chad said. "Result negative."

"Whaddayuh mean, negative?" Harry asked, his voice rising. "You told 'em what's comin', didn't you?"

Chad and Guss exchanged glances. Clearly, Harry Borg was very tired. The lines of strain were plain around his bloodshot eyes. Even a superman had to rest sometime, and neither Chad nor Guss was sure when Harry had slept last.

"They don't believe the Ussirs will attack during Truce Time," Chad said. "Won't even consider the possibility."

Harry turned on Guss. "You told 'em?"

"I told them."

"Still won't buy it?"

"Laughed it off."

"Sheeeit!" Harry said in supreme disgust.

Chad's tanned face was stiff with self-discipline, his gray eyes rock-steady. He continued the bad news without trying to duck. "They're shutting down, sir."

"Shutting down?"

"Getting ready for the games, sir. Like the Friday crowd at home. They're already on the freeways, heading out of town."

"Holy jumpin' Jehosophat!" Harry was in a fury now. He strode away, waving his hands over his head, then strode back to belabor Guss.

"You people are nuts!" he yelled at Guss, his face only a foot away. And, just as his furious voice was loud and hot enough to blister paint, the thoughts he thundered at Guss were enough to overload every circuit, to blow every fuse in Guss's head.

"No damn wonder you get your asses whipped! You're dreamers! You eat butterflies! You're not plugged in! Good godalmighty! A whole country of idiots! And that includes your president! Biggest idiot of you all! Can't get him to see the facts, king of the dream merchants!"

And he went on like that.

And while he was going on, Guss's eyes were drawn to the stone that was called the Red Flame that was suspended about Harry's neck. *The stone was pulsing!* It was pulsing as if alive! Each raging word uttered by Harry seemed to be generated by the stone. The bright blood-red flamed with each word and flamed higher. It was *burning*! Guss fell back in frightened awe. Suddenly he knew in his heart that the legend of the Red Flame was no myth. It was true! And Harry Borg was the reincarnation!

Guss moved the gray film across his large yellow eyes, retreating to the security of his inner self, his tongue flicking out only now and then, waiting for the fury of the Red Flame to subside. And that took a while. But the Red Flame did finally relent, losing its hot red glow, and as it did, Harry's voice began to lose volume. He strode away and stopped at a distance with his back to Guss and Chad, and then he turned to them, shaking his head in tired self-recrimination.

"I think I need some rest," he said. "What d'you think?"

"I think you're overdue," Chad said.

Guss's eyes cleared. "Long overdue."

Harry turned to the other two. "Eighteen hundred hours tomorrow," he said. "I gave Ros Moss until then to change his mind and okay an order for us to attack them just before Truce Time—to beat them to the punch."

Guss was shocked. "Harry! You didn't!"

"Sure as hell did."

"But—we can't do that! We can't violate Truce Time! Moss would never allow it—never!"

Harry gave Guss a tired grin. "You're probably right. Nice people don't fight wars with dirty tricks, and the Jassans are nice people, by God." He looked at Eddie. "When you hear from Homer, tell 'im. Eighteen hundred hours tomorrow, or it's Katy, bar the door."

"Eighteen hundred hours tomorrow, sir!"

"Some good news, sir," Chad said.

"Hey," Harry said, smiling. "I can use it."

"Mrs. Calder has been defused," Chad said. "She and Tippi are in your quarters waiting for you. I believe they have a small celebration in mind."

A big grin of real pleasure lighted Harry's face. Pleasure and enormous relief. "All right!" Impulsively he put an arm around the shoulders of both Chad and Guss, gave them a squeeze, and shook his head in wonderment. His voice was just a little giddy. "That Sassan—he's something else! We gotta take care of 'im, y'know? He can work miracles. That rejuvenation process of his—just that alone is gonna make us stinkin' rich." His voice trailed off as a new thought occurred to him.

"What about Illia? He do anything for her?"

Quietly, trying not to show any emotion, Chad said, "Illia's disappeared. Kidnapped—gone."

"No!" Harry was hurting.

"No trace. Don't know who took her. Probably the bastards who blanked her. Took Toss, too. Do anything to keep their secret a secret, I guess."

"You got folks out hunting for her?"

"Yeah. But . . ." Chad shook his head. "I'm afraid they killed them both. Be the easiest way."

Harry gave Chad's shoulder a comforting shake. "Now, come on! Y'gotta keep hangin' in!" And he looked at Guss and gave his shoulders an additional shake. "Same for you, old buddy. We're gonna make it, some damn how or other. Trust me."

Then he left them and walked, not quite steadily, away. Looking after him, Chad turned to exchange glances with Eddie and Guss.

"One tuckered turkey," Eddie said.

"Old Never-Quit," Chad agreed.

In his living quarters, Harry did indeed find a small celebration waiting. A table was set, candles were burning, and a bottle of vassle, the euphoria-producing drink, waited in an ice bucket. But there was apprehension, too. Though she was doing her best to hide it with her warmest smile, Harry could see the worry and concern in Lori's eyes, the questions: Had he forgiven her? Did he trust her now? Did he believe she had been cured? And those same concerns, with only small differences, looked at him out of Tippi's eyes: Was he going to take her mother back? Were they all going to be happy again? Harry gave them both his most wholehearted answer. He opened his arms wide.

"Come here to me!"

And they came with a rush, each to be wrapped in a giant arm, to be lifted in a close embrace that all but smothered them with comforting reassurance, with love.

"I'm the luckiest man in the world."

They clung to him. Lori turned her eyes away, trying to hide sudden tears. "Harry, I—I was so afraid."

He set them both down and swatted their behinds. "It never happened!" he said. When they had answered his grin with smiles no longer tremulous, he said, "But Godfrey-mighty! I'm the hungriest man alive!"

The food was good, the wine even better, and the company was the greatest. Add to that many long hours without rest, and Harry found it almost impossible to keep his eyes open after he'd cleaned his plate.

"Mom," Tippi said warningly. "He's too big to carry."

Harry's voice was slurred. "Whaddayuh talkin'?"

"She means you're about to fall asleep in that chair," Lori said gently. "Get up, now. We'll steer you into the bedroom."

Harry let the two females guide him toward the sleeping quarters. At the sight of the bed, open, waiting, he took three long steps on his own and fell forward. He was aware only of his face striking the feather softness, and then the blessed comfort of sleep overcame him.

Lori let Tippi help her remove the weapons belt from Harry's waist, the Red Flame from about his neck, the boots from his feet. She even let Tippi help her bathe him with warm water and cloths, using all proper discretion, to be sure, before covering him for the night. And then, with Tippi safely tucked away in her own bed, Lori lay down beside Harry, secure in the knowledge that the surgeon Sassan had found and erased the evil monster that had been implanted in her brain, and that Harry had forgiven her. He was sleeping beside her now as if drugged, and wasn't that a sign of total forgiveness, total trust? She put an arm around his naked waist, snuggled close, and slept.

And in two hours, she awakened.

She was not completely aware that she was awake. It was, again, a dreamlike state, as if she were watching herself from a distance. And she saw herself rise from the bed, moving very quietly, and cross to the recliner where the weapons belt lay beneath Harry's clothing.

A vague alarm sounded in her mind. "No—you shouldn't."

But the alarm passed. And Lori watched the shadowed, naked woman she knew to be herself draw the short sword from the scabbard, turn, and, holding the sword in both hands walk silently to stand beside the bed. Deeply asleep, Harry was lying on his back again, the covering drawn back to expose his upper body, in a posture that made it seem he was offering his naked chest to sacrifice.

The naked woman held the blade pointing straight up. "For peace," she whispered.

Then she reversed the blade. Still gripping the sword in both hands, she lifted it high and paused, gathering strength for the downward plunge. "Kill!" She heard the naked woman's whisper, soft, reverent.

Then a scream, shrill, blasphemous: *"Mother!"*

The scream awakened Harry and sent him rolling. The sword plunged down, drove through the bed where the instant before his chest had lain bared. The slight figure of the gown-clad Tippi hurtled into the naked woman with force enough to knock her sprawling.

"Mother! Mother!" the child wailed. "You did it again!"

And in an awful moment of awakening, or realization, Lori found herself fully aware again, staring at the sword that stood buried to the hilt in the center of the bed, at Harry, naked, standing on the far side, looking down at her, his face drawn by anger, his dark and intense blue eyes burning.

"Oh, God! Harry!"

Harry strode to her, grabbed her by the upper arms, and jerked her roughly to her feet. He stared into her horror-stricken eyes as if trying to see into her mind, as if he wanted to break open her head, to search and find the monster that possessed her and destroy it with his own hands.

"Harry," she pleaded. "They didn't cure me."

He threw her down suddenly, reached out, and drew the sword

from the bed. He stood a moment, sword in hand, looking at her.

Tippi, seeing what she thought was murder in his eyes, attacked him again, screaming, "You can't! You can't!"

She struck at him with small fists, hitting his chest, his face. But, though he closed a big arm around her, he seemed oblivious to the blows, letting her strike as she would. Then he tossed the sword toward his weapons belt and whispered in Tippi's ear, "Cool it, child. It's going to be all right."

Tippi stopped fighting. Harry set her down. Then, still holding his arm around Tippi, he looked at Lori, half sitting, half lying, on the floor before him, tears streaming down her tormented face.

"I'm not cured, Harry."

"That's obvious."

"You can't trust me—you have to kill me."

"Couldn't possibly."

"But I can't live like this!" she moaned. "I'll kill myself."

"Can't do that, either."

"I've got to!"

"You forget our baby?"

"Oh, my God!" She had forgotten. She covered her face with both hands, wailing like a lost soul. "What are we going to do?"

Harry set Tippi aside. He took the sheetlike covering from the bed, flipping it open, stretched it on the floor beside Lori. He picked her up, laid her straight on the sheet near the edge, put her arms down, then began rolling her snugly, tightly in the sheet.

"What're you doing?" she asked, frightened.

"Gonna give you back to that klutz of a Sassan," Harry said as he worked. "Gonna tell 'em to keep trying until he gets it right."

"Harry—I can't move!"

"That's the idea, sweetheart."

He tossed her on the bed, drew a covering over her. As he straightened, Tippi leaped at him, caught him around the neck, and planted a kiss on his lips. "Thanks, Pop!"

She dropped to the floor and ran away.

"Harry..." It was Lori, still frightened.

Harry bent and kissed her gently. "You shut up now, sweetheart. I gotta get some rest."

CHAPTER 28

"Whoever said, 'It's gotta get worse before it gets better,' sure knew what the hell he was talkin' about," Harry grumbled. "If you can stand a cliché at a time like this." He was waiting with Chad and Guss at Eddie Cole's station, where the radio hummed softly, refusing to come alive with either Homer's voice or Sam's.

"I've got another one," Chad said. "How about, 'When the going gets tough, the tough get going'?"

Harry gave him a punch on the shoulder.

"'When it's too tough for everybody else, it's just right for me'?"

"Even worse!" Harry said.

Guss was looking back and forth between the two as they bandied clichés, reading them through his thought communicator but completely unable to understand why the men reacted to perfectly sensible words the way they did. It had to be a form of madness.

"You're nuts," he told them. "If you can joke at a time like this, you've got to be nuts."

"You want me to cry?" Harry asked.

"I think *I* would," Guss said soberly, "if I could."

"We're just whistling in the dark," Chad said.

"There's a cliché that fits pretty good," Harry said.

The day had begun with an urgent call to the surgeon Sassan

and a conference over Lori. Sassan had brought large and detailed X rays of Lori's brain, and began a long detailed explanation of what was wrong with her brain and where it had been altered— as nearly as he had been able to ascertain and understand the facts.

"Very difficult," he had said, a much-distressed Jassan, his glasses crooked on his muzzle, his large yellow eyes apologetic. "So many, many circuits! Imagine, if you will, a computer board with a thousand chips, each with fifty pins. Which two chips? Which two pins? The possible combinations, to all purposes, are endless."

"Ah, for chrissakes!" Harry had said.

"All I can say is I'll keep trying."

"It's no use, Harry," Lori had said in utter defeat. She had been there, listening. "He can't fix me!"

"C'mon, now!"

"He's just ducking, Harry! You know that. There's no possible way he can straighten me out. I can't be around you ever again!"

Harry had taken her in his arms, felt the trembling in her body as she fought tears. "Give him another chance, sweet. I didn't mean it when I called him a klutz. Look at the record. He's a genius!"

Her eyes had been wide, pleading. "He admits—"

"Don't worry!" He had held her away, looking earnestly into her eyes. "Even if *he* can't do it, there's still one last hope."

"Hope? What hope?"

"Me," he had said.

Whistling in the dark.

And when Harry had asked Chad about the search for Illia, it had been more of the same. No trace of her or Toss had been found.

"You sure about your soldiers?" he had asked Chad. "Y're-member the guards I had quit cold when they saw that giant spider, what'sitsname? Bissi? Laid flat out and let that sucker kill them."

"I remember," Chad had said. "But I think mine'll bust their asses for me. No, I'm sure of it!"

"Okay. But don't give up!"

"I'm a realist, sir."

"Try being an optimist," Harry had said, giving Chad's shoul-

der a comforting grip. "Optimism, pessimism—you get 'em for
the same price. Why buy the misery route?"

Guss had been listening again. "How can you be an optimist
today? We're most probably going to be arrested and executed
tomorrow! The day after at the latest."

Harry had given him a hard grin. "You given up on your all-
wise president, Mr. Ros Moss?"

"Given up? I never started!" Guss had been in genuine despair.
"He absolutely will not give permission to attack right before,
or during, Truce Time." Guss had thrown up his hands. "And
even if he would, you can't get our troops to attack. They've
already laid down their arms!"

"He's right, y'know," Chad had said. "I tried all night to call
them back, just in case. They've even shut down the War Room."

"Somebitch," Harry had said softly. "Here I am, standing in
Custer's shoes again. Everywhere I look, nothin' but goddamn
Indians."

"What are you going to do?" Guss asked anxiously.

"I'll think of something."

Whistling in the dark.

All that had been some time ago. Now the hands of the clock
had moved past three o'clock—fifteen hundred hours. The deadline he had set, go or no go, was only three hours away.

He made a quick circuit of the main monitors and screens
and asked the desperately intent operators the same question:
"Any change?" And they all gave him the same answer: "No
change." Which meant that with all their equipment focused and
assembling data, and with all their computers analyzing and
summarizing that data, the inescapable conclusion was:

*The Ussirs would attack just before daybreak, at about four
hundred hours in the morning.*

Harry returned to stand with Guss and Chad at Eddie's radio
station, his face extremely grave. "Runnin' out of options," he
said.

"And time," Chad added.

Eddie's eyes, shining black, intense in his ebony face, showed
no weariness, though he had been on duty at the radio without
rest for hours beyond remembering. He turned dials slowly back,
then forward, listening, listening, and, though the others didn't
know it, praying silently.

"C'mon, Homer," Harry whispered. "We need you."

Another half hour ticked by.

Then it was not Homer who broke the silence.

"Sam calling Eddie. Over."

"Read you, Sam!" Eddie said instantly. "Over."

"Mission accomplished. Coming in. Out."

"Damn!" Chad exploded. "How about that big slob!" He hit Harry an almost crippling blow on the shoulder, a blow Harry never felt, he was still so very intent on a more important need.

"C'mon, Homer!" he whispered, his voice wire tight, his eyes riveted on the makeshift radio as if he were trying by force of will to make the voice of Homer or Arnie come through. Sam's call was gravy; what Homer would have, if he were able to get it, was the meat and potatoes, their only possible chance, however remote, of being able to stay alive and eventually get home.

"He'll get it," he promised the others.

Once the good luck started rolling, he'd always said, you could hardly stop it. Bad luck the same way. And the call from Sam with word that he had succeeded had to be the turning point.

"Gotta be!" he said. "Gotta be!"

And it was.

Homer's voice came through the speaker a few moments later. "Calling Eddie."

"Read you, Cow Flop!"

"Got it. Tell Iron-Balls it's loaded, operative, ready to go."

"Tell 'im yourself."

"Good lad!" Harry said, fighting sudden elation. "What's your ETO?"

"We're en route," Homer said. "Estimate landing sixteen-thirty hours, sir."

"I'll be waiting," Harry said.

He turned away, raised clenched fists, his face taut and straining with his enormous relief, letting his excitement burst. "Will I *ever* be waiting!" he yelled. He gripped Chad fiercely by the shoulders. "Y'see? Y'see what I mean?"

Chad was equally glad. "Be an optimist? Think positive?"

"Right! Costs the same! Works about as often!" Then he held Chad away, his eyes severely questioning. "What's this 'Iron-Balls'? Who's Iron-Balls?"

Chad's face was innocent. "I wouldn't know, sir."

Harry held him a moment longer. "Hell, you wouldn't!" Then he looked pained. "Iron-Balls! That's what's wrong with this whole operation—I don't get no respect."

Both men roared with laughter.

Guss watched them, puzzled, even hurt. He'd been left out again. "This is no time for joking," he said when they'd begun to quiet down.

"Sorry, Guss," Harry said.

He became serious.

And with good reason. They were a long, long way from being out of the woods. In all truth, what Homer was providing gave them a chance—but no better than a hundred-to-one shot at survival, and that could be counted only as slightly better than no chance at all. They were still a helluva long way from home.

"You going to tell me now?" Guss said.

"Tell you what?" Harry said, feigning ignorance.

"You know damn well!" Guss had lost patience. "What Homer's been after, what he's bringing back. I've asked you twice. You wouldn't answer. *Now* answer!"

Harry looked at him. "I can't."

"Can't, or won't?" Guss asked, very angry.

"Both," Harry said. His voice was not unkind, not rude. It was the tone of a friend talking to a friend. But it was absolutely firm.

"Why not?" Guss's anger became tinged with hurt. "We're in this together. I thought we were close friends. Our lives depend on what each other does."

Harry caught Guss by the shoulders and looked him squarely in the eye. "Like I told Moss, if I don't tell you what I'm up to beforehand, you can't be held in any way responsible for what I do."

"You're going to do something violent?"

"Whatever it takes to keep us alive."

"Harry, you're scaring me!"

"Another reason I'm not going to tell you."

"Damn it, Harry—"

"Wait," Harry said. "You'll know soon enough—before any other Jassan. That's a promise."

* * *

Homer and Arnie brought their aircraft in to land only a few moments over their predicted ETO of sixteen-thirty. A battered, worn, hollow-eyed pair, they got out of the aircraft to stand on the landing pad before Harry and throw him a couple of wobbly salutes.

"What took you so long?" Harry asked.

It wasn't a criticism; it was the kind of backhanded compliment the two young men understood best, and one they couldn't fail to know came from the bottom of his heart.

"Finding a tech," Homer said.

"Couldn't keep a tech alive in a museum for three hundred years," Arnie said, his tough face wearing a glow of triumph. "But we finally found a live one that could read the book on the sucker. Homer coaxed 'im."

"A little manual persuasion," Homer said mildly.

"And it's 'all systems go'?"

"Guaranteed. All we got to do is drop it, sir."

"Not 'we,'" Harry said. "Me."

"But, sir—" Both Homer and Arnie began a protest.

"No!" Then, to soften the blow, Harry said, "I won't live long enough to ever thank you enough, or to finish telling you how proud I am of both of you. 'Champions' doesn't half describe you."

Angry disappointment stared at him out of their bloodshot eyes.

"Crap!" Arnie muttered.

"Didn't hear that," Harry said. "Fall out."

A ground crew was already at work transferring the load from the battered transport Homer and Arnie had used to the finest and fastest craft the Jassan Air Force had to offer. They promised the task would be finished by seventeen hundred hours. Harry and Chad went back to the satellite War Room to make final preparations. Guss, whom Harry had excluded from the landing pad, was waiting, seething with anger and anxiety.

"Harry!" he said warningly.

"Hang on, old buddy," Harry said. "I'm not making a move until the eighteen-hundred-hours deadline I gave Moss. If he comes through—and I don't think he will—there'll be no need for me to act, and no need to tell you what I was going to do. Okay?"

"I'm *scared*, Harry!"

"Makes two of us."

They still had time to wait before the deadline, and it was the hardest waiting Harry had ever done. It was particularly hard because he was sure Ros Moss would not give an order to attack during Truce Time, and that it wouldn't be any use if he did, because his troops had already dispersed. It was simply a base he had to touch, so that whatever came after his flight, history would show that he had given the Jassans every last chance to do it their way.

While waiting, Harry and Chad plotted a flight plan, checked times, and rehearsed details—all in whispered conference, still excluding Guss. When this work was done, Chad had a statement to make.

"Sir, I've got to tell you, I'm a better flyer than you are."

"Think so?" Harry said.

"I damn well know so, sir."

Reading Chad clearly, Harry felt a sudden surge of warm admiration for the young man. *By God*, he told himself, *we're still making them right back home!* "And you want to make this flight?"

"I insist on it—sir!"

Harry put a big hand on Chad's shoulder.

"No!" The negative was final.

"Sir!" Chad said. It was cheerful and willing obedience, as he knew it had to be when an order was given by a superior officer. But he could not hide his deep disappointment.

"Stand by," Harry said, his eyes holding pride.

Harry turned to Guss when the clock finally showed him eighteen hundred hours straight up. "Time's gone," he said.

"Finally!" Guss said. His large, vertically slitted eyes burned with intensity, his forked tongue was a blur under flaring nostrils, his many-fingered hands were clenched. He knew Harry would not have made him wait until this last instant unless what he was going to say would be devastating.

"Guss, let's get this clear: The way it stands, the Ussirs are going to attack in the morning. They'll win easily, because your dream-merchant leaders refuse to accept the cold, hard facts.

You'll die. I'll die. Your country will be totally wiped out—as a country."

"I'm not absolutely sure—"

"I am. So I'm gonna get them first."

When Guss realized what Harry was going to do, he screamed. Literally. A high, keening wail of sheer horror and anguish came through Harry's communicater, mental pain almost beyond bearing.

"No—no—no!" he cried, when he could find any words at all to transmit. "You can't! You *can't*!"

"I've got no choice," Harry said.

The tension in his face, in his eyes, in the set of his jaw, told of the extreme emotional hammering Guss's reaction was causing him to endure. And adding to it was his own barely controllable guilt, present from the start, burgeoning now inside him.

"You barbarian!" Guss screamed. He put his gaping muzzle close to Harry's face. "You savage! You'll drive us back a thousand years—to the fires!"

"Can't be helped."

"I won't let you! I'll warn them—"

He began a lunge toward the communicating equipment, but Chad, who had moved behind Guss, closed powerful arms around him, lifted him, kicking, struggling furiously, and carried him away.

The air was very thin and still at fifty thousand meters, and except for a soft clicking of the autopilot answering commands from the inboard computer that held the aircraft on course, the cockpit was silent. Below, the land was distant, bare, and cold in darkness silvered by the light of an almost full October moon.

There was little for Harry to do, and little for him to see, on his way to the target. But there was time—and to spare—for him to think.

The anguished cries of Guss in the moments before he had left still rang in his mind. And the cries of his own conscience echoed with them. But there were times in the affairs of men, and in this case in the affairs of Essans as well, when it became necessary to commit the most awful crimes against a few so that the majority could live. But it made those crimes against the few no less horrible, no more bearable, to rationalize them thus. They had to stand, with those who committed them, as utterly despicable.

And in these moments, again a time of great need, he closed his right hand around the stone of the Red Flame; and again he found it throbbing, and, staring down at it, he saw the Red Flame burning. Whether real or fancied, what he saw gave him comfort, said to him somehow that he was indeed following the right course. And he needed that very much, because what he was about to do he knew beyond any shadow of a doubt would most certainly change the life of this strange planet forever.

For good or ill?

That was yet to be discovered.

In a very short while he saw the vast city and military complex of Usso begin to advance over the horizon of his scanning screen, each detail revealed with perfect clarity. It was there that the main strength of the enemy lay. It was there, too, that upward of a million civilians were living, both Ussirs and the Jassans who had been subjugated by the occupation. The complex was a city that would have been Chicago at the tip of Lake Michigan in Harry's world, and he thanked God it was not his city and his people, shining silver and helpless beneath him, as he set his aircraft into a screaming dive toward his target.

Chad Harrison, who had been following his progress on monitors in the War Room, spoke quietly, reassuringly. "Right on, sir."

"They watching?"

"Affirmative."

Harry saw his target approach, and with the greatest of care he brought it into his sights. And when he released the bomb, he said a small prayer. "With God..."

The bomb gone, he pulled out of the screaming dive and reached for the heavens again. There was still the possibility that the bomb, centuries old, would not detonate, even though technicians had assured Homer it would.

Detonate it did!

Harry held his eyes away from the blinding flash, and for moments afterward, before turning his head to see the awful mushroom cloud, lifting, blooming beneath him. And then he headed home, a sick feeling deep inside, a sick feeling he knew he would carry the rest of his life.

On landing, he was met by an hysterically triumphant Guss, who screamed at him with insane joy.

"You missed!" Gus screamed, a distinct froth flecking his gaping mouth. "By all the Gods! You missed! You missed!"

They were in Guss's place, in the War Room, where Homer, Chad, Arnie, Eddie, Sam, and all the Jassan high command whom they'd been able to find had been assembled to watch the bombing on the giant screens.

Tiredly, knowing the answer, but wanting the confirmation, he asked Chad, "Did I miss?"

"No, sir. Right on target."

"There you go," Harry said to Guss and the others. "I didn't miss."

"The hell you didn't!" Guss was still wild. "Your evil bomb did *not* explode on Usso! It fell way out in the lake! On that island! That empty island! There wasn't an Ussir there! There was nobody there! You see? The Gods defeated you! They wouldn't allow your evil!"

Harry reached out and clamped a big, viselike hand around Guss's muzzle, and though Guss had no voice, the sudden gesture served to throttle his mental raging.

"I didn't miss," he said when he was sure he had Guss's attention.

It took Guss a moment. "You mean you—"

"That's right."

"But—but—why?"

The explanation took a few moments, and it was not given until there was some measure of calm restored, until they were well into another crucial waiting period. Then, a hot drink in hand, and with a measure of diffidence apparent, at least to the human beings present, he told them why.

"From the time of Hiroshima and Nagasaki," he said, "I've wondered over and over why Truman didn't drop the atom bombs on the side of Fujiyama, instead of on cities. It would have served just as well—a demonstration. A warning of what *could* happen, what *would* happen if the Japanese did not surrender. And they wanted to. The fire-bombing of Tokyo had them on their knees. But no. The scientists, and Truman, wanted to demonstrate what their new bomb could do at its very worst."

Harry sat for a moment, looking at his shaking hands. "I wasn't going to make the same mistake, believe me."

"Do you think the Ussirs will surrender?" Guss asked hesitantly.

"I think they'll back off," Harry said. "Might even pack up and go home."

CHAPTER 29

Harry was right.

The most awful destructive power of the atom bomb had been known to the Jassans for centuries, and had been all but forgotten. What had been forgotten, too, was the determination to defend themselves against invasion, against subjugation by a foreign power—against the loss of their freedom. And when that determination, revived, was demonstrated by a willingness to use any means, even the atom bomb, surely the least deadly of the weapons they had relegated to museums as too dangerous to use, the Ussirs were quick to decide there had to be an easier and better way to mend their economy than by making war against their neighbors.

Before noon the next day the Ussirs answered the ultimatum that had been sent them under the name of Ros Moss. The Jassans were fiends beyond description for using the atom bomb, the answer stated, but rather than risk the lives of innocent people, the Ussirs were going to cease all their efforts to bring new and joyous living to Jassa and retire to the far side of the Eastern Ocean.

"Whatever," Harry said. "They're going."

He was once again in the inner garden with Ros Moss. He had been summoned there only an hour after his return from the bombing mission to wait with the president for the response from the Ussirs. The fact that six of the president's armed guards stood with weapons trained on Harry, ready to blow him away at Moss's command, had bothered Harry only a little.

Moss was still staring at the now blank screen, the capitulation of the Ussirs a thing of moments past. He turned slowly. A movement of his hand sent the guards and their weapons of Harry's destruction away.

The staggering impact of all the news—that Harry had unearthed and used a weapon long ago condemned as too dangerous, that he had used it successfully without loss of life, that the Ussirs had capitulated and were leaving the continent—had been much too much for the old Jassan to absorb quickly. While he was still in the process, he resorted to small talk.

"Your female," he said, his gaze wandering. "Did I understand you to say she has been returned to normal?"

"That's right," Harry said. "One of my men, Sam Barnstable, the biggest one. Remember him?"

"Oh, yes. Frightening in size."

"He went into that bassoe meat-packing plant and found the surgeon who had set her up to kill me. After a little of what Chad calls 'manual persuasion' he was only too happy to show Sassan how to set her right. These two chips, these two pins— that kind of thing. She's all right now. Very loving."

"And the bassoe female—the intelligent one?"

"Her, too," Harry said. "Seems the Jassan Chad hauled out of the black building, the bassoe mind-blanking plant—his name's Toss—wanted to repay Chad for his freedom. He took Illia back to the plant, used their equipment, set her right, and smuggled her out again."

"Glad to hear it," Moss was muttering through the communicator in Harry's head. "I'm going to have to look into your allegations about the mind-blanking."

"Gonna have to do more than that!"

The harshness of Harry's voice brought Moss's attention sharply to bear. He focused his large golden, vertically-slitted eyes on Harry; his forked tongue flicked at the human. "Ah!" he said. "The payment?"

"That's right." Harry got up to pace around the fountain. "I can take it you're a man of your word, Mr. Moss?"

"Indeed you can."

"What I've done has saved your country, your kind, centuries of misery. Am I right?"

"That's a fair statement, yes," Moss responded. "I'm happy to say that my estimate of your character and your ability was proven correct."

"Doesn't hurt your position, does it?"

"Like you, I think I'll be considered a hero."

"And in return for all this," Harry said, sitting on the fountain edge, unmindful of the aquatic insects that came to nibble at his shorts, "I was to be given certain rewards."

"That was the understanding."

"We Homo sapiens can go home."

"Yes. At your convenience. When you're ready."

"And there was more."

"You hoped for more—let's put it that way. Do you want to repeat what you hoped for?"

"Number one: An open door between your world and ours," Harry said. "Allow free trade and communications."

"Absolutely not."

"Still think we're going to blow ourselves up with a nuclear war?"

"We know you are. It's just a matter of when."

"You may be right," Harry said thoughtfully. "If the situation changes, I'll come back."

"You have another request?"

"I have two more."

"One at a time, please."

"I'm not going to be able to get my men to leave until they know your population has been told they have been eating intelligent creatures—like cannibals. Once they're told, your people will put a stop to it. That's what we want."

"And the last one?"

"I want to take Sassan's rejuvenation process back with me."

Moss thought for a moment. "That would mean unlimited wealth for you, wouldn't it?"

"All right. Yeah—it probably would mean pretty good money."

"Nonsense!" Moss said. "We both know you would become incredibly rich." He thought a moment. "Easily as rich as the men who have been selling bassoe meat and hides in our world."

He thought another moment. "I think *there* is the fair exchange.
You can have one or the other. But not both."

"Will you explain that?"

"You can take the riches away from our kind, such as Sos
Vissir, who profits on the bassoe meat and hides, by forcing me
to end their use. Or you can have the riches you would gain
from the rejuvenation process."

"But not both," Harry said.

"Not both."

Oh, you bastard! Harry cursed under his breath.

It took a few days to get all the clearances, to get their packing
done, and to get them all together in a plane and airborne. As
Guss's sumptuous summer home receded into the distance, Harry
found himself whistling a tune he'd last heard played repeatedly
on a troopship, back in 1945, as the ship crossed the Pacific
toward the port of Seattle. A thing called "Sentimental Journey."
It had meant a lot then. And it meant a lot now.

"But you're off-key," Eddie said. "Whatever the tune."

And he probably was.

When he had told them of Moss's deal—one, but not both—
Guss, who was riding with them as far as the gateway, had said,
"I know how much great wealth can mean in your world, Harry.
I don't blame you. And, besides, the bassoes won't know. They'll
just go on as they have for thousands of years."

"Yeah—poor suckers," Harry said.

The craft that was taking them to the rundown estate that had
once belonged to Guss's family slowed, then came to a stop in
midair at about two thousand meters, in that miraculous way of
Jassan aircraft.

"C'mon," Harry said to Guss. "I want to show you some-
thin'."

He motioned the others out of their seats. And they gathered
around him at the viewport: Lori, Tippi, Chad, Illia, Eddie,
Homer, Arnie, and Sam.

"Look there."

Below, in the middle distance, plainly in view, was the huge
black building, one of many scattered across the land, that housed
the centuries-old secret mind-blanking operation. Harry lifted a

small box from which extended an antenna. He pointed the antenna at the black building.

"Watch carefully," he said.

He pressed a button and the black building below them seemed suddenly to swell, to expand, to vomit an enormous cloud of black smoke. An instant later a shock wave struck the plane and bounced them, stumbling, about. When they looked again, the black building was no more than a smoking heap of black rubble.

A bit sheepishly, Harry said, "Moss set it up so I could blow this one—as a special reward. The others went up at the same time."

Guss was incredulous. "There went your fortune!"

Harry shrugged. "Here came my self-respect."

For a few moments military courtesy was forgotten. Chad, Eddie, Arnie, Homer, and Sam set about pummeling their commanding officer in a demonstration of admiration and gratitude. When it was over, and Harry was seated again with Lori on one side and Tippi on the other, he had a complaint.

"That's the worst thumpin' I've had since I've been here. Like to busted every bone in my body!"

Lori had her arms around his neck, her mouth close to his. "Knock it off, you big whiner," she said, her voice slurring with emotion. "Just hurry and get us home."

About the Author

Ward Hawkins, born and raised in the Northwest, began his adult life with a high school education and a wife, and his professional career with the hammer and spikes of a heavy-construction worker. He took to writing as an "easier way," sold to pulp science-fiction magazines, *Thrilling Wonder*, etc., and went on to the *Saturday Evening Post*, *Colliers*, the *American*, etc. When they went bust, he moved to L.A., joined the Writers Guild of America, and began writing for the motion-picture and television market— *Rawhide*, *Bonanza*, *High Chapparal*, *Little House on the Prairie*, *Voyage to the Bottom of the Sea*, etc.

He lives now in the L.A. area with Adeline, the only wife he has ever had, near his children and grandchildren, plays golf to a five handicap, and writes only what he enjoys most.

Winner of the Hugo Award and international acclaim...

JOHN BRUNNER

Available at your bookstore or use this coupon.

___THE CRUCIBLE OF TIME	30235	3.50
___BEDLAM PLANET	30678	2.25
___THE INFINITIVE OF GO	28497	1.95
___PLAYERS AT THE GAME OF PEOPLE	29235	2.25
___STAND ON ZANZIBAR	31212	2.95
___THE SHEEP LOOK UP	29559	2.95
___THE SHOCKWAVE RIDER	30146	2.50

 BALLANTINE MAIL SALES
Dept. TA, 201 E. 50th St., New York, N.Y. 10022

Please send me the BALLANTINE or DEL REY BOOKS I have checked above. I am enclosing $............ (add 50¢ per copy to cover postage and handling). Send check or money order — no cash or C.O.D.'s please. Prices and numbers are subject to change without notice.

Name_____

Address_____

City_____State_____Zip Code_____

08   Allow at least 4 weeks for delivery.   TA-79